FATAL HARMONY

The Vein Chronicles
Book One

ANNE MALCOM

Fatal Harmony
The Vein Chronicles #1
By Anne Malcom

ISBN-13: 978-1542466165
ISBN-10: 1542466164

Cover Design: Simply Defined Art
Edited by: Hot Tree Editing
Cover image Copyright 2017
Interior design and formatting: Champagne Formats

DEDICATION

To my readers, who took a chance on me and gave me everything.

I hope you're ready to take another chance on a sarcastic chick with fangs.

ONE

EVERY STORY HAS AN ANTAGONIST AND A PROTAGONIST. Hero and villain. Good and evil. Yada, yada, yada. Thing is, I bet in each story the villain doesn't consider themselves the epitome of evil. Even the evilest of minds have justification for their acts. They're the hero of their own story; it just depends on where you stand.

I gingerly stepped my Louboutin out of the ever-increasing pool of blood at my feet, wiping my mouth delicately with the silk kerchief I carried for situations such as this. The man stared at me, his eyes glassy, the empty stare of the recently dead. The wound was still gushing. I probably could've continued the meal, but what can I say? I was on a diet.

I shook my head at the pants around his ankles, showing off his less-than-stellar package.

"A death you're worthy of, Stan," I informed the corpse lightly.

He continued to stare.

"Don't look at me like that. You're the one who got his jollies attacking women. Should've expected one would return the favor sooner or later."

I took my phone from my Celine.

"Cleanup on aisle twelve," I greeted the bored-sounding voice, looking around distractedly at a drunken group of women stumbling past the mouth of the alley.

Any one of them could have ended their night with Stan groping them, likely giving them scars that would never heal. I got my entrée and did my bit for mankind.

I'm a philanthropist. Someone get me a Nobel Prize.

"Isla? Shit. Seriously? Another alley job?" the voice perked up, going from bored to fan girl in two-point-five seconds.

I inspected my nails while I walked towards the end of the alley, my heels clicking against the concrete.

"Hey, Scott." I tried to stay patient. It was hard. Patience and bagged blood were two things I wasn't hot on. But Scott was harmless really, like those puppies that humped your leg. It was frowned upon to kick said puppies, so I had to practice the feeble human emotion of patience. He was still getting used to his new world. He was young; another hundred years or so and he might be vaguely bearable. I could deal with the humping puppy for a mere hundred years. Maybe.

"Isla! You gotta take me with you next time. I'll be, like, the best student ever. You won't even know I'm there. Wait, can I turn invisible? Is that a thing? Can you teach me? Then it'll be like I'm really not there. You could do your thing and I'll just be the watcher, taking it all in like a sponge," he babbled.

Forget a hundred years. I'd be lucky if I didn't stake him myself in the next ten seconds.

"Scott, focus. Dead human. In need of disposal so we don't

get humans and, in turn, the slayers on my pert ass," I reminded him. Not that I was worried about the slayers—I could wipe the floor with them—but I'd just gotten a manicure and I didn't want it ruined.

"Right, right, sorry," he said quickly.

"Corner of Smith and Sunderland, dingy alley, terrible decorator, dead guy at the end of it. You can't miss him," I said. "Short, pants around his ankles, gaping neck wound, sideburns that should be illegal."

"Yes, yes, I'm sending someone now." His keyboard tapped in the background with frantic speed.

"Great," I responded with only the teeniest bit of sarcasm. I scanned the street. It was reasonably deserted at three in the morning, just the odd taxi screaming past full of partyers dragging their inebriated bodies home. I could tell, since the one who hurtled past reeked of mojitos and the girls were babbling to each other about men who were assholes.

"Amen to that, sista," I muttered under my breath.

"What?" Scott piped in.

Shit. I'd totally forgotten I was still on the phone with him. He didn't hang up and treat me with coldness bordering on disgust like the rest of the dispatchers did. That was on account of the fact that my lifestyle fascinated instead of disturbed him. Give him time and education that half breeds didn't get until they were turned. He'd come to despise me like the rest of my race and my family.

"I wasn't talking to you, Scott," I replied in a tight voice, directing myself to my cherry red convertible across the street.

I was strictly meant to blend in and not call attention to myself, but hey, why try to fit in when you were born to stand out? Or more accurately died and then came back to life as a bloodsucking monster created to stand out. Potato, potahto.

"Do you have someone with you? Like a sidekick?" he asked quickly.

I paused at the door to my car. "No. I fly solo. And don't ever say the word 'sidekick' again," I ordered.

I could practically taste his sigh of relief over the phone. "I can totally do that. Not say sidekick, I mean. Shit, wingman? 'Cause wingman seems totally more appropriate considering there's this man I know who would like to be your wing." He paused. "He's me," he clarified.

"Good-bye, Scott," I said into the phone.

"But—"

I hung up before he could finish his no-doubt Pulitzer prize-winning sentence. Not that such a gesture would offend nor hamper him. The kid seemed to *like* it when I was a bitch to him. I shook my head and threw my bag on the passenger seat.

I should have probably been nicer to him; he just wanted to be my friend. *Sidekick*. I mentally cringed. I wasn't exactly full to the brim in the friends department. Actually, that particular part of my life was decaying with cobwebs. I had one person on the entire planet who I could say with almost absolute certainty didn't want me dead.

Well, at least not this century.

I pulled out of my parking space and hurtled back into the night, heading for my penthouse in Upper Manhattan.

Although I had plenty of others that were overflowing, *one* area of my life was lacking. In addition to my closet, there was my kickass apartment in New York, villa in Italy, cabin in Sweden—you get the picture. I was also gloriously attractive, had great fashion sense, and was forever frozen in my fashionable and attractive state. Immortality didn't suck. Though I did. Har har.

"I'm hilarious. How do I not have friends chomping at the

bit to have late-night hangs?" I asked myself.

Maybe because I talked to myself after snacking on a rapist.

More likely it was because the only particular humans I snacked on were of the disgusting variety. Dregs of society: murderers, child molesters, rapists. Scum that the world deserved to be rid of. I made sure every soul I took was one that was heading for a long, hot stay in the underworld.

I hoped the day would never come when my own immortality was snuffed out. There was no doubt I'd be heading to the underworld, and I'd be facing a lot of pissed-off vengeful douchebags when I got there.

A nice motivation to keep breathing. Or not breathing, as the case may be.

Plus, Chanel had a new collection coming out in a month.

My phone rang in the Bluetooth system of my car as I pulled into the underground parking of my building. I cringed at the caller ID.

"Why, God? Why?" I asked the almighty.

I got no answer, mainly because if the almighty *was* up there and gazing at my auburn head, he'd most likely be trying to figure out ways to smite it, abomination that I was.

"Mother," I greeted through gritted teeth, maneuvering my way towards my parking space.

"Isla." Her terse voice dripped with disapproval, regardless of the fact that she'd not even started speaking to me. Like the big man upstairs, my entire existence was a disapproval to her. She'd smite me in a second if she could.

"To what do I owe the displeasure?" I asked, pressing a button so the phone was to my ear as I got out of the car. "Let me guess, you want to book a spa day with me? Or perhaps go see the latest Nicholas Sparks movie?" I continued in a sickly sweet tone, my heels reverberating on the concrete in the deserted building.

There was a loaded pause at the other end of the phone. I could practically see my mother rubbing her temples together, even though she couldn't get headaches. "I am calling to make sure you haven't forgotten." She spoke tightly, ignoring my previous words.

"Forgotten what? To floss? Don't worry, Mom, dental care is my top priority. Gotta take care of my fangs," I replied seriously, my brows knitting at the human I sensed rapidly approaching behind me.

Another pause. "You *refuse* to act with any semblance of maturity, nor show our race the respect it deserves, and you constantly sully our family name," she said, her voice even.

"Gee, Mother, I do love your little pep talks," I responded sweetly, stopping my journey to the elevators as I felt the presence behind me. I sighed, turning.

The human was dressed all in black, a black beanie yanked over shaggy, dirty hair. His eyes were darting around the empty lot, stubble obscuring half his face. He pointed a gun at my head.

"Give me all your money," he demanded.

I stared at him, raising my brow, the only warning he was going to get.

My mother was oblivious to my current situation, though I bet she would have been pleased it was unfolding on the off chance that a garden variety mugger might be equipped with copper bullets and handy with a head shot. "You are expected at the event to—"

"Hold that thought, Mommy dearest. I've got the nicest man pointing a gun to my head right now," I interrupted her, my voice bland.

"Bitch! I am not fucking around!" the man roared. "Give

me your fucking purse, and those earrings." He shook the gun at the direction of my head and my beautiful diamond earrings.

"Dude, you do not want to do this," I warned.

"I'll fucking shoot you. You want to die today?" he snarled.

I rolled my eyes. "I'm already dead," I muttered, stepping forward and snapping his neck. It didn't seem fast to me, but to his useless human eyes I would have been nothing but a blur. The blur would be the very last thing he saw on this earth.

I regarded the crumpled body. I probably shouldn't have killed him. Yes, he was planning on mugging me, and potentially killing me—I could smell the rage and desperation leaving his lifeless body—but still. I normally researched the humans I killed, made sure they deserved to die, but I was cranky. My mother did that to me.

"I don't have all night, Isla." I could picture my mother tapping her foot.

"Don't worry about me. I'm fine," I told her, my gaze darting around to make sure no pesky witnesses would be a complication. I was slightly pissed off that this guy could even make it in here. We were in an upscale part of town and the security in this building was meant to be tight, yet a tweaker with a gun managed to get in. I'd be writing a strongly worded e-mail to the building manager on the morrow.

"Tomorrow night. The new king is holding a feast. It is imperative that you do not continue to besmirch the family name. Your presence will bring only slightly less shame than your absence," she informed me coolly. Only my mother would call the monarch who'd been reigning for almost a century 'new.'

I didn't flinch at the venom in her tone. I'd been getting it for hundreds of years. A girl got used to it.

"Sorry, I think..." I pretended to pause. "Yep. I'm washing my hair tomorrow night. Say hey to the king for me," I said breezily while I dragged the body of my would-be mugger to my car.

"If you do not come, your brothers will deliver the bodies of three dead children to your apartment at dawn. Children who will have died because of your disobedience," she stated, as if she expected nothing less than my refusal.

I paused, my blood running cold. Colder, anyway. "Why?" I choked out. "Why don't you just disown me? Instead of blackmailing me into attending events such as these every few decades?" My voice was devoid of any sarcasm or humor. My mother's threat was not an idle one. I knew from experience.

"Because as much as I hate it, you are a Rominskitoff. One of the greatest families of our race. That name will always stick to you, no matter what I do. So I do what I must," she snapped. "You know where it is. Dress appropriately," she ordered before hanging up.

I sighed, sagging against the door of my car and dropping the body I'd been holding. It didn't matter that I was hundreds of years old; I was still a slave to a psychotic mother. One who despised me. Along with most of my family, of course. I was surprised to hear they were even in the country. They hated America, found it tacky and vulgar. They usually stayed as far away as possible, hence my residence here. Their social climbing and power-hungry aspirations caused them to forget their hatred for the country, and for me as well, if I was being summoned to the gathering.

One I was loath to attend.

But I did not want to have three more bodies on my conscience that night. The death count was enough to damn me ten times over already.

"Fuck," I hissed into the air.

Vampire politics. I wanted to stay out of it. Far away from

it. But I was a member of one of the *greatest families of our race.* Despite the fact that I was a disappointment to not only that family, but my entire race. Change the record.

"Yo. Need another cleanup," I sighed into the phone.

"Isla?" an overexcited voice greeted. "Another one? You're busy tonight. What's going on?"

I pinched the bridge of my nose. "Just another fun and exciting night in my world," I muttered. "Get the cleanup crew to the basement of my apartment building. I really don't need a murder investigation fucking up my night any more than my mother already has."

I heard the tapping of keys. "On it."

For once he didn't babble, didn't ask questions. I was grateful for it.

"Thanks, kid. They got no one else manning the phones tonight?" I asked, unsure of why I was even making conversation with my not-so-secret admirer.

"No. I mean, yes, but I kind of... *requested* your calls," he stammered shyly.

I looked to the roof for patience. Though I should've been looking to the ground.; the king of the underworld was going to be the one granting me favors, not his estranged daddy. "Of course you did."

New vampires, especially half breeds with no connections to the old families, were given menial jobs in our public sector. Jobs like manning the phones at the cleanup centers. Manning the cleanup crews themselves. Doing the dirty work of the so-called superior families, or older vampires who had clawed their way up the aristocratic totem pole. It was a shitty job. One Scott seemed to think was the freaking best thing on the planet. I seriously wondered if he was the first vampire to be born missing a chromosome.

"I meant what I said. I want to help. Learn from you. Do what you do," he pleaded in my ear.

Maybe because I had just been verbally lashed by the reptile that was my mother, I was feeling unusually charitable. Or maybe I was feeling uncharitable to said mother.

"You free tomorrow night?" I asked with a grin.

Scott's response was in the realm of excited teenager at a One Direction concert.

After I hung up, I looked down at the dead guy and grinned. Mom was going to hate him. Perfect.

"Stop fidgeting," I commanded Scott as we walked through the opulent double doors of an ostentatious mansion on the outskirts of New York.

He immediately stopped yanking his shirtsleeves. "Sorry," he muttered sheepishly.

I glared at him. "Don't fucking apologize, to anyone. You're a vampire, for Lucifer's sake. Act like it."

He swallowed. "Sorry." He paused. "I mean—"

I waved my hand to shut him up.

He pursed his lips and moved his head, his eyes turning to survey the room. They popped out in amazement. "Holy shit," he exclaimed.

I rolled my eyes, already regretting my choice of date. I guessed to his sparkly new vampire eyes, the grandeur of the place was something. Something incredibly tacky. They had strung up various tapestries, centuries old and blood-red, of course. *Everything* was blood-red—the tablecloths, the waiter's outfits, the fricking carpet. I wrinkled my nose in distaste and immediately snagged a glass of champagne off a tray that was coming past me. I avoided the red liquid that was mixed with the champagne, my stomach turning at where it came from. Definitely not free-range blood.

"Is the king seriously going to be here?" Scott asked, his eyes darting around as if he was expecting a man with a crown to jump out from behind a curtain and cry "Worship me, peasant!"

I surveyed the crowd. Most were familiar, some were not. I grew up around these stuffy, bloodthirsty assholes. Went to school with a lot of them. They say the world was small, but when you've been on it for a few hundred years, it felt tiny. The same people seemed to circulate these wretched things. People I loathed, and by the looks I got, the feeling was mutual. The downfall of being immortal, you couldn't even look forward to death taking someone you hated off the guest list.

"So I'm told," I replied, downing my first glass and procuring another. Increased metabolism meant I had to drink fast in order to get drunk enough not to rip someone's limbs off before midnight.

"The real king? Do you think we'll get to meet him?" Scott asked with excitement.

I took a huge gulp of my champagne and rolled my eyes. "Only if you've been a really bad boy."

"You don't want to meet him?" His question made it sound like I was proclaiming I drank animal blood. I didn't. No vampire did. We couldn't survive on the stuff. Though, now that vampires were trendy sex symbols, popular culture had to make us a bit less… icky. Hence making up the fact that we sucked on Bambi's blood rather than Martha's.

Not an improvement, in my humble opinion.

I pretended to ponder, cradling the flute to my chest. "Do I want to meet the high and mighty majesty of our race? A man who most likely grew up being fed willing young blood bags on a platter and expects everyone to bow down and kiss his alligator loafers? And obey his every whim? Of course. I can think of no other way to spend my Saturday, I wouldn't rather claw out my own fangs or anything," I responded, my voice saccharine sweet with sarcasm.

Scott's face turned positively pale. More pale than it already was, anyway. He wasn't gaping at me, but at the space right behind me.

Shit.

"He's right behind me, isn't he?" I asked through gritted teeth.

Scott nodded slowly.

"Fuck," I muttered under my breath. Though why I muttered it was anyone's guess; everyone in the room most likely could hear, if they so desired.

And they'd desire nothing less than to watch the king strip the skin from my arm for daring to disrespect him at his own party.

I wasn't just making that shit up. Apparently that happened to some vampire who criticized his choice in blood.

"I'd hate to disappoint you, but I'm not wearing alligator loafers, though I'm sure I could command someone to procure them for me so you could kiss them." A deep voice floated into my ear. It was smooth and pleasing, with no underlying hostility suggesting imminent skin flaying.

I glared at Scott. "A hand signal, a freaking warning. You couldn't give me anything?" I hissed at him before downing my drink and slowly turning. I tried to plaster an apologetic look on my face, though I worried I just looked deranged. Technically I could be severely punished for my little monologue. Monarchs were stiff like that.

I was momentarily shocked with what I was presented with. The king was hot. Like *smokin'*. It looked like he spent his days tanning instead of ruling, and his features were dark and masculine. Eyes the color of two shiny emeralds and a thick smattering of stubble covering his sharp jaw. His hair was shaggy and brushing his shoulders, a jagged scar sweeping through his brow.

Pre-turning, I thought to myself. Vampires could get injured, by someone very determined or very stupid, but we couldn't scar. At least not after we'd come of age, died and turned into our immortal selves. Before, we were a little more breakable, though we didn't exactly like to broadcast that, which had me wondering why our king hadn't found a little witch to take care of the scar. Though, it was sexy as sin.

Maybe that was why, though I'm sure his crown already got him a lot of tail.

He was huge. Like *huge.* He towered over me, and I was tall for a woman—and in six in heels, no less. Though his tailored suit covered all his body, save his corded neck, it didn't hide his muscular form.

I swallowed, not expecting to be attracted to the monarch I loathed on principle.

"I'm sure your lackeys have better things to do than help perpetuate crimes to fashion," I responded evenly. I glanced down at his feet, but no snakeskin to be found. Only very expensive, very classy midnight Gucci dress shoes with a slight point to the heel. His slacks were black, Armani if I wasn't mistaken, as was the black shirt that was unbuttoned, showing off the thick cord of his neck.

My eyes snapped up to meet his once more. "Plus, your shoes are a comfortable surprise." I swallowed. "Your Majesty," I added with effort.

I supposed I should curtsey or something, but thought better of it. We had gathered a bit of an audience, so everyone had obviously heard my little speech. I wasn't going to demean myself by trying to suck up to my king like the rest of the masses. I'd just have to hope he wasn't feeling particularly wrathful.

His eyes weren't full of wrath, only amusement. "I'm glad my choice of footwear pleases you…." He quirked a brow at me in question.

"Isla," I said quickly, though I didn't think for a second that he was ignorant of who I was. I wasn't arrogant… well, actually I was, but I figured his ever-present aides and advisors warned him about potential troublemakers. I'd been at the top of that particular list for well over four hundred years.

"Isla," he repeated, my name sounding delightful in his raspy tone.

Oh my God, I was getting all squidgy at this guy. I didn't get squidgy.

Stop. Now.

The squidgyness intensified as his gaze traveled the length of me. I was wearing a pure white gown, mostly to piss everyone off. Vampires seemed to think it compulsory to wear dark and violent colors in order to perpetuate stereotypes.

I wanted to stay as far away from stereotypes as I could. My dress was skintight and strapless, molding to my body, and had a slit up to midthigh. White strappy stilettos snaked up my calf. At his gaze, I was totally happy I didn't skimp on the hair and makeup. My auburn locks tumbled around my shoulders and down my back in soft curls. I had gone for a smoky eye to accentuate my green irises and went nude for lipstick instead of my signature blood-red. A girl had to keep *some* stereotypes alive. Or undead.

"I'd have to say, your choice of footwear pleases me greatly too," he said finally, once his eyes met mine once more.

We held this long intense gaze for a split second before he gave me a polite nod and turned to disappear into the crowd. Two men trailed him. Bodyguards, I suspected. He looked like he could well and truly take care of himself, but these were uncertain times.

"Isla," a sharp voice hissed.

"No respite," I muttered, my back going ramrod straight.

A firm hand snatched my elbow. I met eyes identical to mine, narrowed into a look of almost pure hatred.

"Hey, Mom, how's death?" I greeted with a grin.

"Tell me that was not just the king you were speaking to," she demanded.

"Okay, that was not the king I was just speaking to." I sipped my champagne, my eyes already scanning the room for the closest waiter. I needed to be drunk to stay dead for this evening, and thanks to my accelerated metabolism, I needed about twenty more of these to be sufficiently sloshed.

Her grip tightened and she glanced around, mindful of the various eyes on us. She smiled tightly. "We'll talk about that later."

"Can't wait." I smiled tightly, draining my glass.

Her eyes moved behind me, taking in Scott.

He scrubbed up well, if you asked me. I honestly expected him to be some overweight kid with spectacles and red hair.

Yes, vampires could be overweight. All shapes and sizes, not just tall, dark, and sparkly.

Actually, not sparkly at all. Unless you counted my personality, which I did.

Scott was none of those things, but he wasn't bad to look at. Like, I wouldn't need the paper bag in the bedroom. He was shorter than me and a little on the skinny side, but he worked it. His blond hair was artfully messed in the way the kids loved to do these days, and his features were sharp and defined. He had a scattering of freckles, no doubt inherited from his human father.

"Who's this?" she asked, her mask of society vampire slipping back on. "You've finally found a man to survive your company longer than twelve minutes, congratulations."

I snatched another glass off a passing waiter, ignoring the Devil's Mistress's glare. "Mom, this is Scott," I introduced, glancing at my watchless hand. "Been in my presence for approximately… fourteen minutes. Though I doubt we'll get to fifteen with you around."

My mother ignored me and held out her gloved hand. Not for Scott to shake, but to kiss. Seriously.

He stared at her outstretched limb in confusion before he jumped forward and clumsily executed the kiss.

"Ma'am, nice to meet you," he fumbled once he'd released her.

She gave him an appraising eye. "Charmed," she murmured, though her tone betrayed she'd be more charmed to be chewing on a dishrag. "You're…." She stared at his cheap suit, then at his freckles before she bristled.

You could taste the ice in the air, originating from her utter distaste of half breeds. I reasoned if she could find a way to discreetly and immediately burn the glove he'd set his mouth on, she would.

Me? I thought he needed to spray antifreeze on his lips.

"Half human and he works the phones at the Sector," I finished for her, enjoying the way her face froze immensely. "Now, if you'll excuse us." I snatched Scott's hand. "We've got something very important to do, over there." I gestured vaguely to the farthest side of the room.

I didn't wait for her to say anything else, dragging Scott out of reach of her fangs, both literal and figurative. She most likely wouldn't do something as uncouth as lunge at my date at such an event, but I wasn't taking any chances.

I nodded to the various people who stared at me, grinning at the ones who openly glared.

"So, that was your mom," Scott said, swallowing tightly.

I snatched another champagne off a passing tray, handing it to him. "Yes. A total peach, isn't she? A shining example of the wonderful people who attend these glorious gatherings," I said, grinning inwardly at the people who stiffened as they heard my hushed tone. Vampires. Great hearing meant I could insult a huge group at one time. Totally awesome.

I directed us to a corner of the room where we had the best vantage point to look down on the rest of my vampire kin.

"This is.... These are all of the families?" Scott asked, glancing at the sea of attractive, eternally young bodies wearing an array of black, crimson, and other equally depressing colors.

I nodded, scanning the group and locating my brothers and father, though they were hard to miss. My family was tall. Yep, vampires had genetics, just like any other living, or technically dead, species. Every member of my family had thick, auburn hair—though mine was the best—and a statuesque frame. However, unlike me and my mother, my father and brothers weren't slender; they were built with muscle, like they spent hours in the gym. They were just one of the 'great families,' good looks and favorable physiques part of the deal. These traits were ensured by 'selective breeding' of only the purest of blood.

Mixing or dirtying the Vein Line with anything that didn't err on the side of blue was an ideal way to get yourself shut off from the ruling elite quicker than you could say 'shotgun wedding.'

They all looked like GQ models, and the same ages, despite there being a couple of thousand years between them. You'd have to cut them open and count the rings if you wanted to distinguish age. Though, my father's hair was slicked back and he was leaner than my brothers.

"There's the rest of my cuddly family." I nodded to them, giving them a finger wave and a smile.

Father glanced at me with an empty gaze, the chasm of his eyes betraying nothing but perhaps the smallest bead of distaste. Viktor and Evgeni just ignored me.

"Don't let their good looks fool you. They're fucking psychopaths," I said through my smile.

"Aren't all vampires?" Scott muttered, surprising me. His tone was somewhat jaded and full of revulsion, as if he was distancing himself from those in the room whose legs I'd been certain he was going to hump.

I glanced to my side to regard him. He was staring at the room, that puppy dog look gone, replaced with something older and arguably wiser.

"I think we're going to get on just fine, Scotty," I said, looking back to the room.

We had only been swimming in the shark-filled waters for about half an hour before a thick silence blanketed the room. One that had me looking up from the tray where I'd just snatched my twentieth, or fortieth champagne.

The king stood in front of the crowd, slightly raised on a small stage in front of a tapestry depicting The Battle of the Four, where the four supernatural factions fought against each other. Casualties on all sides were heavy before a peace treaty was signed. Then every faction's respective rulers commenced in dividing every major city into four sections, so no such battle would be fought again.

There were summits every decade to reevaluate with the growing cities. From the whispers I'd heard throughout the party, one had just ended in Prague, where some controversial decisions were made.

I wouldn't know, it was New York Fashion Week last week and the only big decisions I knew about was the decision to bring back velvet. Obviously the vampires at this party loved that particular choice.

The king radiated a cold sort of authority that made the greatest vampires—I use that title with a heavy dose of sarcasm—quiet and focus on him. Some did it begrudgingly, like my mother with her pinched face, but all still gave him the most precious thing an immortal could give—their attention.

His emerald eyes darted over the room before they settled on me for a moment. Then they were gone.

"I appreciate your attendance," he started, his smooth tenor traveling over the crowd of vampires in the ballroom. "I know many of you have come far to be here and hear the announcement I brought you here to make." He paused, long enough to be uncomfortable, yet not a vampire muttered a thing. They wouldn't dare. The king's menace was legendary and every vampire there had too much self-preservation to interrupt the king's speech with an ill-timed whisper.

"With traitorous factions causing trouble for themselves, an alliance has been made."

The words settled over the room with such a force that I couldn't hide my grin. Even I couldn't piss off every single vampire so easily. Kudos to King Markandeya.

Vampires considered themselves to be at the top of the food chain. We were created by gods, for Pete's sake. Our Vein Lines had the Ichor, the substance of eternal life running through them. Werewolves were just freaks of nature, witches were pagans, and demons were merely soldiers of a long-forgotten king. Vampires were elite. Or that's what the attendees of this soiree thought.

"This alliance between supernaturals has been a long time coming. The world is changing and so must our society if we are to maintain our position," the king continued. "But be warned, this isn't, and never will be, a democracy. You may disagree with this decision, but I do it for the good of our race, so you must find a way to accept it. Or you face the punishment that those rebels caught after the explosion in Prague." His threat held heavy in the air as cold eyes focused on various members of the marble-faced crowd.

Silence thick with malice and anger filled the room. The king remained at the front of the space, daring anyone to challenge him. When the silenced yawned, he nodded once. "Enjoy the blood, the company, I urge you." Then he nodded and glided off the stage.

Muted conversations resumed after his exit, but no one dared to criticize the king's decision, though I was sure there would be more than enough outrage behind closed doors.

Me, I lapped up the discomfort of the vampires I'd long despised. I held my glass up to my mother's blank face. Her eyes flickered with rage before she masked it.

I grinned, sipping from my glass.

Scott leaned in. "Did something bad just happen?" he asked, oblivious as a child.

I gave him a look. "Oh no, something great just happened."

"I need to get some fresh air," I muttered to Scott as we walked away from a conversation so drenched in verbal barbs, I was surprised I wasn't bleeding.

Though if words could wound, the vampire we were walking away from would have been a headless corpse added to the décor.

Centuries of this meant I had been able to hold my own.

"You gonna be okay in here?" I asked Scott, who was now on his fifth champagne. He hadn't touched the amber liquid either.

He glanced to me, grinning. "Of course."

I shook my head. "I may have been wrong about you, my friend." I was serious. He'd handled the vipers perfectly, insulting them in ways just veiled enough to be considered good manners as a response to every comment about his lineage, or lack thereof. He was from an unknown family, and a half breed to boot. His father was human, or had been. That's the thing about those humans; they had a nasty habit of dying. And there was nothing his mother could have done, since all that shit about vampire blood being a mystical cure was pure Hollywood. Humans died, vampires lived. It was that simple.

Half breeds like Scott were still technically immortal but were a lot more breakable than their full-blood counterparts, which was only a small reason why those in proper society tried their best to shun them away to desk jobs. Mostly it was because the assholes of the 'superior race' considered humans to be little more than meals with a vocabulary. Some, of course, did the horizontal tangle with them, before they sucked them dry. But falling in love with one, *breeding* with one? Well, that was akin to filing down your fangs.

"Stay cool." I winked at him, clinking my glass with his before wading through the sea of assholes.

Luckily, the balcony leading off the French doors of the ballroom was deserted, which meant I could have a moment to myself and shake off the filth that came with attending such things.

The estate was outside New York, sprawled on acres of manicured gardens. It was dark, but that didn't mean much to me; heightened eyesight and hearing were one of the things setting us apart from the human race.

Oh, and immortality and the fact that we sucked the blood of the aforementioned human race to stay undead.

Small things.

I leaned against the railing, resisting the urge to vault over it and run from this godforsaken party. It wasn't just the damage to my outfit that stopped me. It was Mother's words.

"If you do not come, your brothers will deliver you the bodies of three dead children to your apartment at dawn."

It wasn't an idle threat. I'd learned that the hard way.

I'd never been the prodigal daughter my parents had wanted, even before I turned. I spent my childhood reading human literature instead of the vampire gospel, which of course wasn't something you found in Barnes and Noble, or its sixteenth-century equivalent.

I cried when I was six and saw my father and mother kill a human. Something a vampire, even before they'd fully matured, should never have done.

From then, my family made it their mission to hide my habits of humanity from the rest of the society. All done through force, obviously. If I didn't act how they wanted me to, they'd kill children, entire families, in front of me. And then made me sleep in the same room as their corpses.

It had worked for a while. Their methods were grisly and designed to make even the most devout saint into a sinner. Since I hadn't been devout, nor a saint, I turned dark, sinning enough to make even Ted Bundy blush. I'd turned after they killed the life I'd made for myself and after, I escaped the cold and unfeeling atmosphere of Russia.

When I turned twenty-three and the chance presented itself, I ran. Didn't look back. I had planned on going as far away from the motherland as possible, chasing the sunshine while I could live in its warm rays, before I was sentenced to a life in the shadows.

I arrived in post-war Paris at the end of the 1600s, when Louis was crowned and the city was blooming with their newly grasped peace. Both the Parisians and I were blissfully ignorant of how fragile that peace would become. How it would shatter and be replaced with blood, death and anguish.

I was quickly besotted with the growing city and the pulsating life that emanated from its streets. Despite goals to travel to the edge of the world to escape my family and try in vain to hold onto my humanity, I stayed. Made friends with aristocrats, thanks to my mystique, Russian accent, and apparent lack of family.

A young, attractive and wealthy woman in those times did not travel alone.

Times were delicate, as was life. Women in such a time were considered the most delicate of all. I wasn't concerned about the horrors or dangers the human world offered me; it was nothing compared to my childhood.

I was naive and somehow thought I was invincible, although I was at the most fragile stage in my immortal life. Many vampires died when their life force was the closest to a human's as we ever got.

I didn't worry myself with such things at that time, I worried about sunshine, dresses, champagne and parties. And it was at one of the parties at the newly constructed Versailles that I met him.

I floated around the grass, my skirts trailing on the ground as I smiled up into the sunlight, basking in its glow and in the slight fuzz at the edge of my thoughts thanks to the excellent champagne.

The hum of conversations calmed me, the lack of murders and screams I'd grown used to jarring yet comforting.

An electricity snaked up my skin with the telltale sign of a stare landing on my back. I glanced across the garden to see the owner of that stare sidling through the crowds, nodding at men and bowing at ladies as he approached.

His caramel eyes never left me as he came closer. I did little but gape at the young man with skin kissed by the sun. His auburn hair curled around his face in shiny waves, setting him apart from the other men I'd met. His attire was less unusual, the stark white ruff snaking up his neck, contrasting with the intricately designed leather jerkin worn over the matching doublet. His paned hose matched and added to the crisp and opulent look. I wasn't impressed by his tailoring, nor his resources which made him able to procure the finest fabrics. It was the warmth that seemed to travel with him, the eyes focused on mine which were two tiny balls of light, comforting me with their heat.

He made it to me, bowing low and eating me up with his gaze.

The heat of my blush crept up my cheeks. It wasn't unusual to be the subject of male attention. I had had my experience with it since my arrival in the strange and vibrant city and though it had excited me, nothing had curled in my stomach at a mere gaze like it had right then.

I forgot my manners momentarily and scurried to curtsey as was proper.

A shadow of a grin lit up his boyish face as I rose.

"Mademoiselle," he greeted.

I dipped my head, if only to escape the pull of his gaze. Immediately I yearned for it. "Monsieur," I returned. I feared my greeting was not as smooth as his. The way his tongue rolled over the single word betrayed him as a native and me as a foreigner.

He glanced around me, as if expecting someone to come and snatch me from his very presence.

"You do not have a family, a chaperone to protect your honor?" he asked, as if he expected to have to unsheathe the dagger at his belt to take up the post.

I laughed. "Protect my honor? No," I replied softly. Damn it, maybe.

"Your family, they're dead?" His eyes searched mine, warm with concern.

I nodded, sipping my champagne. "Dead," I agreed.

It wasn't a lie. They just happened to be walking, talking and murdering without a heartbeat. Hence my voluntary seclusion in Paris. I'd been there almost a month and they hadn't come to fetch me. I was surprised, figuring the wayward Rominskitoff daughter who mingled with humans would be the scandal of the century.

They weren't quite ready to turn me themselves; I'd bet they were hoping this dirty and death-filled mortal world might snuff my existence from the planet before I had the chance to permanently besmirch their legacy as an immortal. Or they were hoping my rejection of cold-blooded murder and sadism was just a phase. Humanity a nasty rebellion, instead of a way of life, or undeath.

Whatever it was, I was glad to be without them, and I felt confident enough to manage life in Paris alone. Even this stuffy society party was somewhat enjoyable, especially with this sharp-jawed gentleman with riveting eyes and a lean body under his attire.

He stepped forward. "It is a crime that a young lady such as yourself is in society without protection. I'm honor bound to provide my services."

I quirked my brow, mostly to hide the strange feeling his lack of hesitation had brought. The way his proximity, slightly closer than was proper, made my heart flutter like a sparrow.

Made me forget that I could turn at any time into a blood-sucking monster that he would need protecting from.

"It's not exactly a position that needs to be filled," I argued. "I'm quite capable of taking care of myself, Monsieur."

His eyelashes fluttered. "I disagree. You, in society, beautiful as a rose in spring? I would not let anyone pluck you and tarnish that beauty."

I swallowed. I should politely excuse myself, pick up my skirts and run from those whiskey eyes and his endearing scent. But it was as if those eyes had lassoed me and I couldn't leave his presence.

I didn't want to.

"You flatter me, sir," I murmured.

His eyes twinkled. "No, I tell the truth my heart commands me to tell. Otherwise, I shall drop dead, right here at your feet. And since I have renewed motivation not to do that, namely to spend more time in your presence and learn your name, I must tell my heart's truth."

My blush crept up my neck, my whole body humming with a reaction that would have been impossible if I had turned. But I hadn't. Which meant my body was controlled by whatever human impulses lingered before we turned and they were all extinguished.

"I would hardly wish for you to drop dead at my feet, especially here," I remarked, looking around the garden. "It would be most improper at such a party, and a dreadful way to go. Wouldn't you much rather have an interesting story of your demise? Perhaps a duel?" I grinned at him.

His returning grin was blinding. "Yes, perhaps a duel. That is, if there's another suitor I must face for your affections. In that case, it will be to the death. Otherwise, my demise is most suited to be winning the affections of the most breathtaking creature I've laid eyes on."

I sucked in a haggard breath. "Monsieur, I'm afraid you must stop saying such things, for your barely know me and I do not deserve such heartfelt declarations."

He stepped forward, closer than was socially acceptable and I didn't find it in me to care. I didn't care about what the entire vampire race thought about me, so why should I care about French aristocrats murmuring about me standing close to a handsome man unchaperoned.

"I disagree. I know you, for I have watched you glide around this entire wretched party, lighting it up with your presence. You laughed with the children other ladies shoo away, even hitching up your skirts in order to play with them. You bespelled Lord Durand, even made the old man laugh when it is known that Louis himself cried in his presence. Finally, the moment your eyes met mine, my heart stopped and started, for I laid my eyes on the woman I intend to marry."

His declaration, which my twenty-first-century self might have scoffed at and ran from, instead set my whole world aflame with warmth of true, genuine human affection, something that had been entirely absent from my existence.

We married a mere month after the party.

My family murdered him one week after our wedding.

Five weeks. That's what I got. Five weeks of happiness, of the truest and purest form of love that humans live and die for, wrote poems for, and breathed for.

I lived for almost five hundred years, and five weeks of those I had in a box in the bottom of my shriveled heart, a shadow of what humans stayed breathing for.

What I would most likely die to avoid.

Because I couldn't live with having something like that taken from me. Not again. Forever was a long time to live with heartbreak. Humans had it for a blink of an eye, but I had it always.

Four hundred years of the ever-present hole in my heart because I'd spent five weeks in ignorance of true love, thinking it would conquer all.

Then I came home to that house we'd talked about raising children in to see him, and every single person we'd been connected to, lying on the floor. Their throats ripped out.

My mother was wiping her mouth demurely when I walked in, dropping to my knees beside Jonathan's corpse.

"I should hope you now understand," she said evenly, "what will and will not be tolerated in this family." The skirts of her dress bristled as she made her way to me. "And what will happen should you decide to shame our name and your entire race again."

On that note, she'd walked out of the room, leaving me cradling the man who had been the center of my fantasy. The center of my world.

Then I turned. Right then and there. Amidst the blood and remains of what had been my human life.

Every vampire was different when they came into their full selves. Their true selves. Extensive research had gone into the study of how our bodies underwent a natural death in order to bring forward an unnatural afterlife. There were many theories about evolution and Darwinism, but I didn't trouble myself with much of that. It was a fact of our undeath and it was never consistent. You didn't turn twenty-one and have the ability to buy your first drink, grow your fangs and live forever. Some vampires turned when they were teenagers, some middle-aged. Most were early twenties.

Various scientists of our race had tried to pinpoint the reasons behind turning and what the catalyst was.

Well, the catalyst for us all was death.

Our hearts literally stopped beating.

Mine shriveled up and exploded.

I went dark after that. The darkest. Much to my family's delight. I left a blood trail throughout half of Europe. Ironically, my blood spree came at a time of unrest in the continent, when horrors committed by the human race far outweighed the sins a single vampire could accomplish. But that didn't mean my soul wasn't stained forever with the blood of those I killed.

I decided that if I died that day, I would try and kill every part of me that I thought was me. Because if I killed all of it, the humanity, the mortality, maybe I'd kill the pain. Since I couldn't kill myself without great effort, I decided to kill everyone else.

Fifty years I was notorious, respected in my community. Not that I cared. I didn't mingle with any of them. My life was blood, nothing else. My family didn't bother me then. I was towing the family line, so there was no need.

Then it changed. Like I'd been in some kind of nightmare, I'd woken up. Stopped.

I didn't stop killing; I just realized that I was turning right into what my family wanted. I had dishonored Jonathan's memory.

So I changed my life. Or my death.

And the rest, as they say, is history.

Just not the history taught in human schools.

"Thinking of jumping?" a gravelly voice interrupted my journey down memory lane.

Good thing too. That lane was littered with corpses I tried to forget, yet I carried them with me for eternity. Or until someone finally succeeded in killing me.

The source of the interruption brought me out of the frying pan of my memories and into the icy depths of his presence. His voice was flat and cold, yet able to singe my skin with its edge. I didn't turn, just continued contemplating the grounds.

"As tempting as it is, I don't want grass stains on my dress," I replied.

He leaned beside me, regarding the night much like I was, holding a glass of what smelled like well-aged whiskey in his large hands.

He wasn't indulging in the world's finest blood. Curious.

"And that would be a crime that I would have to punish you for," the king said, his voice drenched with double entendre.

I glanced at his profile. He was making me uneasy. No one made me uneasy. "I don't do well with punishments," I replied truthfully, hiding my unease behind my well-practiced bravado.

He turned his head to lock eyes with me. "You would if I was the one administering them."

Well, fuck. Was the notoriously ruthless, callous and coldest king of all vampires *flirting* with me?

"I've heard a lot about you," he continued.

I kept his eyes. "All bad, I hope."

He tilted his head, his gaze speculative, as if he were figuring out a particularly hard puzzle. "No. None bad. All good, in fact." He twirled his crystal tumbler between his hands. "The way I understand it, you only kill a certain kind of human."

I stayed silent, figuring it was my best bet.

"The kind who have committed depravities against the human race," he continued. "You don't kill innocents." He regarded me, no judgment either way, which was surprising. Or maybe he just had a really good poker face. You didn't rule a society of sociopaths for two hundred years and stay undead if you didn't perfect a mask of indifference.

I sipped my champagne. "What can I say? I prefer my meat bitter."

He kept staring. My uneasiness was like a snake slithering in my belly, and I didn't like it. Or maybe I did. Which was why I didn't. I abhorred my entire race. Getting all weak-kneed over the king of them all was a tad hypocritical.

"Stop doing that," I snapped, unable to take any more.

Surprise flickered across his face, his mask cracking. "Doing what?"

"Staring," I clarified. "It's unnerving. And also makes you look like you're a few candlesticks short of the entire box."

Shit. Did I just insinuate that the king of vampires was mentally impaired?

Yes. Yes I did.

Fuck.

"Okay, if you're gonna kill me, can you at least wait until I've touched up my lipstick?" I asked, trying to charm my way out of this.

Respect was big in certain circles. Interestingly, the ones who were the cruelest of us all, the vipers at this party, revered manners, in person at least. All the backstabbing was done in accordance with well-established laws, ones which forbade anyone from spilling another vampire's blood at a gathering where human blood was shared.

I guessed the king could find a loophole if some red-haired idiot decided to let her mouth run away from her and suggest he was mentally handicapped.

He tilted his head so his curtain of hair fell like silk across his shoulder. "Kill you?" he repeated, then downed the last of his liquid. "Now why would I do that? You're much too interesting." He gave me a pensive look before pushing off the balcony and sauntering back into the party.

I watched him walk away, admiring the cut of his suit and the fluidity of his gait.

Then I turned back to regard the midnight air. I so needed to find a way to get out of these things before I was the first person to break a rule that had been in place for thousands of years.

No vampire shall spill immortal blood when Theoxenia has been granted or Zeus shall feast on their flesh.

I scoffed, feeling the premonition of death curl around me like the wind.

TWO

I STARED DOWN AT MY PHONE, TRYING TO USE THE POWER of my mind to make it stop ringing. And to make the person at the other end of the call spontaneously combust.

It didn't stop, which disappointed me twofold; I had to answer, and my mother was still whole and unharmed.

"Mother," I greeted, swirling in my chair to gaze at my view from my corner office. Sunset on Manhattan really was beautiful, but even my mother managed to fuck that up.

It had only been three days since the feast, which meant I shouldn't have been due for another bout of torture for at least fifty years.

"You'll meet your father and me at the Majestic at midnight," her cultured and slightly accented voice snapped.

I'd spent the better part of four hundred years trying to get rid of mine, the only thing—other than blood, of course—that

I had in common with my wretched family.

I succeeded, mostly. It crept out when I was really pissed off.

I took a deep breath, not because I needed to but because that's what those zen humans did in order to stop murdering people.

"Good evening to you too. Hope you're well and enjoying the wonderful city of New York," I replied, knowing full well she hated the city and the country in general. Which was why it surprised me that she and father still remained. The king's party had been days before. It didn't mean good things for me or the general populace that they were sticking around. "And I wish I could meet you but I'm…." I searched for an excuse. "I just really don't want to."

There was a measured pause on her end. "You do remember your incentive to attend the feast, at which you insulted the king and embarrassed your family once again?" she asked in a tone that should have frozen my phone. "Well, that same incentive holds true now."

I clenched my teeth. My fangs punctured my top lip, though I barely noticed. "There's only so long such an incentive holds good for, Mother," I gritted out. "I think four hundred years is long enough."

"Well you surely could just ignore my request, see where that gets you." She was well practiced at delivering a threat without moving from her smooth tone that could cut silver. "Majestic. Midnight."

She hung up. I stared at my phone, then very calmly tossed it across the room with a force that shattered the picture frame it hit and the wall behind it, frame and phone tumbling to the ground in an echoing crash.

The steady background of human heartbeats rose slightly

with the sound, and then the door to my office opened.

My assistant Ashton's heartbeat stayed steady, as did his gaze as he regarded me and the shattered remains of a Warhol and my phone.

"Your mother?" he guessed.

I nodded once.

I didn't make a habit of making friends with employees, especially those who were of the human persuasion. However, I didn't detest Ashton nearly as much as the rest of the people working for me, so we occasionally indulged in a full-bodied red after work.

"I'll get you a new phone and call up to get this mess taken care of," he said calmly.

I nodded again.

"You need anything else? A Xanax? A hit man?" he asked.

I grinned. He knew of my relationship with my mother because he too had a nightmare who sired him. Growing up Mormon and gay wasn't a breeze for him, especially when his fanatic mother locked him in cupboards for hours on end and bathed him in scalding water to 'wash away the sin.' The ribbons of scars underneath his silk shirt were reminders of that. I'd paid her a visit the previous year, the night after he told me that story, in fact.

He hadn't seemed too broken up over her death.

"Oh I don't need a hit man, but thanks for the offer. It's really sweet." I knew plenty of people who dealt in death—a hulking Scotsman came to mind—but killing one of the ancient families was a crime punishable by death. Even if it was your own. Loopholes were if a vampire openly disrespected your Vein Line, killed a human on your property, or spilled blood under your roof. Aristocracy was still rampant in a society that was as immortal and unchanging as the vampires that made up that society.

Ashton gave me a smile and then left me to my rage.

Another reason why I liked him—no small talk. I detested small talk.

I walked into the lobby to the Majestic at quarter past midnight. I may have not had a choice to attend, but my mother hated to be kept waiting and I had to take small pleasures where they came.

The lobby was bustling with vampires who came not just to stay at the exclusively undead hotel, but to see and be seen in the opulent bar that boasted the best blood this side of the Pacific. Humans whose diets ranged from all raw meat, to only certain kinds of fruit, to an overabundance of sugar. I knew they had some meth heads hidden in the back for those after a high. Of course, those humans would lower the tone of the snooty and historic hotel; it was only the beautiful and sober ones weaving through the tables, offering themselves up.

I knew they were paid handsomely and found the lifestyle exciting, but it didn't mean I liked it. Secrecy was paramount, which meant any human who posed even the slightest risk of blabbing was eliminated. Those who 'retired' when they got too old, fat or anemic were either bespelled by the resident witch to forget their employ with the Majestic or drained at one of the less-opulent establishments that the hotel chain owned. No connections to such establishments existed on paper, of course.

"Ms. Rominskitoff, I'll direct you to your table," a vampire dressed in all black and sporting a severe bun and excellent bone structure addressed me. She smiled warmly and, kudos to her, didn't blink at my outfit.

I gave her a look. "Must you, though?" I asked.

She gave me a quizzical look, then turned to glide through the oak tables scattering the high-ceilinged bar area to one of the private booths at the back, separated by a red velvet curtain.

Of course.

The hotel had existed since Manhattan had been birthed, and it'd been exclusive to vampires since the night it opened its doors. Witches were paid handsomely to maintain the cloaking spell that urged most humans to stay away. Though in the age of Yelp and Google Maps, that was proving harder.

The waitress pulled the curtain aside to reveal my scowling mother and stoic father.

"Can I get you anyone to drink?" she asked. "Our special tonight is a twenty-three-year-old female who has cacao and cinnamon undertones."

"A vodka in a water glass filled right to the top will suffice," I replied, savoring the slight curl to my mother's lip as I ordered my uncouth drink.

The vampire inclined her head and then left us.

I sidled into the booth. "Mother, Father. A displeasure, as always."

My mother tapped her fingers on the wooden table and narrowed her eyes in response. She really was classically beautiful, if you didn't know what an evil bitch she was. Her hair was cut in a severe bob that brushed her chin, blood-red like mine. Her smooth face was pale and free of wrinkles with delicate features, like the Russian doll she was. She was the daughter of a tsar, after all. She looked little more than twenty-five but her soul, shriveled and blackened as it was, would betray her true age and nature if one were to cut her open.

My father was much the same, though he made the transition closer to thirty. His skin had a slight tan to it, black hair slicked back against his head, highlighting his harsh and angular features. He always dressed in a suit, no matter the occasion or the weather.

"Isla," he greeted, only a fraction more cordial than my mother. He glanced at my attire, which I'd chosen specifically for the event. The tight tee tucked into my high-waisted leather pencil skirt read "I'm not weird, I'm a vampire." I had pulled my hair into a messy ponytail and gone for a blood-red lip to match my fire engine-red thigh-high, heeled boots. It was hooker chic.

"Five hundred years old and your maturity level is that of a toddler," he observed flatly.

I gratefully took the glass offered to me by the waitress, thankful at least for the quick service. "I resent that. I'm pretty sure maturity is when you really, *really* want to kill someone but then you don't because it would be immature to do so in such well-regarded establishments." I gave my mother a smile as I sipped my drink.

No response. Though if I weren't mistaken, her eye twitched just slightly.

The silence yawned out between us, distaste and disappointment filling the air better than any words could have.

I glanced around the room, not perturbed in the slightest at the lack of conversation. I preferred it.

The night was still young, which meant the room wasn't bursting with well-dressed vampires as it would be towards the early hours of the morning. It was more of the civilized sadists there at the moment. Businessmen conducting deals, high-ranking city officials of the fanged persuasion enjoying their nightly brew of warm blood while reading the *New York Times*.

I glanced back to my statuesque parents. "As much as I'm

enjoying the riveting conversation, I'm sure you didn't have me drag my ass all the way down here to spend time with your only daughter," I said.

Mother pursed her lips. "You are correct. We don't subject ourselves to this"—she waved her hand at me—"for no reason at all."

I smiled at her. "Glad to hear it."

She glanced around the room before laying her long-nailed hands on the table, one atop the other. Something flickered in her cold eyes, something I didn't like at all. Something akin to satisfaction. Like that of a predator when they had their victim cornered.

"It's coming up to your half century," she began.

I clapped my hands. "You remembered," I exclaimed. "Please tell me we're planning my party. I want a pony." You would be forgiven if you'd assume I was turning five years old, not five centuries young if you spent time with me. After the first few hundred years, wisdom was not something I'd gained. It was a reversal, in fact. I was Benjamin Button in my mind. Or I was slowly losing my sanity. But at least I was having fun.

Mother's brows knitted together. "As it is, it's past time for you to be playing around like some common street vampire, or a half breed." She spat the insult like it dirtied her mouth. "We are losing patience with you, Isla."

I sucked my drink back in one swallow. "Patience?" I repeated. "Is that what you call your continued threats and violence and various attempts to bring about my untimely end?" I asked, my voice flat.

"We are of Ambrogio's Vein Line," my mother hissed. "Noble blood. The blood of the vampire blessed by Artemis herself. The blood of gods run through our veins. You will not dirty that blood with your *humanity*. We will not allow that."

I met her gaze. "And what are you going to do, Mother? Kill me right here, right now? Even you aren't that bold. Or stupid, unfortunately."

She glanced at my blank-faced and mute father. It was a familiar scene, Mother spitting her venom while Father sat there, silent and sentinel, the pulsating power from his age and strength daring me to go that little bit too far.

I always went a little bit too far, obviously.

"No. We shall not abandon our only daughter in such a way," she said finally. "Our Vein Line must continue. Through both the paternal and maternal offspring."

My blood ran cold. Or colder. I reasoned the waters in the Arctic would seem balmy compared to the ice in my veins.

My brothers were yet to marry and continue the line. I reasoned that they could never maintain a relationship with a woman long enough for her to carry a child to term. Even the mere four months it took for vampire women to cook a child in their oven. I had always assumed my family had reasoned my womb would be far too warm and accommodating to produce a vampire worthy of the Rominskitoff Vein Line.

My mother's, on the other hand, was the perfect barren and icy environment to grow little sadist vampires like my brothers. I had just been an unfortunate freak of nature.

"You have already had one Awakening," my mother continued. "And practiced your juvenile antics to ensure that we couldn't utilize that." The venom in her tone was still as fresh as when I'd finally emerged from my self-induced seclusion after my first Awakening two centuries back.

She'd been so furious she'd sicced both of my brothers on me and I'd barely gotten out undead.

I'd honestly been surprised at the depth of her fury. I'd disappeared the moment my rib cage had vibrated with the pulsing beat of my heart signifying my first Awakening, merely as a precaution. I thought it would be an off chance that my parents would try to get me impregnated with a Rominskitoff child that could work as my replacement.

Every female vampire had two Awakenings, the vampire version of puberty. When her heart started to beat again, her body turning… alive, for lack of a better word. Accommodating enough to conceive and carry a child to term. Male vampires were always able to and ready to father a child—don't ask me how, since I flunked anatomy—but for one year, a female vampire was able to fulfill her duty to further the vampire race.

That had been the last thing I wanted to do. Plus, I'd known if I had birthed a child it would have been snatched from my cold, dead, headless body from my parents.

Not a fate I would bestow on any child, nor myself.

So I'd slipped off to the Caribbean and drank a lot, sunned a lot and stayed celibate for a year. Even human men could technically give me a little half-vampire baby at that point. I was not risking it.

Now it was coming up to my second Awakening and my mother's words were a chilling realization that they planned on ensuring I didn't head off to a beach this time.

She grinned at me, as if feeding off my revulsion and slight panic. "We will not let you disappear this time, Isla. You will finally rid yourself of this wretched and treasonous humanity. Or *we* will find a way to do it," she informed me, voice pleasing—to an outsider, at least. To me, it was a snake slithering up my spine, constricting the bones with its brutal promise of destruction if I didn't find a way to rip off its head.

I gripped the table so hard small cracks erupted in the marble. Yet I stayed silent, fearing if I spoke I would do something stupid like lunge at my mother. Such an action would not ensure my continued survival. And I needed that.

My father leaned forward slightly, eyeing me as if he half expected the attack. As if he'd welcome it. "You've had your fun, Isla," he said, his voice smooth and accented. "But now you will serve your Vein Line. You will choose a partner before your Awakening. It does not need to be said that their Vein Line must have the Ichor of Ambrogio." He paused. "If you do not, we will choose someone and guarantee, by any means necessary, that you produce a Rominskitoff heir."

I met his cold eyes, and every single cell in my body seeped pure hatred and fury. "*Rape*, you mean," I spat. "You noble members with the blood of gods will procure an equally noble vampire to rape me while my brothers hold me down."

Mother pursed her lips and gathered her bag, standing. "You must always turn everything into a spectacle," she hissed.

I laughed, long and cold. "A spectacle is what you'll get if you even attempt to make good on your promise," I threatened. "A fucking exhibition of just how far I'm willing to go to ensure you never rent out my womb to grow a child to replace the one you're staring at right now."

Every single word I uttered dripped with venom. With the death I'd rain down to make sure that never happened.

My father stood, his hand on my mother's lower back as they exited the booth. So chivalrous.

His unfeeling eyes flickered to me. "You know this is inevitable, Isla. Better you learn to be more accommodating. Then this will be more pleasant for you."

And then they left, slinking around the corner, to spread their venom all across the city.

I sank back into the plush seat as the couture-clad back of my mother disappeared. Fury simmered in my stomach, as was normal with meeting my parents, but this particular occasion had me shaking with it. I seriously considered looking up a Scotsman, knowing he cared little about ancient laws and a lot about money. I had enough to pay for the assassination of my family ten times over, but I didn't think it would go without a hitch. My mother and my brothers were snakes; she would expect me to lash out and would therefore have a trap ready for me to walk into.

So I had to have something I was not known for—patience.

I couldn't run either. It would be exactly what they'd expect. The odds were stacked against me, but there was a time to cut the apron strings. Right about the time my parents promised to get me raped in order to impregnate me. Yep. Right about then.

I gestured to the waitresses who hovered close by. We were the Rominskitoffs; giving us bad service was tantamount to suicide.

"I'll take that cacao special after all"

She nodded. "Right away."

Every girl needed chocolate after a particularly testing evening.

I had to find some form of calm in order to produce a rational plan. Letting the evening eat up every part of me was not the way to win. I had to play the long game. My Awakening was years off, precisely why my parents had chosen now to make their move. To rattle me.

I was not easily rattled.

And they'd just made their biggest mistake.

Underestimating me.

That was going to be fatal to the entire fucking Rominskitoff Vein Line.

After I'd sated my tastes and managed to somewhat swallow my rage, I emerged from the curtain to run into the last person I expected, yet wanted, to see.

"Isla." His voice ran over my name in a throaty caress.

"Your Highness." I addressed him with his honorary title but didn't bow. I'd only likely do that if I had a severed spine. This had the stick-thin, gorgeous vampire beside him sucking on her lips in distaste. Though maybe it was just my general presence. We had history.

The monarch didn't address this slight and if I wasn't mistaken, amusement danced in his eyes. It increased as his gaze flickered down to my chest. "It's most pleasant to see you again, in the midst of…." He glanced at his consort for the night. The king was a notorious lothario, never seen with the same vampire twice. The current one was decidedly forgettable, another beautiful, pinched-face vampire dripping in couture and diamonds. "More of the same."

I bit my lip to hide my smile at the open insult. Selene didn't react to it, too well bred for that. I should know, as she was the daughter my mother wished she had—in other words, a murderous shrew with a borderline personality disorder who made it her life's work to claw her way to the top.

We went to Mortimeus together, the vampire version of college. Only with more blood and less keggers.

We weren't friends.

"Well, I pride myself on being unique," I replied evenly.

His brows rose slightly, but other than that his handsome face remained impassive. "That you are," he agreed.

I frowned slightly at the interest in his gaze and at my reaction to it. As in, I didn't want to stab myself in the eye to escape this conversation, even with Selene's glare in the mix. I was enjoying his presence.

Luckily I didn't have to continue the small talk with the disconcerting monarch, since a barrage of gunfire and blood-curdling screams interrupted it. Someone was obviously looking out for me.

Out of nowhere, four vampires in black suits surrounded the king, fangs out, clutching copper blades.

The king's eyes turned to stone and his gaze darted to the open bar area, the smell of fresh blood filtering from it. His stare was calculating and calm, much like a soldier would assess the situation.

"What do we have?" he asked amongst the spattering of gunfire and continued screams of the previously serene and composed patrons. Most aristocratic vampires were cowards, only preying on those who couldn't fight back.

Me? The only fun was fighting creatures who *could* fight back.

"Attack from all entrances and exits, unknown amount of hostiles," the one closest to him replied, pausing as he listened to the device in his ear. "Assailants are of an unknown species. We have a report of a werewolf in the lobby while others describe vampires."

The king's gaze hardened with a glazed film that I recognized. He was preparing for a fight.

I was impressed at not only this look but at the impression that this wasn't the first time the king had fought. Though monarchs were of a different class than the softer 'great' families that served them, they needed to be strong enough to kill their previous rulers.

Selene whimpered, but everyone ignored her.

This wasn't good. The Majestic had stood for as long as Manhattan had, a pillar of vampire society and a justifiable Switzerland throughout any civil wars or infighting between families. Only human blood was to be spilled there.

Until now.

And reports of vampires and werewolves working together? Not good at all.

The uncertain times that we had been living in for the past decade seemed to be defining themselves more concretely, with the smell of war filtering through the perfumed air of the Majestic.

I yanked two matching copper blades from the inside of my boots and braced myself for the battle.

The king glanced at my blades and where they came from with a slightly raised brow.

I shrugged. "Necessary when meeting my parents for drinks."

He shook his head. "Unique," he muttered to himself.

Selene tugged at his sleeve. "Why aren't we running?" she whined. Her eyes darted to the king's guards, who were surveying the room. We were slightly removed from the general populace, so we could only hear the attack happening in the main room, smell the blood and death. We had yet to embrace it.

"Shouldn't you be ushering your king to safety?" she snapped.

I rolled my eyes.

The king regarded her evenly, then backhanded her with enough force to send her crumpling to the ground unconscious.

Right on.

I didn't have much time to bathe in that moment because a werewolf chose to come barreling into me, slamming into my midsection and sending me flying into the booth I'd just vacated. Even the wet dog smell and the snapping of teeth at my jugular were preferable to the company I had just enjoyed in the same booth minutes before.

I slammed my first blade into the shoulder section of the giant creature and reveled in the yelp of pain. When it was distracted, it gave me enough wiggle room to move to snap its neck. It fell limp against me instantly, the dead weight pressing my back painfully into the shattered glass on the table. I pushed it off me, jumping back to the Persian carpet that had become a bloodstained battlefield. The king's guards were fighting off attacks from every side. And instead of hiding behind them, the king was front and center. His body jerked as a barrage of gunfire scattered the area, a bullet finding purchase in his flesh. I darted forward to yank the gun out of the shooter's hands.

"Bringing a gun to a fang fight?" I hissed at the masked vampire as I crushed the weapon in my grip. "That's just bad form." Then I snapped his neck. It would take him out of action for a good ten minutes, hopefully half the length of the battle.

Battles between immortals rarely lasted for an extended amount of time. To human eyes, it would have been little more than a blur and a cacophony of noise and blood.

More gunfire roared through the thumps and tearing of flesh. Fire erupted in my shoulder, the realization that they were using copper rounds pissing me right off.

Ambushing a sacred and historical landmark and bringing weapons? The youth were really cheapening a good fight. After dispatching another two vampires and plugging them with their own weapons, I glanced back to who I guessed the reason for the attack was. The king was holding his own with not a hair out of place, apart from the blood staining his neck where the bullet had hit him.

Close. If that had gone through his skull it might have been bye-bye monarch.

A flash of movement behind him caught my eye. Selene had woken up, and obviously didn't take kindly to be ignored, if the gun directed at the king's temple was anything to go by. He was still distracted and didn't count the pale socialite as a threat, the vampires with guns and pet werewolves more pressing in his mind. She grinned wickedly at that realization. Though she wasn't grinning when I snapped the bones in her wrist, causing the gun to tumble to the floor and her to cry out in pain.

"Assassinating the king, Selene?" I asked conversationally. "What *would* your mother say?" I didn't wait for a response, just slammed my fist into her chest, satisfied as her rib cage shattered with the force of my blow. She tumbled to the ground, immobile.

I grinned at her prone form as the battle quieted around me.

Then, as if someone flicked a switch, silence reigned. It was how it usually ended; nothing like the movies, with dramatic openings and closings and cries of victory. Death was rarely triumphant, even for the victorious. There was only one true victor in a fight—the shadow that lurked at the corners, taking the fallen into its embrace.

The king's icy presence tickled the side of my arm. I continued to consider Selene, frowning. "You really need to pick better dates, Your Highness," I said, breaking the silence.

His emerald gaze was no longer empty with his practiced coldness. Instead it glowed, full of the blood that had been spilled. As it settled over me, it danced with the own sparkling in my veins. A fight did that to you. As did the gaze of a hot vampire king, if I were being honest.

He searched my face, ignoring the chaos that had settled in around as his guards snatched up groaning bodies and such. "I had you pegged as a lover, not a fighter," he rasped.

I grinned, letting my fangs brush my top lip in a brutal

caress. "Oh baby, I'm both."

Before I could get in any more trouble and ruin my boots, I darted out of the room, dodging fallen bodies as I did. I was only successful because it was likely the last thing the king expected me to do. He'd probably assumed I'd erupt in feminine hysterics or use me saving his life as currency to further my position in society.

But what could I say? I'm unique.

One week later

"Hey, Lewis, what have you got for me today?" I strutted through the door the detective held open for me, wandering around his office as he closed it.

I picked up a document at random from his stacks, frowning at the coroner's report. I was just getting to the part about unusual toxins in the blood when the paper was snatched from my hand.

"That's confidential," Lewis snapped, frowning at me and rounding his desk.

"Touchy." I rolled my eyes and sat across from him, crossing my legs.

His eyes flickered to my bare pins before moving his gaze up my body. It wasn't appreciative like the rest of the men, and some women, in the station had been. He didn't think of me that way. He knew what I was. What I really was, apart from a knockout redhead with decent tits, an immaculate fashion sense and a great ass.

And fangs.

He focused on the fangs.

Let's just say the great detective was not exactly turned on by the fact that I drank blood to keep that ass fed.

"Must you dress like that when you come here?" he growled, stacking the papers scattered across his messy desk in an attempt to get them out of my reach.

I glanced down to my white pencil skirt, strappy Manolos and sleeveless gray silk blouse. "Like what? A model? Fashionista? Sex symbol?"

He shook his head. "You're drawing attention."

I grinned. "Well, of course I am. I exist."

"Fuck," he muttered under his breath, running his hands through his graying hair. The detective was pushing forty and although he was pretty well maintained in the body department, he wore his age and exhaustion on his face. It was as if ten years had passed since I'd seen him last, not a month.

"When was the last time you caught some *z*'s, detective? Or at least snorted some cocaine?"

He glared at me. "We're understaffed and there's been numerous unsolved murders around the city. The grisly kind. The kind that even seasoned detectives have been shocked by. Not to mention missing persons." He gave me a look, one full of accusation.

I held my hands up. "Hey, don't look at me. I clean up after myself. Or, more accurately, I call the person to clean up after me."

Technically I could get seriously punished for even *speaking* to a human about such things, but what could I say? I didn't give a shit.

"That doesn't mean your kind is not responsible for these depraved acts," he hissed, his eyes haunted.

I bristled and leaned forward, laying my hands on his desk. "Depravity isn't uniquely a vampire condition," I informed him. I grabbed the closest file on the messy desk, running my eyes over the report on a couple of teenagers torturing and killing a homeless man. I met Lewis's eyes. "In fact, if we got down to it, you'd find that humans might have the monopoly over that. Even the most sadistic vampires kill for an underlying reason—sustenance. Their methods may be flawed and archaic, but there is some natural explanation." I held up the file I was clutching. "Humans, on the other hand, have slaughtered each other through the centuries for what god they worship, the color of their skin or for resources. That in itself is cause for you to maybe rethink your unwavering hatred for the undead and check out the living."

He regarded me, his eyes not giving away much. "I don't have an unwavering hatred for you, Isla," he said quietly.

I restrained my surprise at the warmth in his tone.

Lewis and I went way back—twenty years, in fact. I'd been minding my own business, out for a stroll to grab a bite, when I was accosted by a group of miscreants with less-than-noble intentions. I'd decided they were a perfect dinner and went about ensuring they wouldn't try and gang rape a woman alone in an alley in the near future. Unfortunately, a rookie cop had stumbled upon the scene and witnessed too much.

His eyes and the way they danced with shock and disgust and the tiniest bit of excitement told me he'd seen it all. They weren't focused on the three men lying tangled at my feet. No, they were on me and, more precisely, my fangs.

I retracted them and wiped the underside of my lip with my thumb.

"I couldn't convince you to turn around and go about your life like you didn't just see that, can I?" I asked hopefully.

His silence served as my answer.

"Great," I muttered.

Before he had the chance to do anything like use the gun at his hip, I darted forward, clutching his arm and dragging him into the empty warehouse beside the alley.

He reared back the second we stood in the middle of the cavernous room, smelling faintly of urine and narcotics. A quick scan told me that the homeless humans using the place as lodging weren't currently in residence. Thankfully.

The young cop with a baby face and a spotless uniform looked like he might throw up.

"Hold your breakfast there, Officer. No one wants regurgitated doughnuts ruining your shiny shoes."

He didn't hear me, probably trying to get his bearings. Instead of spending time looking for them, he did what all humans seemed to do, reaching for a weapon instead of sense.

The hand holding the gun was shaking uncontrollably. If he managed to squeeze off a shot, it wasn't likely to hit me, even though I was standing a few feet in front of him.

"You're...."

I folded my arms. "A vampire," I finished for him.

That word succeeded in sucking all sound from the room. His heart even skipped a beat.

The officer took time to digest. Think on it. Though he didn't lower his gun.

"This... this is unbelievable," he stammered, finally. His voice echoed through the room and if his hand hadn't been shaking and heart not been pumping frantically I would have been under the impression he was calm. His voice was, at least.

I did appreciate that he didn't cry or scream or shout 'Back, devil.' I'd gotten all three a multitude of times.

I gave him a look. "No, it's incredibly believable, which is what makes you reject it with all of the force of your incredibly narrow mind. We aren't aliens from outer space, nor are we disfigured monsters. We're touchable within your human narrative.

We look like you, talk like you, like the same TV shows. We just live a lot longer and feed on blood instead of burgers. Don't get me wrong, a double cheeseburger is pretty darn good, but it's not going to keep me immortal. We need the essence of what makes you mortal to do that."

His body was frozen, though his trigger finger twitched slightly.

I grinned. "Try it."

His brows furrowed. "What?"

I nodded to his belt. "Plug me with the entire clip, if that's what you need to do to grasp a concept that isn't exactly outside the realm of possibility. That's what makes it so impossible."

He regarded me, his grip still tight on the gun.

It could go either way, I wagered. I'd seen a lot of humans, good, bad and everything in between. They were almost never always completely 'good' or 'bad.' I was loath to believe in such concepts, similar to how this cop wasn't going to believe I was four hundred and forty years older than him. Such ideas belonged in fairytales, alongside tales of bloodsucking monsters. Only one thing existed in the 'real' world, and it wasn't the good and evil binary. Even bloodsucking monsters were more realistic than that, if you thought on it long enough.

But this guy, he was the closest to the fantastical concept of 'good' that I'd encountered. I'd been around enough humans to smell the depravity seeping from their pores. Decency was just as easy to spot, even if it was decidedly rarer. Every instinct was telling him to shoot me, but he was fighting it. His eyes were weathered and old for such a young rookie, but not yet hardened by the horrors he'd no doubt encounter if he lived through this.

"I'm not shootin' an unarmed woman," he gritted out finally, his posture relaxing slightly as he lowered the gun.

"I don't need weapons to kill you, rookie," I told him before

stepping forward, letting my mouth open and my fangs elongate.

His eyes widened and he went back on one foot as if to scuttle back, but he stopped there, holding his ground.

I grinned at him. "Stubborn, brave, or stupid," I observed, retracting my fangs. "All three would have gotten you killed if you had been in the company of any vampire but me." I glanced to his gun and then the eyes that, if I weren't mistaken, seemed to have hardened within the length of our conversation that no doubt blew his tiny, ordered mind. "I get that it's a lot to swallow—pardon the pun." I winked. "But this"—I gestured around the room—"the world, is so much more than you see through those blurry mortal eyes. You're blind because we want you to be, and more importantly because you *want to be .Your alternative, entertaining ideas about immortal beings – the supernatural underpinning and influencing all of the history you've thought you humans were responsible for?" I shook my head. "That would not go well with you trying to find understanding in the world. Plus, your mortality is of enough trouble for you. Finding that there are those not plagued with that burden might just get you angry enough to decide to wipe out those who have the gift of eternal life."*

I narrowed my eyes at him. "Which would not end well. Bit of advice for free. You know that what goes bump in the night can drain you dry in the blink of an eye, so don't decide to be a hero and go on some sort of mission to save mankind. It's not possible. Plus, saving mankind is not going after the supernatural, but fighting mankind itself. Your species seems intent on killing itself. Wars, diseases, murder, global warming, you're doing everything in your power to make sure your life span is even shorter than it already is. Which doesn't bode well for people like me, who need at least some humans around, you know, to snack on, and to give me fabulous shoes. So, how about we make a deal? You hand me over every human you can't lock away and I'll make sure they pay."

We'd been working together ever since.

"Can't you at least tell your friends that they need to find a new hunting ground?" he clipped.

I picked up his paperweight, turning it in my hands. "They aren't my friends, just fellow members of my species. I'm not asking you to march over to have a chat with Kim Jong-un and kindly ask him to stop with all those human rights violations, am I? And me telling them where to dine would most likely land me six feet under. For good. And I rather like being top-side." I glanced up. "So instead of talking about things we can't change, how about you tell me what you've got for me?"

He sighed, rummaging through his files.

"You need a system," I observed.

He ignored me.

"Color coding is always good," I continued.

More silence.

"Or how about you try this newfangled technology, you know, the one that's being utilized as modern art right now." I nodded to the computer on the side on his desk, covered in dust and not emitting a low hum that would mean it was actually turned on. "I know it's hard to get into the twenty-first century, but I adapted and I'm much older than you."

He threw a file at me, ignoring all my comments. He didn't exactly like to be reminded that I had about four hundred years on him, despite looking like his daughter. Or his midlife crisis. I knew his contemporaries speculated on both.

I knew there was also talk about how I'd been in and out for years and hadn't seemed to age a day. I'd encouraged Lewis to tell them I had a really good plastic surgeon. We rarely met in his office anymore, but I was starting to feel annoyed and slightly homicidal after the whole debacle at the Majestic. Not the battle—that was rather pleasing actually, but the bloodbath that was the conversation with my parents.

Needless to say, Lewis did not like me entering his place of work and causing a stir. Which was precisely why I did it.

"Joseph O'Malley. We got him on three child assault charges. Or we did, until every single kid retracted their statements. Now it looks like the fucker'll walk."

I opened the file. "Not for long," I muttered, then raised my brows. "*Father* Joseph O'Malley?"

"What, priests violate your moral code?" he asked dryly.

I grinned. "The only things that violate my moral code are sneakers and jeans. Draining the priest, I can get right with." I memorized his details along with his address and place of worship. I glanced up. "Anyone else?"

He shook his head.

"Slow day for scumbags."

"No, just managed to lock the rest of them up. You know, do my actual job," he said, his voice hard.

"Your job is to punish those who do wrong?" I asked.

He nodded curtly.

I shook the folder before tossing it back to him and standing. "Well, you're still doing your job, just outsourcing. So you can keep your own moral code. You're helping people," I said, my voice softer.

He frowned at me. "Yeah," he relented.

I blew him a kiss. "Stay classy, Lewis. And if you're not going to get some shut-eye, I recommend cocaine. I can put you in touch with a good supplier."

He scowled at me. "Good-bye, Isla."

I grinned and walked out the door.

My eyes locked with crystal blue ones across the room, so

blue they flickered to silver. The moment they caught sight of me, they illuminated in hatred, glittering pure and so certain I had to blink a couple of times to make sure the attractive man was not, in fact, my mother.

Nope, his strong jaw and beating heart communicated that he was not the female vampire who birthed me. His considerable form tightened and a sharp masculine jaw turned granite. The change was palpable, even from across the room. Rage rolled through the desks and files until it washed over me with enough force that I could sense its texture.

Vampires couldn't read people's minds; Hollywood had taken liberties with the fact that we could sense emotions or auras, though. Humans emitted them every hour of every day, even when they slept. One of the first things I'd perfected as a new vampire—after my murder spree, of course—was how to block them out. I didn't need to be emerged in the sea of insipid human emotion all day every day. It was bad enough I heard snatches of their conversations on a twenty-four-hour basis.

Sometimes it was irritating enough to question whatever screwed moral code I had. I just wanted to kill every loud, unintelligent and oblivious one of them.

This human, though, his emotions were different. They tore down my shields like they were paper and urged me to inspect them, taste his hate.

He was still glaring at me in shock.

Of course, I'd sensed him the moment he'd set his motorcycle boot into the open precinct. Obviously he didn't have my mad skills, as he was now only just clocking me.

I smiled at him.

He glowered further, which made him even more attractive. He was sitting, so I only saw half of his body, but it was a good half, although arguably not the best. His hair was midnight and short, tousled and spiky in a way that looked like it took hours, but I'd bet he just rolled out of bed like that. His features were strong and masculine, harsh enough to stop him from being classically handsome, his clipped beard adding to the 'bad boy lumberjack' thing.

Yeah, he was hot.

And also a slayer. I probably should have mentioned that first. They actually called themselves Praestes, but come on, how obnoxious was that? Using the Latin word for protectors to fashion themselves as some sort of heroes? No one called them that; we all had much more colorful, derogatory names for them. Slayers was the most recent, and most kind. They were part of a sect as old as vampires themselves, existing purely to kill our race, or at least try to dampen down the numbers. Mortal enemies, blah, blah, blah.

A lot of vampires, my brothers specifically, made it their mission to hunt down slayers to the point of extinction.

Me, I tried to ignore them when possible, break a few bones when not.

This one, I didn't want to ignore, despite the murder in his eyes.

This one sparked feelings similar to, but a lot different than those the king of all vampires had spiked a few days prior.

I didn't have time to go on a stare-down death match type of thing.

It was time to go to church.

THREE

LIFE IS SUPPOSEDLY ABOUT BINARY OPPOSITIONS. YOU know those two people I talked about in the beginning? The hero and the villain? Binary oppositions. Like good and evil. Black and white. They're a cultural construction. Who knows when the idea of life being so simple, so definable, began. Maybe sometime, way back when, life *was* that simple. Easily categorized. Though I doubted that; even in the beginning simplicity was a luxury bestowed to Adam and Eve. It sure wasn't now. It wasn't black and white. Heck, it wasn't even black, white and gray.

Heroes and villains existed solely to sell movie tickets. To fuel ideas about life to keep the ideological machine chugging away, to distract humans from what was going on behind the curtain. What the powers that be were doing, the struggles for that power and the atrocities committed in pursuit of it. To distract humans from that, and from their own mortality.

As an immortal, maybe I needed distracting most of all. Wasn't it those of us who held the possibility of eternal life in our hands the people who were most likely to be consumed, obsessed, with death? Humans who had but a scarce moment on this earth and were fragile as feathers were easily distracted from their impending doom. Distraction in the form of binary oppositions.

I might see through the construction. See more. But I was also a slave to those ideas myself.

For me to exist—the soulless, evil, immoral, immortal creature that I was—someone else needed to balance me. To counter me. My binary opposition.

A slayer.

First used as villains in our bedtimes stories, slayers were what went bump in the night for us. The only thing that could kill us. *Designed* to kill us. I didn't know how it worked because I didn't share lattes with beings who existed solely to hunt my kind into extinction, but I knew they could sense us. We passed unnoticed to mere mortals, although some with the touch might see us for what we truly were. Witches too, and shifters—let's blanket that to all supernatural creatures that most humans were blissfully oblivious to. But slayers weren't of the supernatural world. They were mortals, as far as I knew. Hybrid versions, for sure, but human nonetheless. Less breakable than most, but my brothers had made it apparent that they could die rather easily.

Scientists on both sides had puzzled for a century as to why we could sense one another. Countless slayers and a handful of stupid vampires were caught by their respective enemies and dissected to see what it was that caused this connection.

None could be found.

My theory? Nature.

Yes, many liked to preach—maybe this preacher right before me, in fact—that my race were unnatural and ungodly creatures. But we were born, not made. Part of the natural world. Top of the food chain. So something had to exist in nature to counteract us, to balance.

Hence slayers.

That's just my two cents.

But this slayer was really pissing me off. He'd followed me from the police station to the church, where I'd made it just in time for afternoon mass.

"It is not without sin that we must strive to live, but through faith. God forgives all of his children who hold faith in their hearts and love in their souls. 'The righteous will live by faith,' Romans 1:17." He spoke softly but with an underlying echo that boomed through the whole room. With a quiet grace that cloaked the dark evil soul underneath.

I barely restrained a snort. Actually, I barely restrained myself from bursting from my seat and draining him right there and then. But even I must have some limits. So I settled for glaring at the white-haired man in the collar with his hypocrisy. It made me even angrier that the church was crowded, almost full.

I licked my lips at the prospect of sending this guy into the afterlife, where he would most certainly not meet the god he pretended to worship. Nor would he be forgiven for his sins that even a merciful god could wash away.

I just had to get rid of the slayer first.

I'd positioned myself on the edge of the altar for this precise situation. I'd hoped he'd lose interest, reasoning that he might have, I don't know, a life other than following me around. Though, I guess following me around was technically his life.

Rather inconvenient when I planned on draining a priest.

I pushed open the double doors to the church, shoving my heavy black sunglasses down on my face as the sunlight assaulted my eyes. It had been weeks since I slept. The raw sunlight's effect had me realizing I had to pencil in some shuteye.

Another small thing the lore had taken liberties with. We didn't burst into flame with the presence of sunlight, but it became an annoyance when we hadn't slept. Though it helped with the monster image for humans to think we slunk in the shadows, holding dominion over the darkness while they held the light.

The streets weren't busy in this neighborhood in early afternoon, and the slayer made it no secret that he was following me.

I guessed you couldn't really be stealthy when the person you were stalking was born with an instinct to sense your presence.

Bummer for him.

I passed a homeless man outside a grocery store and tossed a fifty in his pan.

"God bless you, miss," he exclaimed, fingering the money with wide eyes. I hoped he wouldn't drink or snort it all. Though he smelled sober enough, if not in need of a shower.

"Or Satan damn me," I muttered.

I kept walking past the grocery store and veered down an alleyway. It was off the street, quiet and bathed in shadows.

Perfect.

I leaned against the brick wall by a dumpster, hoping the rough stone wouldn't catch threads in my blouse.

It was only a few seconds before I smelled the woodsy scent of tobacco and something else almost as enticing as fresh blood—his scent, filled with tumultuous emotions, and a steady undertone of rage.

I ignored that.

"You know, you could have just asked me on a date instead of following me," I said blandly, glancing up from my nails. "Though, my ass does look great in this skirt, so I'm guessing the view from behind wasn't bad." I winked at him. He glared at me, splaying his feet wide as he came to a stop in front of me, dangling a long silver knife from his hand. I glanced at the carvings, registering the gentle hum in the air surrounding the blade.

"Blessed by a witch," I observed, then clapped. "This isn't the slayer's first rodeo." I didn't move from my position against the brick, my body relaxed. The way he was standing, so close, using his size to take up the alley, would have given the outsider the illusion that I couldn't escape.

Of course, I was a vampire. I could escape in a second if I wanted.

But I was a vampire. I didn't escape from anyone.

Even a slayer with one of the only weapons that had the chance to fuck up my day.

"What were you doing at that police station?" he demanded. His voice was a low baritone, manly and rough. Where the king's voice sent shivers of ice down my spine, the slayer's rough gravelly tone had heat shooting from my toes to the hair piled atop my head.

Up close, he was even more delicious. His downstairs area, the one I couldn't see at the precinct, was impressive, powerful thighs encased in faded blue jeans. And the tee under his leather jacket was molded to his torso, hinting at the ridges of his abs and a physique that I bet could have graced every cover of *GQ* on the planet.

I'd known he was built, but he was *built*. Muscles apparent even under the leather jacket, and he easily towered over me, even in my heels. And his scent, tainted with the fury and hatred he was nurturing for me, was woodsy and distinctly masculine, stirring the most basic instinct every creature had—arousal.

I was so deranged, checking out the guy who was moments away from trying to end me.

Trying being the operative word.

"I was reporting a crime," I answered. "Keeping the streets of this fair city safer." I quirked my brow. "I hear there're men accosting women in alleyways with knives."

He stepped forward, gripping his knife tightly. I didn't react. "What the fuck do you have on Lewis? He's a good man," he hissed.

His rage surrounded me, but instead of revolting against it, my body sank into it, welcoming the bitter musk.

Jerking myself out of the fog his anger had created in my mind, I nodded. "That he is."

His eyes were marble, glistening with fury. "You need to leave him the fuck alone."

I held up my hands. "Dude, he called *me*. I'm not one to disobey a detective. I respect the law and those who enforce it. There're too many heathens out there who don't in these archaic times." I gave his knife another pointed look. "Why, a mere hundred years ago a well-bred man would never have even entertained the thought of approaching a young and, might I say, stunning young woman and confronting her with a weapon." I resumed my gaze down his thighs to his black boots and then back up again, past the beard and crazy hair to the wild eyes. "Then again, I'm not exactly in the presence of a well-bred man, so the point is moot."

I watched in amusement and maybe slight arousal as his anger intensified.

He was hot when he got all murdery. Granted, I'd only seen him murdery, but that's how I liked my men: broody with a side of homicidal.

"Why were you at the church?" he snapped, giving up on his last line of questioning.

"It was closer than McDonald's and I was after a snack," I responded. I wasn't even going to bother telling him about Father Kiddy-fiddler. No way he'd ever believe me. "What's with the third degree? All the slayers I encounter lead with that, getting all stabby." I nodded to the steel at his side. "Granted, theirs don't usually have those fancy scribbles on it, but they like to go straight for the kill, don't even take me to dinner first."

Something flickered in his eyes, the rage disappearing for a few seconds before hard resolve replaced it. "You're right. I'm not getting anything from this conversation, so it's about time it ended."

He stepped forward again, that time with purpose, and I sighed heavily before straightening. Then Duke's "Vampires" punctured the air, taking away the drama and making the slayer momentarily freeze. I guessed my choice in ringtone wasn't exactly tasteful, but I found it amusing and that was all that mattered, right?

I smiled at him, holding up my finger. "Let's pause this death match. I've really got to answer this." I glanced down at my bag to retrieve my phone. If he had decided to strike while he thought my attention was diverted, it would have been a mistake. I could have disemboweled him with my pinky finger while reading *War and Peace* if I so desired. Many rookies had made such mistakes.

He didn't.

Definitely not this slayer's first rodeo.

I put the phone to my ear, smiling apologetically to the

man with the knife. The really hot man with the knife.

The one I should have itched to kill instead of wondering what his lips tasted like.

"For the thirty-fourth time, Scott, I am not coming to ComicCon with you," I answered. After the party Scott had this warped idea that we were friends, and the annoying little twit wouldn't leave me alone. I assigned him a ringtone so I could prepare for his calls.

"Why not? It's kickass," he whined.

I didn't take my gaze off the ice-blue eyes which were now flickering with something other than homicide. Amusement? No, it couldn't be. The stoic slayer types weren't capable of such a thing. It was all kill, kill, kill.

Yawn.

Even I, a vampire bred and birthed for such a reason, had other hobbies. I was an avid shoe collector, for one.

"Because I consider it to be the epitome of evil," I responded. "You know, present company excluded. It's an insult to our very existence. The fact that you want to go makes me want to stake you myself, except staking doesn't do shit apart from piss a vampire off." I paused, seeing the slayer's eyes flicker again. Definitely amusement. "So stop asking me to come. I'm personally insulted every time. And I can't talk about this right now. There's this marble-faced slayer in front of me anxious to get his *Bladerunner* on. If you're not careful, instead of kicking his ass I'll just give him your address where he can punish you for harassing me about this stupid human convention."

There was a gasp at the other end of the phone. "Fuck, Isla. A slayer? Hold on. I'll get your location and be there to help." The rapid typing on a keyboard filled the phone.

I laughed. "Dude, I got it. I can handle *one* slayer. I'd have to let you take me to this convention if I couldn't and sacrifice myself to the Twiharders, or whatever they're called." My eyes met those iceberg blue ones that were flickering with quicksilver. "Now how about you go shopping for a new date to your convention and your Captain Kirk outfit? Got to go."

I hung up on him.

I slipped the phone back into my bag and shrugged at the man in front of me. "Sorry about that. He would have just kept calling if I hadn't answered, and it would totally ruin the vibe you've got going here." I waved my hand down his body. "He's a pain, but I just don't have the heart to kill him. What can you do?" I stood a little taller. "Now, where were we? Right, you were going to try and get all stabby. Then I'd have to kick your ass, and it'd be embarrassing for you to limp back to the slayer clubhouse. So how about we save my manicure and your pride and just go our separate ways?"

He blinked away the amusement and if I wasn't mistaken, shock shuttered his gaze once more, his muscles pulsing in his neck. "Not fuckin' likely," he growled. "It's against my nature to leave a vamp breathing."

"Well, I'm not breathing, so there we go. You're not going against your nature," I informed him chirpily. I stepped forward with deliberate slowness, showing my intention to slip around him, just to see what he'd do.

Surprise, surprise, he moved his body so he could block my way and bring himself closer to me.

It pissed me off that I enjoyed the proximity, the way his heartbeat vibrated through my own body with its force, so much stronger than regular humans.

Obviously I couldn't give my preference to that away. In fact, I should kill him on principle and to stop my body from working against me.

I straightened my shoulders. "It's always the hard way with

you burly types."

I could taste him, the scent bitter and sweet at the same time. Interestingly, his heartbeat was even, a steady thump that vibrated the air. Even the most experienced of slayers had a slight increase in beats per minute during confrontations with vampires. Experienced slayers more so; they knew enough about vampires to fear them.

Either this one wasn't threatened by me, and therefore very stupid, or else he was… something else. Something that was the reason for his strange alluring scent that almost wasn't human.

But it had to be. What else was there? Every instinct in my body told me this was a slayer, my cells almost rejecting his presence at the same time as welcoming it. Yeah, he was a slayer. And by that very fact, it ruled him out from being anything but human.

"I don't want to hurt you," I stated honestly.

His brows rose. "You think I look fuckin' stupid?"

I grinned. "Do you really want me to answer that?"

His lips thinned. "You're a bloodsucker. Of course you don't want to hurt me. You want to drain me dry."

I rolled my eyes. "Don't flatter yourself, buddy. I'm not suicidal like you." Another pesky part of the slayer's genetic makeup: their blood was toxic, to vampires at least. Only uneducated or stupid vampires actually died from sucking their blood, since it wasn't exactly a secret. But they were inventive in the ways they used it.

I'd heard whispers that they were developing bullets that were injected with their own blood and copper-coated. If that was true, they might stand a semblance of a chance against our race.

His eyes stayed locked with mine, his body taut and ready

for attack. Instead of doing so, he just stood there, a hair's breadth away, imprinting his scent on me, those piercing blue eyes unnerving in their intensity.

The stillness between two naturally opposing creatures such as ourselves should have been uncomfortable. It shouldn't have been like this. Like the swirl of quicksilver in his eyes was urging him against killing me. Like that swirl flickered with something that crept up my spine and urged me to lean forward, not to bite but to....

"Hey!" The loud shout tore the moment and both of our heads snapped to the direction of the voice. It was coming from the mouth of the alley where a man was stopped, staring at the two of us.

I jerked back, the interruption giving me exactly what I needed. Clarity. And distance from the slayer that spelled disaster.

"What the fuck are you doing? Get away from her!" the man yelled.

Then he started to briskly jog in our direction when the slayer didn't move.

I realized what this looked like: a hulking man with a beard, leather jacket and a knife backing up a well-dressed woman in an alleyway. Needless to say, this woman was far from helpless, but to the mortal's eye, I was a delicate flower.

"You should run," I whispered to the slayer, who bristled.

"Like fuck I'm going anywhere," he hissed, the man almost on us. "I'm not leaving you alone with a human."

I put my hand to my chest and watched as his eyes flickered to my ample assets. I grinned inwardly. "I would never drain a man who's riding in to save the day. That's just bad taste."

His eyes darkened but he didn't have the chance to say anything before the man roughly pushed the slayer out of my orbit. I was both glad and pissed about that. Slayers in the immediate vicinity weren't usually ideal, but this one… well, I was getting used to it. Liking it.

"What the fuck are you doing?" my knight in plaid yelled at my villain in leather. The man whipped his ponytailed head to me. "You okay, miss? Do I need to call the police?"

I straightened, doing my best not to grin at the muscled hipster who would so not win in a fight with the brawny and dangerous man he was currently shielding me from.

"I'm okay," I said, trying my best to sound all breathless and vulnerable. "Thank goodness you were here. I hate to think what would have happened had you not happened upon us." My eyes flickered to an ice-blue gaze. "Blood could have been spilled. And blood makes me queasy." I glanced at my watch. "I've got a plane to catch so I can't stay to make a statement to the authorities, whom I urge you to call. Detective Lewis at Precinct 15 is an old friend. He'll make sure to put this scumbag where he belongs." I hitched my bag up on my shoulder and leaned to give the hipster a chaste kiss on the cheek. A cheek which reddened, his heartbeat speeding up.

Totally still got it.

"Thanks so much for saving me. If I didn't have to fly to Tokyo, I'd thank you properly," I purred with a wink.

I noticed another heartbeat quicken, one that drowned out hipster's. Swallowed it, in fact. It seemed to bounce off my skull in a way that was not at all normal. My gaze narrowed but didn't leave the hipster's.

I turned on my heel and hurried down the alley, not listening to the slight ruffling of feet and cursing from both male voices. No, the heartbeat drowned it all out. Even as I walked back onto the street.

That unnerved me.

Something was different about that slayer.

And not just the fact that he got me tingly in the worst ways.

I was accosted by two burly vampires the second my elevator doors opened. I would have most likely sensed their presence had I not been daydreaming about a certain slayer and imagining what I thought his denim-clad ass would look like.

Especially since I had gotten a text from Lewis not one hour before.

Lewis: *Is there a reason why I just had a call to an alley where a woman matching your description specifically asked for me after a man interrupted an assault on the aforementioned woman?*

This guy was a hoot. Who used the word 'aforementioned' in a text message? I was almost five hundred years old and didn't use it.

Me: *Please tell me you gave him a full cavity search. And then describe the outside of the aforementioned cavity.*

Lewis: *Such a man actually exists? The good citizen was found unconscious once I got there, and neither you nor the man was anywhere to be found. Did you… you know?*

Hmm, the not-so-little slayer harmed a human to escape the authorities. Not very slayerlike. I thought they were meant to protect those masses, not assault them. Disturbingly, I liked him even more now. I grinned down at the message.

Me: *What does 'you know' mean? Did I… get his number? Alas, no. He was too busy waving a scary knife to exchange digits.*

Lewis: *Not funny. Is he battling a case of anemia?*

Me: *Nice euphemism, Lewy. He's got all his platelets, so don't worry your pretty graying head about it. Have attached my dealer's number for that cocaine we discussed.*

Obviously I didn't get a reply after that.

"Stop," one of the burly vampires in my hallway demanded, snatching my bag.

"Hey!" I protested. "Were you born in a fucking crypt? You don't snatch."

The other one got in my face when I reached for my bag. I gave him a once-over. "Your friend wants a Birkin, he better just get on the waiting list like everyone else. I'm not averse to ending you both if you try to take it from me."

"She's clear," the deep voice of the handbag snatcher declared.

His stoic friend stepped back.

I snatched the handbag, glaring at both men, who stepped to either side of the elevator, staring straight ahead like that hadn't just happened.

My gaze flickered forward, deciding not to even bother with the confrontation. Whatever 'that' was, it was something that I'd deal with later. Or never. It wasn't like I couldn't take care of myself, and two vampires who looked like they snacked on steroid-laden blood were not something for me to worry about. So I stepped forward, my view unobstructed by said roid freaks so I could see a much smaller vampire barring my way.

"You don't live here," I informed the vampire standing at the door of my apartment.

It had been a fricking long day and the last thing I wanted was a visitor with fangs. Or a visitor full stop. I wanted a bucket of wine, a rare steak and a season of *Prison Break*.

The slayer had fucked up my hunt and the priest was gone by the time I got to the church. Which meant that I had to call Scott to get him to dig up info. Which also meant that now Scott thought that he was involved in this hunt, which had led to him making a 'date' for us to stalk and murder said priest the following night.

And the handbag I'd been eying at Bergdorf's was out of stock.

I was cranky, to say the least.

Plus, I couldn't erase two ice-blue eyes from my head. Nor those arms. Or shoulders. Or thighs. I hadn't even gotten to see the butt.

I totally needed to get laid.

Not by this guy, though. The vamp at my door was bald, tall and skinny, wearing a black suit and tie. He looked like a funeral director or an aged Beatle. He'd turned old too, maybe early forties. His face was screwed up in what looked like a permanent grimace of distaste. I'd be pissed too if I had to spend eternity with crow's feet.

"The king requests an audience," he said in answer.

I stopped in front of him, quirking my brow. "Tell him to talk to my assistant. I'll try to pencil his majesty in for an 'audience.' Though, I'm sure his schedule is full with killing babies and severing hands, so how about I send him a Snapchat video and we'll call it a day?"

Funeral vamp obviously didn't get my humor because his mouth didn't even quirk. His face barely moved. Vampires were notoriously unemotional and cold, but this guy was statuesque. The only thing apparent was his clear distaste of me, though it wasn't communicated through facial expressions; it was like he excreted the emotion into the air.

Totally creepy.

But also kind of cool.

I needed to figure out how to do that.

"His majesty does not make *appointments*," he stated, looking down at me. "He is inside the door. I am here merely to notify you of his presence."

I raised my brows. "He's in there? *My* apartment? The king requested an appointment with me is what you said. But what you meant is that he broke into my apartment and has thrust said appointment on me," I snapped. I wasn't like Mr. Creepy here; I couldn't seep emotions, so I needed a glare and a snippy tone to communicate how pissed off I currently was.

He didn't answer me.

I hitched my bag on my shoulder. "Right," I huffed, pointing my heeled toe towards my door.

Before I could shove it open angrily, the vampire stepped forward, opening it for me.

He faced the interior of my apartment. "Ms. Rominskitoff for you, Your Majesty."

I pushed past him. "Yes, by all means, announce *my* presence in *my* apartment to the vampire who broke in," I snapped, glaring at the emotionless face. "Who else would it be? Britney Spears here for an impromptu concert?"

"That will be all, Sven," a deep voice rumbled through my apartment.

The vampire did a little half bow, flicking his disapproving gaze to me for a split second before he closed my door.

I glared at the attractive man who just happened to be the king of all vampires lounging on my white suede sofa in my all-white living room. My sanctuary with a ten-million-dollar view from the floor-to-ceiling windows. Central Park was framed by the glittering towers that still amazed me with their magnificence. Mankind had come very far in the blink of an eye. Though vampires had a hand in the evolution of technologies and the like, it was still hard to believe such a civilization could create and adapt to a totally different way of life in a mere century. Vampire society was a lot less malleable; after all, we still had a monarch who boasted absolute rule over all immortals.

The man in question had both arms stretched out to the back of my sofa, his inky black suit juxtaposing the pure white and his patent leather dress shoes resting on my coffee table. His emerald eyes were focused on me.

"Sven?" I said, nodding to the door that just closed. "Are you sure it's not Jeeves?" I stomped into my living room, throwing my Birkin onto the ground. That's how pissed I was, treating such a beautiful item with violence it didn't deserve. "You think it's appropriate to break into my house, put your feet all over my pure white, ten-thousand-dollar coffee table and station a vampire butler outside my door, giving me permission to enter *my own* apartment?" I asked mildly, my tone sharp enough to shave the small amount of stubble kissing his strong jaw.

Side note—yes, vampires got stubble.

I held up my hand as he opened his mouth. "What if I'd brought someone home with me? Then not only would you be ruining an already shitty day, but you'd be cramping my style when I really needed to get laid."

His eyes, once expressionless, darkened just a fraction,

enough to send a small shiver down my spine.

He moved his shoes off the coffee table with a pointed stare but remained sitting. "You think that is an appropriate way to greet your king?" he asked mildly.

"No, I think that's the appropriate way to greet the vampire who broke into my apartment. The polite way, in fact. The less polite way would have Jeeves flying out of that"—I nodded to the far wall—"window and your pretty face getting another scar. So, Your Highness, consider yourself greeted." I did a little curtsey, scowl on my face.

He was off the sofa and in my space in a split second. To human eyes the movement would have been little more than a blur, but I watched his entire journey, observed how lithe his movements were, the way his muscles moved underneath his custom-tailored suit, open at the throat, exposing thick cords and smooth, tanned skin.

I could have moved back, but I'd been too busy perving to retreat.

Also, I didn't retreat. Ever.

So I did my best to lift my eyes from the wide and impressive chest to meet his emerald orbs, full of heat and authority. Considering I was centuries old and could school my expression, you'd think I wouldn't be a slave to my baser instincts. But you'd think wrong.

"I'm your king," he rasped, his voice strong and rough. "Therefore, that threat of violence to me and my person is considered a punishable offense. With death." His breath was hot on my face, somehow making a death threat seem seductive. "But since I'm intrigued by you, I could think of some alternative punishments that would be the most exquisite form of torture. You'd be begging me to keep going and yearn for chains instead of freedom."

His words hypnotized me for a hot minute, I'm ashamed to say. Yes, I was vehemently against the monarchy of my race that promoted elitism, glorified and romanticized murder and genocide and were just all-around assholes. But he was just so freaking *hot*.

I stepped back, keeping my leveled gaze on his. "I'm rather attached to my freedom, and my head—I just got it colored," I deadpanned. I crossed my arms, mostly to hide the physical evidence of his little monologue, hoping it came across as a pissed-off gesture. The way his eyes flickered to my chest area and the side of his mouth ticked up made me think he sensed the former.

"You going to kill me, punish me, or tell me why you're here?" I probed. I thought I'd gotten away cleanly after the battle at the Majestic, but obviously, I was wrong. "Because I'm sure the king of all vampires has better things to do than threaten mere peasants. And I know this peasant has better things to do." I needed to call Dante to relieve some of the energy this guy had just pent up.

He watched me for a second longer before his face transformed to full-on king mode. He crossed his arms and turned his back to me, wandering over to my stainless steel, vintage bar trolley that held crystal decanters of liquid.

He unstopped whiskey, my favorite, and poured two glasses, extending one to me.

I stared at it, not moving.

"It's customary and polite to take a drink when offered."

I met his eyes. "It's also customary and polite for the *host and owner* of said drinks to offer refreshment to a guest she invited into her apartment, not one who broke in and is now raiding her hundred-year-old whiskey," I retorted. I so needed to realize I was talking to the king and choose my words more carefully, but in almost four hundred years, although I'd learned a lot of things, how to control my mouth was not one of them.

"Take the fucking drink, Isla," he commanded roughly.

The way his mouth wrapped around my name had my legs disobeying me.

My hand touched his briefly as I took the glass. I didn't visibly react to the spark that came from the contact, but his eyes darkened a fraction beneath his king mask.

I took two measured steps back from him, wandering to regard the twinkling lights of Manhattan to make it seem like I was enjoying the view instead of escaping his presence.

The sharp twang of the whiskey slithered down my throat as silence descended heavily over the room.

His form filled the corner of my eye as he came to adopt the same position as me, thankfully a reasonable distance away. That didn't stop my hand shaking slightly around my glass.

"I owe you a debt," he murmured, breaking the silence. "You saved my life at the Majestic, fought for me."

I gave him a look. "I fought for *me*," I corrected. "If I'm not mistaken, I didn't have much choice when a werewolf spear-tackled me. Plus, I've been itching to give Selene what was coming to her for centuries. You did me a favor by almost letting her kill you."

He regarded me, his brows narrowed only slightly, the rest of his face impassive. "Your rapid exit made it unable for me to offer my thanks," he said.

"I hate cleanup," I said. "I hire people for that, and I did rather make a mess. Plus, like I already said, you don't need to thank me."

His stare didn't waver and it unnerved me. "You don't want anything in return for your actions?"

I scoffed. "At the risk of sounding disrespectful, Your Highness, you don't have anything I want."

His face changed slightly, eyes widening in surprise. "You're serious."

I waved my hand. "I'm rarely ever serious, but on this occasion, it's the truth."

He twirled the tumbler in his hands, the only movement as his body stayed statue-still. "You really have no desire to align yourself in any position in society, like your mother and brothers crave?" His voice had a note of disbelief.

I smiled. "You're referencing their ruthless pursuit of power and influence, so you've met my family, I presume?"

His eyes turned hard as he nodded once.

"Well then you must understand my immense desire to position myself far, far away from them. And any undead contemporaries clinging to an archaic and outdated feudal system." My thoughts caught up with my mouth. "No offense intended," I added, attempting to put a verbal Band-Aid over the bullet wound I'd created.

He merely sipped his drink. The silence yawned over us and I turned to glance at the skyline, the lights like floating diamonds.

"You're aware of the current situation within our society?" he asked finally.

It was a leap from our current topic, but I was one who regularly spoke about puppies one minute and nuclear bombing my parents' house in Russia just for fun, so I rolled with it,

I didn't take my eyes off the horizon. "Politics bore me," I responded. "But if you're referring to the sect of vampires vying to be supreme rulers over their race and to enslave humankind as the current 'situation,' then yes, I'm aware."

It was hard not to be. I didn't add that I was reasonably

sure my idiot brothers were probably involved in said sect somehow, nor would I be surprised if my cunning and manipulative daddy was a founding father of the little group that had been causing trouble for the past ten years but now were engaging in coordinated attacks against established forms of vampire governance and humankind in general. A lot of their mass murders were marketed as national disasters, disease epidemics and even one war. Publicity for that must have been a bitch.

"I've got a team investigating the instigators and leader of this faction," he began.

I glanced at his profile. "What? You don't support it? I was sure you'd be their main cheerleader. Human enslavement, vampire dominion over the entire world? I was thinking that's exactly the kind of thing a ruler would be on board with," I remarked.

His cold gaze settled over me. "One thing to learn about me, in addition to the fact I'm your *fucking king*, is that you do not make assumptions about me. Such things are dangerous, even for women like you, who have my attention," he said, his voice even but sharp. He turned his attention back to the skyline. "I do not condone nor appreciate challenges to my authority. I take it as a personal insult," he continued. "I will personally pull apart every vampire involved in this pitiful thing they call a rebellion." The cold promise in his voice unsettled me, and I'd seen and delivered a lot of death. "We coexist with humans. Yes, we are superior to them. That's a fact of nature. As is the fact that we rely on them for sustenance. But it does not mean we will take over their civilization, pitiful as it is."

I hid my surprise by taking another sip. "I fail to see what this has to do with me. Unless you consider me to be an instigator and are here to tear me apart?"

His gaze bore into me. "That would be a crime in itself, so I'll try not to do that. I know you would have no affiliation with such a group considering your… relationship with humans."

I glared at him. "I don't have a relationship with humans," I argued sharply. "Apart from the ones who make red-soled shoes and exquisite handbags. The rest are of little consequence to me."

He saw through me. "And what of your abruptly stopping one of the most notorious murder sprees of the seventeenth century to get your meals only from humans evil enough to be vampires by nature alone?" He paused, twisting the glass in his hand. "Could it be the relationship you had with a human in Paris in 1676, one that was solidified in marriage, if I'm not mistaken? One that ended with you becoming a widow at a tragically young age and was the catalyst for your final transition into immortality?"

Centuries of solitude with those memories didn't make them any easier to hear out loud. In fact, in all the centuries that had passed I didn't think I'd ever heard it out loud. Not in a handful of sentences. I could scarcely believe that pain and suffering not even small enough to package into four hundred years could be surmised so coldly. I stiffened, my only reaction to the words piercing skin thick enough not to be punctured with any blade.

I drained my glass and calmly walked over to my bar, pouring three fingers into it. I was sorely tempted to drink from the bottle but vulnerability was dangerous, even deadly in situations such as this. My family already knew about mine, and it was the string they tugged at when they wanted to use me as a puppet.

I didn't need anyone else adding their own strings to my back. Especially not this monarch. Or any monarch.

I took a considerable gulp of the liquid. He'd stayed silent, regarding the view the entire time. Calm. One might even say relaxed.

"You've been doing your homework," I observed, my voice light. "You want a gold star to go with your crown for such extensive research?"

He turned his back on the windows, giving me his full attention. Such an action was unnerving in my current state, when all I could see was Jonathan and blood.

I blinked away the images.

"I'm not surprised that your family was behind the murder of your human husband," he said. "Their stance on humans is not exactly a secret, and your brothers have already received many warnings as to their discretion in procuring their meals since I've taken my position."

I snorted. "You've met my brothers?"

He nodded.

"Well then, you've got your explanation as to why they don't consider discretion laws around human kills as applying to them. Haven't you heard? They're part of the 'great families.' Things like high-risk humans and kill quotas don't apply to them."

There were rules in our little society around killing humans. It wasn't outlawed, of course; in fact, it was encouraged. We only had to call the Sector to get them to clean up whatever bloodbath we'd created. But there were strict rules as to how such kills were made: nothing in public, and if there were witnesses, they must be taken care of. No pack kills in urban, population-dense areas. Vampires could own humans as property, and those humans were not to be harmed by anyone. If they were, their owner had justifiable means to start a blood feud. Rare, as vampires weren't usually willing to start such things over something as insignificant as human life. It was mostly the principle of the thing. Vampires were big on that.

And the rules went on. Most were rarely enforced because humans were too stupid to realize that the majority of their missing persons and murders weren't the work of the people they locked up. They'd be more than a little shocked to learn that vampires were not only real but a large majority of them held high-authority positions in the human world.

Secrecy was the biggest rule of the race; no one was coming out of the coffin any time soon. That would make eating out that much more political. Better to live in the shadows.

"I'm the king, so I make the rules. And I know that the families with Ambrogio's Vein Line think those rules don't apply to them. Which is why most of them are frontrunners for leaders of the sect," he said, clutching his glass.

"So that's why you're here? You want me to snitch on my family?" I deduced.

His face betrayed nothing, yet his eyes swirled with something I couldn't grasp. "No. I do understand how loyalty works."

I grinned. "Oh no, I'd snitch on them in a second. Less than a second. It would be my immense pleasure to do so. Unfortunately, I'm not invited to family dinners to overthrow the vampire king." I shrugged. "I'm the white sheep of the family, you see? So it's been a wasted trip." I turned towards the door. "I'll let you get back to your night of draining virgins and ruling the masses from your ivory tower. I'm afraid I don't validate parking." I fastened my hand against the knob and prepared a glittering grin for Jeeves.

"That's not the reason I'm here, Isla," he said.

My hand paused. "Well then, Your Majesty, please educate me. Because as much as I love dancing, and I do, it's preferably in nightclubs full of juicy humans, not around subjects."

"Emrick." His voice was rough.

My hand snapped back from the door and I turned. "Seriously?" I didn't display my shock outwardly to hearing the king's given name. It was knowledge only a few possessed. Yes, they were that pompous that they didn't even let those they ruled know their first names. That and there were whispers of their blood being the closest to that of Ambrogio; spells could be weaved by witches who knew their true names. If so, Rick was going out on a limb—all of them, actually—by giving me his name. He had always been known as King Markandeya. It was a family affair, and the current king was usually crowned when he killed his father.

No shit. They were that ruthless.

Granted, his father had been ruling for a few millennia, so I guessed it was time for a change.

"Of course you'd have a name that literally meant 'immortal.' Ever heard of subtlety?" I teased.

He didn't respond, though I didn't expect him to. "You should take the knowledge of my name as a gesture of trust on my part."

"The only person I trust is the woman who does my Brazilians. Sorry, but murderous monarchs don't even make it to the people I kind of trust." I paused. "Actually, they and vampires in general are on the big old 'don't even trust with my great screenplay idea' list."

His eyes flickered and then his face hardened. "Not surprising. But you can trust me and I'm trusting you. Betrayal of that trust—"

I waved my hand. "Yes, pieces of me. No need to quote Ashlee Simpson."

His brow furrowed. It was quite novel, the confusion on a face most likely always connoting authority. "I don't follow."

"Of course you don't. I didn't expect you to listen to bad pop songs in your spare time."

He resumed his mask. "I don't have time for this conversation, as entertaining as it is. I'm here because of your friendships with those in both the supernatural and human communities."

I raised my brow. "Well, someone's giving you dodgy info, Rick."

His eyes narrowed. "It's Emrick. Surely you haven't forgotten your own king's name in a handful of seconds?"

I quirked my brow. "No way in heaven I'm calling you that." I downed my drink. "Back to your original statement. I don't have friends. I'm a lone wolf. I walk this world alone. Haven't you heard? The entirety of the vampire world hates me, just as I like it. And humans annoy me, werewolves smell, witches are pesky, demons are just plain selfish and the rest don't interest me."

I thought of Scott, but he most certainly didn't count. He was more like an annoying stray puppy that followed me home than anything else. I still hadn't ruled out killing him.

Even mentioning Sophie to the king was out of the question. He did not need to know about my friendship with a controversial witch; he already had enough reason to punish me. Plus, Sophie was my one and only friend, and I didn't want her to be on the receiving end of any death sentences.

Though I didn't completely rule out telling him, since his 'punishments' sounded like my kind of fun.

He took measured steps towards me, placing his glass on my coffee table.

Once more, he was back in my bubble. I tried not to like it. I really did.

My resolve was failing. In the space of twenty-four hours I'd been far too close to two men I found inexplicitly attractive, both of whom I should've stayed far away from.

One because he was born to kill me.

One because he was born to be something that I despised.

"The *entirety* of a race hates you?" he repeated. "I think you're being overly dramatic."

I quirked my brow. "Oh, I'm really not. Three assassination attempts in as many months would beg to differ."

My tone was light but he didn't take it so. His entire body stiffened and his eyes went to stone. "What?" he ground out. "Assassination?"

I shrugged. "No big. Well, actually the last one did ruin my favorite pumps, so that was kind of a big deal."

"I'll put a protection detail on you."

I blinked at him, first shocked at his sudden anger and subsequent declaration, then insulted. "I don't need protection," I snapped. "I'm more than capable of snuffing out any vampire stupid enough to try and mess up my day with a murder attempt. Especially ones who ruin my favorite heels. That one's death was particularly slow."

He stared at me, his face impassive. "Then I'll find the vampires behind it."

"No need. I know who's behind it."

His silence communicated his question.

"It's my darling family," I continued.

"Your family?" he repeated.

"It's a game we play. They hire various vampires to kill me on the off chance they'll succeed and they'll be able to breathe easier. I continue to survive for a multitude of reasons, mainly because I like it, and it comes with the added benefit of pissing my mom off. I'm hoping that my continued existence will be the catalyst for the first vampire case of wrinkles." I held my crossed fingers up.

"Your family could quite possibly be more fucked up than mine," he observed dryly.

The tone was so natural it caught me off guard for a second.

I grinned. "You can bet on it, Rick."

He stared at me, something behind it that time. Some sort of shared connections at our bloodstained lineage perhaps.

Whatever it was, I was betting the attraction between us was more dangerous than our respective families.

"You would be surprised to learn that in some circles within our race you are respected."

I raised a brow. "What circles would those be? The ones that the brain-damaged vampires draw?"

Various vampires had been documented as going mad. Some purely from old age, which made sense. Thousands of years of memories and emotions could only fit in one mind for so long without going a little hinky, twisting to accommodate more of the world. Existing on earth indefinitely also got a little tiring. Others were captured by hunters or cursed by witches and went batty through curses or torture.

"Ones who hold the same amount of respect for humans that you pretend not to have. We won't count the men who have for centuries been lining up to spend even a night in your company," he rasped, his voice thick.

"Well, I choose my bedmates carefully. I don't want to add to the number of vampires in the silly house. I'm too much for most." I winked.

He stepped forward. "I believe that."

I didn't say a word. This flirting thing was getting far too real.

"Despite what you think about your reputation, you have one. And connections, if not friendships, with almost every sector of the supernatural world. Which is valuable for me.

And my goals."

So maybe he already knew about Sophie. He had a better poker face than me.

It was worrying. And annoying.

"Sorry, but I drive a Mercedes, not an Aston Martin, and there are no zeros before my name," I stated.

His brow rose in question. "I'm afraid I don't follow."

I scowled. "You want me to spy for you. And my name isn't Bond, James Bond, so I'm not up to the task, unfortunately. Try Daniel Craig. He does do a charmingly good job."

He folded his arms, the seams on his suit stretching to accommodate the motion, and his considerable biceps. "I would like you to acquire information for our mutual benefit," he corrected, obviously choosing to ignore my pop culture references.

"You mean *spy*," I argued. "I'm Switzerland. Completely neutral." I paused. "Despite killing humans for food and any other creature that doesn't like my fashion sense. Regardless, I'm not adding 'spy' to the long list of things that I am."

He gazed at me, menace flickering around him like smoke "I'm your king. I could command you."

I stared back, refusing to flinch in the face of what a lot of vampires would have bowed down to. You know, to avoid a beheading. I was not a lot of vampires. "You could try," I challenged.

To my utter surprise, he grinned. "I believe I would enjoy every moment of that. But you're not stupid, Isla. You know that this faction is gaining traction and momentum, despite your feigning ignorance." He paused. "Though if you repeat that I said that, I'll have your tongue cut out." His voice was smooth, cultured as it wrapped around the promise. The cold resolve in his eyes told me he wouldn't blink twice while doing such a thing, despite the witty repertoire we seemed to have or his increased tolerance for my bullshit. His cold eyes continued to focus on me. "You're very concerned with your own survival, so I'll let you do the math as to how long a vampire like you would survive in the new world order that despises humans and any vampires who sympathize with, or marry them. I'll make sure they don't succeed in overthrowing me, but that doesn't mean they won't take a few choice targets down with them. You're at the top of their list with your dead human husband, despite the years that have passed." The verbal barb found its purchase. "Vampires don't forget," he murmured.

He stepped around me, his arm brushing mine. "In addition to that, think of the lack of assassination attempts you'd have to field if I were to exterminate all of those responsible." His eyes didn't change, the emeralds glittering with cold resolve.

His implication of the knowledge of my family's involvement was crystal clear. I wasn't surprised, as I'd learned a lot about King Rick in this few minutes. He smelled like soap and expensive cologne. He could make my panties wet with one stare. His biceps were impressive. He wasn't cruel but wouldn't hesitate to maim or execute me if it suited his needs. And he wasn't stupid.

"You'll do this, Isla," he murmured in my ear. "I'll be waiting for you to come to me with what I need."

Then the door opened and closed, and I was left alone with my empty apartment and the smell of cologne and monarchy.

"Well, fuck me sideways," I muttered.

I heard a masculine chuckle descending in the elevator.

FOUR

"THANK YOU SO MUCH FOR LETTING ME COME, ISLA."

"I didn't *let* you come," I reminded him. "You turned up at my apartment and wouldn't leave despite me threatening to give you a wedgie with your Captain America underwear, and then deciding to kill you with it when you still didn't leave."

He grinned. "Well, I'm here. So, thanks."

I rolled my eyes in response and focused on the house in suburban New York.

I despised places like this. A big collection of the 'American Dream'—a thin veil for unhappy wives who chewed Xanax like Skittles, husbands who banged their secretaries in the city and kids who were glued to those stupid iPads and probably would grow up with drug habits and taint the world with their presence.

But the priest I'd been tailing lived out there, so there I was.

"I've got to give it to the sicko. He's picked a prime hunting ground," I observed as two small humans wandered down the street pointing their phones at a bush, mumbling something about a Pokémon. Whatever that was.

"Humanity is so fucked if *that's* the future of tomorrow," I muttered.

My focus flickered to the door of the house we were parked outside of. A small boy and his plump mother emerged. The mother clutched the old priest's hand, a grin on her splotchy face. I could smell the belly full of chocolate almonds she most likely ate to escape her fucking horrific life, which she wasn't doing the best at if her small pale child's rapid heartbeat was anything to go by.

I toyed with the idea of having her for dessert for being such an oblivious shrew but quickly tossed it. I didn't do moral gray areas. Let the man upstairs figure that out when she died during complications from a gastric bypass surgery.

"That's him," Scott whispered.

"You don't have to whisper, idiot. They're not vampires, so they can't hear us," I said.

"Right." He nodded, then thrust a flask at me. "Entrée?"

I gave him a sideways glance before grabbing the flask. After taking a swig, I screwed up my nose and thrust it back at him.

"What the fuck was that?" I hissed. "Is that even blood?"

He frowned at me. "Yes," he protested. "I guess it's an acquired taste."

"Acquired taste?" I repeated.

"I've got a deal with a human at hospice. A buddy of mine, actually. He lets me drain the patients in the last stages. It benefits us both, taking them out of their misery and keeping me kicking."

I stared at him, listening to the menial conversation of my mark and the idiot mother distractedly.

He shrugged, his face reddening slightly under my gaze. Since he was a half breed he still had blood flow and the ability to do things like blush. On chicks it was probably endearing but Scott looked like an idiot, albeit a loveable one.

Wait, did I just say loveable?

"It's how we lost my dad," he explained. "Cancer." His voice shook just the tiniest bit. "Though it was fifty years ago. Who knows if they could have given him more years with today's technology." His eyes were faraway. "But the time he had left was excruciating. He begged for death in the end. Mom couldn't do it so…."

My eyes bugged out. "You drained your own dad?" I surmised.

He nodded.

"Well, shit, Scotty. That is ruthless. You'd fit in with our unholy ruler any day."

Now why did I mention that unholy ruler? Couldn't be that he and his emerald eyes were on my mind? More precisely those emerald eyes battling with ice-blue ones. Though it wasn't the eyes that were battling but the sinewy, muscled, oiled-up and naked bodies.

"It was what he wanted. He'd always known he wouldn't outlive us both. He and mom had a deal, but she couldn't do it… in the end," he explained, eyes sheepish, oblivious to the fact that I was imagining a pornographic death match between a vampire and a slayer while he explained how he'd drained his cancerous father dry.

Unsure of what to do in the face of such emotion, I

patted his head. "There, there. I think it was totally honorable. Draining your father to save your mother having to do it. Majorly fucked-up, but honorable. Honor is a rare thing in our race." I tilted my head, regarding him. "You only feed on dying humans?"

He nodded.

"Because of your father?"

Another nod. "I hadn't met another vampire like me. So when I heard how you cared about humans too—"

"Nope. I do not care about humans. They are stupid, lazy, clumsy and have the tendency to die, like your dear old dad." I was being needlessly callous, but I was a vampire for fuck's sake. I eyed the priest who was closing his door. "So how about I show you how much I care about this particular human while you stay in the car and try not to fuck anything up."

On that note, I darted out of the car and schooled myself to walk a mortal pace past the chubby mom and the kid who would most likely be fucked-up for life. I barely resisted the urge to throat punch the oblivious twit. I only restrained because such a move would crush her windpipe, which may help her waistline but wouldn't help the kid's psychological scars, of which he already had many.

My heels clicked along the walk and I rapped my blood-red nails on the door that the father had just closed.

It took him a suspiciously long time to answer. I didn't even want to think about what he was doing.

The second he opened the door, I shoved him back and slammed it behind us. I technically didn't need to wait for the door to be opened, but I had manners.

"Whargt—" He let out garbled protests as I circled my nails around his neck and held him against his wall. His eyes were widened in terror and my hand covered his little white collar.

"Forgive you, Father, for you have sinned," I whispered.

His hands scratched at my own as he gasped for air.

"I'm sure you've been operating under some warped logic that by wearing that suit and preaching the good book you get a free pass to the pearly gates despite your sickening sexual preferences," I hissed. "I'm here to tell you that's not the case. I'll be sending you to meet the guy downstairs, who has some truly delightful rewards for those who steal things like childhood innocence."

I released my grip a fraction so he could gulp in his last breath of air, then stepped forward. "Say hey to him from me, you know, between the screams," I murmured, my lips at his neck.

My fangs pulsed as they elongated ever so slightly in preparation to feed. I sank them into his wrinkled flesh and marveled at his grunts of pain and feeble struggles.

The blood flowed warmly into my mouth and I drank deeply and greedily. It had been a few days since Stan and I hadn't even finished him, so I was due for a binge.

Despite what movies or books showed a vampire to be like, it was not an act of pleasure for those being bitten. The ones doing the biting? Heck yeah. Imagine the nirvana of eating your favorite chocolate cake after a bad bout of PMS and you've got it.

But for the almost not-so-dearly departed priest I was attached to? Not so much. It pissed me right off that those idiotic humans at the many blood bars around the world actually volunteered to do it, with *Twilight* in their minds. I was sure they must have been missing a brain cell if they thought someone tearing into their neck and sucking their blood would be the same as getting an orgasm from Edward Cullen.

The priest's vein ran dry far too quickly and I dropped the

shriveled corpse at my feet with a scowl. I should have made it last, did it over a matter of days, weeks even, to give him a punishment he was worthy of. But I must have underestimated how hungry I was.

"Oh well," I muttered.

I wiped my face and straightened my black silk shirt.

I didn't even bother looking around his small house of lies and no doubt terror before leaving. Instead I whipped out my phone, firing off a text while I walked back to my car. I didn't have to call the Sector for this one; my very own pet detective would have it covered.

Me: *Priest just took his last confession. Hit me up with the next sucker. Get it? Sucker?*

Sometimes I did wonder about my maturity levels. Well, for a hot minute, anyway; then I figured it was my afterlife and I was the one who had to find a way to make it through. If juvenile jokes and sarcasm got me through, who was I to try and be something as utterly dull as mature? I put my phone back in my bag, not expecting an immediate response, or any kind of response. Lewis didn't seem to like my blood humor.

"It's done already?" Scott exclaimed as soon as I sat my booty in the car.

I started it and pulled off the street. "I don't like to play with my food," I informed him. "Plus, the finale of *America's Next Top Model* is on tonight and I don't want to miss it."

"Can I come in next time?"

"No."

"Please? I can help."

I gave him a look. "Tell me how the infant half breed would help me do something I've been doing for half a millennium?

Having you even in the car with your hospice blood is more of a hindrance than a help."

As soon as I said the words, the dumb little smile snapped off his face and his eyes went all sad and doey.

And it bothered me. Usually I saw such expressions as a victory, but not that time. I felt… bad? The feeling was foreign and I didn't know what to do with it. I rolled my shoulders, trying to rid myself of the uncomfortable prickle of guilt, if I weren't mistaken. *Is this what people have to deal with when they worry about other people's feelings? Jesus, no wonder humans drop like flies.* Compassion and empathy were the most fatal of emotions. And feeble.

"Fuck," I muttered, sucking in a breath. "You're good with computers, right?"

Scott's sullen head snapped up, his eyes alight once more. "Yes, the best in the Sector. That's why I've been promoted to senior call analyst despite my… lineage. Some of the other full blood—"

I held my hand up. "I don't need your autobiography. A simple yes would have sufficed." I stared at the road that was hurtling past. I had good reactions, couldn't die and was impatient, so of course I drove fast. "Well then, you can use those computer skills to navigate the Interweb, or whatever it's called, and find me some new marks. Lewis is too slow for my taste."

Scott beamed, and fuck me if that didn't give me some kind of warm and fuzzy. I worried that I was getting soft. Maybe I'd have to go over to the werewolf side of town and kill some puppies to find my edge again.

Scott's brows furrowed. "The Interweb?" he repeated, tone teasing.

I scowled at him. "I don't need to know the ins and outs of such a horrific technology. I know how to order shoes, and that's enough for me." Though I could use all of the new technology, I didn't like it. More so, I didn't like that it turned humans into even more mindless zombies than they already were. Previously, one could hold a conversation with another about fine arts and literature for almost ten minutes without wanting to rip their throat out. Now? Their cellular device was attached to their hand and they viewed the world through a screen, a frame. Everything was a distortion on reality. I doubted they'd even rip their eyes from the screen until half of their blood was slipping down a vampire's throat. Or until a demon had sucked out what little soul the device in their hand had left.

"No more words from you," I commanded, "or I promise I will feed you to a slayer."

Scott zipped his mouth shut, though he was still grinning. I could taste his amusement the entire road home, despite the silence in the car.

Which was actually rather dangerous, considering at the mere mention of a slayer I was consumed by thoughts of a particular one with a great beard and murder in his eyes.

I was walking out of my office downtown when the hair on the back of my neck prickled. An ancient instinct had my system tight, ready for attack, for death. Not mine, of course.

The steady thump of his heartbeat reverberated through my body. Never mind the handful of other humans scurrying through the lobby of my building; his drowned them all out. It was troubling, that little fact. It wasn't a slayer thing. I'd known, and killed, my fair share, and their heartbeats had been nothing but background noise.

Until they were nothing at all.

I stopped in the middle of the lobby, locking eyes with him. He was leaning against the wall of the entrance, sinfully good-looking and out of place. This was just one of the many businesses I owned; I was immortal and smart, so I'd amassed a lot of wealth. We were technically meant to keep a low profile, but I couldn't exactly do that, considering I was one of the only female billionaire CEOs in the security industry.

I'd made the *Forbes* list the previous year. And the year before that.

The Sector had not been happy about that.

It was brilliant.

This particular company employed Ivy League assholes who wore ten-thousand-dollar suits and had most likely date-raped girls at frat parties in their heyday. He didn't look anything like them.

Which was a good thing.

His jeans were so faded he'd probably worn them for years, and they most likely weren't designer. Ditto with the leather jacket; it wasn't worn for fashion, but rather for purpose, as blood didn't stain leather as much. Yet it molded to his biceps, clinging to them and his muscled body for dear life like it was alive. I would too, if he wouldn't likely kill me for doing so.

His wild hair and beard made him look like a lost bounty hunter or an alpha werewolf, without the shapeshifting quality. Or the general air of arrogance. He had an aura about him that wasn't human, but there was only werewolf, vampire, demon or human, and I was certain he wasn't the first three. Process of elimination had him human, just a strange one.

He pushed off the wall after giving me the same once-over I'd given him, though his eyes didn't betray any appreciation for my skintight white dress that was tailored to perfection. My red hair tumbled down my back in long soft waves, and my signature red lipstick slathered my lips.

That kind of pissed me off. Yeah, so I was a monster to be killed in his eyes, but surely he could appreciate this monster's killer body before he tried to put holes in it?

I folded my arms once I'd come to a stop in front of him, close enough for his scent to wrap around me. For his emotions to roll into me and nearly choke me with their complexity, though anger was an overriding quality. "A little public to try and stab me with that trusty knife of yours, isn't it?" I asked, quirking my brow and glancing around the people who gave me a wide berth. I wasn't exactly the boss who took her employees out for drinks or cared when their grandmothers were sick. They were terrified of me. It was brilliant.

Though, they probably wouldn't care if he stabbed me right there. They might even cheer. Or join in.

"I heard you were all about the secrecy, or are you a rebel without a cause? You've already got the leather jacket," I continued.

His eyes danced with hatred. "You killed him," he growled in a low voice.

"Who? I've done a lot of killing over the past week, so you're going to have to be a little more specific."

Of course I knew who he was talking about, but if he wanted a monster, I was happy to play along.

"The priest," he gritted out. "Went to mass, he wasn't there. The new pastor said he's on vacation."

"Well even priests deserve a break. What are you, a sadist? Let the poor man have his blowout in Cancun. What happens in Mexico stays in Mexico. You know, he may never come back." I winked conspiratorially.

He stepped forward, engulfing me in his scent and making it hard to focus on anything but the roaring rumble of his heartbeat. I struggled with my composure.

"You see, I did some digging. Turns out there're some failed charges against the priest." His eyes changed, advancing beyond hatred. "From young boys."

His emotions swirled with something else cutting through the anger. Something that was difficult to taste because it was decidedly different than the rage and hatred that had become characteristic to the slayer's aura. When he was around me, at least.

I shrugged. "Well, I guess sometimes the stereotypes are true. Catholic priests and little boys. Vampires and slayers." I paused, narrowing my eyes. "That being the vampire will kill the slayer if he doesn't stop following her around," I threatened, my voice hoarse.

He didn't move. Didn't blink. "You were at the police station. Lewis was the officer in charge of those complaints."

I tilted my head. "I'd stop my digging if I were you. You might just find out you're digging your own grave."

I stepped out of his orbit and sauntered off, feeling the heat of his gaze on my back the entire journey.

I wasn't lying. I would have to kill him if he unveiled any more of my life. Slayers couldn't be trusted.

But the question remained: why hadn't I killed him already?

"I'll have a scotch on the rocks, barkeep. And a shot of O-Neg, if you've got any fresh from the vein." I winked at the demon leaning on the weathered wooden bar.

He quirked a brow at me.

I grinned back.

"You sure you want to be in here, Isla?" he asked, setting a glass on the bar and reaching for ice. "The last time you damned me with your presence, it cost me ten thousand dollars in damages after you were attacked by two werewolves."

I rolled my eyes. "You're already damned, number one." I put a single, blood-red fingernail up. "This entire establishment isn't even worth ten K. Two at a stretch," I continued, holding up a second finger. "And if you don't recall, both of those werewolves are still growing their fur back. The publicity for that little incident had this place the most frequented bar in all of the under and overworld. The way I see it, you owe me a drink. Or twenty." I tilted the freshly poured drink in his direction before draining it.

He shook his head. He was attractive—you know, for a demon. Obviously he didn't have pointy horns or anything like that; demons looked like humans, on this side of the earth's core anyway. I'd heard the ones downstairs were like a beauty queen without her makeup—in other words, downright terrifying. I was not hip on finding out any time soon.

Which was why I was there. I'd chewed on Rick's proposal for a couple of days and begrudgingly decided he was right. I'd never tell him that, mind you. I'd let him believe I was doing this under the influence of blackmail. But it was in my best interests to find out who was behind this little rebellion. And the promise of punishing my family once I got concrete proof against them was a mitigating factor. Their shadow was getting a little too suffocating since the conversation at the Majestic.

I needed to be rid of it, and them, for good if I hoped to remained undead for the foreseeable future.

"Yeah, well it's not stupid dog brains I'd be worrying about if I were you," he said, laying his tattooed forearms down in front of me.

My gaze went to the sinewy corded flesh, remembering the need for my little itch to be scratched.

I must have been mad to be considering going back in Dante's direction again. I'd gone there, once. Having been on the earth for as long as I had, it was hard to find someone I hadn't slept with. Especially in the supernatural community, with all the politics and shit. I also had a scorched-earth policy: one rumble in the hay, then out.

So even though Dante's inky black hair framed his modelesque face perfectly, and the 666 tattoo under his left eye was weirdly erotic, as well as the tongue ring and muscled body covered in flames and hellfire was totally swoonworthy—if I swooned—I was not that desperate.

Yet.

It would have been smarter to work out my frustration with a not-so-harmless demon instead of risking something with the king of all vampires or the human who was born to kill the vampire race, but I wasn't exactly known for my smart decisions.

Hence the werewolf fight in there ten years back.

Dante's bar, Inferno—yes, he was that much of an arrogant ass—was situated at the nexus of all five sectors of New York, the place at which werewolf, vampire, witch and demon territory converged, where Murray Hill straddled the Garment district. It sat at the end of a dirty alleyway, spelled so no humans could stumble in. It was nothing special—rusting paint and Metallica and Grateful Dead posters littered the walls, and the tables were rickety, but he had good booze and it was one of the only places in New York were all supernaturals could share a brew and not a body bag. Dante had a strict 'no murder in his bar' policy. Not for humans, of course, he didn't care about that, but no supernaturals. Brawls weren't uncommon but were usually broken up quickly enough, by Dante himself. He was one of the strongest demons in the world; why he chose to tend a bar was anyone's guess. After thousands of years on earth, maybe he just needed the simplicity of pouring beers.

I pushed my glass back for a refill. "And who do I have to be scared of? Little men from the hottest place on earth with a boss who has daddy issues?" I asked sweetly.

His eyes glowed, bright red flames flickering in his irises. Demons were literally born in firestorms, so they had this pesky habit of bursting into flames when they got pissed. Or horny.

I'd experienced both.

Only one was fun.

Who was I kidding? They were both fun.

He pushed the drink my way and I didn't even flinch when my hands fastened around scorching hot glass. The ice completely melted, and the glass had softened slightly under the pressure of intense heat. And that was him on low. He could technically flatten New York if someone pissed him off enough.

It didn't stop me from annoying him whenever I came in, though. I lived on the edge.

"You gotta be careful, Isla. Half a millennium of arrogance without retaliation has made you complacent," he threatened.

I threw back my warmed-up whiskey, then leaned forward, baring my elongated fangs in such a way that Dante reared back, just a bit. They weren't just the most well-formed biters this side of the underworld; they were deadly. Despite my avoidance of killing innocent humans, I wasn't averse to doing the same to anyone else. I had a reputation. Of course, there were those who didn't heed that reputation and reasoned my diet made me weak, and they tried, and failed, to challenge that. I was glad; death matches were my cardio. What was five hundred years on the planet with exceptional strength and great bone structure without a good old duel every decade or so?

"You forget yourself, Dante. I don't blame you, since chauvinism is hard to kick and the males of your species still think you've got the upper hand." I grinned at him. "Problem is you've never actually had it. The fairer sex has always been stronger, more cunning and a fuck of a lot more dangerous. We'll rip out your spleen when you're too busy checking out our fabulous racks."

Dante's gaze flickered up from my chesticle area. I leaned over, brushing his washboard abs just for kicks and snatched the bottle from behind the bar.

"It's quicker this way," I said, pouring my own glass. "And as much as it's a nice change to have whiskey at one hundred degrees Celsius, I prefer it chilled, like my heart." I winked.

He shook his head and looked around the bar. It was quiet. Ten o'clock on a Friday was early morning for most creatures that crawled to this establishment. Most were having breakfast, dining on virgins and such.

Dante's bar was one of the most infamous in Manhattan. It was close enough to the trendy nightclubs and Times Square that all kinds of supernatural assholes could snatch a drunken human off her Manolos and feast on her Chanel-laden body.

I didn't frequent the place because they didn't serve cocktails, and because I almost always left with blood on my clothes after saving a drunken damsel in distress from being someone's snack.

"Now, you were implying about my life being in mortal danger, but that's far too boring." I waved my hand. "I', here to talk to you about other, much more entertaining things."

His gaze darkened. "I knew you'd be back for another taste," he growled. The arm warmed up once more, kissing me with its heat.

I rolled my eyes. "Don't flatter yourself. I'm here to ask if you've heard any whispers about the rebel vampire faction vying for world domination."

I guessed spies were meant to be more subtle about obtaining information, but you could only be so subtle while wearing a blood-red pencil skirt and six-inch heels.

"Shh," he hissed, waving his hands while he glanced around the mostly empty bar.

The only patron, apart from me, was a shaggy-haired, muscled werewolf, hunched over a glass at the edge of the bar.

He was kind of hot, if you liked that tortured hero kind of thing. And didn't mind the smell of wet dog.

"Chill out. You'll give yourself an ulcer," I said, taking another sip of my drink. "No one's here. Wolverine over there is too busy dreaming about chasing tennis balls to even know what's going on."

I grinned at the growl that got me.

Dante glared at me. "Your overconfidence is going to get you killed."

"Or get me a date with Johnny Depp."

He stared at me. I stared back.

"I don't have time for a Mexican standoff," I exclaimed. "I've got a date with a murderer in about"—I glanced at my watch—"half an hour, and that's all the way on the Upper East Side. Stockbroker who doubles as a prostitute killer. Dude took *American Psycho* way too literally."

Lewis had texted me the address and the link to the news story about the Manhattan Slasher. I was tempted to stop by the reporter's place who coined that train wreck and have an entrée.

His text had told me the man had been brought in for questioning, though he'd had the best defense lawyer in the city get him off without charges, and what little evidence they had against the guy had conveniently disappeared. Deep pockets could buy innocence in this world. He'd also mentioned being careful with something called thorne.

Me: *Don't worry, I don't prick easy. Also, you added an E where there isn't one. I know cops aren't meant to be literate, but that's a little worrying.*

Every rose has its thorne.

He hadn't written back.

"I don't know anything. And if you want that shiny hair to stay on that obnoxious head, you'd stop asking questions," he bit out.

I touched my hair. "Shiny? Really? I was worried my new shampoo was drying it out."

"Seriously, Isla. Even you have to have a little self-preservation." His grave expression was starting to freak me out. Dante was either joking, murderous, or horny. He was never… scared.

"I have a lot of self-preservation, hence me asking questions."

He narrowed his brow. "You in some kind of trouble?"

I was surprised at the concern in his voice. We'd bumped uglies two hundred years back and had been friendly acquaintances since. I'd even shared Jack the Ripper with him when he just happened to be in London.

"I'm always in a little trouble," I said breezily. "Thing is,

I'm not in *enough.* I need the lowdown on the vamps looking to enslave humankind. Because their first target would be *moi* if they somehow succeed in this little coup. So I've got an investment in them failing."

He tilted his head at me, not buying my words for a minute. Which wasn't a surprise, as Dante hadn't stayed alive on this earth for thousands of years by being stupid. First rule of immortality: never trust anyone else who has unlimited time on this hunk of rock.

Some creatures lied only to keep things interesting.

I, of course, was much better than that.

But Dante was my best bet for information. He may have been a bartender, but nothing happened in the supernatural world without him knowing about it. You could either buy information from him, if you had a few human souls in your pocketbook, or you could flutter your eyelids and embellish the truth, like I did.

"Plus, I have it on good authority that they're planning on taking over Lucifer's hood as soon as they're done with Planet Earth," I lied. "So it's in your best interests to stop the innocent act and tell me what you've heard."

You want to learn about a species? Go to its bartenders. No need for comprehensive ethnographies. The ones who poured the booze always had the goods.

He sighed and took a swig of my bottle. I hadn't paid for it, but I'd stolen it which was pretty much the same thing.

"I didn't tell you any of this," he said gruffly.

"Of course not. A generous leprechaun popped out of a subway grate and blessed me with the information."

He ignored this. "All I know is that they're gaining numbers, and quickly. Not just with vampires." His eyes flickered to the dog in the corner. "Since the king's alliance with King

Filtiaran and the elders of the Raven witch coven, there's been a lot of pissed-off people coming in and rumbling about a revolution. Immortals don't like quotas on kills. Witches don't like caps on black magic. Werewolves certainly don't like having fences around their doggy parks."

I grinned as the stench of wolfy anger filled the air.

"Down boy. I'll give you a belly rub if you're quiet," I murmured with a grin. I had my own itch that needed scratching too.

We didn't have a huge beef with werewolves like history liked to exaggerate. The handful of fights that were just a result of stolen prey or general disagreements could have happened between any two beings, but because it was a vampire and a werewolf, it started some terrible myth. I didn't particularly like them because they were too brooding and serious about things. Bureaucratic too—"we must obey the alpha," blah blah blah, yawn.

Vampires only had one natural enemy.

Humans.

Or more specifically, a slight variation on the normal model.

Slayers.

"Anyway," Dante said, jerking me into the present before a certain slayer could hold my mind hostage like he had been lately. "There's something coming. Something big. Factions between species are unheard of, at least in this century." His eyes flickered, probably to the wars that immortals had waged every couple of hundred years. The last one had been particularly nasty. Or so I'd heard.

I'd been sunning myself on a little island in the South Pacific. I didn't get involved in epic wars. Not good for the complexion.

"Okay, so we've got a few pissed of sociopaths who want to suck, spell and sprint on their paws without restriction," I surmised.

"It's worse than that, Isla. I don't know specifics, but I heard a vamp in here a couple of nights ago talking about a 'game changer.' One that would seal the fate of the monarchy and...."

I perked up. "And?"

He gave me an uncertain look.

"Spit it out, Dante. You're like a teenager asking the cheerleader to the prom hoping he'll pop her cherry. Newsflash, my cherry was popped four hundred years ago. I'm a sure thing."

"And that Rominskitoff slut, race traitor will become our own private blood slave before we dismember her," he parroted, his voice flat.

I gave him a hurt look. "You didn't even think to call and warn me about such a threat?" I asked with a fake pout.

He narrowed his brows. "I was considering warning them about you if they would try something as stupid as attacking you," he answered.

I gave him a blinding smile. "These vamps, you got names?"

He leaned back, crossing his arms. "You know I can't give out that kind of shit. Even for you, Isla. I don't get involved."

I rolled my eyes. "This goes the way you think it will, you'll have no choice, Dante. Business could seriously dry up if we're in the midst of a war."

He scoffed. "Seriously? I'll do my best business. There's nothing more than the prospect of a fight to get people in the door. Looking for booze, blood and sex." He grinned at me, a blinding smile that I was sure had lost plenty of dull-witted humans their souls. "The three most natural things on this planet."

"So you're not all cut up about this war?" I asked. "Maybe you even support those in this little rebellion? Demons do seem to get left out of all the little alliances and summits. Maybe you're looking for a place at the table."

The temperature increased rapidly, like we were inside a furnace instead of a bar. I stared at the condensation on the beer taps turning into steam before focusing on Dante's attractive and vaguely pissed-off face, if the red irises were anything to go by.

"We don't need a seat at the table because if we so desired, we could burn the table and this whole fucking world down," he rasped, his voice deeper, more dangerous. Not entirely human. I'd heard it before, but we were more horizontal and had fewer clothes on.

The temperature dropped rapidly, as did his fury. Though the air stayed brisk, like we were in the middle of a California heat wave, not November in New York.

"Touché." Demons could technically wreak hell on earth if they were feeling bored with the current status quo. I didn't think it was as easy as all that. Lucifer didn't stay downstairs for the weather; he'd been banished. Getting him topside would be a challenge.

"But I doubt you really want Father Darkness up in here, watching your every move," I continued. "It's like your boss following you around and making sure you can't skimp money from the register, or kill patrons." I shrugged. "Not my idea of fun, but I have problems with authority."

He shook his head, a smile teasing the corner of his mouth as he laid his tatted arms back on the bar. Demon mood swings could rival a woman with PMS who'd just been dumped by her boyfriend.

"Yes, which is why I'm wondering why you're doing the king's dirty work," he mused.

I failed to hide my shock but masked it quickly. "I have no idea what you're talking about. I'm just trying out a new hobby. What insanity took you to that conclusion? Or at least, who told you?" I planned on killing whoever had the big mouth. I'd bet it was Jeeves.

"No one told me. But I happen to know you, Isla," he replied, eyes darkening. "Intimately. And I know that you never do anything with a specific purpose or plan. Insanity doesn't do well with a schedule."

I scowled at him. "I prefer spontaneity."

He grinned. "Whatever you call it, it doesn't line up with this little mission you happen to find yourself on not a week after your attendance at the king's party and your little heroics at the Majestic."

Silence followed his words as I considered how many other immortals would string such events together. I needed a number; it was always good to know how many people would be trying to kill you. Not necessary, but handy.

"No one else has the knowledge or the contacts to come to this particular conclusion," Dante cut into my thoughts as if he were watching them unfold.

I jerked my head up. "And what makes you so sure?"

He gave me an even look. "Likely because you're sitting here right now, not dismembered or being raped by the faction vying for war with every supernatural on the planet opposing them.

"Well, the night's still young. But your faith in me is disappointing."

He took a swig from my bottle. "Faith is for humans. But I do work on logic, and the logical thing for you to do here would be to get the fuck out of this war. And out of any dealings with the king. I've heard he's a right ruthless bastard to anyone who slights him. Frankly, I'm quite surprised he hasn't had you executed already for saying something... well, saying anything."

"Well *I* don't work on logic. I have fun. The two are never mutually exclusive," I replied. "And I resent that comment. I know when to hold my tongue."

He gave me a look.

"I said I *know* when. I didn't say I actually used that knowledge."

Dante shook his head. "I'm not going to talk you out of it, am I?"

"Nope. The best thing you can do is give me names, numbers, addresses."

He sighed. "I can't do that, Isla. But I'll tell you that they were talking about a master, John."

I rolled my eyes. "Well thanks for the great info. A guy named John. Awesome. He shouldn't be hard to find at all."

"You really want to go looking for the vampires who are looking to torture and kill you?" Dante asked.

I raised my brow. "Is that even a question?"

"Fuck," he muttered. "You need to watch your six, Isla. This is growing, and fast. And you're at the top of the hit list. Right below the king."

I twirled my finger along my glass. "Interesting. I'm flattered that the future leaders of the not-so-free world consider little old me such a pressing matter after world domination and dismembering a millennia-old royal family," I mused.

"Of course you wouldn't take this seriously," Dante grumbled.

I glanced up, snatching my clutch and standing. "Oh, I

don't take life too serious. I'd never get out undead otherwise. Thanks for the info, Dante. I'll try not to mention your name to the rebels when I have a chat with them. Can't make any promises, though, since I'm 'insane' and all that jazz."

I blew the moody werewolf a kiss before strutting out the door.

FIVE

"IS THIS TIFFANY?" I HELD UP THE SILVER LAMP, inspecting it in the light.

"Please, I'll do anything," he cried. "I've got money. You want money?"

I rolled my eyes, putting the lamp down after deducing it wouldn't fit in my purse. "Look at my shoes. You think I need money from you?" I shook my head, wandering around the ostentatiously decorated living room. Then to the man crumbled on the ground in front of me, unable to move on account of his broken kneecaps.

"It's literally like Burberry threw up on you," I muttered. "No wonder you had to pay for it." I crouched down. "You think you've got a lot of power, don't you, Dick?"

His name was Richard. Of course it was.

"No," he spluttered.

"Don't lie to me, Dick," I said. "The only thing I hate more than murderers is liars. And you're both. Yahtzee!" I threw my hands up. "It's shaping up to be a great Saturday night."

"Wha-what?" he stuttered.

"The girls, Dick. Six of them, if I'm not mistaken. You picked them up in your hundred-thousand-dollar car, no doubt giving them *Pretty Woman* vibes. That is until you drove them to an empty lot, stabbed them, mutilated their corpses and then afterwards defiled them." I screwed my nose up. "Dude, I drink blood to survive and even I think that's deranged." I tilted my head up in thought. "You'd get along so well with my brothers. You know, if you weren't a human with less than two seconds to live."

His groans muffled when I attached myself to his neck, snapping the bone so I didn't have to listen to his cries. I liked to eat in silence.

After I was done with my meal, I closed the door on his brownstone, hoping whoever got it in his will was worthy of it.

"Yo, Scott. I've got something for you," I said, wandering through the balmy New York night. Pedestrians were lacking in the area, as mostly stuffy Wall Street types were either sleeping with their trophy wives or out at some charity gala. Or, like Dick, rotting in their apartments.

"You went without me?" he whined, tapping at the keyboard. "It was the Manhattan Slasher, right?"

I rolled my eyes. "Don't call him that," I snapped. "It's not my fault you have to work for a living. I don't work around people, people work around me. If you wanted to come, you should have gotten the night off."

"I would have if you'd told me."

"Well, if you were that committed to going, you would have learned how to read minds," I retorted, pausing as something caught my ears.

"I can do that?" he asked, excited.

"Good-bye, Scott," I said, not wanting to tell him that he could, if he paid a witch enough.

Doubtful that he'd have enough for even the deposit for such a spell, or the mental strength. Plus, they backfired more than they worked, leaving the idiot who paid a couple hundred k to hear if their spouse was sucking some other human instead of the one you shared drooling with their fangs falling out.

On second thought, maybe I'd give him the money for the spell.

My step froze as my instincts perked up.

I stood, listening at the sounds coming from the side of a building, behind a dumpster.

Don't do it, Isla. Go home, ring Dante and rethink the scorched-earth policy. You've done enough for the pathetic human race tonight.

My feet went in the direction of the noise. Of course I didn't listen to the logical side of my brain; where was the fun in that?

"Seriously, Earnshaw? A miniature human? That's just embarrassing," I stated, staring at the back of a very well-tailored suit.

The vampire in question turned, revealing a human child of indeterminate age. It couldn't have been that old, considering its shoes were lighting up and was wearing a pink backpack.

"Stay out of this, Isla. I'm eating," he snarled.

I inspected my nails. "I can't. Not in my nature."

He stepped forward, away from the paling creature with the stupid shoes. "Your nature?" he spat. "Your nature would be snacking on this." He gestured back to the frozen rabbit. "Children always have the best blood." He grinned so his fangs glistened in the moonlight.

"What can I say? I like mine matured." I shrugged. "Also, your crazy is showing. I'd advise you to tuck that back in and go on your not-so-merry way. You don't want that suit getting ripped. Custom, isn't it?"

He stepped forward again, slowly, most likely because he was underestimating me.

"Bitch, I'll rip that whore's hair out of your scalp," he snarled.

The second he'd uttered the threat, I moved—not slowly like him, but so my heel found itself embedded into the fleshy part of his cheek, muffling his insults and filtering a wet noise into the night.

"You *never* insult my hair if you want live to see another moonrise," I said casually.

He tried to struggle off the concrete but I was stronger than him. Laughably so.

"I'm *really* not in the mood to get my hands dirty tonight," I continued. "So I won't kill you. As long as you get out of here, like now. I'm sure you know that it would be embarrassingly easy for me to kill you, which I'm tempted to do just for you getting blood all over my favorite Jimmy Choos."

There was a squidgy sound as I lifted my foot from his cheek. He darted up the moment I released the pressure, the wound in his face already healing.

His bloodstained face was etched in hatred. "You'll get what's coming to you, race traitor," he hissed.

"Yup, uh-huh. Someone's already passed that on. Tell me something I don't know. Or better yet, run off into the night." I shooed him with my hands.

For a second, I thought the idiot was actually going to make me kill him, but then the air emptied as he scampered off into the darkness.

"Yeah, that's what I thought," I muttered.

I turned on my heel, planning to stop by the little wine bar down the street from my apartment. I was in the mood for a full-bodied red.

Then I'd pick up the bartender of that wine bar and have a nightcap. He and I had a delightful agreement; the weirdo actually liked getting bitten.

A tug on my sleeve stopped me. I glanced down to see the little human had somehow unstuck itself from its 'rabbit in the headlights' position. And instead of running, the little twit was looking up at me, freckled face stretched into a grin.

It was missing a front tooth.

Ick.

"That was awesome," it breathed. "You totally *owned* that vamp."

I scowled at it, yanking my sleeve from its grasp and inspecting it for stains. Children always had sticky hands.

"Of course I did," I said in distaste. "Now run along." I gestured down the alley much like I had for Earnshaw.

It didn't move.

I tilted my head. "You're not crying," I observed. "And you haven't lost control of your bodily functions." Most humans reeked of urine after a near-death experience, at the mercy of such useless emotions as fear.

It shook its red ringlets. "Nope. My brother said crying will get you two things, dead and drained."

"Your brother sounds smart. How about you go and annoy him, let him know you've made him proud with your lack of tears and the fact that despite everything, you still have blood pumping through your system." I paused. "Though he doesn't seem to be a very good one if you're out here about to be someone's next meal. Don't you have owners or something?"

I peered down the alley to see if its parents hadn't already been drained, then back to see if it had a collar around its neck or anything. Nothing, not even a telltale wound. Earnshaw hadn't even had a taste. He most likely was waiting for glutamate to pulse around the human's circulatory system. Fear changed the way the blood tasted, made it slightly tangier, enriched the flavor of it. Some vampires liked to feed on that fear, while some preferred the ecstasy of orgasm—hence why so many humans were drained in the midst of sex. It wasn't just about the blood. Some humans liked cheeseburgers at those dirty fast food chains with the bad fluorescent lighting and others liked fine dining with snooty waiters and overpriced wine. Same thing with vampires.

"My parents are dead," it, a girl, said, no nonsense.

I folded my arms. "Yes, well they do tend to do that."

"My brother, he takes care of me now," she continued.

"Well he's not doing a very good job," I observed.

She gave me a strange look. "I snuck out. He doesn't know I'm gone, and he would kill me if he knew I'd almost gotten eaten by a vamp."

I nodded, knowing all too well about homicidal brothers. "I'd suggest killing him first. You know, hit him before he can hit you.... Wait, *vamp*?" I only caught on midsentence because I was half listening and half figuring out if I could knock her out and leave her outside a firehouse. But that was three blocks out of my way. Also, I didn't quite know how breakable small humans were, so I'd probably inadvertently kill her instead of knocking her out, rendering this whole fucking scene redundant.

She nodded vigorously again. "Obviously he was a vamp, on account of the teeth." Her voice muffled as she opened her mouth, pointing to her non-pointed incisors.

I screwed my nose up in distaste.

Her gaze on my red lips, she continued. "I'm pretty sure you're a vamp too, although I don't have the sense, you know, not yet. They said you grow into it or something, but I'm pretty sure that's what you are. Even though you haven't bitten me yet. Thanks for that by the way."

I folded my arms. "I wouldn't thank me yet, kid. The night's still young, and I haven't had dessert."

I was going for threatening, but the little cretin smiled at me.

Smiled! In the face of the most fearsome creature known to man.

And demon.

"Wait…. Oh fuck," I cursed.

"You're not meant to swear," she chided.

"Yeah well, you're not meant to be alive. Stupidity normally means death," I snapped. "By the sense, you mean you're a—"

"Praestes," she finished for me, then squinted. "Well, I'm not technically… yet. I'm in training. But that's because I'm a girl and my brother doesn't think a girl can fight vampires at ten years old, even though he did."

"It's a shame gender equality hasn't come to the slayer community either," I said. "Vampires seem to have the same warped ideas, despite us women being the fairer and far more dangerous sex. Humans seem the most progressive out of us all which is just downright embarrassing, considering how stupid the entire race is."

"Yeah." She nodded vigorously. I started to wonder if she'd snap her little neck from all that motion.

One could only hope.

"That's why I'm out here," she said, yanking her backpack

off her back and rifling through it.

I considered leaving while her attention was diverted, but I was intrigued to see where this was going.

The baby slayer had my interest.

"I'm here to show him I'm just as strong as he is," she exclaimed, whipping out a silver blade.

"Careful," I snapped as she waved it too close to my blouse. "I've managed not to get a stain on this all night."

She paled. "Sorry."

My eyes narrowed on the blade and the subtle pulse coming from it.

"Fuck," I muttered. That blade was all too familiar. I really hoped her brother was not who I thought he would be. I mean, those blades were rare, but there was a chance another slayer with an idiot for a sister owned one too.

Then I felt it, the prickle at the back of my neck. A slayer was there. A real one. One who smelled of man and sex. And whose heartbeat echoed through the alley.

"Get the fuck away from my sister," he growled.

The little human's eyes bugged out and she moved quick for a little thing, standing between me and her knife-wielding, hot-as-fuck brother—but the latter was neither here nor there. I was so entranced by… whatever he was doing to me that I let the little gnome get the better of me.

"Thorne, please don't kill her. She saved me," she begged.

I blinked. "Thorne?" I repeated. "Your name is Thorne?"

The slayer—who I may or may not have had bath-time fantasies about the night before—glared at me, then his sister.

"Lucille, get away from the vampire," he ordered tightly. Emotions rolled off him in waves, raw and unbridled. There was the familiar taste of his fury, but something entirely new, with a taste like an overripe peach.

Fear. For his twit of a sister, presumably.

That's who Lewis was warning me about? He's not illiterate, just purposefully vague. He's so not getting a fruit basket this Fourth of July weekend.

"No." Lucille put her hands on her hips, nearly stabbing herself in the stomach in the process.

"Shouldn't you, like, keep the small, idiotic human away from the pointy objects?" I nodded to the knife.

Cue another hauntingly erotic death glare. "Shut the fuck up," he snarled. His eyes moved from me. "Did she hurt you?" The transition of his voice was enough to give a girl whiplash.

He went from Hannibal Lector to friggin' Santa Claus in zero-point-five seconds.

"I'm fine. Thanks to her." She nodded her curls at me. "She saved me from a vampire."

His eyes bugged out. "She *saved* you? She was about to drain you," he growled.

I rolled my eyes. "*She* has a name, and a much higher intellect than both you and your forefathers combined," I cut in. "And I would like to add at this juncture that I don't drain miniature humans. Not enough blood, you see," I lied through my fangs.

"Do you expect me to believe that?" he spat.

I shook my head. "Of course I don't, much like I don't expect you to believe the world is round. Stupidity is, unfortunately, incurable." I glanced at a strawberry blonde head. "And genetic, obviously. I'd tell little sis to lay off the slayer practice until she can actually… slay. Now if you'll excuse me, I'd rather be… well, anywhere but here, actually." I wiggled my fingers. "Toodles."

Then I darted off. Full speed. Thorne, the ape, was quicker than he looked and almost snatched my waist to stop my exit.

But he was human and I was a vampire.
If only my uterus would get the memo.

Me: *You could have elaborated on what, or who, 'Thorne' is. You know, part of a race of humans out to exterminate my kind? A heads-up would have been real nice.*

Lewis: *I did give you a heads-up.*

Me: *Saying 'watch out for Thorne' without any explanation doesn't count. Your mother should spank you, or if she, likely, has kicked the bucket due to old age, I'll do it. Though only one of us will enjoy it, and I won't tell which one.*

No reply.

No fun.

I was in desperate need of fun. Which was why I was heading for drinks with Sophie and was going to get her to curse demons while we watched.

Two days since the 'incident' in the alleyway with Thorne and his weird sister, and I was frequenting all the bars around town trying to get info on this weirdo sect planning on killing me and everyone else who didn't toe the line.

It was getting utterly dull.

Hence me texting Sophie and telling her to meet me at the bar.

I ruled out the cursing demons part, for the time being.

She was late. And since I was always fifteen minutes late, and this time she was twenty, she was really late.

I'd already had three cocktails and was toying with taking

the human bartender home.

Then the door opened and Hurricane Sophie came in. You'd think a witch would be wearing those criminally long gypsy skirts, too many scarves, with plaited hair and smelling like incense.

Not Sophie.

She looked like she should be trailing after Metallica concerts. She was almost always wearing a band tee, spelled or just altered to be skintight across her huge breasts and showing a hefty amount of midriff. Bottoms were always short and tight. Today it was leather hot pants and thigh-high black boots. A fringed leather jacket, a tumble of blonde hair and a heavy hand with the eyeliner topped it off.

"Sorry," she breathed, leaning over to drain my drink.

I shrugged. "No problem. I'm totally sure Alice Cooper needed that blowjob."

She scowled at me.

I grinned at her.

She shook her head and tapped her fingers on the bar. The bartender put two drinks in front of us moments later.

I picked up my cocktail. "It's so handy having a witch around, especially one who breaks all the utterly dull witchy rules for very important things, such as drinks."

She sipped her own. "Those rules are archaic, and I'm opposed to any form of authority. Stupid coven council just can't seem to get that memo. Never mind it's been a century or so," she groaned.

"They just can't handle change, young one," I said. "Wrinkly old witches who are stuck to the old ways. They need to get progressive. 'Times, they are a changing,' to quote Bob Dylan."

Sophie was young, a baby really. She was only about one hundred and fifty, and had been rebelling against authority for about one hundred and forty years. I'd met her when she was running from a building she'd blown up in London after the witch coven had forbidden her to use her newly discovered pyrotechnic power.

We'd been friends ever since.

Witches weren't exactly immortal; the coven council, who needed shots of Botox like I needed a warm blood bag, were examples of that. They aged, just at a much, much slower rate. With the help of sparkles and fairy dust, I was sure. The secrets of the witch community were locked up pretty tight. After the disaster that was Salem, they needed it that way.

"They giving you trouble?" I asked.

The council was pretty big on their rules, and the punishments that went with them. Sophie had been able to escape the most severe on account of her lineage and witchy talent, something about birthrights, yawn. But I was thinking the more powerful she got, the more the council would want to chain her up, control it.

A loose cannon was one thing but a loose nuke, which was what Sophie was in the witch world? That could fuck everything up.

Precisely why I liked her.

She nodded. "What's new? The threat of a cell, binding spells, unimaginable pain if I don't toe the line." She smirked. "I'd like to see them try."

"So would I. Text me when they come to inflict that unimaginable pain," I said. "Especially if that bitch Hazel is going to be there. I've been itching for a reason to rip her throat out since the nineteenth century."

Hazel and I had history.

Another problem with immortality: you had history with everyone. And in my case, it seemed like all of mine was bad blood.

"You got it. But I have to say I couldn't officially have anything to do with condoning a vampire killing one of my own. My Miss Congeniality crown would fall right off."

Sophie was somewhat my counterpart in the witch world. Supernatural societies were old, established, set in their ways. In some ways, humans were more progressive than us, able to accept drastic shifts and changes in society. Mortality did that, I guessed. But difference, changing the status quo, took small increments over centuries.

"We here to troll for guys?" Sophie asked, sucking the cherry out of her glass. "Human bar for once? You haven't fallen off the wagon, have you?" Her tone was casual but I didn't miss the slight bite—excuse the pun—to it. She may not have been around for the murder spree of the early seventeenth century, but she'd heard about it in detail after she made me bewitched cocktails in the sixties. My whole tragic past poured right out.

"Still firmly on the wagon. Don't shoot me with any sparklers out of your fingers just yet," I answered, glancing down to her silver-drenched hands. "This is about business, actually."

Sophie raised her brow.

Along with being a rebel of the witch world, she was also a well-known PI for hire in the supernatural one. She did have a distinct advantage using spells, but there were some laws against which spells you could use for commercial gain or something equally boring.

Like Sophie, I didn't do well with rules.

"Business?" Sophie repeated. "I'm intrigued."

"That's me, intriguing and barely breathing." I finished my drink. "Do the tappy thing," I ordered when she just looked at me.

She sighed dramatically and did it again.

"I'm looking for you to find someone. I could probably do it, but it's time-consuming and also I don't want to. I don't actually want to be involved in this whole mess, but here I am, so I'm going to delegate as much as possible."

I already had Scott pushing his friends—yeah, I was surprised he had them too—for information regarding the rebel group and their membership quota. My family were obviously at the top of the list, but I'd wait a while before going to a reunion. They were back in Russia, and I wasn't in the mood for vodka and depression just yet.

"A certain vampire. And some information," I told her.

"You're looking for a vampire? Am I matchmaking?" she teased.

"Careful, witchy. I may have said I was on the wagon but the road suddenly got bumpy and there's a delicious-looking blood bag in front of me," I threatened.

She didn't look at all concerned.

"Actually, can you do that, but in reverse?" I asked suddenly, my mind jumping from the task at hand. Surely it could wait; there wasn't likely going to be a war this very second.

She frowned at me. "Do what?"

"Make me… unmatch with someone," I clarified, thinking of the slayer I'd been daydreaming about since the week before, and the alley.

The king may have had an effect on me when I was in his presence, but the slayer haunted me in the dark corners of my mind.

She slammed her glass down with such force it cracked. A couple people stared but she didn't notice. "You've got a crush on someone?"

I scowled at her. "I'm almost five hundred years old. I do not get *crushes*," I spat the word. "I have an unsavory connection with an equally unsavory character, which I would like that severed before I sever his head in order to break it. I thought this would be a better, less bloody alternative."

"Right," she said, sounding far too amused. "Who is he?"

I stared at her. "Can you do it or not?"

She shrugged. "Depends. Species?"

I gritted my teeth. "Human. Slayer to be more precise."

"Blow me down with a feather," she breathed. "Slayer? The vampire and the slayer. This is like that show, you know, the one with Sarah Michelle Gellar.... What was it called?"

"If you mention that show, I swear to everything that is unholy that I'll rip your spine out through your throat," I promised.

She grinned. "Yeah, like you could."

"Try me, Hermione. You may have a few little improvements on the base model, but you're still human," I snapped. "Now what can you do?"

She waved her hand. "Oh nothing. A spell like that doesn't even exist. You can't screw with human, or even inhuman, emotions," she said, her gaze flickering up and down my body. "I just wanted to know who you were crushing on."

"So you lied to get that information?"

She nodded.

"I knew there was a reason I liked you," I said. "But this information leaves this little bubble, you'll—"

"Become your next brunch. Yeah, I get it. Girlfriends keep secrets. It's in the vault." She tapped her head. "Now, which slayer is it? I will say I'm not familiar with them all, since they're pretty staunch and serious and I stay away from that like I do pastels. But I'm sure I can do some research. Give me a name," she demanded, pulling out her phone.

I snatched it off her. "This subject is closed. We need to get down to business now."

She screwed up her face. "You're no fun."

"I'm loads of fun," I argued. "I'm just more fun when I don't have threats like dismemberment hanging over my head."

"Dismemberment? Bummer."

I nodded. "Bummer indeed. You can find a vamp, can't you?"

She looked offended. "Of course."

"Vampire by the name of John," I said.

She waited for a beat, but then I didn't speak. Her eyes widened. "That's it, a vampire named John?"

I nodded. "I realize it's not much to go on."

Her brow rose. "Isla, it's *nothing* to go on."

"Well, you can try after I tell you more about what he's involved in. Will that help?"

She sucked her drink down, nodding.

"Good. And now I need some inside intel," I said, leaning forward. "Of the delicate kind."

"Will me telling you this information get me a threat of dismemberment of my own?"

"Don't you always have something like that from the council?"

"Good point," she said. "Go on."

I glanced around. We were surrounded by humans, drinking the sorrows of their pitiful lives away. Or sucking down liquids in order to make themselves more attractive to drunken stockbrokers and land themselves an orgasm. They weren't paying attention to us. They would, I was sure, if Sophie hadn't cast a glamour over us the moment she sat down. It stopped those orgasm-seeking humans from coming in our direction.

"What do you know about a rebel faction of vampires, witches, demons, werewolves and a variety of the supernatural vying for world domination?" I asked, cutting to the chase.

Her eyes flickered and she was silent for a moment. "What have you got yourself into, Isla?"

"Trouble, of course."

She shook her head. "This isn't just trouble. You need to stay far away from this." Her face was serious.

I frowned. "Everyone's telling me that. What's so bad about a bunch of fanatics with a fairytale of an idea? It's not like they're actually dangerous."

Sophie's eyes bugged out. "Are you serious? Have you been paying attention to anything going on in the supernatural world for the past decade?"

I rolled my eyes. "Of course not. It's all such a bore." I narrowed my eyes at her. "When you've been around for as long as I have, you learn that it's all a cycle. It's useless. I focus on fashion trends, not political immortal ones. By the way, do you like my boots?" I lifted my foot to reveal my spike-heeled lace-ups.

She flickered her eyes to the boots and then back to me. "This isn't just a bunch of fanatics," she corrected. "At the beginning of the century, perhaps, but now, with technology and such making it harder to be an immortal in hiding, they've gained more unhappy followers with the status quo. To whom the idea of not being a slave to secrecy is more than a little enticing. The promise of a society in which each supernatural race can embrace their baser instincts without rules. It's a tempting idea."

I scoffed. "It's a utopian idea. They'll always be underlings of someone. How can people who have lived through numerous revolutions and dictatorships not realize that they never end well? Someone's always at the top and then everyone else is usually at the bottom."

Sophie shook her head. "Reason and revolution are never

in the same narrative. The party speech is pretty convincing if you're stupid enough to believe that exterminating all 'race traitors' and enslaving the human race is actually a possibility." She sucked on her drink. "Think about it. No rules that we both hate, no secrecy, no politics. We get to just… be."

I stared at her. "Are you fucking serious? You think this whole thing is a good idea? That killing humans and supernaturals en masse is necessary for some new world order? I thought you actually *liked* humans."

"Chill, Isla. I in no way want any part of this crazy war." She raised her brow at me. "And that's what this is, a war. It may not be just yet, but the air has that bitter taste to it like during the demon uprisings of the early twentieth century. You can't tell me you haven't noticed."

I rolled my eyes. "Of course I noticed. Ten vampires were killed at a bloodletting bar in London not three days ago. Then in a similar establishment in Prague. Humans going missing in record numbers and the human press citing some endemic disease? Yeah, the world is going to shit. What's new?"

She placed her hand over mine. "What's new is I think this one's going to blanket the world in blood that will stain almost every being in the supernatural community before it's over." Her grip tightened almost to the point of pain, which surprised me. Apart from her magical prowess, the little witch was 100 percent human, as breakable and weak as one too.

My question at her suddenly inhuman strength was swallowed when I caught her eyes.

They weren't hers.

No. The spark, the mischievous glint that lingered in those green orbs had disappeared in the short moments I'd glanced from her face to her hand and back.

They were vacant. And ancient. The chilling depth in those

eyes had me flinching.

"Hell," she declared, her throaty voice replaced by something flat, emotionless. "Hell will rise up from the flames of the underworld and will reside in those who are chosen." The vacant eyes focused on my frozen face. "The one vampire and the other will intertwine. This will become the point at which the worlds hang on the precipice. Blood. It's in the blood that life and death are decided."

Silence descended heavily, like a cloak over the bustling bar. It was like whoever that was—it certainly wasn't Sophie—had sucked all the noise out.

Then, like an elastic snapping back into place, it returned. The noise, the glint in Sophie's eyes. Her hand left mine.

She blinked a couple of times and shook her head, as if to clear it.

"What were we talking about again? The slayer whom you want to do naughty things to, ones that don't include killing?" She grinned mischievously, sucking down the last of her drink.

I gaped at her. "Please for the love of Lucifer tell me you're playing me right now?"

She tilted her head in confusion. "No, I'm seriously going to put a spell on you to make you reveal the identity of the slayer who has captured your attention."

"Holy shit," I muttered. "You honestly don't remember going all Nostradamus and talking about hell, demon fire and the chosen? And maybe the end of the world?"

Her eyes hardened and the grin left her face like I'd pulled the plug on her amusement. "What?"

"You don't remember," I surmised, cool unease snaking up my spine. "Okay, this is totally creepy. Not in the good way. Are you possessed?" I leaned forward, peering at her eyes again for the telltale flicker of flame that would signify demon possession.

It was saying a lot that I hoped my friend was possessed by a demon rather than the alternative.

She leaned back. "No, I'm not possessed by a demon," she snapped.

I frowned. "Yep. We're not that lucky."

She raised her brow. "Lucky?" she repeated. "How would me having a slimy asshole in my head be lucky?"

I drained my drink. "Because that would have been relatively easy to deal with. That"—I gestured to her face in a circular motion—" is not easy to deal with."

"What exactly did I say?" she commanded.

I dutifully repeated it, word for word.

By the time I'd finished, she was paler than me.

"Fuck," she whispered, her voice barely audible, even to my ears.

I nodded. "My sentiments exactly. You had no clue you had the sight?"

She shook her head. "No. I've never had it. But my powers have been changing lately," she said slowly.

"Changing?" I probed. "Like you deciding to spout out ominous prophecies after a couple of cocktails?"

She shook her head again. "No. This is going to be a first." Her head snapped up. "This doesn't go any further."

I crossed my heart. "I'll take it to the grave."

She scowled at me, then took a deep breath. "I've been getting stronger for a few years now. I've been hiding it from the council because I know more power means more danger for me. There's already the threat of binding, imprisonment, and maybe even death on my head, and they only sense a tiny amount of my power." She held her thumb and forefinger together. "If they knew how much I actually had…." She shuddered.

"What are we talking here?" I asked, suddenly interested. "Were you holding out on me? Could you actually make the slayer become repugnant to me?" I paused and thought on it. "And a vampire too, while we're at it."

"Okay, we're so going back to that, but it's a little more than that," she replied. "I kind of… time-traveled the other day."

I spat out the sip I'd just taken. It took a lot to shock me. I'd wager before that moment that it was actually impossible.

"Time travel?" I yelled.

She snatched my hand. "Shush," she hissed, glancing around.

No one had moved, had even noticed. "Chill, your little glamour is doing its job. The humans are too focused on forgetting their miserable lives to notice they've got a real life Marty McFly in their midst."

She narrowed her eyes. "Yes, *humans*," she clarified. "But this might not hold against another witch or demon." She glanced around again before relaxing when she was satisfied no one was spying.

"Okay, now I need more information," I commanded.

"I don't have it," she admitted. "One second I was in my living room playing *GTA*, the next I was in England. In 1902," she said. "It was only for a split second, but long enough for me to seriously shock some aristocrats with my boxers and Harry Potter tee shirt."

I gaped at her.

And not just on account of the Harry Potter tee shirt.

Time travel wasn't something that happened, even in the supernatural world where the laws of nature were a little more flexible than humans believed.

There were legends, of course, but everyone had legends.

Vampires had the origin story that we began with Ambrogio, the first vampire, cursed by an angry Apollo to never feel the warmth of the sunlight on his skin. Then he sold his soul to Hades in order to bathe in that light once more. Then Apollo's sister, Artemis, the goddess of the hunt, decided to grant the soulless creature the punishment of immortality, to walk the world alone without a soul. She fed him her blood, with the Ichor of the gods to sustain him. Since that first taste of Ichor, the only thing that would continue his strength and immortality was human blood.

Before long, Ambrogio pleaded with Hades for a companion. He was bestowed with Lilith, the ancient temptress from a garden where apples were eaten. And thus began the vampire Vein Line, tracing back to the gods.

Or so the story went.

Werewolves also had the Greek gods to thank, or curse, for their existence, as the legend went. A human king, obsessed with the idea of immortality, was advised by a witch that eating a human heart on every full moon would ensure him eternal life. Of course, that was utter bullshit, but it did have its intended effect. Jupiter was angered by such atrocities against the people of his country, deciding that if the king were to act like an animal in order to live forever, he would undergo the painful transformation every full moon to gain that immortality. And he had to snack on human hearts.

I had no clue what demons had. They locked their shit tight.

Guess you could say the Bible, if you switched it all around.

But time travel.... My mind went to sixteenth-century Paris.

Sophie gave me a look. "I can't control it," she said softly.

"I don't even know if it'll ever happen again, and if it does it's not exactly a science. I doubt I'll be able to pinpoint times and locations. Sorry, Isla."

I glowered at her, only because I couldn't glower at myself. Weakness, even in front of friends, could mean death.

Because friends could turn to enemies in the blink of an eye.

"Can you read minds too?" I snapped.

She shook her head. "No. Not vampire ones, anyway. But I can read my friend's face, and I know that the ability to manipulate time is that much more covetable when time was the only saving grace for someone."

"I don't have grace to save," I snapped. "I'm graceless. And the only way I could make that time travel thing handy was if I could go back and not walk into the fifth precinct on the first Friday in November."

She gave me a long look but didn't say anything.

Friends still. For now at least.

"So that, combined with what I just saw…." My skin chilled even more.

She nodded grimly. "Yep a one-way ticket to seclusion for my prophet ass," she finished for me.

Witches had prophets. People with the sight were slightly different. They did spells, saw a limited future that was hardly ever reliable. The future was a fickle thing, determined by free will, which could change in a heartbeat. Even the smallest decision was a rippling effect over all the futures available.

Prophets, people who didn't need spells to see the future and spoke in codes and tongues like Sophie just did, were something different altogether. From what I heard, their predictions almost always came true. Granted, it was most likely because they were vague and tricky.

But they were sparkling assets for any supernatural. Countless cases of prophets getting snatched and milked for predictions were present over the years.

You couldn't put a price on knowing the future. And what can't be possessed with money is usually stolen with blood.

Witches took steps to 'protect' their prophets. I say 'protect' because those wicked bitches were only protecting one thing, themselves. They all had prophets on some island cloaked with magic, little more than prisoners.

I could see why Sophie wasn't too hot on going for an indefinite holiday there.

"Well, this conversation never happened," I declared, standing.

She stood too. "You're leaving?"

I nodded, hitching my bag up on my shoulder. "I don't want to be treated to any more prophecies. I hate those things with a passion. I'd suggest you buy a ticket to Timbuktu until you figure this out and can control it so you don't go blurting out predictions all over the place. That little gift is a loaded gun, pointed right at your head." I paused. "I already have a murderous vampire faction to investigate and try not to get killed by. I don't want to get on the witches' interrogation and kill list too. My calendar is super full."

I may have sounded flippant, but distance was a luxury I was affording myself. My friend was in deep shit. My mortal friend. Which meant most likely death. I would have loved to do what I could to make sure that didn't happen, but I didn't have a magic wand.

She folded her arms. "I'm not running away," she decided.

I quirked my eyebrow at her.

"We're in the midst of a revolution, right? Well, it's time to revolt." She grinned wickedly.

"Oh no, you're not going to join the cause and try to dismember me too, are you?" I moaned.

"No, I'm going to fight it. And the witches council."

"Aces," I said immediately. "On second thought, my calendar just cleared. I'm in. Once I get the info on these supernatural idiots, it's war. I feel like I've been out of the game for long enough. A good battle might spice up my life, as long as it doesn't ruin my manicure."

She grinned at me. "I'm happy to hear. We haven't had fun since… forever. Plus, I can investigate the witches' side of this faction, and get back to you."

"Sounds like a plan, Marty," I agreed. *Less work for me. Awesome.*

She scowled. "Don't call me that."

"Okay, Marty."

She shook her head. Her face turned quizzical as we weaved through the bar. Our glamour must have dissolved because all male and female eyes went to us as we passed. I didn't blame them; we were smoking.

"Why are you suddenly yanking yourself out of your narcissistic bubble to trouble yourself with this?"

"I'm not narcissistic," I protested.

She gave me a look as we stepped out onto the street.

"Okay, I totally am," I relented. "I've decided to embrace my inner philanthropist."

She didn't buy it for a second.

I huffed. "Let's just say the newest member of the royal family has made me feel all warm and cuddly towards monarchy and doing their bidding as long as it keeps my head on my shoulders," I relented.

She gaped. "That's a story for another twelve cocktails."

I nodded. "Yeah. But we've got a rebellion to quash,

witches to kill and battles to fight. Let's not get too carried away, shall we?"

She smiled. "It's just another normal year for us."

"Yeah. Let's hope it's not our last one on this earth."

SIX

"BROTHER. TO WHAT DO I OWE THE DISPLEASURE?" I asked, exhibiting no surprise that he was standing in the middle of my living room. I was more than a little irritated, though. I'd had enough excitement for the night, what with prophecies', battle plans, and a certain slayer taking up prime real estate in my head. Was it so much to ask to not have my psychopathic brother drop in for tea?

"There are no infants in here for you to drain, nor humans to terrify and defile. I'm afraid no fun at all for sadistic pleasures." I paused. "I do have a red room of pain but I'm thinking even you wouldn't go that far… and I'd have to fling myself out of that window rather than deal with what I'm sure is the most horrible last fifteen seconds of some poor young human's life." I wandered over to my bar, intending to pour myself a drink to get through extended periods of time in my brother's presence.

A firm grip on my wrist stopped me. The dull pop of my bones snapping echoed in my living room.

I glanced up at him with gritted teeth. "You never did know how to play nice."

His glassy eyes flickered with rage as his face stayed impassive. "What have you been telling the king, Isla?" he asked, squeezing harder.

I didn't cry out, though the pain was most unpleasant. Most vampires didn't have the strength to hold me in such a position, let alone shatter most of the bones in my wrist, but my brother unfortunately shared the purest vampire blood on the planet with me and was three hundred years older.

"That you shave your chest and injected yourself with steroids before you turned," I said sweetly. "But it was under duress, I promise. I'm meant to obey my king, right? And he asked."

He squeezed harder before letting me go so he could backhand me, sending me flying across the room and crashing into the wall beside my television. I struggled to get up as he leisurely walked towards me.

"Centuries you've been a disgrace to this family," he said, his voice cold. "An embarrassment, what with your feeding tendencies and proclivity for *humans*." He spat the word as his boot connected with my stomach. Pain radiated through my midsection as my rib broke and punctured a lung. "You will behave until your Awakening, if I have to visit you daily to remind you."

"Why couldn't Viktor be the one to deliver the beating?" I wheezed. "He wears loafers."

Evgeni knelt down, gripping my hair and yanking my head back so the muscles in my neck screamed in protest. "You think everything is a joke. That you're untouchable because, although our family may despise you, you still share our blood. But we will not tolerate your disloyalty."

I punched his jaw, sending him flying into my glass coffee table, shards littering the room. I grabbed a steel leg that had conveniently landed beside me and limped to his body, holding my ribs. He was still recovering from the shock, which gave me the chance to embed the steel into his midsection.

"For murderers, rapists, sadists and sociopaths, your fixation with loyalty is laughable." I pressed the steel further.

My upper hand didn't last for long, but I did feel a small amount of satisfaction at the grimace of pain on my brother's harsh features. He could never have been called handsome, what with angular cheekbones that cut too high on his face, a jaw that was too pointed, a bald head that accentuated all those features and those eyes that glittered with empty cruelty.

He yanked the steel out without a sound and pushed himself up. In one move he had me against the wall by my neck.

He flexed his hand, straining the bones of my windpipe. "We're the Rominskitoffs. Our name, our family, is *everything* we have. And you disgrace that. Vampires should be rulers, not ruled. Certainly not the great families. Humans should bow down to us. They are our lessers," he hissed. "Nothing more than oxen. Your love for them is sickening."

I glared at him. "I don't love humans," I snarled back. "I will *never* make that mistake again, brother. They are nothing to me. Just like our ridiculous family name. Though I do enjoy these little visits to let me know how valued I am in our great family, what's your excuse this time?" I rasped as the pressure intensified.

"Like you don't know," he growled.

"I don't do well with guessing," I snapped. "Or mind reading. If I did I wouldn't even want to venture into the bag of crazy that's your consciousness."

He squeezed tighter, snapping a small vertebra.

"You know why. You've been traipsing around town, poking your nose where you shouldn't. You'll stop if you want to stay on the face of this planet much longer." He abruptly let me go and I tottered on my heels at the impact.

"I don't traipse. I glide gracefully," I argued, rubbing my neck. "What do you care how long I stay on this planet? Isn't that what this little visit is? Daddy sent you here to finally rip my head from my shoulders?" He wouldn't, if I had anything to do about it. I wasn't fighting now, but I would when he tried to get real. This violence was nothing. Child's play.

He hadn't stepped far from me. "I'm not here to kill you, Isla, though it would bring me much pleasure to do so."

I put my hand over my heart. "Your love for your sister is utterly beautiful."

He scowled. "I'm here to tell you to stop whatever you're doing for the king. Stop before Father decides to stop being so sentimental and insane to think that this little rebellious streak is temporary, and I rip your heart out myself." He stepped forward, thrusting his fist into my chest, clutching my heart in a firm grip.

I gasped and made some seriously unladylike sounds as he squeezed, pain making my vision blank. He couldn't kill me this way, but he could make things unpleasant. I was basically paralyzed.

"I will tear you to shreds once we get the power to do so. That's a promise, sister."

I met his empty eyes with a measured gaze. "Ditto, brother," I hissed, hatred rendering my voice unrecognizable.

Empty air replaced his hand as the door to my apartment slammed.

I slumped to the floor, clutching my chest. Blood poured out steadily.

I groaned.

"This is my favorite sweater," I whined to my empty apartment.

The blood would stop. It was already slowing, but my sweater was ruined, just like my coffee table.

I sat with my head back, closing my eyes for just a second.

Visits like that from my brothers weren't exactly rare. Whenever I did something particularly human I was treated to more of the same. It wasn't just to make sure I teetered on the right side of immoral that motivated such visits; my brothers enjoyed it. The violence, inflicting pain. They were sadists.

I used to think with youthful hope that it was their way of showing they cared.

Now I knew better.

A banging at my door made me jerk.

I ignored it.

It didn't stop.

I sighed, pushing up. "Can't a girl bleed out in peace?" I cried, limping to the door.

There was only a couple of people it could be. I was hoping for Sophie; she could heal me, repair my coffee table and maybe save my sweater. Maybe she could click her fingers and rid the earth of my family with her new powers. Such a comforting thought.

Or it could be Scott, who was still stalking me. He'd probably faint or something equally pathetic at the sight of me. That would almost be worth the excruciating pain.

Almost.

I didn't think it would be him banging so loudly, though.

I did not expect to have a grim-faced, then horrified slayer at my doorstep.

"No, thanks, I don't want any Girl Scout cookies," I said, trying to shut the door in his face.

His motorcycle boot stopped it and he surged in, taking me in with wide and slightly panicked eyes. "What the fuck?" he growled.

I glared at the door he just barged in. "I so need Sophie to hex this place against unwanted guests," I muttered to myself. I could have done it ages ago to keep my brothers out, but I kind of liked their little visits. I could give only slightly less than I got, but it was still satisfying. Once I even ripped Viktor's entire arm off. It had taken a week to grow back.

It was brilliant.

And my father had even called me after to say that maybe I wasn't lost after all. Yes, that was my family. Dismemberment of my siblings was tolerated, if not encouraged, but not killing humans whenever the mood struck me was tantamount to treason.

Though it seemed like they were already committing treason if my brother had been sent to scare me off. Interesting. I had suspected as much, but that was almost concrete proof.

I made a mental note to call the king and hand over my family, then request a front row seat to the execution.

"What the fuck happened here? Are you fucking dying?" Thorne demanded. Surging forward, to my horror and slight delight, he grasped my neck with one hand, pushing my hands from my midsection away with the other.

"Holy fuck," he seethed, eyes zeroing in on the hole in my sweater.

"I know. It's cashmere," I moaned.

"Isla, your fuckin' chest is *open*." His stoic face betrayed little, but his eyes were wild, face pale. The grip on my neck bordered on violent. But it wasn't, which puzzled me. Violence I understood, expected. But this?

I nodded. "Yeah, my brother is a total dick."

He pressed his hand into my wound, as if to stop the bleeding. In the process of his needless first aid, he'd brushed my breast. The contact had me forgetting all about the vaguely painful fact that my ribs were knitting themselves back together.

"Your brother did this?" he spat.

Regretfully, I circled his wrists with my hands and yanked them away from my chest. "Yes, he's a frightful prick," I said, limping over to the bar which was thankfully still in one piece.

"Fuck, Isla. Sit the fuck down," he all but roared at me.

I glanced over my shoulder at his marble face. "Why? If I were sitting down I wouldn't be able to get a drink, and I *really* need I drink."

He strode over to me, gripping my hips and forcing me onto the sofa. I scowled at the overturned one, then down at the bloodstains I was getting on the one beneath me. "Great. These were flown in from France. This is why I can't have nice things. Blood gets on everything. This is the fourth sofa they've ruined. Plus, that vintage mirror." I nodded over to the corner where the mirror had smashed on my carpet beside my ruined wall. "Seven years' bad luck," I muttered.

Thorne stared at me, his mouth slightly open in shock or confusion. I wasn't sure which since I was focused on that mouth and the sharp jaw, wondering what it might taste like.

Not his blood, no just *him*.

Maybe Evgeni had shaken up something important. My marbles weren't locked up tight and I reasoned it would be quite easy to lose them in the midst of a skirmish.

"I'll get your drink," he clipped after he schooled his

features. His hand went up to brush my cheek, which I guessed was an angry shade of purple. In an hour or so it would be flawlessly pale once more. “Don’t you need some sort of medical attention?” he asked, his voice only slightly above a harsh whisper.

I sucked in a breath; his touch was tender, his proximity bordering on uncomfortable.

I wished he was holding a knife at my neck. It would’ve made things so much easier.

I didn’t get easy, though, and I had a part to play. One that meant I had to act like his mere touch wasn’t having me feeling some type of way. The wrong type of way.

I laughed. “A slayer asking me if I should get medical attention? Shouldn’t you be taking advantage of my weakened state and plunging a dagger in my heart or something?” I paused. “Although, I’m pretty glad you’re not doing that. I guess this is just rounding out a particularly strange day.”

“Is getting brutalized by your fuckin’ brother what you call a ‘strange day’?” he hissed.

I shrugged, hiding my wince at the movement. Not well enough if his narrowed eyes were anything to go by. “I call it a Saturday.”

He scowled at me, his eyes a cocktail of emotions. Instead of answering me, he turned his back and stomped to my bar. He was back in a second, holding out a whiskey.

I took it with a raised brow. “How do you know what I drink?”

He didn’t lower his gaze, nor did he answer.

“You’ve been following me,” I guessed. For a moment, I panicked at the thought of someone overhearing my conversation with Sophie. A slayer, no less. That would not do. It would also mean I’d have to kill him, and the thought of doing such a thing actually made me taste bile. I may have avoided killing humans carte blanche like the rest of my race did, but it didn't mean I wouldn't. I couldn't afford to feel sick at the thought of ending one. Yet I did.

I relaxed slightly when I realized I'd have known if he was tailing me. "No, the pesky slayer sense I've got would've hampered that." Not to mention the Thorne sense I seemed to have. "You've paid a human to follow me. I would say a witch or demon, but I know you slayers keep to yourselves. Well, unless you're killing, that is."

Slayers were built for the purpose of killing vampires, but they'd diversified in the past few hundred years, deciding to go after any supernatural creature they deemed a threat to the human race.

Which was all of them, coincidentally.

So they went from a pain in a vampire's ass to a pain in everyone's ass. Public enemy number one in the supernatural world.

Right below me, obviously.

"I can understand the reason for the tail, if I put myself in your self-righteous motorcycle boots, of course," I said, my voice light but with an edge. "In no way do I appreciate it, though. But let's just forget my simmering fury right now. We'll circle back to me using my powers of persuasion to make certain you have the desire to follow me again."

The threat rolled off my tongue as easy as a sweet nothing. Who was I kidding? Death threats *were* my sweet nothings. "I assume you're conducting surveillance on the nefarious activities you're convinced I partake in. Devil worship, killing children, the usual. But I wouldn't think my drink preference would factor into the reports you get," I continued with a raised brow.

He stared at me, his gaze unwavering.

I sipped my drink, shifting uncomfortably as my body went through the healing process. I obviously wasn't going to betray the extent of my pain to him. He'd already acted on manly instinct that I was an injured female instead of an injured vampire; I couldn't count on him forgetting the vampire part for this whole conversation. Hence me acting like the hole in my chest was little more than a paper cut.

Never show weakness, physical or emotional. It was of the upmost importance that I continue hiding my feelings towards his little show of tenderness, or his presence in particular. If I let even a sliver of that show in my eyes, I feared it would be more fatal than a dagger to the heart.

"It must get boring," I continued, "being the most hated sect of humans in the whole of the over and underworlds. You don't get invited to any of the good parties."

He stepped forward, his fury cloaking us in its thick musk. Used to the bitter twang, I didn't revolt against it; in fact, it relaxed me. "Stop the shit," he commanded. "You're sittin' here with a wound that looks disturbingly like someone has put their fist through your chest, acting like it's fuckin' nothing."

I smiled at him. "Oh my dear, sweet, naïve slayer. It is nothing." I pointed to my almost-healed chest. "Vampire. Means I heal rather quickly. I know you humans get touchy about such things as 'mortal wounds,' but no need to worry your gruff little head about me. I'll survive. Always do. Perks of being immortal." I paused, straightening my shoulders. "Now you can tell me why you're here, if not to kill me. You'll see someone has already attempted that tonight, and failed. My patience is wearing thin."

He stepped forward, bending down so his hands circled my just-healed windpipe. The gesture itself was threatening but the pressure was little more than a pinch. More erotic than homicidal.

"I should," he whispered. "I should be killing you. I should have killed you in that alleyway the first moment I laid eyes on you. The second I found out you murdered that priest. I hesitated because…." He paused and I stilled. Has he yet to try—and fail—to kill me because he felt this weird thing too? I didn't know if the thought comforted me or freaked me out further.

"Because you threw me with his history, and I had a little chat with Lewis," he continued, and I deflated. "He wouldn't say shit about you, but he did warn me against embedding a knife in your chest." His jaw tightened. "Even fuckin' *threatened* me, should I try. Lewis is a good man. He knows what you are and still he defended you. That gave me pause."

I grinned. "Lewis and I go way back," I said sweetly. "He's like a father to me, though more correct to say I'm like a mother to him. No matter how correct it is, you won't even say that if you don't want me to rip your throat out," I seethed.

He didn't flinch at my empty threat. That worried me. So did the way he was regarding me. Murder was in his eyes, but that confusing concern still lingered, a strange and unnerving combination. He gritted his teeth and schooled his expression. "I don't give a shit what kind of spell you've got him under, or whatever a man I respect says about you. It doesn't change what you are. I should have ignored him and ended you the instant I found you with my fuckin' sister." His grip tightened.

I could have extracted myself from the situation as easy as breathing, but I was kind of enjoying it. I knew he was too; his eyes danced with desire and hatred, the most beautiful of combinations.

"How is the little cretin?" I inquired casually. "She still alive? I would imagine her chances aren't good if she keeps doing idiotic things like chasing after vampires. You should make sure her cage is locked at all times."

My words caused one emotion to win in his eyes.

Hatred.

He squeezed my neck once more before letting go and stepping back abruptly.

"You're a monster," he spat, his eyes dripping with disdain. The change in his aura was immediate, a shock of hatred cutting through everything as he let his natural instincts take over. I needed to follow suit.

I scowled. "I resent that. It's been a while since I've had a solid day's sleep, that's true, but I think I look pretty good. Blood and guts aside, obviously."

It did worry me slightly that my wound was taking longer than was favorable to heal, which was connected to the lack of sleep I was joking about. It might turn dangerous if I didn't sleep soon, but it was even more dangerous to fall into the abyss that was. The phrase 'sleep like the dead' did originate with vampires, considering we did a very convincing corpse impression when in laevisomnus. Since our bodies were immortal and our strength supernatural, our slumber captured us and dragged us into what a human would liken to a coma. We weren't able to awaken easily and were at our most vulnerable. Which was why, at this tumultuous time in my life, with assassination attempts more common than offers for dates, I had to put off laevisomnus, despite how dangerous it was to put it off any longer than I already had.

I'd just have to hope no one else punched through my rib cage for the next few days.

Thorne's form tightened, as did the grip on the solid silver knife he'd yanked from his leather jacket. I wasn't hugely bothered; if he was planning on using it he would have tried, and failed, by now.

"I was born and exist to exterminate your kind. The abomination that you are. The murderer that you are. The only reason that red head isn't lying at my feet right now is because I need what's inside it. That's the only thing quelling my overwhelming urge to rip your evil, unnatural, disgusting head off."

I tilted my head and smiled at him. "It's sonnets like that every girl needs to hear. That'll keep me cold at night."

I pushed off the sofa, keeping my smile in place as pain radiated through my upper torso. I didn't like being on unequal ground, him towering over me like he had the upper hand.

He stepped forward so my pointed heels were toe-to-toe with his biker boots. I had to look up to maintain eye contact. That meant my gaze traveling up his neck, inspecting the pulsing veins snaking up to his sharp jaw. I wasn't looking at them hungrily. Well, I was, but not the blood kind of hunger. Something I sure as shit shouldn't be feeling for the man who would attempt to kill me the moment he had the chance.

You'd think my body, even my downstairs parts, would realize that. Obviously not.

"You're not a girl," he growled, his eyes flickering up my body. I felt the gaze rake up my hips, my nipples hardening as his dark eyes held them to attention. "No matter how much you try to show that outwardly. Trying to look like a fucking wet dream doesn't change that fact."

I sighed and rolled my eyes. "Ugh. Your mood swings are giving me whiplash. This 'you are an unnatural monster and I must annihilate you' crap is getting old." I whirled my finger around. "Can we wrap this up? Threaten my soulless self a couple more times, damn me to eternity, and then tell me what you came here for. I've got things to do."

His jaw ticked as he breathed in my face. That would

normally piss me off. Some sweaty human blowing their regurgitated carbon dioxide in my direction. With him, it didn't. The opposite, in fact. I licked my lips despite myself.

Mustn't bite the slayer, Isla. There's the nasty side effect of getting dead after that little snack.

He watched my lips, and his face changed. Now, I saw a lot. Namely because my eyesight was one hundred times better than any human. And I'd been on this earth long enough to become an expert at social cues. If I wasn't mistaken, hunger, mirroring my own sexual desire, lurked in his gaze.

Then it was gone and he stepped back, shaking himself as if he was covered in poisonous dust.

He folded his arms and I did my best not to watch the pulsing of his muscles as he did so. I did try my best not to lust after men who threatened death. Some considered it foreplay, but I was an old-fashioned girl. I preferred my men not to be homicidal. At least not towards me.

"There's a vamp goin' around the city, turning humans." He scowled at me, then started to pace the room. "At least tryin' to. What's left." He paused, his eyes flickering with something before they turned back to hardened silver. "It's not human or vamp, both yet neither. They never survive. At least not yet. They're getting stronger. Latest one survived long enough for us to get it back to the doc and for it to try and drain him."

All thoughts of sex and homicide left my brain. "That's impossible," I snapped. "Vampires don't turn humans. Despite it being illegal to even try, it's biologically impossible. Sounds like something a stupid human who'd watched too many television shows would do." I gave him a pointed look.

His eyes narrowed. "I'm not lying. You think I'd come to you if I had any other option?"

I tilted my head. "Of course, because you can't get enough

of me. A tiny lie about something impossible is nowhere near the most outlandish thing a man has done to get in my company. One even started a military coup to get my attention."

"I'm not lying. I don't lie," he gritted out.

I laughed. "Oh that's cute. Everyone lies. You trying to tell me you're some sort of saint? Here's the secret from an immortal who's got centuries on you. No one, not even a sexy, self-righteous slayer, is a saint. *Everyone's* a sinner."

My brain caught up with my mouth the moment I stopped speaking and his frame jolted.

Crap. I just called the slayer sexy. Abort, abort!

I jumped up the second I realized the change in the air. "Now that I've educated you on your lack of sainthood, I request you leave now."

He stepped forward, his eyes focusing on mine. "I'm not leavin'," he murmured, his voice velvet.

I stood there frozen like a big dumb idiot. I decided to blame it on the hole in my chest and my healing wrist, not his sensual gaze.

"I'm not goin' anywhere till I get answers," he continued, voice firm.

I schooled my expression. "Answers? To what? I'm not an oracle, and you can't come running over here whenever you need to know which pill to take. I'll advise the red, then maybe you'll take those fucking self-righteous blue-tinted glasses off and see the world for what it is."

He stepped forward. "I see the world for what it is," he hissed. "Monsters running around the world, killing, maiming, torturing without any justice."

I glowered at him, stepping forward so I could enshroud him in my own cloud of fury.

"You want to see what monsters look like?" I whispered.

"You're in the wrong place, Buffy. Don't go searching for vampires, or werewolves or demons. The only thing they have in common with monsters is that their depravity is on the outside. That's not a monster—that's reality. You want a real, 'hide under you bed, break out the crucifix' monster? How about you open a newspaper, turn on the TV, have a fucking browse through your history books. You'll find your monster there." I gestured to the twinkling skyline, then leaned forward even further so his breath was hot on my face, his fury like a space heater. "But that one's far too scary to take on, so you stalk us instead. We're different enough that it seems justifiable to kill us. Humans, on the other hand, are just too darn similar to you to be damning and slaying. What with all those gray areas, you might find the worst monster you've ever faced staring back at you in the mirror."

Our gazes were locked in the intensity of my monologue, the truth hanging in the air. Or whatever version of it was closest to reality.

His eyes swirled like quicksilver. "I'm not here to debate the fucking depravity of the world," he growled finally. "No, I'm gettin' real answers. We can't have vamps runnin' around the city drainin' humans as well as turnin' them. So I need to know who's behind it."

I folded my arms. "What drugs have you been taking to think that even if I knew, which I don't, I'd go blabbing to a slayer? What made you think you'd even get out of here alive?"

He stepped forward again, so close his thumping heartbeat actually made my teeth chatter, the taste of his proximity rivaling even the bitterest of blood. "Because I've been in your presence three times," he rasped. "Been around enough vamps to know that's two times too many. You were gonna kill me, you'd be dead."

I raised a brow. "*I'd* be dead? You sure think a lot of yourself. Arrogance coupled with stupidity is fatal, you know."

"I'm still breathin', ain't I?" he asked, voice hoarse.

"Don't ask me how," I retorted.

He stared at me a beat longer before his gaze went to my mouth, his eyes hooded. I couldn't read minds but I was certain he was considering what I tasted like.

He shook himself, then stepped back once more. "Decided to take a calculated risk by coming here," he said after he'd cleared his voice and his expression.

"You must be shitty at math because your calculations are *way* off. In fact, you'd be a pile of blood in the corner if you'd turned up not three minutes before you did. My brother does not like humans, and slayers don't last a second around him. Unless they're a lot prettier than you. Then they wished for death before the end."

He quirked his brow. "Way I see it, the very fact that I missed him means that something is workin' here, making me think I've made the right choice," he observed. "Though I am sorry I wasn't here when he was, so I could have given him the taste of copper for doing that." He nodded to my chest, jaw taut.

I laughed. "And you'd do what? Protect my honor? Clue in, baby slayer. He's centuries older than you, so I'd inevitably be the one protecting *your* honor."

He narrowed his gaze. "Doesn't look to me like you came out on top."

I changed my gaze. "Honey, I *always* come out on top," I purred.

His eyes flickered before they hardened. "You're gonna tell me about vamps turnin' people," he commanded.

My mood changed and I soared forward, pressing one

hand against his neck and another at his wrist, exerting enough pressure so his enchanted knife clattered uselessly to the floor. I squeezed just hard enough to obstruct his airway. "You don't come into my home and command me," I whispered. "Especially when you have some warped idea that you are any match for me." I squeezed tighter. "Which you're not. You'd do well to remember that."

I let go and he went back on one foot, his breath frantic as his lungs sucked in the oxygen they'd been deprived of. He narrowed his eyes at the floor. I followed his gaze, picking up the knife before he could move. I gritted my teeth at the pain that radiated up my arm with the contact. I pressed my finger to the tip. "You got a witch with serious juice to enchant this," I said, regarding the knife. The pain was getting close to uncomfortable, especially coupled with my recently healed injuries.

I glanced up to see his intent gaze on me and the knife. He obviously knew what it was meant to do and how it was designed to repel vampires from even touching it. Breaking the skin and drawing blood meant hellish amounts of pain. Puncturing the heart or brain meant death.

Limbs didn't grow back when cut off with such blades, either.

"Nifty little weapon," I observed. "I'm sure you can't pick these up at Slayermart. I'm guessing it's valuable. A family heirloom, perhaps?"

He didn't say a word. Maybe he couldn't. Maybe I'd squeezed too hard and damaged his vocal cords.

My bad.

"Though it seems you're parting with it a lot, considering you let a little human get her sticky hands on it." I made a tutting noise with my tongue. "You really must keep better watch of your supernatural priceless weapons. I'd hate to see what you did with your keys." I paused, my eyes turning hard. "I'm also sure it would most likely damage your pride to have to limp back to the clubhouse with your own knife embedded in your midsection, so you should tread carefully with the commands. Better yet, *never* command me again. You don't have that right."

"How the fuck are you still holding that?" he demanded, aghast.

I grinned, tossing it to my other hand so the pain evened out to the bones that had only just healed. "Oh, I'm much stronger than the baby vampires I'm sure you tangle with. You're hunting big game now, and you're well out of your depth. I'd advise you go back to the shallow end before you drown," I warned.

He clenched his teeth. "I'm not goin' anywhere."

"Stubborn," I observed.

"Determined," he countered.

Commence stare off. It started all serious and death match-like, but somewhere in between it turned carnal. The air charged around us so much you couldn't cut it, even with his fancy knife.

Then we weren't staring. We were kissing.

Not romance or soft and sweet. It was a clash of our mouths and tongues. He tasted bitter enough that I yearned for more. He took control in the battle. I let him.

For a moment.

Until the boom echoed in my skull.

Heartbeat.

Human.

I detached immediately, scuttling to the corner of the room, my hand at my mouth.

He stood there, in the middle of the carnage of my living room, eyes wild and on me. I was afraid he might stalk to me once more, but he didn't. He just stayed there, staring.

"I think it's time you took that." I nodded to the knife on the ground. "You know, the weapon your kind uses to fight their formal enemies, AKA me. And you leave." My voice was strong, firm, detached.

He stayed there for a moment longer, frozen in place, the rapid rise and fall of his chest betraying his emotion.

Mine was locked down tight. That and I didn't need to breathe.

Then he moved, picking up his knife and turning towards the door.

The thump of his boots did little to drown out his deafening heartbeat. He paused at my front door.

"This isn't over," he murmured, low enough that he knew a human couldn't hear but that I could.

Then he was gone.

SEVEN

"YO, THE WITCH COUNCIL BURNED YOU AT THE STAKE yet, Marty?" I asked while I hustled down Fifth Avenue, my phone glued to my ear.

"Nope. And don't call me that," Sophie hissed.

I rolled my eyes underneath my glasses. Even though they covered half my face, the sun still smarted.

I *really* needed sleep.

It had taken my injuries like three hours to heal. And then another two to feel properly recharged. It felt like human speed.

I'd spent most of my time at the office, working. I didn't trust myself to even try to catch a nap. I had this weird itch at the back of my neck like someone was watching me. Like I was well overdue for another assassination attempt.

I scratched my neck absently. "Whatever. Look, I need some intel. You are not allowed to laugh at this question," I ordered.

"I make no such promises."

Sometimes it was irritating how alike we were. I sighed. "How impossible is it to turn a human?"

There was a pause and no laugh. Which wasn't good. Laughter meant the whole idea was ludicrous. I'd take the hit to my pride for long-term reassurance.

"Into a vampire?" she clarified.

I nodded.

She seemed to have sensed my nod; maybe that was part of her new witchy powers. I so needed a list of those so I could see which ones suited me to manipulate.

"Who told you?"

I bristled. "How do you know someone told me?"

"Because I know that, had you stumbled on some hybrid or vampire trying to turn someone, you wouldn't be speaking so calmly nor expecting me to laugh. I'm deducing it was a tip-off that had you calling me."

I whistled. "You're not just a pretty face and a handy ball of magic."

I felt her scowl through the phone.

"So it's possible? How can that be? I feel like, as a vampire, I should have known about this." It was long understood that 'turning' humans was in the realm of the fantastical. Some love-crazed vampires attempted it in desperation after they'd fallen for a human and wanted to share immortality, but you couldn't *make* someone immortal. You could kill them by trying, though. It was so bad that, at one point, the Sector had to outlaw it altogether.

Obviously someone was out there breaking the rules.

Normally I'd be the first to congratulate them on it, but this was leaving a bad taste in my mouth. And it wasn't to do with the wife beater I'd had for breakfast either.

"No. At least it wasn't until recently," Sophie answered. "I've heard murmurings about it, but passed it off as junk."

"Until?" I probed, hearing something in her voice.

She sighed. "Until a client, a *human* client, had me looking for their son. I found him this morning."

I heard a rattling of what sounded like a cage in the background and a string of curses.

"You have a human locked up?" I deduced.

"No. I have a *vampire* locked up."

"Please tell me it's a member of my family."

"Isla, follow the conversation. I know you're getting old and senile, but even you can put two and two together."

I scowled. "Watch your mouth, young one. Didn't anyone ever teach you to respect your elders?"

"Only everyone. And then this smartass, crazy vamp came into my life and told me to 'fuck 'em all.'"

"Shit," I muttered. "I did say that."

There was a pause as I got my thoughts together.

"The vampire I have locked up was, until three days ago, a human," Sophie said.

I stopped so abruptly a man in a suit with a toupee walked into me.

He scowled up from his phone. "Watch it, lady," he snarled.

"You watch it before I decide that toupee is crime enough for me to drain you dry," I returned, smiling with fang.

He blanched and scuttled away.

I turned my attention back to Sophie. "Now, you're saying you have a fucking turned vampire chained up in your office?" I didn't wait for her reply. "I'll be there in ten."

The clang from the rattling of the bars and the hiss from the human/vampire's mouth mingled together to create some sort of disturbing melody.

I started at the wild thing, which was bashing its head against the bars, red eyes on Sophie. More accurately, Sophie's neck.

She was standing beside me, eyes on the same *thing* as me. It wasn't human; the elongated fangs and blood-red corneas communicated that. It wasn't vampire, either, despite the fangs and obvious bloodlust. In all my years I hadn't seen a vampire like this, even the crazy ones. This was an abomination. I was tempted to call it an animal for the lack of any form of humanity in its eyes, but animals were natural. This was something entirely different. My body revolted from its presence, my blood curling in my veins.

"Is there any specific reason you have a solid steel, reinforced cage in the middle of your office?" I inquired casually, watching as the thing decided to stop smashing its head, trying to yank the bars instead.

Sophie turned her head. "You would not like to know how many times this has come in handy. Paid for itself within a week."

Her office was in an industrial area of Brooklyn, nestled between warehouses and most likely places where mafia hits took place.

It was cozy.

The room in which her cage resided was decorated in pure Sophie. In other words, rock 'n' roll.

The cavernous warehouse space was industrial, with exposed beams and brick walls. The glass-walled office in the corner juxtaposed the entire theme, but it worked. A treadmill and flat-screen were in one corner of the room, a huge bookshelf and Union Jack-embroidered chair in the other. Abstract prints littered the walls, my favorite being a sketch of a jewelry-clad wrist holding up a middle finger.

Weirdly, the cage actually suited the whole theme.

"It's spelled?" I guessed.

She nodded.

"How did you get him in here?" I asked, tilting my head. It was like every ounce of humanity or conscious thought had left him, his red eyes vacant and frantic.

"With love, good thoughts, and fairy dust."

I turned my head to her.

She grinned. "Okay, with a Taser and maybe a weensy bit of magic," she admitted.

I gave the cage one more glance. "Can we talk somewhere else?" I requested. "It's freaking me out."

Sophie nodded and we headed to her office. I sank down into her matte black sofa, loaded with pillows of contrasting prints. I gratefully took the scotch she offered me.

"Where'd you find him?"

She sat across from me. "Fricking sewers. Draining rats." She screwed up her nose. "I ruined my favorite combat boots."

I leaned over and squeezed her hand. "We'll just take a moment for all of the lost accessories lost in the line of duty," I whispered, thinking of my bloodstained Jimmy Choos.

After a beat, I thought on it. "It was lucky he was in the sewers. I'm surprised. He's almost crazy with bloodlust, and letting him loose on the populace would blow the supernatural cat out of the bag. No council, vampire or otherwise could hide that and the multitude of bodies it would create. Not in the age of camera phones."

This very fact had me suspicious. After five hundred years on Earth I'd learned there was no such thing as luck.

"Yeah, that's where this gets weird."

I rose my brow at her. "*That's* where this gets weird? The turned vampire with the scary eyes and the fact that it's the first of its kind is just another day at the office for Sophie Walker?"

I was only half sarcastic; this witch got up to some crazy shit.

Hence why we were friends.

She grinned. "Hear me out. He was contained, like someone had set him up in there, made sure he had just enough rats to keep him fed, though not enough to actually sustain him. But they did, even though all other vamps can't survive on animal blood. I don't know how long he'd been in there, or if that"—she nodded through the glass in the direction of the cage—"is a result of being locked in a sewer and starved, but I'm thinking not since he hasn't been missing long enough to go nutty. I'm guessing insanity is a lovely side effect of turning a human into a vampire."

I sucked in a breath. "Yeah, though it's been done now."

She nodded gravely, knowing this was something pivotal to our race, and the human race by proxy. If it got out that humans could be turned, it would not only screw with millennia of belief, but I'd wager it would result in a lot more of the red-eyed freaks running about.

Which was why it couldn't get out.

I already had a theory of why they had been created and by whom.

"You find them? Whoever was holding him?"

It was too much to ask, really, to grab not only the first human turned vampire before he could become infamous and the one who created him.

Sophie shook her head. "No. But I'm thinking they might find us since their pet is missing."

I stood, draining my glass. "Well that's a good thing, since we can kill them both and pretend this day never happened." I could only wish, but there was a little more than a one percent chance that this wasn't connected to the current assignment I was on. I really didn't need it to be. This was turning out to be complicated enough.

Sophie stood too, looking surprised. "You want to kill them both and bury this?"

"Well duh. Is that not how you want to play it? You want to try and spell him and turn him human again? Can you do that, even with your new juice?" I wandered over to her office bar, contemplating another drink.

"I've already tried," Sophie admitted. "Nada. Only thing I did was seriously wipe myself out. I just figured you'd want to… I don't know, tell someone. Then we'd have to fight about it."

"Tell who?" I asked. "All my friends in the vampire community who I'm oh-so-loyal to?" I paused, thinking of the sexy-as-sin king vampire I technically should tell about this. Then I focused on the sexier-than-holier slayer who'd turned up at my apartment, talked about this very situation, and then kissed me. My lips flamed at the memory and I shook them away. Not the time.

The time was never.

Neither the king nor the slayer was getting anywhere near this.

I turned. "You were testing out your funky new magic without me?" I pouted. "Please at least tell me you blew something, or someone, up."

She laughed. "No such luxury. Need to keep this on the down low, remember."

"Oh yes. How dull."

She quirked her brow. "We sure *dull* is the word we're going to use right now?"

I shrugged. "It's all relative. And this could be a touch more exciting. He's already in a cage. It's like shooting fish in a barrel."

A crash of metal and gunfire sounded below as shouts echoed up the stairwell.

Sophie rolled her eyes. "You just had to say it, didn't you?"

I grinned and placed my glass down. Sophie leisurely drained hers and pushed off the sofa at a lazy pace.

"How many?" she asked conversationally.

I focused on the voices getting closer and the thump of boots on the stairs. "I'd say four," I replied.

"Supernatural?"

I shook my head. "Human." The heartbeats were soft flutters against the grating sounds below, but they were unmistakable.

Sophie sighed. "It *is* like shooting fish in a barrel." She stepped forward slowly. "I've just refurbished my office. Can we try not to break anything?"

I nodded vaguely as I focused on the itch of my spine, freezing as an echoed thump drowned out the sound of them crashing through the last door.

"Slayers," I said to Sophie's back.

She turned, her mouth quirking. "*Your* slayer?"

"He is not *my* slayer," I snapped.

"Sure," she teased. "If he was going to pick you up for a date, he could have just buzzed up, or does he have a flare for the dramatic?"

I scowled and pushed past her. "Shut up and let's go mince slayer meat."

Her retort was lost as the men waltzed into the room. Their gait was easy, measured, though the four of them held their bodies and their weapons taut. My gaze traced over them in a millisecond. All stocky and muscled, of varying heights and races. Humans were much of a muchness, cookie cutter versions of each other. Apart from *him*.

Thorne was heading the little crew. His ice-blue gaze settled on me and his body jerked before he schooled his expression, tightening the grip on the gun hanging at his side.

Though he may have blanked his face, his eyes were locked on me. Electricity seemed to saturate the air as the memory of his lips on mine surfaced.

"Are you guys looking for the S&M club?" Sophie's voice sounded from beside me. "You got it wrong. That's next door." She grinned.

I wrenched myself away from Thorne's magnetic and stoic gaze to regard the slayer squad. They were all attractive, in the conventional, no-neck, 'I eat steroids for breakfast' kind of way. Most were wearing tight tees and fatigues. Apart from Thorne, who was wearing those faded jeans that did wonderful things for his ass.

Focus, Isla.

The slayer standing beside Thorne gave me pause; he wasn't wearing the look of steely hatred like the rest of him. His blue eyes were hard and focused, but a shadow of a smile touched the corner of his mouth.

He was young. Very young. He looked barely old enough to drink, and like he belonged in California pumping iron on Venice Beach. His sandy blond hair was artfully styled in spikes all over his head, his skin tanned just a little too much to be tinted by natural things like sunlight. His tank top dipped way low, exposing a muscled and hairless chest. He had sunglasses hooked haphazardly at the top.

I shook my head with a shadow of grin, then moved to

Thorne. "This stalking thing is getting downright creepy, dude. Plus, I think stalkers are meant to be subtle and invisible. Shooting up the place and bringing in your four gym-rat buddies kind of defeats the purpose," I said blandly.

Thorne's jaw tightened but he didn't say anything. His no-neck friend cut him off. That one took himself far too seriously.

"You know this bloodsucker, Thorne?" he hissed in disgust.

I tilted my head. "You haven't told your friends about me?" I put a hand on my chest. "Now that's just hurtful." I regarded the bald-headed slayer. "Thorne and I go *way* back."

The man narrowed his eyes. "Why does it still have a head?" he gritted out in fury.

"Brother—" Thorne began.

"I'll rectify this right now," No Neck growled. Then a knife hurtled through the air.

I snatched it by the handle inches away from my forehead.

I grinned at No Neck, then at Thorne. "I like him," I decided. Leading with throwing knives instead of niceties was one way to make an impression.

I tossed the knife in my hands, hiding the discomfort that came with the motion.

The slayers were obviously surprised at the fact that I could do that, their masks slipping slightly into disbelief. Apart from Thorne, whose expression was still carved from marble.

Sophie was grinning beside me.

"Don't be too hard on him, buddy," I addressed No Neck. "He has tried, and failed, many times." I didn't know why I was lying for Thorne. Lying came easy to me, but it was usually to benefit myself, not others. No, it was *always* to benefit myself, and never humans. Never slayers.

There was a first time for everything, obviously.

"I'm just faster, better, stronger and all around more

awesome than any slayer. It's just a fact of life. Or death, in my case." I tossed the knife back to him with dizzying speed. It was a kind of experiment to see if his reflexes were fast enough. He would either catch it, or the knife would embed itself in his skull. I was kind of hoping for the latter.

He fumbled with it, but stopped it from ending his life. Just.

"You ought to be more careful with those fancy blades," I instructed. "I was under the impression they were kind of rare and important in the whole slaying vampires part of your job description, and you seem to lose them more than I lose my marbles." I winked. "Which is often. You know those riots in London? All me."

Sophie let out a choked laugh as the muscled child gave in to a small grin. The rest of them didn't crack a smile.

Thorne stepped forward, eyes glittering. "Enough," he growled.

I pretended the pure rage and authority in his tone didn't get me the teensiest bit hot.

"You're right. We've got things to do, and I'm sure you've got vampires to slay. Now that we've established I'm too much for you, it's time to run along and let the adults get back to their jobs," I said.

The rattling of the cage behind me reminded me of the pressing job.

All eyes went to it. The kid's peepers widened, as if it was the first time he'd noticed the huge metal cage in the center of the room. Though, I was pretty noticeable, so I understood while I stole the show.

"Don't mind him," Sophie cut in. "He's just cranky if he doesn't get his morning coffee."

Thorne stepped forward again, as did his posse, who

tightened the grips on their guns.

Sophie and I stayed relaxed, but I noticed the slight glow to her right hand. She was ready to zap these guys five ways to Sunday before they could even say boo.

Thorne wasn't focused on that, his steely gaze on me.

"You fuckin' lied," he growled.

"And?" I asked, not getting why that was a big deal. "Wait, what did I lie about? Five hundred years is a long time. I can't keep track of them all."

He stepped forward once more, closer to me than was comfortable, Sophie's hand glowed brighter and the men behind him noticed, raising their guns. Thorne's eyes were still on me, as if nothing else in the room was important.

He pointed his chin behind me. "About him."

I turned my head; the thing had one filthy arm outstretched as if it was reaching for Thorne. It could obviously smell the blood, too far gone to realize this particular meal would be his last if he attached himself to the delectable sinewy flesh of Thorne's neck. Or would it? I wondered idly whether these things would die from drinking slayer blood. If I had time, I'd toss No Neck in the cage to conduct an experiment.

"You said you didn't know about turned vampires. You fuckin' refused to believe they even existed." His breath and the weight of his words floated through the air. I could taste his fury—bitter and delicious. "You're one fuckin' fine actress," he accused.

I screwed up my nose before regarding Thorne once more. "Thanks, but the Academy has never recognized me. A huge oversight on their part." I sighed dramatically when it became apparent that he didn't find me amusing. It was looking like his friends might start shooting if I didn't cut to the chase. "I didn't know about that"—I nodded to the cage—"until about thirty minutes ago, and you're not exactly first on my speed dial. In fact, I don't even have your number. I doubt looking up 'grumpy and broody vampire slayer' in the white pages would work." I paused. "Or maybe it will."

"You're expectin' me to believe that?" he hissed.

I sighed again. "Quite frankly, I couldn't give a flying fuck about what you do and don't believe. If it keeps you warm at night to think that a big jolly man with a weight problem comes down your chimney and watches you sleep, have at it. But I've got shit to do, so take this show somewhere else. I bet you guys could make a killing at a bachelorette party." I waggled my eyebrows at the kid. "Just a suggestion."

"We're not leavin' without him," he declared tightly.

I bristled. "Sorry, we've got dibs. We found him first. Finders keepers, losers weepers. Better luck next time."

His eyes alighted with fire. "He's not a fuckin' object," he hissed. "That's a human being."

I stepped back so the rest of his posse could get a good look. "You think *that's* a human being? Take a good look, boys." I let their gazes roll over the red-eyed, long-fanged thing that had stains of blood around its mouth and a trail of red trickling from its forehead. The white button-down shirt that he had worn in life was torn and stained with I didn't want to know what. Nothing about it betrayed any sense of conscious thought.

"That is not a human," I declared. "That's not even a vampire. That's an animal that is dangerous to that very race you boys get all hyped up to protect. Therefore, it needs to be put down."

Thorne gripped his gun. "You're not fuckin' killin' him. That's a *person*. We're taking him."

I straightened as the men behind him stepped forward,

prepared for a fight.

I raised my brow. "You and what army?"

No Neck scoffed. "One vamp and a little witch? You don't stand a fuckin' chance."

I smiled. "Oh, it's so nice to see misogynistic cockiness has endured through little movements like feminism. Makes things so much more interesting."

I gave Sophie a look.

She grinned. "You sure you don't want to run along and train your legs, suck down a protein shake? Last chance," she offered.

No Neck glowered at her, stepping forward.

Sophie's hands stayed still at her side, but one finger jerked.

No Neck froze midstep, his combat boot hovering in the air. The only thing that moved was his eyes, wide in their sockets as they darted around in panic.

Sophie kept grinning as the men around him were slow to catch on, looking between him and Sophie in confusion.

Another finger jerk had his combat pants around his ankles. I choked out a laugh as his tight white briefs were revealed.

She tilted her head. "Tighty-whities. What a surprise," she declared sarcastically. Then her gaze moved down to his small calves. "You totally should have taken me up on my offer," she added. "You really shouldn't skip leg day."

"Parlor tricks won't save you," the man beside him hissed, stepping forward with his gun raised.

Sophie flicked her hand again and all of their guns flew in various decorations, hurtling through the air to float in front of her, pointed at their previous owners.

"You're totally right," Sophie said sweetly. "Parlor tricks won't save you. Arrogance and stupidity certainly won't."

The air was thick with tension as angry eyes settled on

Sophie. They weren't dumb enough to move, though.

Thorne's gaze was blank as he looked to Sophie, then to me, hand on his own gun that hadn't managed to fly away. I wondered if that was deliberate of Sophie. He was measuring the situation calmly. He wasn't stupid.

"See what I was telling you about?" I asked him. "If only you all weren't so set on becoming the supernatural public enemy number one. Not only would you go to all the good parties, but you'd probably have a longer life span." I gave him a look. "As it is, you're intent on crashing parties you weren't invited to, making demands that you don't have the power to enforce, and then you get bested by two females."

He stared at me, then focused on Sophie. "You don't want to kill them. They're humans."

She glanced at him. "Humans who smashed up an office I just got remodeled. I'd maim them for that alone." Her grin intensified. "Oh my goddess. You're the slayer," she exclaimed, her eyes lighting up.

I glared at her. "Not now, Sophie."

She laughed. "I totally get it. He's hot," she said appreciatively.

Thorne stiffened.

Just before things could get uglier, an explosion rocked the building and sent everyone flying. It wouldn't have done so to me because of my superior supernatural balance and because I was awesome, but it wasn't a naturally occurring explosion. As it was, I hurtled the farthest, smack-dab in the center of the steel cage.

My spine crunched as the impact crushed bones and my head whipped back, jarring my consciousness.

I crumbled to the floor in a moderate amount of pain, but still conscious, which was more than I could say for my human brethren. My worried gaze found Sophie's prone form six feet away from me, only relaxing when her dull heartbeat reassured me that she wasn't dead.

The thump echoing in the back of my mind remained, but still I found myself glued to Thorne for reassurance that he was still alive. His large body lay half upright against the wall of Sophie's office. He'd cracked the glass on impact.

Sophie was going to be so pissed about that.

And the explosion in general, which had caught her unaware.

And me, which I was pissed to admit. I'd been too busy focusing on the stupid human whose heartbeat obviously drowned out coherent thought.

I pushed myself up, ignoring the shooting pains down my spine as I did so. My gaze was focused on the four vampires and one witch strutting through the door.

On one in particular.

"Earnshaw, how nice of you to drop by," I said sweetly. I didn't betray an ounce of surprise but I was. He was from a middle-class Vein Line, not important enough to be anyone at all. Or so I'd thought. My earlier worries came to fruition with his presence. "Now this is a party. Not the guest list I would have chosen, but still."

The slayers scattered around the room had begun to stir, most jumping up and commencing battle stances.

Including Thorne.

Sophie was still unconscious and that worried me, especially with the witch's dark gaze on her. I didn't doubt she was working something to keep Sophie down.

I swallowed the worry for my friend, hoping she could take care of herself, and focused on Earnshaw.

He was certainly focused on me, his black eyes narrowed in disgust. "I told you I'd be giving you what was coming to you, race whore," he spat.

I tilted my head. "Hello to you, too. You're looking well. Snacking on more children does wonders for that complexion. I can't say it will do well for that black, ugly shriveled-up thing that is lucky enough to be your soul," I responded.

The cogs were working in my mind. He was a prime candidate for the new revolution. Someone cruel, stupid of the belief that he was Satan's gift to vampire kind despite his poor lineage and less-than-impressive looks.

"You're so self-righteous, thinking saving one human child is going to do anything but bring about your final death that much faster," he hissed.

I watched Thorne's body jerk as he caught on to the meaning behind Earnshaw's words. His gaze blackened at the vampire's Armani-clad back.

Earnshaw wasn't focused on the slayer, though. Luckily. No way Thorne would be able to take him on in his current state, though I knew he'd try to exact revenge on the vampire who attempted to murder his sister. Humans were big on such things.

"You think *you're* the one who's going to bring about my final death?" I laughed. "I think you've forgotten that the last time we met I ruined a pair of shoes. By embedding them into your face and demonstrating just how easy it is for me to gift you *your* final death." I looked to the three other vampires, standing deathly still, as was their nature, their predator eyes on each slayer they'd decided to stand in front of. I didn't recognize any of them. Soldiers, I guessed, most likely from second-class Vein Lines. Disposable. The aforementioned slayers were crouched, ready to attack, despite only a couple of them having weapons.

Kind of my bad. I glanced at them scattered around Sophie's

prone body, which the witch was circling while muttering.

Ignoring Earnshaw, I darted to the side, intending to break the witch's neck. We had enough to deal with without her muttering curses to make everything that much more complicated. Plus, she was responsible for that little explosion and it pissed me right off. Which was why she had to die.

My movements would have been little more than a blur to human eyes. Earnshaw was too slow and dumb to stop me, and I doubted he would have expected it.

But just as I got to the witch, I hit an invisible wall and a clawed hand squeezed my heart.

She turned, revealing a pale and beautiful face. Red lips stained with the color of blood, a curtain of black silk tumbling down her shoulders.

She smiled, the beauty flickering for just a moment, long enough for me to glimpse her true face. The wrinkled, paper-thin skin, dotted with age spots and glassy eyes, a mouth full of rotted death.

It was gone again as she stepped towards me, her long black gown trailing on the floor.

I scrambled against the invisible hands, the depth of her power pulsing through me. She'd masked it until that point. Black magic had a bitter quality to it, rotten and dirty. The taste of death. Death was the only thing that made such magic possible. The death of countless people, and the a deal for the witch's soul as she surrendered herself into the abyss of the dark arts.

Death wrapped me as the hand squeezed tighter, a choking sound erupting from my mouth as I fought against the magic.

She was old. Quite possibly older than me. Which was not a good sign.

Old witches, especially ones who practiced dark magic, could theoretically kill a vampire.

The ice in my blood and the small rupturing of the cells in my body, little deaths, all of them were communication this.

The echo of Earnshaw's heels sounded through the death-cloaked room as he made his way over to me.

"Your overconfidence always was frightfully unattractive, even when we were children," he stated, his breath hot on my face.

Earnshaw had gone to Mortimeus, the ancient school that still operated in the plains of Siberia. The one place any vampire child who had a prestigious Vein Line went. Earnshaw had never been popular because his blood wasn't nearly as pure as most of the rest of the class.

That and he was a total dick.

"Your face was always frightfully unattractive," I hissed.

I struggled inwardly as his long-fingered hand trailed up the side of my hips, brushing my breasts. "No matter how desirable the outside of you is, you will always be repulsive to the *true* vampires. Your death will make me a hero." He glanced at the cage. "Among other things."

Until then, I'd been preoccupied with the soul-wrenching pain of the dark magic pulsing through me that I hadn't noticed the silence. The complete silence.

The gaze of everyone in the room, including Thorne, whose heavy stare had been on me, went to the cage.

The animal inside it was no longer wild. It was standing still, statuesque, its face blank and its red eyes focused on Earnshaw.

I'd thought the wild and carnal thrashing had been disturbing, but this, this was worse.

Especially because I knew what it meant.

"You're its sire." The cold chill of realization settled over me with what that meant.

Earnshaw clapped his hands, the sound bouncing off the concrete walls in a taunt.

"Yes, Isla. I am the first vampire in existence to turn a human."

I sneered at the prideful look on his face. "You're not going to get any medals, psycho," I hissed through gritted teeth. "That is not a vampire. Or a human. You've succeeded in polluting our race more than I ever could. That's an abomination."

He stepped forward, his eyes flickering with fury. "No, this is saving our race," he murmured. "I'm creating soldiers that will answer to one master and will destroy those who oppose us with unyielding ferocity."

I narrowed my gaze at him. "You're never going to do anything of the sort. Insane vampires don't ever make the history books. But they do die. A lot. Here's hoping I'm the one to make that happen."

Earnshaw was no master. He was a guinea pig. Whoever was running the show was smart enough to use someone disposable and deluded enough to try such a thing.

He smiled at me, his fangs elongated just slightly. "How will you kill me when you'll already be dead?"

His eyes moved to the witch, and there was a loud clang as the cage unlocked. I watched as the creature moved, slithered almost, towards Earnshaw and me.

The smell of death and rancid blood intensified as it came to a stop, vacant gaze on Earnshaw.

"Master," it croaked, voice raw and distorted, as if it couldn't quite taste the word properly.

Earnshaw stroked the matted and dirty hair that had once been blond, then turned to me. "The cause will win. The world will burn. And vampires who are traitors to our race will get punished. We will take our rightful place as rulers."

I struggled against the pain to grin. "That's a nifty little speech. Did you write it yourself? I bet they made you practice it at headquarters before they let you out."

He backhanded me with a speed I easily could have dodged had I not been paralyzed by the witch's magic. As it was, the impact sent my body hurtling to the ground.

The pain was barely noticeable against everything else in my system, but the gesture in itself was important. Earnshaw was trying to show his strength. Though strength was not what such a gesture connoted; it was weakness. As was taking a helpless human and turning them into… that.

"Hitting me when you've got your pet witch rendering me immobile is rather similar to preying on helpless human children. Rather pathetic," I hissed. I was trying to bait him to getting the witch to release me. Then I could kill the prick, and then maybe he'd stop talking.

He stood above me, grinning, his gaze traveling the room to the stoic slayers. Thorne was watching us, breathing heavily through gritted teeth, the veins in his neck pulsing. His fury mingled with the death in the air.

"Maybe we won't kill you… yet," Earnshaw mused. "I think I need to notify the movement of just how depraved your relationship with humans has become. In the company of slayers," he spat. "Even for you, that's despicable. I enjoy being a part of whatever punishment the master conjures up for such a betrayal."

He glanced to his witch, giving her a brisk nod before turning on his heel.

I struggled to get up, the weight of magic still a lead force of pain, rendering me little more than paralyzed.

"Kill them all," Earnshaw ordered flatly to the vampires facing off with the slayers.

He gave me one last grin. "I'll be seeing you soon," he promised.

Then he, his pet and the witch were gone.

I got Earnshaw's rapid exit, but the witch's was puzzling. They couldn't disappear into puffs of smoke, nor did they have the increased speed that vampires had.

Troubling.

But at least I wasn't paralyzed with excruciating pain and had a grip on my motor functions.

The thud of flesh against flesh, grunts and the smell of fresh blood had me jumping upright.

The slayers were facing off with the remaining vampires. Even without their weapons they weren't doing too bad. No Neck with the knife was doing okay, and Thorne was holding his own, but the rest were most likely going to die.

If I didn't do something.

I bit my lip and glanced to Sophie. She was still motionless but breathing.

I looked back to the fight.

Was I really going to save slayers? I mean, I'd made some questionable decisions and never really stuck with mainstream vampirism, but this was going off the deep end.

Earnshaw was already running off to his master, if I didn't catch him first. I could leave them to their fate and trail Earnshaw to find out who the 'master' was, or at least kill him before my dirty little secret got out. It would be the smart thing to do.

The kid took a savage blow to the chest and hurtled past me before crumpling to the floor.

"Fuck," I cursed, then extended my arm to stop the vampire intent on finishing the kid off.

My arm jarred slightly at the impact, which sent him back

a foot.

The vampire's eyes flared in disgust.

"Race traitor," he hissed.

I rolled my eyes. "Come up with some new insults, please." I stepped forward and gripped his neck, then commenced the icky job of detaching his head.

Once he was lying in two pieces below me, I commenced in further damning myself in the eyes of everything that was unholy.

The rest of the vampires were young. Stupid. Weak. Even still recovering from the witch's magic, I was able to beat them. Sure, they got in a few lucky hits and messed up my hair, but it was child's play.

After I'd snapped the last neck, the deafening sounds of battle diminished in a surge, as if a vacuum had come to suck all sound from the room.

The bloodied slayers were scattered around the room, breathing heavily. No Neck was holding his arm against his chest, which suggested it was broken. The bone sticking out from the skin was a dead giveaway too. Kudos to him, though; he had yet to make a sound, even though his face curled slightly in a grimace of pain.

The other two were standing slightly dazed, looking to the bodies on the floor in confusion.

Idiots.

The air changed, the thump that had been the background to this entire event becoming deafening.

Thorne was in front of me, looking slightly winded but otherwise unharmed. And totally hot.

I glanced down at the way his tee clung to his abs before I reminded myself that it wasn't the best time to be wondering what they'd taste like. The fog of death was heavy over the room, pulsing with its weight.

On the other hand, maybe this was precisely the time. My stomach tingled with the thought.

"Are you okay?" he asked, his gaze flickering over me in concern.

I scowled at him. "I'm immortal. Is my head still attached to my body?" I didn't wait for an answer to my rhetorical question. "Then I'm okay." My eyes darted to the corner of the room. "Though I can't say the same for your little friend. He seems to be bleeding out," I added in a bored tone, dusting off my jacket. It was fricking custom. If it stained I was raining hell down on those assholes.

He moved quickly, and I tried my best not to drool at the fluid movement of his bulging muscles. He was all sweaty and covered in blood from the fight. I licked my lips.

"For fuck's sake, Isla," he shouted, pressing his hand into his annoying friend's shoulder. "A little help?"

I rolled my eyes and moved over to the corner of the room, stepping over a groaning body as I did so. I didn't behead all the vampires, just broke their necks; it usually rendered them immobile for a decent amount of time, but that one was healing too quickly. He would still be paralyzed for at least another twenty minutes. My heel may have slid into his palm, and he emitted another grunt of agony. "That's for my jacket," I informed him.

Thorne glared at me, all concern gone from his features. Only irritation and hatred remained. Good. I could deal with that. Concern and warmth were troubling and a trifle unsettling; we were immortal enemies, after all.

"By all means, move at a leisurely fucking pace," he growled. "It's not like his life hangs in the balance."

I rolled my eyes again, bending down gingerly to escape

the worst of the blood. It wasn't like I was tempted to take a bite or anything; it would take some pretty extreme starvation to forget slayer blood equaled painful and slow death. No, I just didn't want my jacket ruined anymore.

"Why must things like this happen on days I wear white?" I asked no one in particular.

Both he and his pale friend glared at me. He looked like he might try to stake me right there.

"All right, all right, don't get your panties in a bunch, boys. You humans are always so serious about mortal wounds." I slapped Thorne's hand away, inspecting the kid. He'd been unlucky enough to be stabbed with his own blade by the looks of it. Either that or the vampires had carried their own weapons. Vampires didn't need weapons. That gave credence to a slightly disturbing theory that they had expected slayers to be there. Since we couldn't bite slayers without the nasty side effect of certain death, some vampires decided to go all human with guns and knives. Ones who were young or weak and didn't know how to fight if fangs weren't involved.

I was not one of them.

"It hit an artery," I murmured, watching the blood flow and the kid's tan dissipate at an alarming rate.

"Fuck," Thorne hissed. It was one word, uttered quietly, but it had enough weight as if he'd yelled.

The kid's eyes darted around the room, unseeing before they settled on Thorne. "Am I going to die?" he asked, his voice thick and wet.

"Most likely," I told him honestly.

Thorne clutched his chin. "No, you are not going to die," he promised. His voice was so firm, so full of authority that I might have believed it, had the kid not been losing enough blood to contradict him. I'd seen enough bleed-outs in my time. Had been the cause of most of them. He had about two minutes left, tops.

The kid's eyes went vacant again.

Thorne's gaze narrowed at me. "Can't you do something?" he hissed.

I shrugged. "I'm usually the one causing these types of wounds. My expertise doesn't translate to healing them. And before you ask, my blood doesn't work either. That shit's only real in Hollywood."

He scowled at me.

"I can heal him," a voice croaked from behind me.

I glanced up at a shaky-looking Sophie. She was almost as pale as the kid. "Hi, sleeping beauty," I greeted, then frowned at her. "If you don't mind me saying, you're a lovely shade of gray. I don't like your chances of saving this one. Death's in the job description anyway." I put my hands up in a 'you win some, you lose some' gesture.

Thorne's glare was heavy on the back of my neck but I ignored it.

She poked her tongue out at me, a signal that she wasn't completely tapped out, and pushed me out of the way.

Thorne bristled as she approached. The men behind him, who had gathered around their dying comrade, fastened their grips on their newly retrieved guns.

I gave both them and Thorne a look. "What do you think she's going to do, make him even more mortally wounded?" I asked sarcastically.

They scowled at me.

Sophie gave Thorne an even stare. "I'll save your friend. Despite what you think of me, I value human life. Even slayers. Even slayers who waltz into my office and get all confrontational. I'm a peach like that. I've got the power to save him. Are you going to let him die because of your pride or arrogance?"

Credit to him, Thorne didn't even need a millisecond to think, immediately leaning back to let Sophie in as he lifted his hands to the men behind him.

They didn't look happy, but he must have been in charge, as they obeyed.

Sophie started to murmur under her breath and the taste of her magic was immediate. The rancid, bitter taste of death that lingered in the air was replaced with the light and sweet flavor of life magic. Not exactly white magic, which would suggest that Sophie was pure and good, but the dusky gray kind that was more complex.

The hardness left the humans' bodies. I doubted they could boast the same awareness of the magic that we could, but it didn't mean it didn't affect them. Even oblivious mortals would notice the difference, the thickness to the air. They would recognize it but it would settle into their brains, turning thoughts soft at the edges.

Well, this stuff anyway.

Minerva's shit that had clutched me before would almost certainly have made them go insane, even indirect contact with it. They'd been lucky that the initial blast had separated me enough from them that they weren't polluted by the magic.

I wasn't as lucky obviously. Even with the sweetness of Sophie's life magic, my thoughts were sharp and uncomfortable at the edges.

I was dancing with madness myself, but luckily I was already on the wrong side of sane, so I could resist it. Or at least accommodate it. That was the thing; completely sane people were usually the weakest, the ones who went crazy the easiest. Because they lived life on a sword's edge, sanity wasn't something they could grip with both hands. It was better to be a little crazy so when the world threw you a lotta crazy, you knew how to deal with it.

Fire with fire and all that.

In the blink of a human eye, the kid regained his unnatural tan and coherency came back to his sparkly blue eyes. The blood staining his skin and ruined tank remained, but its source had dried up.

He sat up abruptly, Thorn put a hand to his chest. "Easy, Chace," he murmured.

Of course his name was Chace.

The kid blinked. "Am I alive?" he asked.

I rolled my eyes. "Yes. I can't say the same for your sunglasses," I cut in, nodding to the crumpled mess beside him. "You can't have everything, though. Unless you're me."

Sophie leaned back, frightfully more pale. She dusted off her hands before pushing up. "Okay, you can leave now. And let's never do this again. There's a reason why no one likes slayers. They ruin perfectly good offices and make it so my latest case gets stolen from me." She looked pointedly at the empty cage, then stumbled slightly.

I moved to put my hand on her elbow. "And you suck the power out of my favorite witch," I added, frowning. "Fun ones are really hard to come by." I winked at her, though an undercurrent of worry tainted my voice.

She gave me a weak smile.

Thorne helped the kid up. He regarded Sophie, his eyes softening.

Was I a bad person for being jealous of pretty much my only friend for being on the receiving end of that look? Yes, yes I was.

"Thank you," he said quietly, his voice smooth and rough at the same time.

When his eyes moved to me they hardened instantly. And damn if that didn't smart a little. "That vampire. The one who sired that…."

"Thing? Atrocity? Abomination?" I finished for him as he struggled to find the word.

He glowered at me. "That *human being*," he said through gritted teeth. "You know where to find him?"

"No," I said sweetly. "I don't associate with those types of vampires. You know, the ones who promise to kill me. Call me crazy. You wouldn't be the first. Or three hundredth."

Of course I knew where to find Earnshaw. More accurately, I knew where to find someone who knew where to find him. No way in hell I was telling the slayer that, though. He was already far too involved in this. And he shouldn't be involved for a multitude of reasons, number one being it put him in my orbit and subjected me to the weird connection we seemed to have. The more I saw him, the less I was able to think about things that didn't involve him.

Or his abs.

Or his large hands.

Or his undoubtedly large—

"We're not killing her?" No Neck hissed, interrupting my train of thought. He gripped his knife with his uninjured hand.

I put my hands on my hips. "Well, that's just rude. Talking of killing me right after I saved your worthless lives."

Thorne opened his mouth to say something but the kid beat him to it. His blue gaze had darted between me and Sophie since he left death's door.

"We're not killing them." His voice was deeper and much more adult than he looked.

All heads turned to him.

"She saved us." He nodded to Sophie. "And the witch saved

me."

No Neck stepped forward an inch, and Thorne positioned his body slightly so he was between us.

The gesture was obviously instinctual, and puzzling. Puzzling because it almost seemed it was to protect me.

But that was insane. I didn't need protecting.

His friend did.

"Do you not have any idea what she is?" He didn't wait for a response. "A *vampire*." He enunciated the word carefully and with distaste.

"Good spotting." I gave him a slow clap.

"It would sell its own mother for a pint of blood," he hissed, as if I hadn't spoken.

I scowled at him. "Of course I wouldn't sell my own mother," I retorted with mirroring distaste. "I'd give her to you for free," I added sincerely. "In fact, I'd pay you to go and slay her."

Sophie let out a choked laugh. Chace's eyes twinkled as if he hadn't almost kicked the bucket moments before. Thorne's arms were crossed firmly over his chest, his face carefully blank. But his aura lightened slightly, with amusement if I weren't mistaken.

No Neck was not amused. "She's everything we're trained to kill."

I rolled my eyes. "Lucky they've got you here to remind them of their entire purpose in life."

Chace shook his blond head at No Neck. "We're trained to kill evil," he argued. "From where I stand, she's not evil." His voice was firm. Resolute.

I laughed. "Child, there is no such thing as evil. Or good. That's what you self-righteous slayers need to learn. Not that you will. Now, you were just leaving?"

I glared at Thorne, who looked like he was going to push

the issue of the turned vampire.

We commenced in a stare off and so help me, I would snap No Neck's vertebrae if they gave me any more trouble. I was bone tired, had just almost been killed by a witch and ruined my favorite jacket. I was not in the mood.

"We're findin' that human," he promised before turning his back.

"Good luck with that. If you do, I won't be there to save your bacon and you'll all undoubtedly die." I paused while No Neck sneered at me. "I'll text you with any location I get, just to speed the process along."

That got no answer except the echoed bang of the steel slamming shut.

"That all turned to shit very quickly," Sophie declared, eyes scanning the pieces of vampire littered around her office.

I couldn't shake the chill in my bones from the dark magic; it seemed to have punctured them and settled into my marrow. That and the fact that I was feeling sick over what I'd done. Killed vampires in the protection of slayers.

That was far even for me.

The target on my head would increase a lot when that went public.

Which meant I needed to find Earnshaw stat.

Which meant laevisomnus needed to be pushed back another day. Not good. Especially if I was going to be doing any fighting, as the longer I went without it, the slower I'd heal.

Another motivation not to get physical. That and my wardrobe did not need to be suffering so unnecessarily.

I glanced to Sophie. "You okay, witchy? Minerva mistress of the dark reserved most of her ickiness for me, but she was muttering some ominous-sounding Latin over your sleeping form." I gave her a weary once-over. "You're not going to go dark side or grow horns, are you?"

She rolled her eyes at me. "Eat me."

I gave her a look. "Careful there, Hermione. It's been a while since I snacked and the fight took it out of me. Though I'm not one for wounded meat. Tell me you're not about to drop dead or anything so I can go along with my undead existence."

She grinned. "I'm fine. Takes more than four vampires, four slayers and a bitchy black witch to get me down."

"Glad to hear it. Though technically I'm the one who took out the four vampires, and kept the witch busy. You pretty much napped the whole time," I teased.

She poked out her tongue at me.

My mind wrapped around the witch, thoughts unpleasant. The mere presence of her in my mind was wrong, unnatural. "I'm thinking that's not the last we've heard of her. And I'm thinking she'll be hanging around Earnshaw, who I have to now go and kill because I can't have him blabbing about me killing vamps to save slayers. It'll massacre my image."

"Your image?" she repeated with a heavy dose of sarcasm.

I scowled and nodded. "*Anyway.* Any tips or spelled grenades I can throw at her to stop round two of the mind-rape thing? I wasn't a fan of it the first time around."

The chill that had settled over my bones and the taste of the grave on my tongue was yet to recede. I did not like that. At all. But I had to push through.

Sophie frowned at me, her emerald eyes turning hawk-like and glowing slightly as she regarded me. "What exactly did she do?" she asked slowly.

"Got an invisible hot poker, jammed it in my heart, then froze my blood and played Hacky Sack with my psyche," I told her cheerfully.

I needed to find myself a snack, stat. Warm blood would do

wonders for a chill. My journey to Succor would work twofold: get me a snack and to retrieve my information on Earnshaw. I didn't usually like the blood whores employed by such establishments, but I wasn't in the position to be choosy.

My frazzled mind bright up an image of Thorne, unbidden. More precisely Thorne's pulsing neck. White-hot desire burned through my body at the prospect of tasting him. Some very foreign part of me was certain his blood would chase away the chill that had drilled into my bone marrow.

Luckily a less foreign part of me still remembered how toxic his blood was and that such a meal would welcome the grave, not fight it off.

Sophie stepped closer, still regarding me while I made dinner plans. "I can taste it, her magic. It'll stick to the air here, imprinted on it for weeks. She's powerful," she deduced, her face pinched up. "And what she worked on you isn't anything I've seen before."

A gentle warmth tickled at the edge of my brain.

I stepped back, holding my hands up. "Whoa! If you're going to probe me with magic, at least take me to dinner first."

Even though I trusted Sophie—well, as much as I trusted anyone—I didn't want any more magic up in the bag of feral cats that was currently my consciousness. I'd had them tamed for close to five hundred years and this witch had set them wild once more.

I'd rip out her spleen for that alone. It seemed that the corner of my mind that held whatever was left of my heart and cradled those forbidden warm memories had been unlocked. The gritty tang of loss permeated the landscape of my mind.

I could smell his blood. His death. The faltering of his heartbeat and then the deafening silence that followed.

"Isla." Sophie snapped her fingers in front of me.

I jerked, only half of me coming back into the moment, the other half still held in the clutches of the past.

"I'm fine," I spat defensively.

She frowned at me. "I don't think you are. There's something about that spell.... It was blood magic. Death magic. I'm not sure I can understand what she did." Her gaze went glassy as she looked inward, not seeing the room anymore. I could see the ripples in the air as she manipulated it to reveal the threads of magic that wove through the world, unnoticed to most. It was creepy, and I didn't like the flicker of shadowy blackness hovering around my body like a bad smell.

I snapped my fingers in front of her face. The shadow disappeared but its chill remained.

"Well you don't have to understand. You need to get rid of this." I swept my hands around the bodies.

She quirked a brow at me. "I'm guessing you're not volunteering for cleanup?"

I looked at her in shock. "I don't clean up messes, just make them. Plus, I've got a vampire, a witch and a human-turned-vampire thing to kill. And a war to end." I glanced back around. "Can't you just, like, snap your fingers and magic them away to limbo?"

She laughed, a musical, pleasing sound. Such a sound should have been coming from an English lady in the 1900s who blushed around men and was as pure as the day was long, not a slutty witch with tattoos who was currently wearing a ripped Def Leppard tee as a dress.

"It doesn't really work that way."

I waved my hand as she opened her mouth to no doubt talk about physics and Mother Nature and the pulsating force underlying everything in the universe. "Save the magic lesson. I've got pressing matters. I'll call you if I haven't been killed or turned insane."

She stepped forward as I began to leave, grapping my arm.

The touch of her magic made me flinch slightly, and she frowned at the movement before moving her eyes to mine. "I'm coming."

"Oh no, you're not," I said firmly. "You just got knocked out and I'm thinking you're not at full witch. I'm not going to be responsible for your death. I've got enough blood on my hands." I glanced down. "And my jacket. Plus, where would I find my next drinking buddy who's fun and not afraid to use her magic for bad? You're staying here." My mind tickled with a cool sense of unease. "I have a very bad feeling that this is all far from over, so we'll keep you on the bench for now. Let's play the long game."

She scowled at me, crossing her arms. "You're not going alone. You're no match for that witch. I am. There's only one bloodsucker who I can also count as one of my only friends who will rip someone's throat out if I ask them. You won't be able to do that after you're drooling from a spell that sucked your brain out of your ears."

I paled. Or I expect I would have had I already not been that way. "They can do that?"

She gave me a look.

I shelved that one for later, to use on one or both of my brothers.

I straightened my spine. "I've been around the block. I know how to handle myself. And I know when someone is dead on their feet, pardon the expression." I gave her gray face a pointed look. "You're in no state. Stay here, call my—" I caught myself before I said the word 'friend.' "Call Scott and get him to take care of this." I gestured around. "He's got this villain worship thing for me, so he'll do it no questions asked.

Fair warning, he gets irritating after five seconds of being in his presence, so try not to hex him," I instructed. "And then have a Gatorade or get laid, recharge, and we'll make a new plan to stop crazy vampires who seem intent on turning humans into vampire warrior slaves."

I winked at her and walked out the door.

Her scowl burned into my back but she didn't follow me.

Because she knew I was right.

I always was.

And I was feeling that the night was going to get much darker before we saw a red dawn.

EIGHT

"That was amazing," a throaty voice purred as soon as I released him.

I rolled my eyes, wiping my mouth demurely before standing from one of the plush sofas they had in the back of Succor. The lighting was low and décor was 'bloodsucker chic'—in other words, a lot of red and velvet and eighteenth-century tapestries.

Yuck.

"Wait, don't go. You can keep going," the voice continued, the edge of desperation mildly sickening.

I glanced over my shoulder at the man sprawled on the sofa. His muscled arms were extended toward me, a junkie looking for a fix. Blood trickled in a thin line down his sculpted torso. Our fangs had an anticlotting agent in them should we consider to use it, but he'd requested not to.

Despite his outward appearance, his classically good-looking face, sandy blond hair and aesthetically pleasing physique, he was an addict. Twin incision marks scattered around his neck in various stages of healing, some snaking up his sinewy forearm, glowing in the low light.

I scowled at him. "Keep going?" I repeated. "I've had my fill and you're seriously anemic already. Get yourself a steak dinner and maybe a life? One that doesn't include getting accidently drained to death as a job hazard."

His glassy eyes communicated that he'd barely heard me, his arms still outstretched.

I rolled my eyes and turned on my heel. I was sated, but still peckish, if I were honest. I'd stopped purposefully, even though every instinct in my body had urged me on, to keep filling myself with the warmth of his lifeblood to chase away the cold touch of death that still gripped me from the witch's spell.

Not cool.

You weren't supposed to kill the 'hosts' there. It was pretty much frowned upon by Fabian, and I was already on thin ice with my fellow vampires, waiting for the whole 'me and slayer' thing to come out. It was best not to break the rules. Which sucked because the only fun to be had with rules was breaking them.

I also had that rule about not killing innocent humans. While this was a pathetic one, he wasn't a murderer or rapist, so he didn't get to die by my hands.

I glanced back one more time at the slumped form on the sofa.

He'd die by somebody's, though.

When the structured rules of Succor became too strict for his addiction and he went to the streets looking for a longer, deeper high. When he went to the clubs that had no rules against murder.

I sighed as I closed the door.

"Not your problem, Isla," I murmured to myself as the thumping bass of the main club filtered through the low-lit hallway.

Succor was one of the most popular and mainstream clubs in the city. It straddled the border with the wolves so the clientele was always interesting. A lot came here to juice up before doing something stupid like strolling onto Third, looking to cause some trouble with the wolves.

Okay, that was me. I did that once. Okay, twice, but I was bored. The third time I had a good reason. I can't think of it now but I'm sure it was valid.

But this visit was all about business. Which I had told Fabian when I'd walked in and surrounding conversations had muted just slightly. Not enough that a human would notice; in fact, the barely clad ones wandering around with drink trays and scarred necks didn't even stutter in their steps. But I heard the murmurs.

"Isla Rominskitoff. I heard she mates with humans," a voice hissed.

"There's no bounty that would be worth taking her head."

"Someone said she can turn into a bat."

That one made me snort. Vampires couldn't turn into anything but ash if someone had a flamethrower and enough gasoline. Shapeshifting was something the furry part of the supernatural community had dibs on.

I whirled around my newly found stage as the undead eyes flamed on me with their fear, disgust, unease and hatred. "And I married a werewolf the other day," I exclaimed to no one in particular, then rubbed my belly. "Now I'm carrying his child. I'm taking bets on what a fanged werewolf cub will do—"

Fabian snatched my hand before I could completely run with it, shamefully.

"Isla, I don't want any trouble," he hissed, yanking me into a dark corner, eyes darting around.

I rolled my eyes. "Now, that's a total lie. You love trouble."

He glared at me. "No. I don't." He paused, licking his lips. "Not when I have important clients in here tonight. You need to leave."

I pouted. "I promise I'll behave," I lied. "I just came in for a little drink, and then I'll be out of your hair." I looked to his smooth bald scalp and back down at his eyes. "Or out of your… eyebrows," I corrected, focusing on the furry caterpillars framing his small pinched face.

His glare deepened and he stared at me for a long time. I smiled back. He sighed and lifted his arm to jerk a chubby finger.

An attractive, sandy-haired human appeared, his lazy eyes intent on me.

"Tristan, will you take care of Isla in one of our private rooms," he asked tightly.

Tristan sidled up to me. "It would be my honor," he purred.

Jesus.

And he'd led me off into a private room that reeked of blood and lost dreams.

Now that I was sated on Tristan and felt like I needed a shower, I was ready to break my promise to Fabian about the trouble thing and scout around the bar for info on Earnshaw. One of these vampires would know where he tucked himself away. Or maybe that was wishful thinking. I'd most likely have to go to Six, and I was avoiding that place. It didn't have a no-violence rule and was more than likely full of vampires who wanted to kill me. I'd had enough of death matches for the day. Plus, I needed a nap something wicked. Blood could only recharged me so far.

It was getting hard to fight the pull of laevisomnus since I'd gone too long being consecutively conscious, but I had fear of missing out, okay? You couldn't blame me considering all the excitement I'd been treated to lately. If the world was going to end so brilliantly and violently, as Sophie had predicted, I wanted to have a front row seat and a cocktail while watching, not miss out because I had to take a disco nap.

But it was better to miss the 'end of the world' than be permanently in the ground because my lack of sleep translated to slower healing and reflexes. Not good with so many darn humans, vampires and witches trying to kill me.

I thought fondly of the werewolves for a second; none of the furry brethren had tried to kill me in at least a decade.

Maybe I could use one to scratch the ever-present itch that had been simmering since I'd met Thorne.

Ick. On second thought, I'd never be able to stand the wet dog smell.

Because I was retreating in my head, the pair of beady and disapproving eyes that seemed to appear from the folds of the shadows caught me off guard.

I steeled myself from jumping back. Just. "Jeeves," I said smoothly. No way was I giving him the satisfaction of knowing he'd surprised me. "Not somewhere I'd imagine you would be eating dinner." I jerked my head back to the door. "But I do have an inkling that you like them young, muscled and male." I winked at him. "He's ready and waiting. I've cooled him down for you."

I tried to step around him but he matched my movement. I frowned up at the wiry vampire in his three-piece suit that looked like he'd snatched it from the set of *Downton Abbey.*

They didn't make them like that anymore. Then again, he was the real-life—or real-dead—version of the butler.

"My usually paper-thin patience is now nonexistent, as I've had a trying day filled with too many people trying to kill me and not enough people I've killed. I wouldn't push it, Jeeves."

He bored down on me with a blank face. "The king wishes to see you."

I raised a brow. "The king is here? Why would he want to slum it with the vampires who frequent such places? Surely he could just order in." I paused, pondering. "So he's the important clientele Fabian was speaking of. Well, if I were him I wouldn't have let me in the door. Letting me in while he's got the king under his roof? I admire that insanity."

Jeeves stood stoically, impatience radiating off him.

I looked him up and down. "That's a neat trick. You communicating your unreserved distaste and disapproval of me without uttering so much as a curse. Admirable."

He pinched his lip slightly. "Will you follow me to the king, or must I persuade you?" he asked tightly.

I grinned. "Oh I'd love to see you try and persuade me, but I'd hate to ruin your suit." I gestured ahead. "After you."

He gave me one more stare before gliding forward, his feet barely touching the blood-red carpet.

We ventured to the end of the corridor, past doors on each side shielding subtle moans and the wet sounds of blood. Two ornate double doors sat at the end of the hallway.

I tilted my head. "I always wondered what was behind these. I thought that's just where Fabian stashed the bodies."

His only slightly blood-spattered track record had always been suspect to me. Humans were just so fragile; I didn't believe only a handful had died in the years he'd owned and operated this place.

Jeeves ignored me and opened the door.

The sweet scent of blood mingled with the woodsy scent of our fair ruler assaulted me as soon as I stepped inside.

The room had not been decorated by Dracula's interior designer, rather a refreshing modern take. The lights were brighter than the dim ones in the hallways and the furniture was white and plush. It made me think of my forgotten sofas fondly. Maybe I could buy them from Fabian. Or at least arrange to have them stolen for me.

The room was much bigger than it appeared, but even then the man sitting in the middle of the sofa with a barely clad human sprawled over his lap seemed to take it all over. There was a small, sleek kitchen in the corner and a four-poster bed hidden slightly by a transparent curtain.

The presidential suite.

The king was smoothly shaven, wearing an ink-black suit and a black shirt unbuttoned, exposing his thick and muscled neck.

"Isla, what a pleasant surprise," he greeted, voice smooth. It caressed me with its smoothness, so different than the throaty assault of Thorne's.

I straightened, pushing the slayer from my mind. "Your Grace, the pleasure is all mine," I said sweetly.

He quirked his brow at my greeting, knowing me well enough to understand that it was drenched in sarcasm.

"I wouldn't think this would be an establishment you would frequent," he continued. "Considering your… dietary habits." His eyes twinkled and even though he kept his voice even and smooth, it was apparent that the king was teasing me.

Not such a stuffy monarch after all.

I sauntered into the room, his eyes traveling the length of me as I did so. I mentally congratulated myself for dressing for battle and fashion. My skintight black leather jeans and heeled Balenciaga boots hugged me in all the right places, as did my black bustier-style tank.

I was going for Kate Beckinsale in *Underworld*. Despite my hatred of pop culture movies that pretty much butchered our history and ancestors, I liked the costumes.

"Ditto," I said while I sauntered in and poured myself a drink from the solid silver drink stand. The whiskey was the good stuff, in a crystal decanter much like my own. Everything in the room screamed money. From the sheepskin rugs to the marble floors. Fabian didn't filch on décor to make the club look elegant, but even he wouldn't spend this much dough. Not unless it served a purpose.

I met emerald eyes. "I don't need the clichéd 'come here often,' because I'm guessing this"—I twirled my finger around the room—"is made and purposed especially for you."

He followed me with his eyes while absently stroking the human who was sidled up to him. It was slightly disturbing the way he did it, the way humans would interact with an animal. Not enough brains to garner your complete attention but a kind of distracted attentiveness.

Though the woman wearing a backless red dress covered in sequins wasn't doing much for intelligence; she was nuzzling his neck silently, much like a feline.

"It's nice to get out and escape the bureaucrats every now and then."

It was my turn to quirk my brow. "And you come here. And associate with that?" I nodded to her. "It just warms the cockles of my heart to see that you're just like us commoners. A sucker for a pretty face, empty head and a willing vein."

"It's the empty-headed ones who cause the least amount of danger," he said smoothly, his eyes moving over me pointedly.

"They may not be as satisfying as the ones who promise chaos, but at least they don't start riots in this very establishment over a human pop star, if I'm not mistaken?"

I grinned. I did do that. I just couldn't stand vampires insulting my girl Britney.

I smiled. "Haven't you heard? Chaos is the most utterly orgasmic thing on offer in the immortal world." I trailed the tumbler from my lips down to my breasts, rolling it along the skin and reveling in the heat in the king's gaze, the only thing on his impassive face giving away his reaction. "So the rumors are true, then?" I asked casually, moving my glass back up to my lips.

Rick's gaze stayed at my chest for a split second before he met my eyes once more.

"You've fed her your blood." I nodded to the girl. "And it has some kind of quality that makes it err not only on the blue side but on the hypnotic side. Here I was thinking that the fairytales about king's blood being able to transmit the original Ichor from Artemis herself were all bullshit."

His eyes went blank, his only reaction. "And what made you come to this conclusion? One that most vampires in society would dismiss as part of your insanity, and one which may provoke your timely death," he added, his intent clear.

Don't tell anyone, or not only will everyone think you're even crazier but they'll say that at your funeral.

I grinned and tapped my auburn head. "Not just a hat rack, Rick."

A shadow of a grin tickled his mouth, though there was an edge that came with me pointing out my knowledge.

It had been a lucky guess, honestly. And I was more than a little blown away that such legends were true. If I were smart, I would've kept my questions to myself. But curiosity did kill the cat.

I was just hoping it didn't kill the Isla.

"The experience of drinking from a human who has metabolized vampire blood is rather… unique," he said after a long silence, his voice thick and rid of whatever kinglike detachment his death threat had reeked of. He tilted the girl's neck so her blonde hair fell like a curtain over her face, revealing her porcelain and blemish-free neck.

I regarded that with surprise I didn't betray. No fang marks. Yet the slight flush to his cheeks and raise in body temperature meant he'd fed recently.

Curious.

"Now that you're working for me—" Rick continued.

I narrowed my eyes. "I'm working for *me*," I corrected. "Your interests and my interests just happen to align, and now I have added incentive to ensure I hand you the culprits. I assume that your promise to wipe them off the face of this earth, regardless of their Vein Line, still stands?"

The more I'd thought on ways of making sure my family didn't make bad on their promise regarding my Awakening, the more I realized handing them over to the king after I'd uncovered their treason was the best way to be rid of them. And to make sure I wasn't strung up by the other 'noble families' and the connections my father had in the Sector if I did succeed on ending one or all of them.

The king would have no choice but to execute me under continued pressure from the prominent Vein Line and the Sector itself. Though vampire society wasn't a democracy, it wasn't a dictatorship either. If the king didn't listen to such families and the Sector, he wouldn't stay king for long. Which wouldn't be good in the face of the rebellion that would gain more supporters.

He didn't move from his position on the sofa, but his eyes hardened. "I'm a vampire of my word," he answered. "What added incentive?" His voice had an edge to it. "Are you in trouble, Isla?"

I sipped my drink. "No more than usual. And any trouble I'm in is due to the little assignment I'm on from my king."

He rose a brow. "The king you must serve," he pointed out.

"Yes, apparently," I agreed flippantly.

His eyes darkened. "Your utter loyalty does not go without reward." His hand trailed down the flawless neck of the mute human. "Have you ever fed from a human who has metabolized vampire blood?" he asked, voice thick.

I watched him caress the female's neck, felt the pulse of her heartbeat carry across the room, the scent of her blood something more than anything I'd experienced.

"Can't say I have," I answered, my own voice thick.

His eyes held mine. "Few without the purest concentration of Ichor in their blood have," he told me. "It's an experience unlike any other in the world. One I feel you have earned."

I put down my tumbler, fangs already extended slightly as the chasm left unfilled by Tristan opened up once more. The aroma of blood in the air, mingled with the king's own scent, promised something that might chase away whatever chill remained from the day's events.

I moved closer, my eyes hooded. "I never say no to dessert," I murmured, moving to sit on the other side of the human. She smiled up at me, her eyes swirling with euphoria. Mine touched the emerald oceans of the king's, then focused on the pulsing vein below her chin.

Without another word, I sank my fangs into the supple skin of her neck, ambrosia exploding on my tongue. Tristan's blood was a two-dollar bottle of wine compared to the sweet priceless vintage I was treating myself to. I edged my body closer, and the feel of another being feeding as well gave me little room for pause.

Neither did the king's grip on my arm, soft and erotic, mixing with the sensation unlike anything I'd ever experienced. Her blood was sweeter than any human's, running through my system with a depth of warmth that could not be mortal.

Rick's hand moved to my back, pressing into me so my body plastered against the woman's as he fed on her wrist.

I was swallowed with the experience in itself, tumbling down the rabbit hole and flying at the same time.

As quickly as euphoria assaulted me with its magnificence, it was gone. The sluggish labor of her heartbeat signified the end to the experience. I longed to drain her dry, to hold onto this forever, but I found it in myself to stop. The king's presence hinted at something else, something erotic that didn't belong to him.

Thorne's face assaulted my mind before I banished it to the corner.

I leaned back, my body singing with the blood and craving more at the same time. Every instinct I had was sharp, my senses picking up every aroma in the air. Rick's enticing scent overwhelmed me, but didn't drown out the cheap perfume of a 'host' down the hall, or the spilling of a sickly sweet cocktail as two vampires had a small disagreement over who got to taste a human first.

It was as if I'd been given the gift of laevisomnus, and the benefits that came with it, without the extended vulnerability.

Rick pushed the half-drained woman aside with little more than a flick of his wrist.

His hand remained at my back, eyes glued to mine. "Remarkable, isn't it?" he asked, breaking through the bloodlust in the air.

I was consumed with his gaze for a moment. Then I darted up from the sofa, at the door in a second.

"Rather," I agreed. "Better than the espresso I was considering to get me through this evening."

He didn't seem surprised by my sudden movement, his face a carefully schooled mask. Though his eyes glowed.

I stood at the doorway with Rick, my eyes refusing to leave his as the warmth of his blood and the human's pulsed around my body, separate from myself altogether. The pulse traveled downwards and had me digging my nails into my palms to the point of pain not to jump him right then and there.

The cords of his neck moved fluidly as he swallowed, not out of necessity of course, but because he could taste it, my arousal. His eyes were almost black with his own.

I blinked and welcomed the familiar cold of anger mingling with the foreign blood. "Did you just try and date rape me with a tainted human?" I snapped in indignation.

His own eyes stayed dark but turned hard. "I would never take a woman, human or vampire, unwillingly to my bed," he informed me, his voice liquid steel, stepping forward so our bodies touched.

Even though I didn't breathe in, the scent of his own arousal clouded me, as did the pulse from his body.

"Your feelings aren't from her blood. No vampire has had this reaction to mine. Even the few who have experienced it didn't do this." He tilted his head at me. "You're different. Special."

I flicked my hair in order to ward off the impact of that word and the power behind it as it settled under my skin. "Yes, I'm well aware. I'm one of a kind, which is why you have blackmailed me into some spy mission that's quickly turning into a suicide mission. Trying to see if I'm still special from beyond the grave?"

His transition from seduction to king was quick even to my eyes. His body went rigid, eyes blank with the subtlest hint of malice. "Someone tried to kill you again today?" The blandness of his tone didn't connect with the fire in his eyes. "This is becoming a habit."

I crossed my arms. "Yes, a nasty one at that."

He regarded me. "Death threats mean you're getting somewhere. What do you have?"

I chewed on his question. "A vampire who may lead me to more information, and the knowledge that the rebellion isn't exclusively vampire in nature. Though that was already apparent by werewolves working with the vampires who attacked the Majestic." I paused, refusing to lower my eyes from his. "Which begs the question as to why you've got little old me involved instead of calling some supernatural UN conference. Or creating an elite task force with your new allies."

I left out the part about the turned vampire. And the slayer who had managed to become embroiled in this whole disaster. And who would most likely be executed by the king the second he found out Thorne was involved. Hence my silence on the matter. Thorne's death had the grave chill creeping up my spine once more, battling with the warmth of the blood I'd just consumed.

Rick's eyes searched mine, as if he had the ability to taste my deceit. That he could reach into my mind and pluck my treasonous thoughts of slayers from the depths.

Such a quality didn't exist, despite his funky blood, which was good considering that parlor trick would result in my head being separated from my shoulders.

"Even someone as narcissistic as yourself must know each

species does not play well with others. Getting them together without starting another war proves difficult. It took everything not to turn the current alliance into a bloodbath and even now, politics takes too long to get things done," he said tightly. "While they attempt to do the logical thing, I always do the illogical. It usually works out the best."

I tilted my head. "I'm the illogical?"

He gave me a look.

"Yeah, okay, not a surprise. But I'm not going to be any use to you if you stand here trying to seduce me instead of letting me do what I came here to do."

"And what was that?"

I forgot for a second, his voice liquid sex.

"I need information from a patron," I said finally, after searching the reaches of my brain not held hostage by Thorne and Rick.

He stayed where he was for a sliver of a second before stepping back from the door silently.

I guessed kings didn't say good-bye.

I grasped the handle before the sex voice returned, a chill at the nape of my neck with his presence.

"And this isn't seduction, Isla. Seduction would result in you writhing naked underneath me while I take your pussy and your neck at the same time so much that you don't even remember your own name."

I gave myself a mental pat on the back for not even pausing as I opened the door and walked down the corridor at a measured pace.

Kings might not say good-bye but they definitely made you not want one.

"Are you sure you don't know where Earnshaw is?" I asked the bleeding vampire pleasantly. "I was so certain you two are chums. Why, according to a source of the undead variety, you killed a preschooler together not one week ago." My conversational tone succeeded in hiding my distaste.

It wouldn't do well to show weakness, such as disgust for the murders of children in front of anyone. Most certainly not Glint.

He was the one I currently had tied to a chair in Fabian's office, the copper wire bonds making steam erupt from the patches of skin it touched directly. It'd been ready and waiting for me in my purse, and stayed there while I'd breezed around the main room of Succor.

Most of the patrons gave me a wide berth and then a wider one once they knew I was looking for Glint. He and I weren't exactly on all the best guest lists. Him because he was from a working-class Vein Line and his sadism was even blanched at by vampires; he didn't have the aristocracy to fall back on. Me because I did have the aristocracy to fall back on but had a nasty reputation for not being sadistic enough. Kindred spirits we were. Or at least that's what I'd convinced him of when I lead him into Fabian's office with fluttered eyelids that promised sex. The fact that he came so readily and acted surprised when I snapped his neck and restrained him made me feel all warm and fuzzy. Earnshaw was yet to tell him I was public enemy number one.

Well, he'd already known that, of course. I'd have no doubt he'd have most likely tried to have his wicked way with me and then behead me afterwards. That was not happening.

I'd already chopped five of his fingers off and had to give it to the guy; he was yet to scream through them getting chopped off and growing back.

"Not a sound, eh?" I asked his marble expression. "All that baby blood make you a big bad vampire?"

I bent over so my breasts spilled into his vision, making quick work of his designer belt before freeing the hardening flesh from his pants.

It was good to know the girls still got a rise from the vampire I was currently torturing.

I palmed his unimpressive length, giving it an unenthusiastic look. "How about I start chopping things off that will prove much more difficult to regrow?" I offered, my voice a purr. The blade sliced at his base, a small bead of blood blossoming as his body stiffened.

"Fuck," he hissed. "You're a bitch."

I tilted my head up at him. "That's the best you can do? Well color me utterly disappointed."

He sneered and I dug the blade in. He let out a muted grunt.

I smiled.

"Fuck," he repeated. "He'll kill me for telling you."

"And I'll kill you if you don't. But not before I cut off your most unimpressive appendage and make you grow it back again and again until it bores me." I gave him a look. "And when it comes to two of my favorite things, torture and" – I gave him a squeeze that emitted another pain filled grunt – "I rarely get bored."

His gaze was saturated in hate. "He will kill you."

I put my hand to my chest, still holding the blade. "So you haven't told me because you're worried? Aren't you just the sweetest psychopath that I ever did torture? Don't worry, chum, I can take care of myself. Especially with someone as pathetic as Earnshaw."

Cue another glare from Glint. Unfortunately, he was quite

attractive, even beneath the veil of pain and hatred. He was tall and lean, not much with big muscles, but strong, proved by the struggle to get him tied to the chair.

His face was angular and harsh in a way that stopped him being conventionally handsome but made him endearing if you didn't know he drained babies. He shook out the curtain of black hair that had fallen over his eyes.

"Not with what he has. Not with the army we're building," he snarled. "We're going to wipe all half breeds and race traitors off the planet. And the master will make sure everyone has a turn with you before he grants you the mercy of death."

I laughed. "Well that's a date I just can't look forward to enough. This 'master' sounds like he'd be a blast. Care to tell me who he is?"

He stared at me in a way that would have melted the skin right off my face.

But he couldn't, so I was golden.

I squeezed harder. "I've got all night and there's nothing good on TV," I purred, my intention clear. "Torture is so much more entertaining than zombie TV shows, no matter how hot the human with the crossbow is."

His resolve lasted one more brutal squeeze and one arguably more brutal dismemberment.

Then I had a location to meet up with Earnshaw. It was turning out to be a particularly productive evening.

NINE

"YOU DON'T TELL ME WHERE YOU ARE, I'M DOING A tracking spell on you right now," a very irritated Sophie shot through the phone.

I rolled my eyes, watching the seemingly abandoned mansion just a few miles out from where the final edges of New York City surrendered to the wilderness.

The sprawling brick mansion sitting desolate behind bent and broken wrought iron fencing was a shadow of opulence and vigor that had long left this place. Instead, a stillness that even the dead couldn't reproduce remained.

That was their first mistake.

An empty night was never quiet. The absence of humans, or vampires for that matter, gave the air a different quality, and wildlife and creatures that slinked away from unnatural presence thrived with dominion over the darkness.

Not a blade of grass moved on the balmy night.

The quiet was unnatural.

The sprawling grounds removed from New York proper might not be a place even homeless people looking for shelter would stumble upon, but the sheer inconspicuousness of the echoing silence worked as a flashing beacon. I didn't need but to glance upon the house that seeped menace in its stillness to know Glint had given me the goods.

And I had returned the favor by granting him a much quicker death than he deserved.

"You wouldn't be that stupid to waste a spell on finding me," I retorted. My voice carried over the still air and it recoiled from the disturbance. "Plus, I'm guessing my current location will be cloaked from magical eyes."

Sophie's sharp indrawn breath cut through the magically silent night. "The witch is there?"

I gazed into the darkness, little issue to me as I watched the edges of the overgrown garden for signs of life. Or death.

There were none. But there was no mistaking the bitterness to the air that mingled with the stillness, sending waves of foreboding down my back.

The warmth of my snack with the king disappeared as soon as that feeling cloaked my skin and that yawning chasm appeared once more, death too tangy on my tongue.

I didn't tell Sophie all that, of course. "I'm thinking so. Earnshaw is too weak to be somewhere without magical protection and he's not stupid. He'd know I'll be coming for him."

"Yeah well, he isn't the only one who isn't stupid," Sophie snapped.

I straightened. "What's that supposed to mean?"

"It means that I think you're incredibly dense to waltz into a situation with no backup and no idea of what you're facing.

Oh yeah, apart from a witch who practices death magic. You know, some of the only magic that could actually *kill* you," she hissed into the phone.

"I'm hanging up now. You sound like I imagine my mother would sound if, you know, she didn't want me to die. As it is, I'd assume she'd be encouraging me to go in and hope my bad decisions got me killed. I'm going to follow her advice and still hope to disappoint her for coming out undead. I'll see you soon. Or never. Catch you on the flipside, witchy. All my handbags and shoes are being left to you in my will."

On that, I hung up, shoving my phone into the pocket of my jeans. I fingered the copper knife at my belt.

I didn't like having weapons with me. At all. In fact, I was embarrassed to be carrying that, plus the sword strapped to my back Samurai-style. But although Sophie might think me dense for going into such an uncertain situation, I wasn't suicidal. The opposite, in fact. Catching Earnshaw and pumping him for information that would hopefully lead me closer to proof my family was in on this was a very enticing prospect to continue to bless this earth with my presence. I knew my best bet would be to kill the witch before she had the chance to wave her magic wand.

Hence the gun at my other hip.

Witches were still human in the mortal sense of the word. They didn't require special weapons, like vampires needed copper, or werewolves needed silver, or demons needed a knife blessed by a true priest. No, anything would do. Heck, they could trip on a bath mat and break their neck if they were unlucky enough. Their only protection against death was their magic. The stronger the witch, the less likely she was to die.

I did enjoy a challenge.

After careful consideration on how to conduct a stealth

attack, I made my decision to strut right up the broken cobbled path and knock on the crooked wooden front door. I'd already made an almighty racket kicking through the wrought iron fence, so if they did have magic burglar alarms, I was sure I'd already set them off. No need to look like a twat creeping around when they knew I was there.

Just before I was about to take my first step down the path, a familiar boom echoed in my head and my senses exploded, the taste of death replaced with something different. And equally dangerous.

I let out an exaggerated sigh and whirled around, hands on my hips.

"Buffy, what are you and the Scooby Gang doing here? Didn't you get enough of a hint at just how out of your league you are earlier today?" I asked, irritated as Thorne and a couple slayers from earlier stalked towards me.

They had the stealth thing down pat. If I weren't a vampire with an unnatural connection to the hard-faced and hard-bodied slayer currently glowering at me, they would have seemed to melt out of the darkness.

"Isla." The growl of rage, the way his anger rolled over my name, had my knees weaken in an irritating reaction. "What the fuck?" he continued when he stopped his boots a few feet from me. His slayers had pointedly stopped much farther away, their hands on the weapons at their belts. They had much more than me. Then again, I was stronger than them.

And more attractive, and intelligent. Just all round better than them, really.

"Those will just slow your boyfriends down, you know," I said by response to Thorne, nodding to the arsenal on their belts.

I spied a grenade and decided it would come in handy.

I had plucked it off No Neck's belt and was back in front of Thorne before any of them could even blink. It was vaguely impressive that he was still there, although he had a cast on his arm betraying his injury, and stupidity. It would take a vampire a gentle squeeze to rip that off and take advantage of him. That vampire could turn out to be me.

I tossed the grenade between my hands as they took the usual human slowness to understand what happened.

Well, most of them. Thorne's eyes had seemed like they followed my entire journey. Which was impossible, of course. His human eyes would have seen nothing more than a blur.

Then why did it feel like he'd watched it all as if time itself had slowed?

Rick's drugged blood, I decided. That could be the only option.

I grinned as No Neck cursed at me, stepping forward abruptly until Thorne's hand at his chest stopped him.

"Thanks. I totally forgot explosives. They're usually always in my purse but"—I gestured down at my skintight outfit, illuminated in the dim moonlight—"a purse doesn't go and I don't have many pockets." I winked. "So I'll send you a fruit basket as thanks."

My sarcasm was a shield from the sudden molten heat coming from Thorne as he took in every inch of my outfit.

Not the time.

Never was the time.

He seemed to shake himself out of it, stepping forward and leaving No Neck fuming and breathing heavily through his nose like a bull.

"What are you doing here?" Thorne asked, his voice rough velvet.

"Out for a moonlight walk. Maybe some murder. You

know, the usual. You should go before one of you trips over and breaks a neck." I glanced behind Thorne. "Those of you who actually have necks, that is." I gave No Neck a pointed look before focusing back on Thorne and his flickering irises. "This neighborhood is dangerous for those with a heartbeat." My own voice smoothed over the threat like it was a seduction.

"You know what's in there," he deduced instead of addressing my words.

"In where?" I played dumb.

The glistening anger in his eyes told me he didn't buy it.

I rolled my eyes. "Yeah, I know what's in there. And I also know it's none of your business, unless you want to check out of this world early and not see your next birthday." I shrugged. "But whatever, at least then I won't have to worry about getting you a gift."

His breath tickled my face in a violent caress. "That's the second time you've threatened me and mine. There won't be a third," he promised.

I quirked my brow at him. "I'm not threatening you. In fact, I'm *helping* you. Or trying to. You humans seem heaven-bent on your own destruction. Meddling with things much stronger than you, that could snap your necks in the blink of your useless eyes."

With one hand on the grenade, I darted around the rough semicircle once more, stopping with my mouth at a slayer's neck. "Dead," I murmured. I was gone before anyone could even gain purchase on my shadow. Moving to the next one, I did the same. "Dead," I repeated. When I moved to No Neck, I may have given his cast a gentle squeeze—you know, for fun. "Dead," I told him cheerfully, feeding off his pure fury and frustration.

And then, in what would have been a flash of nothingness

to him, I had my hand around Thorne's neck, not even properly circling the muscled cords, but gripping it hard enough to communicate my point.

"Dead," I murmured. My eyes locked with his.

To his credit, he barely even flinched.

I couldn't say the same for his boy band.

The air filled with human hostility and the unmistakable sound of exposing weapons. The slayers had found their attack stances, only about four seconds too late.

I glanced behind him at the two men who had advanced and the third who was trying to come behind me.

I used my other hand to pull the gun from my belt and point it at him. "First, I'd thank you for making sure this weapon is actually used, as I was frightfully afraid I'd have brought it for nothing. Second, I'm sure you'd like to not be plucking a bullet from your cornea, so I'd stop if I were you." I glanced to No Neck and the other human. "And one step guarantees your stupidly fearless leader's pretty little neck being snapped."

They stopped.

"There's a good slayer. Not so hard, is it?" I glanced back to Thorne, who was staying remarkably calm. His steely gaze had yet to leave me. And the comforting cloud of his anger was a pleasing scent to kiss the edges of my psyche. My hand was already exploding with heat at my grip on his skin, vibrating as his heartbeat jerked my hand with its steady cadence.

"I won't kill you because I've got bigger fish to fry. But I would advise you to be on your merry way and go look for kitties to be saved from trees or something equally human that has nothing to do with vampire politics." I let him go with a grin. "Run along."

He didn't run. Nor did he move a muscle. The only thing he did was speak. And not to me.

"Stand down," he clipped at the men still crouched to attack. There was a loaded pause before they did so.

"That's the second time this bitch has threatened our lives and the fuckin' second time you've stopped me from putting the cunt down," No Neck growled.

I frowned at the ugly language, and in an unexpected turn of events, Thorne moved quicker than me, slipping out of my grip with an ease that should have been impossible.

His hands were around No Neck's… well, neck, large enough to circle the expanse and even lift him slightly off the ground.

"And that's the second time you've questioned a *direct fucking order*," he bit out, his rage like an open flame.

Interestingly the taste of it, the sheer volume, dwarfed his earlier fury with me. Swallowed it.

I didn't have time to inspect that little irregularity because he'd dropped No Neck, who let out a splutter.

When he straightened, the fury was palpable, but the silent night was silent once more. Apart from the scream of male testosterone, that was.

"You and Stephens take the back, recon only. Go in through there. Wait for my signal." He glanced to the man I still had my gun pointed at.

"Lenex, I want you on the western perimeter, by the woods." He nodded to where the house jutted into a wooded area, strange for New York, even the outskirts. What wasn't strange about this night, though?

"I'll go in the front," he finished. "With Isla."

His directions were a taunt, a challenge for me to argue. As were the eyes that glued themselves on me as his little toy soldiers melted back into the darkness.

I finger-waved at No Neck's retreating glare. "Have a nice

death."

Once their heartbeats disappeared into the night, Thorne wasted no time in backing me up against the iron fence that surrounded the property.

I let him, curious where it was going. And maybe a little excited. He was like those drugs humans ruined their bodies with. I hadn't understood the allure of chasing a high that only distracted you from the havoc it was wreaking on your body, your life. I did now. All I wanted was a hit, the consequences be damned.

He put his hands on either side of the iron, boxing me in.

"You knew where this vamp was holed up this entire time," he accused through gritted teeth.

I shrugged. I wasn't going to split hairs and say I hadn't at the time.

"You told me—"

"I lied." I rolled my eyes at the expression on his face. "What? I'm not a moral snob. I'm a vampire. I lie as easy as I breathe. Or don't breathe, as the case may be."

His breath was hot on my face. An inferno. "You were going in there, alone?"

I rolled my eyes. "Yes. Yes I *was*. And now I have to sidestep the bodies of your fallen comrades, no doubt. Such an inconvenience."

He furrowed his brows at me. "Why?"

I blew out an impatient breath. "Because I learned something that I'm sure you'll learn through blood and pain because you're far too superior to listen to a vampire. People, vampire or otherwise, slow you down. If you want a job done right, or wrong for that matter, do it yourself. Less people die." I paused. "Or more, depending on the aim. But whatever the mission, it's best not to worry about anyone else's jugular but your own.

Oh, and if you haven't noticed, I'm kind of a lone wolf. The way I like it, of course, and the only being strong and not irritating enough to come with me is currently recharging her witchy batteries. Since she had to use the last of her juice to save your idiot buddy." I gave him an accusing look. "Now, is story time over? Can I please go do what I came to do and also pretend you don't exist, until you actually don't?"

He didn't move and I didn't make him. Despite my protests, the pressing need of killing a witch, a vampire and getting closer to killing my family, plus the bitter twang of magic in the air and the unshakeable cold in my bones—I didn't want to move. Thorne's body was almost pressing into mine, electricity whipping thought the night. The heartbeat that should have acted as somewhat of a deterrent to getting to close to him seemed to yank me closer.

"That's not what I wanted to know," he said, his voice thick. "Why are you here? Doing this? You don't strike me as a mercenary, and you sure as shit aren't a concerned citizen. What's your play here?"

I snapped my logic back into place. "My play is none of your damn business," I snapped. "Slayers don't get the luxury of breathing around me, so I'd keep the questions close to your chest, you know, if you want it to keep containing that fucking loud heart of yours."

At that, I shoved the very chest that was the topic of our conversation. I tried, and failed, not to appreciate the hard ridges of his pecs.

I strode away from him before I could do anything stupid, such as lick them.

"I've got shit to do, things to kill. I'm not having chats anymore. If you're coming in, stay out of my way. And if you die, try not to do it at an inopportune time," I instructed, giving my voice a flat, disinterested quality, so as not to betray any ounce of what this exchange was doing to my insides.

The crunch of his boots on the uneven ground signified his following of my footsteps. That and the molten heat of his stare on my ass and the thundering of his heartbeat, of course.

In my effort to focus on anything but that, I stared at the ground beneath my feet. A good thing too, because it tilted almost vertical and came up to meet me.

Or would have, had iron-like arms not caught me and yanked me upright.

Thorne's eyes glowed with something it took me a split second to recognize.

Concern.

"Isla," he growled, his hands tight on my shoulders.

The grip was stronger than it should have been, to the point that it almost hurt. Which I would ponder later but was grateful for now. Nothing was more useful for clearing the head than pain.

I yanked myself from his grasp. Or tried to.

"What the fuck just happened?" he demanded, his hands clutching my arms as his eyes clutched my attention.

"I tripped," I lied. "These stones are a health and safety hazard. I could sue the owner. I'll kill him instead." I grinned at him, finding enough strength to wrench myself from his grip and resume my journey.

I didn't take careful steps that would betray weakness, though the world was still spinning slightly.

"Isla," he hissed, no longer at my back, but keeping stride with me as we approached the door. It was charged with something strong. Something dark that tasted fouler the closer we got.

"There's somethin' wrong with you," he rasped. "Vampires

don't trip."

I glanced at him. "They do when they're being distracted by a slayer who kisses them instead of slays them. Why is it that you did that, Buffy?" I asked sweetly.

My question had its intended effect of shutting him up. I didn't think he'd like to be reminded of sucking face with the undead creature he was born to slay, no matter how attractive she was.

Trouble was, it kind of backfired, sending heat tingling down my spine at the electric response in Thorne's body. The irritation, fury and arousal created a cocktail better than even my favorite bartender could.

His distraction was only momentary, as just before I got to the door that rippled with the amount of magic cloaked over it, he stepped in front of me. The view was arguably better, but I wasn't there for pleasing and confusing vistas of slayers cut from marble.

"Are you sure you weren't born merely to piss me off, not kill me?" I snapped. "You're succeeding, and I might even drop dead just to get away from you."

His jaw hardened. "You're not goin' in there," he declared.

I laughed at the way he folded his arms, as if such a gesture cemented his word as law.

Males.

"Yes. Yes I am. And I would snap your collarbone for even *thinking* that you had any sort of authority over me, but I've got better things to do."

On that note, I waved the grenade I'd just pulled the pin on in front of us.

"I'd step back a little if you like all your limbs attached to your body," I instructed blandly.

I threw the grenade at the door. To the unpracticed eye, it

looked rundown, but the magic was tangible. Unfortunately, I didn't have a witch, so I was hoping for a grenade to work.

The air vibrated and debris from the door flew through the air with the flames that flickered around me.

Not enough to singe my eyebrows, luckily. And not enough to rival the heat of Thorne's gaze.

Troubling, but a thought for later. Or never.

Maybe the blast had killed him; then I wouldn't have to worry about the attraction and the unwavering panic at the thought of his death.

"Jesus," his muted shout loaded with fury was enough to satisfy my worry that he'd perished.

I stepped forward through the rubble, bracing myself as I crossed the threshold.

A slight prickling and shadow of the excruciating pain of earlier that day, but nothing I couldn't handle.

Grenades doubled as spell breakers when one wasn't in possession of a witch. Handy to know.

"Hello, anyone home?" I called into the dark foyer. "The door was open."

The beat of silence didn't fool me; the entrance was empty, but the house was not. The cavernous space had been disturbed in its afterlife, by creatures as dead as the house was grand.

One heartbeat upstairs.

"Witchy poo, please come down," I called sweetly.

"If you didn't realize, that was the signal," Thorne hissed into the device at his wrist.

Three heartbeats entered the lower levels from various entrances. They weren't what I focused on.

"You think the element of fuckin' surprise might have given us the upper hand considering we're outnumbered," Thorne hissed, his body tight in what I guessed was his battle stance.

I gave the rippling veins in his forearms an appreciative glance before being slightly surprised that he'd clocked the number of vamps so quickly.

"You lost the element of surprise the moment you and the bumbling oafs you call friends set foot on the perimeter, with all that breathing and blood circulation," I replied, stepping through the foyer into a living room. "Plus, I did surprise them. Grenade instead of doorbell."

The foyer was large and decorated with crumbling opulence, a stale smell of mold and dust weaving through the bitter magic that had disturbed it.

The vampire that darted in front of me, hissing and attacking, was little more than an annoyance.

The next two were slightly more of an effort to subdue, and I scowled at Thorne as he yanked the third out of the air and embedded his blade in its temple.

"I don't need your help," I protested, just as another vampire got a lucky kick into my chest which sent me hurtling through a wall.

I landed in a sitting room, covered in dust, my ribs protesting from the chunk of wood protruding from them. I yanked it out, gritting my teeth at the pain as half of my insides, and fabric from my tank, went with it.

Luckily I was wearing a replaceable outfit that time.

Thumps of flesh on flesh and the unmistakable sound and smell of death from the other room echoed and then there was that unnatural silence once more.

Thorne appeared in the archway I'd created.

"You were saying?" he asked, his voice even, though I glimpsed a twinkle in his eye.

I pushed myself up with a scowl, wincing at the protest from my healing midsection, then stormed past him and the GI

Joes who'd wandered through the carnage, breathing heavily.

I pushed No Neck's chest and sent him to the floor to appease some of my irritation.

It did help.

As I ascended the stairs, I turned. The silence of before reigned once more, as the vampire welcome wagon had been dispatched. The increase in heartbeats and heavy breathing behind me was a telltale sign that the slayers were unfortunately still alive.

"This is where you get off," I said to Thorne, who was my shadow on the step behind me.

His grin, or the shadow of it that couldn't have been due to me manhandling his friend, disappeared.

"We're not goin' anywhere."

"Just because you've shown that nature didn't completely fuck up by making you able to roughhouse a couple of baby vampires doesn't mean you can handle what's up there." I pointed to the roof.

"And you care?" he challenged.

"No, but I know once I take care of all of that, I'll have to either kill you all or knock you unconscious in order to get what I came for. And I *always* get what I want. As long as you know that, be my guest. I'd advise you to keep your arms inside the ride at all times, or they're likely to get torn off."

I made it to the top of the stairs quicker than the rest of Robin Hood and his merry men but not as quick as I could have been. I'd sensed them waiting at the end of the long hall.

Thorne's gun was raised, his body slightly in front of mine as soon as he caught a glimpse.

The second time he'd protected me with his body on instinct.

The rest of the slayers gathered behind us, the rapid

increase in their already thundering heartbeats betraying their fear at seeing the bundle of red-eyed freaks standing stoic at the edge of the hall. Waiting.

The loudest boom of them all stayed steady. Either Thorne had exceptional control over his beats per minute or he wasn't afraid.

I didn't get time to think on this, because a silent command rattled through the air and the red-eyed abominations hurtled forward.

I was vaguely surprised and unnerved that there wasn't just the one I was expecting. It didn't bode well that one relatively unimportant vampire had so many in his command.

Now that the tests had been done, they would be making sure that more pivotal players in the rebellion got their very own gang of red-eyed freaks.

Gunshots echoed through the hall and several oncoming bodies hurtled to the ground. Another quickly took the place of the fallen.

They would be on us in seconds.

"Isla," Thorne snapped, his voice a yell even though it sailed through the air on little more than a whisper. "There's too many of them."

I regarded the horde. That's what they were, an oncoming swarm of animals, with no brainpower other than attack and kill.

We may've held more coherent thought, but their numbers and the fact that they weren't weighed down by things like worry for their own survival gave them a distinct advantage.

I grinned, rocking forward on my heels slightly. I glanced at Thorne. "Do I look worried?"

The first who tried to latch onto me said good-bye to their head in a second. Sounds of close-range gunshots still peppered the air, along with grunts of exertion. I dispatched the creatures easily. They were stronger than humans, but not by much. Their danger came with their lack of concern for their own survival. They were serving their master, who had ordered them to attack.

The slayers weren't as useless as I expected; not one had died yet, and the horde was diminishing.

I yanked at the back of a creature who was about to make a meal out of Thorne's neck as his back was turned, fighting off two others.

The tearing of its neck coincided with Thorne finishing the two off in time for him to witness me saving his hide.

I quirked my brow as his eyes blazed to mine. "You're welcome." My gaze darted to the gap in the attacking forces. "I'm going to assume you've got it from here."

"Isla," he roared, but the rest of his yell was lost as I left the diminishing battle behind in search of the more important prey.

I didn't notice the concrete wall of magic until I ran straight into it.

So instead of looking at the grand bedroom with a four-poster antique bed which and a dressing table, I was looking at the cobwebs that cloaked the ornate designs on the ceiling.

My fractured skull made it a little hard to move, as did my broken ribs.

Those weren't what worried me. It was the way my blood seemed to turn to ash and something that I hadn't realized was planted inside me began to bloom.

A spell that I'd half known was there and chosen to ignore.

One that tasted decidedly like my death.

If this were a cartoon, I'd likely have birds fluttering around my head as I blinked away the cold premonition of my own demise.

I darted up quickly enough to fend off an attack by a blur of teeth and snapping.

Not quickly enough. The teeth sank into my forearm instead of my neck, which was preferable but no less painful.

His grip was that of a pit bull, but I rectified that by snapping his neck, flinging his body to the wall.

"Thanks for inviting me around for tea," I said to Earnshaw, who was standing beside his witch. His arms were folded and he was dressed in a three-piece suit, grinning smugly. "You're not fooling anyone, you know. It's disgraceful, really, hiding behind a witch because you're too scared to fight me yourself.

His gaze went feral. "No, it's smart," he hissed. "What's disgraceful is you aligning yourself with slayers."

Obviously, Thorne had joined the party. I had hoped it would take him longer to fight the dregs of the first wave. I needed to stop underestimating him and his team just for being human.

His heat at my side gave away his location and I glanced to him. I could smell blood, and I needed to ensure it wasn't coming from him. I was mollified that he was stained with red, but not his own. I didn't care about the rest of the slayers.

His gaze centered on my bleeding arm, then upwards towards my midsection, where his eyes bulged. I glanced down to where my rib protruded from my skin.

I sighed and put my hand to it, shoving it back in with a crunch and sinking my fangs into my lips to muffle any cry that would totally fuck up my badass routine.

I didn't miss the wide-eyed gaze of Thorne's team as I did so, not having time to smile at my not-so-secret admirers. I moved my attention back to Earnshaw.

"I'm not exactly aligning myself with them. They're kind of stalking me." I shrugged. "Can you blame them?"

I stepped forward pointedly, to get the chitchat over and get out of Thorne's presence.

"Now would you like to surrender now and tell me what your malicious and evil plan is, or do we have to do it the proverbial hard way?"

Earnshaw grinned, his glance going to the adjoining door I'd only just noticed. He didn't say anything, but the way the air thickened with his gaze made some nonverbal command slink over me. It felt wrong, grated against my skin much the way the stench of the witch did. Her spell was tangling in my insides, and I fought to keep the grimace off my face and the memories at bay.

I didn't exactly know what it was, but Jonathon's lifeless corpse was trying to claw itself out of my subconscious, so I guessed it wasn't good.

The door opened.

"Great," I muttered as the countless abominations filtered out, their red eyes wild. The first lot were obviously designed to tire out intruders. This was the kill squad.

"It's the hard way."

Thorne and his men went to work battling the creatures that came out of the door like clowns out of a miniature car. For every one they cut down, more replaced them.

The witch had probably cloaked them so I couldn't sense the impending attack.

There was the silver lining that I was able to unsheathe my sword at my back and whip through the horde with speed to save the brave but idiotic slayers from at least three deathblows. I lopped the head from a snapping woman, or what used to be a woman, just before she sank her fangs into Thorne's neck.

He took out his own opponent before turning to see the blood dripping from the sword that saved his life.

I grinned at him through the prickling of black magic in my belly. "Second time tonight. You owe me a beer. Handle the rest on your own, would you? I've got a bitch to kill."

I whirled, stepping out of the small area designated for battle and into the part of the room where Earnshaw and his witch watched with impassive faces. Earnshaw grinned and my gaze whipped back to see more creatures pouring out, the slayers struggling to keep them at bay. I should have gone back to help, but I feared the dark shadow itching up my spine might consume me if the witch didn't die soon. And the way one of the snapping creatures hit the space between me and them showed I couldn't even if I wanted to; I was in some sort of spell circle with Earnshaw and his pet witch.

The slayers were on their own. To meet their deaths, presumably.

I swallowed the ash at that.

"So, Minerva, we haven't been properly introduced," I addressed the witch in the same flowing black dress as before. She was grinning seductively at me, her glamour at full effect. The moonlight flickered in from the one window in the room to make her skin glitter with diamonds, highlighting her rosy lips and slim figure. "I've seen your true face. I know you're not winning any beauty contests, so this"—I waved my hand at her body—"is completely unnecessary."

Her smile didn't dim as white-hot pain radiated from my hairline to my toes. I didn't make a sound, though it brought me to my knees, the roar of it in my ears drowning everything out.

I blinked the dusty room back into existence to see black lace trailing around the floor to rest at my face. Long-nailed fingers drew blood from my chin as she yanked it up to meet her eyes.

Her black eyes.

"My name is Belladonna, you insolent bitch," she informed me, her words a whip. "It will be the last thing you hear before you meet your final death." She paused, tilting her head. "That's after you swim in the blood and pain of your past."

The room rippled, turned to paper and fell like a fake background in a Hollywood movie.

It was replaced by a house that didn't exist anywhere, except in memories I'd banished.

It moved as I moved, my slippered feet taking unhurried steps towards the door.

My skirts rustled in the mild summer air, and my hand lifted to brush a tendril of hair that had escaped my pins.

"No!" the interior me screamed at the memory, the imprint of my human self.

I was stuck in her head, thinking her thoughts. Inside I was me, but I was trapped in this ghost of a memory that tasted so much worse because it was real.

My corset dug into my waist, my ribs protesting at being constrained in such a way, and I had an ache in my feet as I had walked from town, deciding to marvel at the delight in the day. To bathe in the happiness.

My skin burned somewhat, as I'd gone without a hat and the harshness of midday sun wreaked havoc on my pale skin.

All of that, plus the beat of my heart, felt so real, like the past five hundred years had been a dream and I was still a human in Paris. In love.

I watched in horror as my hand twisted the doorknob, my vision tilting with my head as I remembered the confusion of it being slightly ajar.

I clawed at the edges of my mind, trying to find a way out. This was a spell, magic; there had to be a way, a hidden door out of this prison.

Then the smell assaulted me. Even my weak human senses recognized it. Hurried my steps and turned everything into ice that had once been hot blood in my veins.

Once I saw the first body my stomach lurched with nausea. My eyes scattered around our grand drawing room.

Blood mingled with the rose pattern of our rugs.

"Celeste," I whispered, passing my housekeeper, her throat torn open and her green eyes opened in the final empty stare of death.

My steps were on autopilot. Pain mingled with numbness in the most unpleasant and horrific of feelings.

Scattered on the floor in some sort of brutal decoration was everyone I'd ever known and become friends with in Paris.

People who had given me the gift of hope. That maybe I'd have a life instead of a death.

Their deaths were the surest way to kill that hope.

And when my eyes cast over the final person, I let out a strangled cry.

Pain and agony radiated through my entire body as I wove through fallen limbs.

"No, no, no," the past me chanted, her voice so full of raw agony I flinched inside my own head.

Shaking hands hovered over the bloodied and mutilated corpse of my husband, not touching him. I didn't want to make this real, as if it would be my touch that killed him instead of the puddle of blood staining my white dress.

I steeled myself and placed my hand on his cheek, then screamed. It echoed through the corners of my skull, and I flinched in my spot.

Pain radiated through my body and my heart pounded at a speed that didn't seem human.

Because it wasn't.

I proved that when it stopped and an invisible hand closed around my throat, crushing the bones and robbing me of air.

Still inside my head, watching it happen, I couldn't say how long it took for me to die.

A long time.

I gasped for air, as if emerging from underwater, coming back into the room to the thudding sounds of battle and blood.

Belladonna's sardonic grin was all I saw.

"I'm not nearly done," she whispered.

I thought I heard a masculine voice bellow my name before I was sucked under once more.

"Please," a frightened voice pleaded.

I glanced down at the dirty human on his knees, clutching his young wife to his back, as if he could protect her.

I laughed in the face of their terror, finding it amusing. Or pretending to, at least. Feelings weren't something I was plagued with. Only death. I dealt in it. Tasted it. Survived on it.

I left their lifeless bodies at the mouth of the alley in Prague without a second thought.

A brutal wind whipped around my cold face as I hurtled through time and space. I struggled for a foothold to climb out of the vortex.

There wasn't escape.

Only death.

The English streets were noisy as I battled the urge to murder every human who bustled through the streets like rats. I managed to swallow my rage to keep my eyes on my target.

Another couple.

Laughing. In love.

Fools.

It was my job to educate them on how deadly their happiness was. And to do them the favor of watching each other die.

I gasped at the pain of the deaths my dead self had caused. Drowning in them.

"Had enough yet?" she purred.

I grinned through the pain. She was merely using the memories as a distraction so I didn't realize her spell was rotting me from the inside out. "Fuck you," I hissed.

Her gaze flickered for just a moment before she muttered Latin under her breath.

A fresh and powerful wave of agony washed over me, making the spell at Sophie's office look like child's play. I couldn't hold in my scream, as much as I wanted to. To my amazement, when looking down at my hand, the skin wasn't being flayed from my body. Though I could see the steam rising from my porcelain arms, which now had a red tinge to them.

This bitch was literally making my blood boil.

I was very aware that I was dying, and in front of an asshole like Earnshaw, who was grinning the whole time.

Not the blaze of glory I had imagined.

I wanted to fight more; however, this witch not only had power but she'd obviously been the mean girl at Salem because she knew how to truly bring someone to their knees. How to end someone, make them first mentally weak.

Using someone's brain against her was a surefire way to get their death on the way.

I would have admired her had she not been a sadistic, black magic, hideous bitch.

Not only was my mind weakened, but her spell rendered me paralyzed.

It took me a second to hear past the boiling of my own

blood.

"Isla," a muffled voice roared.

I craned my head with the same effort it would take for me to move a small building. My eyes locked with Thorne's. He was alternating banging on the invisible and unbreakable glass between us while swatting away turned vampires.

Blood trickled from a cut in his temple, his muscled arms decorated in torn gashes on fang marks.

His bloodied fist connected with the wall once more.

"Don't let that bitch kill you," he commanded, his voice a scream through the thickness of the air.

It was the flick of her wrist that sent him flying into the hordes of snapping vampires that did it.

I wrenched through the pain and lifted the gun that I had been so sure I wouldn't use. It wouldn't have worked, had her attention not still been on Thorne. But the bullet hit her between the eyes, breaking the spell and giving me a moment to step away from the grim reaper's embrace.

I didn't take a chance on her coming back with necromancer magic, using the last of my strength to rip her head from her shoulders. The instant I did, the rancid grip of her spell receded like a tide. It wasn't an immediate snap like I expected, which disappointed me.

My blood itched with the aftereffects of the spell and I turned to Earnshaw, smiling.

"Not so smug without your witch's skirts to hide behind, are you?" I asked him.

If vampires could pale, Earnshaw would have been white as a sheet. He blinked it away, grimacing.

"You will die for this," he promised. "*He* will make sure of it."

I tilted my head. "Big talk coming from someone inches

away from their own demise."

I hated that such a statement wasn't rightly true. As much as I wanted to tear off his head and use it as a footrest when I finally did get to sit down, I reasoned the king might want to have a chat with him. Wasn't that the whole point of me almost dying? To give the king what he wanted so I didn't *actually* die? I would have to call Sophie to get her to do some eraser work on Earnshaw's memories of me and the slayers. It wouldn't do well to have him reveal that under torture.

Not well at all.

Earnshaw's wide eyes went behind me as the last telltale crack of bone echoed through the air.

"No" was his strangled whisper.

I glanced back. Thorne's eyes immediately found mine, the cocktail of emotions in them nearly stopping every other thought I had. His chest rapidly expanded and fell with the exertion of breathing.

No wonder, as he was almost up to his knees in corpses.

None of which were of his own men, surprisingly. I was a little disappointed that the only thing No Neck was nursing was a blackened eye and a particularly nasty bite wound near his shoulder.

If only they'd aimed a little higher.

"Looks like all your abominations have gone bye-bye, Dr. Frankenstein," I said, turning my gaze back to Earnshaw. "I would say I'm sorry, but I'm not and you're an asshole who got what he deserved, so I'll just get down to it."

I darted forward expecting an easy fight, but when you corner a predator, you find them at their strongest.

And I loathe to admit that I was at my weakest.

Not only had the witch's spell drained me, but my lack of sleep meant my recovery time was lagging.

Which meant it was all the easier for Earnshaw's fangs to attach themselves to my neck and rip half my throat out.

The pain was white-hot and immediate. Luckily it pissed me off enough to snap his neck and hinder any more mortal wounds.

He crumpled to the ground at my feet.

I stared down at his body, holding one hand to my jugular that had yet to stop bleeding. Cool liquid spurted down my neck and coated the front of my body. The pain had yet to recede, as the blood didn't stop flowing in seconds like was normal.

No wonder humans were so goddamned miserable.

"Isla," a voice growled beside me.

"Please tell me you've got some form of vampire restraints in your Batman belts," I said by response to the concern.

A pause.

"Restraints?"

I nodded my still-bleeding head, ignoring the lance of pain that came with the movement. It was intense enough to turn my stomach. Throwing up blood was the last thing I wanted to do; I needed to hold onto as much of that as I could, considering the only people with pulses in the room would kill me surer than the witch could with merely a taste of their blood.

"Yes. I'm not growing old here but increasingly annoyed," I snapped. "I can't kill him, as much as I'd like to. I need him alive for information." I extended my hand and wiggled my fingers impatiently. "Restraints."

Out of my periphery, Thorne nodded. One of his men darted forward, handing me the copper cuffs as quickly as humanly possible before darting out of my presence.

He was the kid I'd pointed the gun at. Seemed he couldn't forgive and forget.

I fought against the way the room blurred at the edges to cuff Earnshaw, the burn from the copper nothing compared to the inferno that had only just receded from every part of my body. He'd be healed in about twenty minutes, so I needed him in transit, or ideally out of my hair, before that.

I stood, once more trying to convince myself that the world should not be spinning. My blood loss had finally slowed, only a slow trickle escaping from my hands that were still holding my neck together.

"Can one of you strapping young lads carry him down to the car for me? I think that's the least you could do since I did all the heavy lifting for the night," I asked, my voice light.

The air was charged, and it only then occurred to me that I was injured and seriously weakened in the presence of four bloodthirsty slayers riding off the high of cutting down countless vamps.

If I was ever going to serve my head on a silver platter, that was their chance.

Thorne's body stiffened at my side and I could taste the realization in his emotions. Not subtly, he stepped aside, taking me with him and positioning his body in front of mine while keeping his eyes on his men.

Third time. It was becoming a habit. And I was beginning to enjoy it.

"Take him down," he growled at No Neck. He didn't wait for a response before he glanced at the other two. "I want you two to take one of those"—he nodded to the corpses strewn at their feet—"and get it to Silver. We don't want to be here when reinforcements come."

His command was clear. The first two rustled to get going, the muscled olive-skinned one hoisting the body over his shoulder in one smooth move. They gave me one last look of distaste. I winked at them.

No Neck was still glaring at Thorne. "And you, Commander? What are you going to do?"

Thorne stiffened at his side. "Knowing what I'm doing wasn't part of your orders, Erik. Are you going to disobey me?"

The question hung in the air. It wasn't lost on me that Erik was clutching his copper knife so hard his meaty hand turned white.

My vision blurred. I was pretty sure he didn't clone himself, so it was not a good thing I saw two angry roid-freak slayers.

They merged back into one when he took a step forward. Thorne stiffened, only slightly, but enough to make it clear that he'd challenge one of his own if they went for me.

Instead of watching the two slayers fight, which even in my weakened state I would have enjoyed, Erik breezed past us, treating me to the bitterness of his rage before he lifted Earnshaw.

"Mine's the cherry-red convertible on the curb, Mercedes," I told him sweetly. "In the back is fine. And if you scratch my car, I'll rip your throat out." It worried me there was a slight wet undertone to my voice thanks to my throat being ripped out. "And unlike me, you won't be standing here chatting after I do it."

Erik gave me a look so hate-filled the air swirled with the rancid taste of the emotion.

Then he looked to Thorne, waiting for him to challenge my request. Thorne folded his arms. They were covered in blood, snaking up his muscled biceps like some kind of tattoo. It was delicious.

"Do it," he bit out. "Then go back to the compound."

Erik had an internal struggle on whether to drop the bloodsucker, stab his commander and then finish ripping my head off. It was as clear as day. The air charged yet again, but Thorne kept his arms folded.

Reaching his decision, Erik turned on his heel and stomped down the stairs, enshrouded in his blanket of hate.

Thorne and I stood in silence, death permeating the air, the last of the black magic seeping into the floorboards.

My stomach still curled with icy coldness that hadn't been banished with the witch. That and the blood loss from the wound that didn't seem to want to heal.

I needed a fresh blood bag. I glanced at the pulsing tendons in Thorne's neck, his blood calling to me, hypnotizing me with his thundering heartbeat.

Which didn't make sense at all. Instinctively, I should have known his blood would kill me. Instead, I craved it like it was the only thing that would keep me on this earth.

I needed to get out of here. "Okay, well as fun as this was, let's never do it again. You really know how to show a girl a bad time," I said, trying to step around him. He whirled and had me pushed against the wall in a moment. My reactions were dangerously slow, because I let him. Was it the mortal wound at my neck that let him box me into the same position as I had outside, or was it something else? The dark hooded look in his gray eyes, the taste of him mingled with the taste of death? His body that had my blood singing as if it hadn't been boiling underneath my skin moments before?

"You're not goin' anywhere," he growled. The savageness of his tone didn't match how his bloodstained hand reached up to my neck, brushing over the flesh that was knitting back together.

His eyes glued to the wound that was becoming little more than a scratch, the pain that had radiated through my body muted to an uncomfortable itch.

In novels and sonnets and those terrible romance movies, people talked about time stopping or slowing down. I wanted to drain those people, or the person who invented the concept of some sort of emotional connection overriding physics.

Magic could do it, as could some strong vampires, manipulating the thread of time to bend it. Nothing crazy, just a few seconds here or there. All supernatural forces, but there was a reason to the concept.

Reason didn't exist here. In the moment where time became a mold that Thorne sculpted with his breath and his beating heart. His head lowered towards my neck, his inky hair falling around him as his lips softly fastened over the newly healed skin. Kissing it. Laying his mouth over my bloodstained skin as if his human lips had a power vampire blood didn't. They could heal it and chase away the chill that had begun to retreat at his proximity.

The second he made contact, my entire body went alight with a heat that couldn't be rivaled by an open flame. It melted the ice at my stomach like I'd drained a hundred humans dry.

When his head lifted and his hungry eyes met mine, time snapped back and everything happened in a blur. His lips were brands on my own as his hands clutched my sides, a low growl vibrating from his throat.

I wrapped my arms around his neck, plunging my hands into his hair, brutally tugging at it as he lifted me and immediately threw me brutally onto the bed that was all but forgotten in the midst of the battle.

His body covered mine before I had a second to chase whatever semblance of sanity remained in my psyche.

His lips set mine aflame while his body plastered against mine. If this was insanity, then I would happily accessorize a straight jacket.

He ripped my shirt open, then held my breasts for a glorious second before the garment was gone in a tear of fabric and my last shred of reason.

Thorne let out a low hiss as he took in my blood-red lace bra, his eyes glowing.

"You're fuckin' magnificent, Isla," he rasped.

Then he lowered his mouth so it settled atop the thin lace covering my nipple.

I clutched his hair, threading my nails through it and yanking hard while he stoked the flames inside me. I was sure the bedframe would serve as kindling and burn this whole place to the ground. I wouldn't have blinked if that happened, as long as Thorne's body stayed on mine.

I could deal with anything as long as his scent was close enough to taste, his heartbeat rattling through my soul, giving me life that had been absent for five hundred years of undeath.

His mouth moved lower, tasting, relishing and worshiping his way down to the waistband of my jeans. His touch, his lips, the energy streaming through him—none of it was gentle. His teeth grazed my belly roughly, his grip on my hips firm enough to imprint bruises on my pale skin. Bruises that remained longer than usual but that I would happily keep as tattoos of his touch.

The curtain of his hair fell back and feral eyes met mine.

They stayed that way, locked in a brutal gaze, as he ripped off my boots and jeans in a movement that was a blur to even my eyes.

I was too drugged by his touch to register the strangeness of this. My eyes devoured him, blood and bruises peppering his muscled body, remains of a battle that had happened ages ago. I moved quickly, capturing him and turning us so he was on his back and I straddled him, my lingerie-clad core pressing into his rough hardness encased in denim.

My forehead clashed against his. "I told you, I'm best on top," I purred, my voice barely recognizable.

His eyes were quicksilver as he clutched my face with a ferocity that I sank into. Then in another blur and a delicious amount of pain, my back pressed into the rough fabric of the bed, Thorne's entire body pressing into mine.

"This is one place you don't get to be in charge," he growled. He roughly tweaked my nipple and then moved lower, freeing himself from his jeans while the rest of him stayed clothed.

He leaned in, capturing my bottom lip in his teeth and biting down hard enough to draw blood.

"You surrender to no one but me," he rasped against my bleeding lip. Then he covered my mouth with my own, tasting my blood at the same time he surged into me.

Sex and death were the two most natural parts of life. Natural, necessary and best if feelings weren't involved in either.

Yet the moment Thorne and I connected, it was something beyond the natural.

Supernatural.

He pounded into me with a ferocity that rivaled that of any vampire, demon, or werewolf. I gripped his back, holding on with everything I had, sinking my nails through the fabric of his tee so I scratched his skin, drawing blood.

He let out a hiss and his pounding intensified, his mouth hovering inches from mine as his blood lingered in the air. The aroma of it coupled with his smell had me focusing on the veins in his neck, yearning to sink my fangs in and taste his blood on my tongue while he pulsed into me.

I'd even meet the death it promised at the moment.

As if he'd sensed it, Thorne's hand circled my own neck, jerking my gaze up to quicksilver eyes.

"You look at me, Isla," he growled. "Me."

I complied, no longer yearning for the taste of his blood.

Nor the taste of the grave that came with it.

I wanted more. And in the moment when the fire he built reached breaking point, I realized that him, inside me, taking me amidst the corpses we'd created, was nothing supernatural.

It was natural.

And it was fatal.

Then there was nothing but white blinding light as my climax took over every inch of coherent thought, my mind latching onto Thorne's grunts of pleasure as I milked his own end from him.

The air was sweet and bitter and wondrous with our combined scents, with the pulse of his emotion.

I managed to blink away the white light until quicksilver dominated my vision.

With a gentleness that contrasted the brutal grip of before, Thorne brushed my hair from my face with agonizing slowness, watching its journey as it trailed along my cheek.

My world became blurry around the edges, Thorne's face the only thing in stark and jarring clarity. Bruised and stained with the results of damage that would always be done as long as he was human.

The stark realness of his face decorated with the symbols of mortality served as omens that sent a cold force of premonition through the heat he'd created.

"These violent delights have violent ends," I murmured, almost to myself.

He grasped my chin, his steely gray eyes oceans to be lost in. To drown in. "Everything has a violent end, Isla. Life. Death, as it turns out. Even peace is violence packaged differently." He gripped my face tighter, his other hand digging painfully into my hip. "But isn't the violence the best part?" he growled.

The blurring at the edges of my vision became more dominant with his words. The enticing respite from that very violence I craved from his touch. So I gave in.

Surrendered.

In Thorne's arms was both the most fatal and safest place to do so.

TEN

COMING AWAKE IN AN INSTANT OF PANIC AND GRASPING at my burning throat was not my idea of a good way to start the night.

Every instinct in my entire being thrummed with unease as I surged into consciousness in unfamiliar surroundings. The savage thirst of flames stripping my throat of flesh made it hard to take in why I was in a small and sparsely decorated bedroom.

One thing I did note was the woodsy scent that snaked from the gray sheets I was tangled in.

Thorne.

Images of furious bodies clashing together in a brutal coupling amongst the blood and corpses littering the floor had flames lick somewhere else.

Somewhere much lower.

It was only belatedly that I realized I was naked except

for a shirt that imprinted Thorne's scent into my flaming skin, pressing into my breasts.

Had I not been half wild with thirst I might have paused to ponder why I was in Thorne's shirt in what I guessed was Thorne's bedroom. As it was, I thought of only one thing.

Blood.

Not in decades, centuries perhaps, had I been so stripped down to my baser instincts.

Years when the only thing that meant something was filling the emptiness with the lifeblood of as many humans as possible.

Thrumming in the next room had me leaping from the bed and darting to the door before I quite understood what happened.

I caught myself with my hand on the doorknob as lowered voices floated through the air and tickled my ears.

Had I had a smidgeon less self-control, I'd have ignored it and went in search for a big breakfast. Instead, I stopped.

"Normal?" A rumbling voice encircled me in its rough caress and Thorne's unmistakable fury-filled growl echoed through the room. "She's been as still as a fuckin' corpse for almost a fuckin' week," he hissed. "We got no clue if she'll even wake up because she doesn't have a heartbeat. We need the witch back here."

A week? I felt like I'd been on a no-blood diet for at least a year. I glanced down at my arm, still smooth and flawless. But my hands had a wrinkle to them which would have been invisible to the human eyes. When vampires went too long without blood they started to shrivel up like a prune. Young vamps couldn't last a day. Once they'd passed a century they were better.

Me? I could go longer than a week. It was uncomfortable,

but nothing more than emaciated models felt like on a daily basis. However, I couldn't go that long without blood when I'd lost a lot from a gaping wound at my neck and that blasted witch had turned the rest to steam.

"We can't bring the witch here," a deeper, smoother voice argued. The twinge in my neck told me he was a slayer too. "We've got enough heat on us havin' a fuckin' *vamp* in the house. Another in the barn. Sneaking the witch in a second time is going to be near impossible. You know Erik is watching this place. He's still loyal, despite being an asshole, so he's yet to inform anyone outside the unit about you working with a vampire. But if he knew you had one in your *bed*?" There was a pause and a rustle of movement as the speaker paced the floor. "Jesus, Thorne, what were you thinking, bringing a bloodsucker here? You know the council can take your stripes for this." Anger and frustration bubbled out of the formerly smooth voice. "I know she's got somethin' on you, bro, but it's *not fuckin' good.*"

I agreed with him there. Even now, Thorne's mere presence had my body in tune with the wave of fury and undertones of concern rippling through his rigid body like a storm. I could taste his emotions with more clarity than I had purchase on my own. His heartbeat was loud enough to reside in my own chest. And the surge of blood around his system sang to me with a melody that had me gripping the doorknob with enough force to snap it off.

I glanced down, wondering if I'd just announced my presence.

Thorne's thundering shout coupled with his volcanic eruption of my emotions drowned out the sound.

"I fuckin know," he roared.

Silence bathed the room in its tempting and confronting

clarity.

I tried to swallow the flames at my throat.

"Then let's go in there and solve the problem by putting a knife through her temple." The other voice was once again calm.

I grinned against the fire. I liked that guy. Well I would, if he wasn't discussing my murder. But I enjoyed his bloodlust.

Thorne's fury seeped through the walls and drenched the room I was in.

"You touch her, I'll put my knife in your heart," Thorne uttered in a voice so deceptively soft you'd think it was a lover's whisper—if you were dense, that is. Even a deaf person could taste the promise of death in the air.

It swept around me, its meaning permeating my bloodlust.

The other slayer let out a throaty chuckle. "Only *you* would fall in love with the creature you were born to kill."

I burst through the door before my eavesdropping took me somewhere I couldn't come back from.

Love and Thorne?

No.

Love was a death sentence.

I may have already been dead, but I didn't want it to be literal.

I sped through a hallway peppered with photographs to reach a small open-plan living room and kitchen. The glass doors leading to a porch revealed an overgrown lawn that snaked into dense woodlands.

Two masculine gazes focused on me. I returned the favor. Thorne was close to the muscled man in front of him, obviously necessary for his death threat. His hands were still curled into fists, and the veins exposed from his black tee pulsed with the way he held himself. His jeans were black instead of his usual faded denim. I steeled myself against his gray gaze and the wild look etched into his features.

I focused on the man beside him. It was like looking at night and day. Where Thorne was dark, his features carved from marble, this slayer's blond hair was cut short but mussed artfully, his nose crooked from being broken one too many times. He was covered from throat to ankle in tattoos, vibrant and alive on his muscled skin, visible around his tight tank and board shorts. The skin underneath the tats was tanned, and I half expected him to give me the 'hang ten' greeting while drawling "dude" in a Californian accent.

My perusal of them only took a couple of seconds, but it caused physical agony to ignore the pulse in Thorne's neck and the call of his blood. Interestingly, surfer slayer was about as appetizing as wet cardboard.

"I don't think we're in Kansas anymore, Toto," I addressed the imaginary dog at my feet.

Surfer slayer's eyes popped out just a little at my words. Once more his gaze roved over my exposed legs, Thorne's tee swallowing my torso but only just covering my butt. My hair wasn't mussed from sleep because I stayed completely still when I slept, the absence of bed head was one of the great things about being undead. My auburn locks tumbled down my back like I'd just strutted out of a shampoo commercial.

"I get it," he said immediately.

Thorne let out a warning sound in his throat as his gaze mirrored his friend's, though it was followed by a shadow of his phantom touch. Memories of the rough hands pinning me down as he drilled relentlessly into me.

My memories were cut short by another hunger pang that bolted through my midsection with the power to double me over. I stayed upright, but the sardonic smile flickered from my face.

Thorne caught it and was already halfway across the room when it hit. His breath was hot on my face the moment he came in front of me.

"Isla," he rasped. "You're alive."

I tilted my head, ignoring the pain in my stomach and the burn at my throat. I couldn't show weakness. Not even in front of the man who'd ravaged me within an inch of my afterlife a week before, then sheltered me through laevisomnus and threatened what I guessed was a close friend who'd suggested murdering me in my sleep.

And he may or may not love me.

"Not technically," I replied breezily as if that last thought hadn't chilled me to the bone. "But I'm not dead, so kudos for me." I gave him a thumbs-up.

"Could you tell me where we are, how I got here and then kindly direct me to my car?"

His gaze turned thunderous. "Could you fuckin' tell me how you collapsed in my goddamn arms and not even an open fuckin' vein has woken you up in a week?" His emotions flickered around him like a black cloak.

My head snapped up. "Open vein? Hate to break it to you, buddy, but unless you were trying to kill me for real, your open vein wouldn't do much," I lied.

His proximity had me tracing the journey of the blood pumping through him with every beat of his heart. I craved it. To sink my fangs into his neck was the promise of something even more than the blood Rick had given me a week back.

Nirvana perhaps.

Death certainly.

But the urge was so strong I had to dig my nails into palms and cut them open just to stay rooted in place.

His eyes hardened. "It wasn't me," he admitted through gritted teeth.

"Ditto with surfer boy over there." I nodded at the slayer who was watching the exchange with interest. "No offense," I added. "I'm sure your blood would make me all squidgy if it weren't for the whole 'toxic to vampires' thing."

Though his blood wasn't singing to me like Thorne's. Even as I tracked its journey around his body, the scent of it made my starved body recoil. Yet Thorne's was an oasis in the desert. Not good.

He grinned wide. "None taken, beautiful bloodsucker."

The way he used 'bloodsucker' as an endearment had me grinning.

"Sophie," Thorne continued.

I turned my attention back to the stormy gray eyes that searched my face like a man searching for flecks of gold in a pan.

"Sophie was here?" I asked, glancing around in case I'd missed my not-quite-a-wallflower best friend. "She's okay?"

Thorne nodded once, confusion knitting his features at my concern.

"Didn't tell you not to worry about a vase that you broke seconds afterwards?"

His brow furrowed further. "No."

Thorne obviously hadn't seen *The Matrix*.

"Didn't take any unexplained trips to colonial New York?" I continued. It was a risk even hinting to the powers that could get her dead if found out, but if they knew about them I'd sense the lie in the air. Then I'd have to do something about the knowledge.

Thorne looked at me like he was wondering where he could get a vampire straight jacket on short notice.

That was good. It was a look I got on the regular.

"Isla," he clipped, his voice full of the authority he had commanded his men, and my body, with.

My stomach dipped, making way for a new kind of hunger.

Only for a second; then my baser instincts for blood took over.

"Explanation," he demanded.

I let out an exaggerated sigh. I didn't rightly need to but it was the human marker for annoyance. "In case you didn't notice, I was involved in some strenuous activity at the house of horrors," I answered, and his eyes flared. "Killing witches who have a thousand years on me and can boil my blood kind of took it out of me."

I watched as Thorne's eyes flared for a different reason.

"She *boiled* your blood?" he repeated, his low rumble cutting through the air like razor blades.

I nodded. "Not an experience I'd recommend."

Thorne didn't glance behind him. "Silver, out," he commanded. "Go put that vamp in the barn into Isla's car, ready for transport." He paused, eyes never leaving mine. "Keep enough copper in him that he's out of action for a while. A long while."

My stomach dipped with different hunger pangs at his words.

Silver grinned and gave me a chin lift. I winked at him. "Nice to meet you." I couldn't resist putting my thumb and pinky finger up, shaking them in goodbye. "Hang ten, bro," I drawled.

His laugh followed him as he stepped outside the glass sliding door. "Same to you, bloodsucker," he murmured, knowing I could hear.

"I like him much better than No Neck," I informed Thorne. "Why don't you take him on missions? Seems to me he's less likely to get killed than No Neck—by me, that is."

Thorne regarded me. "Silver works in the lab. He doesn't come out in the field unless needed."

I raised my brow. His appearance certainly didn't translate to 'scientist' but then again, appearances rarely gave insight to the true person underneath.

"He's been dissecting the red-eyed freaks we tangled with last week?" I deduced.

Thorne nodded once.

I fought past my need for his blood. And his touch. "Did he find anything?"

The question hung in the air as Thorne watched my face with an intensity that had me rattled. "Later," he growled. "Now he's gone. And you're awake."

His hands moved up to frame my neck and his mouth fastened on mine, kissing me with a fervor that made me forget about my thirst for blood.

Heck, it made me forget I was a freaking vampire.

If it were possible for me to be breathless by the time he let me go, I would've been. Had I been human, his grip on my neck would have snapped my bones.

"You don't do that again," he ordered, his mouth inches from mine. "You just…." His jaw hardened. "You want to tell me why it felt like you fuckin' *died* in my arms the second after you made me feel more alive than a thousand battles could have?"

I jerked at his words, at the delayed effect of the kiss, at the fact that I was being held by a slayer.

"Like I said before, I've gone through a lot. You know, cursed with black magic for the second time in a day, throat ripped out, then…." I thanked everything that was unholy for my inability to blush. Never in my undead life had I been chaste when discussing sex. In this case, however, I felt like a fourteen-year-old virgin.

I decided to skip the fornication part of the evening. "I hadn't slept in…." I paused, mentally calculating. "Two months." Crap, had it been that long? "It usually wouldn't be a big problem, but I've had more injuries and blood loss in the past two weeks than I've seen in the last two years." I paused again. "Oh wait, there was the time that demon broke all the bones in my back. That didn't exactly involve blood, though, or battle."

Fury cloaked the air once more when he read between the lines.

Thorne was the jealous type.

I pretended that didn't get me a little hot as I stared at him. "Anyway, vampires don't need nearly the same amount of sleep as humans. Eight hours every twenty-four-hour period? How do you get anything done?" I waved my hand in a dismissive gesture before he could answer. "Young vampires need it more often, maybe twice a week, but it quickly becomes less necessary as long as you don't sustain too many injuries. If you've never slept with a vampire before"—I gave his granite jaw a pointed look—"which I'm betting you haven't, you wouldn't know that the expression 'slept like the dead' does in fact hold truth. Vampires have a heightened metabolism despite being technically dead, so in order to stay *un*dead we have to enter a sleep deeper than REM. It's the closest we come to taking the 'un' out of undead. The reason for everyone thinking vampires slept in coffins was because stupid humans stumbled upon a vampire taking a nap, stuffed him in a coffin, and then buried them. And vampires have no consciousness when they're under the cloak of laevisomnus, no control. Nothing short of copper through the heart could wake them long enough to kill them." I gave Thorne a look. "Which is why me giving a slayer such information makes my life already forfeit under vampire law, so I'd appreciate you keeping that little piece of intel to yourself."

His eyes blazed but he didn't respond.

I clicked my fingers in front of his face. "Earth to Buffy," I snapped. "Can you let me know you won't go blabbing like a sorority girl with a secret so I can make sure I don't have to rip your tongue out in the near future?"

"I won't tell anyone, Isla," he promised, though his eyes promised more than that.

I stared into them for a fleeting amount of time that was still too long.

Luckily the burning in my throat became too confronting to ignore. "Great. Now I've got to go. "

Thorne clutched my arms the second the words left my mouth. My muscles screamed out in both protest and ecstasy with the grip. My brain idly puzzled over the inhuman strength behind it. "What the fuck, Isla? You're not going anywhere. Not until you tell me exactly what the fuck is going on to make so many people try and take you from this earth," he commanded.

His heart was no longer a steady cadence as it had been before, as it was when he was battling off a horde of blood-thirsty abominations intent on ending him. No, it started to thunder the second he placed his hands on me.

I met his eyes, though his neck tempted me to gaze upon the pulse. I didn't. If I did, it was all over.

"That's just my life," I said tightly. "Granted, it's slightly more exciting than usual, but it's my business. Not yours. And you'll likely get dead if you continue to try and fight in a war that will swallow you in the abyss before it even starts."

His hands flexed. "So it is a war," he murmured.

I stayed silent.

"Between vampires?" he probed.

I eyed him. "Oh darling, it's much bigger than that. Too big for you."

He moved so his body brushed mine. "And yet here I am. Because you're in the middle of it, getting your throat ripped out and your blood boiled when you seem like the last person to be a soldier."

I jutted my chin up. "You're right. I'm not a person. I'm a *vampire*. The soulless creature you're destined to kill, remember?" I opened my mouth so my fangs elongated, the pull to his throat almost too hard to ignore. His eyes were my anchor.

"This has nothing to do with you," I continued coldly.

His eyes darkened. "It has to do with you, which means it has *everything* to do with me."

I couldn't handle it anymore. The thundering heartbeat, the overwhelming desire to commit what was tantamount to suicide just to get a taste of Thorne. Mostly I couldn't handle what he was implying.

Us.

I found my strength and placed two hands on his chest before I pushed him savagely so he all but flew across the room, landing solidly on the wall across from us. Plaster rained down on him from the force of the impact but he stayed upright.

I sauntered forward with a carefully blank look on my face as he wiped the blood from his forehead. All my strength went from remaining impassive and cold to fighting the inferno that his blood offered.

He stared at me, fists at his sides.

"You need to stay away from me," I warned him. "From this war. Because I promise you, if vampires on the other side of this don't kill you for getting involved, then I will." My voice was firm. An outsider would have noted the strength in that promise.

I wanted to believe it was true, yet I knew I'd likely sink my fangs into his neck and drink my death before I'd give him his.

It was a long moment before he spoke. Long enough for me to leave and do the smart thing.

The smartest thing would have been to kill him. Unable to do that, I should have left. I did neither. Merely waited while the sand in the hourglass trickled past.

"You want to lose your humanity because it's all getting just a little too real, fine." His eyes seared into mine. "But I'll hold onto it for you, until you're ready to find it again," he promised.

"You'll be clutching that until your echoing heart stops beating, then," I snapped coldly. "Humanity is a frightful side effect of mortality. And I don't plan on embracing mortality any time soon. Which is where you and I differ. Mortality is inevitable for you, so you have to deal with that pesky humanity. Me? I can avoid mortality altogether and the pain and horrors that come with it. And death. That's the big one I'm going to avoid. To avoid it, I avoid human attachments. Therefore, this"—I waved my hands between us—"needs to come to a conclusion."

"A conclusion?" he repeated, voice gruff.

I nodded.

He surged forward, his hands framing my face in a grip that I guessed might break a fragile human's jaw.

I was not a human. His touch was yet another reminder.

"There is no fuckin' conclusion to us," he growled, his gaze tattooing my soul. "No end. Even death doesn't signify the severing of this. Us. Nothing's gonna do that, baby. Something as inconsequential as a visit from the grim reaper sure as shit isn't gonna keep me from you. And we both know from living in this world that death is far from final."

I scowled at him, lifting my hand as if to caress his wrist holding mine, but instead exerting pressure to make him let go.

"My death is far from final. Yours, on the other fang? Fatal."

On that, I finally found my sense and left.

"Jeeves, never have I been happier to see you." I gave him a blinding smile.

He didn't return it. "The body of the traitor?" he asked evenly, as if asking where I put the groceries.

My grin didn't flicker. I nodded to the trunk. "Careful not to dislodge his head from his shoulders. There's only one tendon keeping it on. I may have got a little knife happy." I winked at him. The liquid copper that Silver had injected in his system was technically enough to keep him paralyzed with gut-wrenching pain, but I was pissed at the time, so I took it out on him.

I was generally more agreeable with a decent amount of blood in me. I'd had to spread out my breakfast across three different campers who'd stopped at a rest stop to consult a map. I'd quelled the burning in my throat and taken their map to find my way out to the city.

I owed Silver a great big favor, considering he'd made it so that Earnshaw was in my trunk and I was able to leave Thorne's isolated property in a whirl of dust. Though I did take a look around and deduced that the reason for the isolated location was because I was deep in slayer territory.

I didn't think on why the slayers hadn't gone against my wishes and killed the vampire; that's what they did, wasn't it? I'd spent the entire hour-and-a-half drive back into the city managing not to think of Thorne. I wasn't letting him invade my mind in the parking garage, in front of Jeeves no less.

I worried he could scent my treasonous thoughts. He'd run directly to his king to let him know I'd bumped uglies with our one true enemy and I'd be dead before my head hit the ground.

I kept my blinding smile. "I'm assuming Rick is upstairs, making himself at home?"

Jeeves kept his even stare. "Your king gives you the privilege of his presence and something nearly unheard of, his patience," he said, his voice the closest to a chastise that I'd ever heard.

I couldn't help but extend my smile. "What can I say, Jeeves? I'm worth waiting for." I winked at him, then turned on my heel towards the elevator. The last thing I wanted to do was share an enclosed space with Jeeves, Earnshaw, and Jeeves's disapproval of me.

My prediction had been correct. Rick was in what I considered to be his normal spot as I walked into the apartment, splayed on my newest blood-red sofa—I figured it might not show blood stains as much—feet on my new coffee table, which was reinforced steel, not glass. He was clad in a suit that was no doubt tailored; the way it molded over every ridge of his body was nothing short of magic. There was a black shirt underneath, open at his throat. He was clean-shaven, making his scar all the more pronounced.

"How'd you get that?" I greeted, feeling bold and suicidal, obviously.

I'd done some subtle digging, but no one knew about how the king got the scar.

He quirked a brow. "My father," he said without emotion. "Being a prince wasn't what the idiotic masses of humans conceive it to be."

I nodded. "I don't imagine it was."

Nothing else was said, though it didn't need to be. The mere fact that he offered the information up so readily was gesture enough.

"No need to dress up for little old me," I said, changing the subject before walking to the bar. "You're making me conscious of my state of undress." I'd had little choice in what to wear, but luckily I kept a change of clothes in my car. Arriving reeking of a human slayer might not have been the best plan if I'd wanted to survive the night. Still, the only thing I could keep in my car and not have wrinkle was cashmere leggings and a white buttery cashmere jumper, which draped to midthigh. It was winter casual chic and contrasted with my milky skin and red hair, but not exactly what one wore to greet the king. Or anyone for that matter. I may have adapted to most of humanity's changes, but this frightful trend of leaving the house in little more than loungewear had me murderous. Jeans made me positively homicidal.

Except on Thorne.

I could taste Rick's hungry gaze as I poured my whiskey. My stomach fluttered, yet it didn't respond as it had to—*Nope, Isla. Shut up.*

Thorne didn't exist for me. He couldn't. Otherwise, he wouldn't exist for anyone.

I drained my glass without even turning.

"I disagree. You do look rather fetching in all white," he argued, his voice velvet. "Innocent and pure. Angelic."

I turned, quirking my brow at the practiced look of seduction on his face. "If I'm an angel, does that make you the devil?" I retorted.

He was off the sofa and in front of me in mere seconds. "Oh no, Isla. I'm much more dangerous than that," he promised.

Why did that sound like a threat? He couldn't read my mind, so I was safe.

Plus, I had stopped by Sophie's office on my way back into the city. Earnshaw's memories of me and any slayers no longer existed.

As did any lingering imprint of his scent on my skin. Sophie had raised more than a brow at that but luckily she read my face and didn't offer any questions. Despite the magic that stole his scent, shadows of his touch lingered everywhere, tattooed on my mind. Sophie couldn't get rid of that.

Unfortunately.

I'd just have to live with it. Or die with it, depending on how this all played out.

I sipped my drink. "You certainly have as many enemies as the man downstairs," I quipped, ignoring the threat and the liquid sex in his voice. "Though you're down one vampire, a nasty witch and about a hundred humans they'd managed to turn into mindless vampires," I added casually.

His eyes turned glacial, all seduction gone from them. This was the king of all vampires in front of me, free of innuendo, and mercy. What remained was a coldhearted killer. You didn't rule millions of monsters without becoming one yourself.

It unnerved me, and though I was loath to admit it, scared me, as well. The wrath wasn't even directed at me. All the more reason never to see Thorne again—certain death.

Now why did pain knife through the cavity where my heart might be at that thought?

"They succeeded in turning humans to vampires?" he asked, his voice low, yet it could have smashed the glass in my apartment if it weren't shatterproof. I'd learned the hard way why that was necessary.

I nodded in response. "They don't have much brainpower

apart from 'attack' and 'serve thy sire' modes," I told him. "But strong enough to cause annoyance in a war, if it comes to that. Obviously they'd need serious numbers, which is a problem in itself."

A couple of humans going missing was one thing, but if they were intent on using them like I thought they were, it would amount to a small country. That wouldn't exactly go unnoticed.

"How did they do it?" he hissed. "Vampires have been trying and failing for centuries. Losing their heads for doing so."

I shrugged. "Sorry, above my pay grade." I realized that Thorne hadn't given me the lowdown on what Silver found with the ones he'd dissected and just hoped that vampire scientists could figure it out. If we couldn't do what humans could, then we deserved to go extinct.

As if on cue, Jeeves walked in with Earnshaw's body hoisted over his shoulder. "But here is the person who can describe in great detail the process he used to create these abominations at the same time as committing treason." I held out my hand. "I'm sure you and your minions have powers of persuasion. I'll leave that up to you." I held up my maroon nails. "Manicure means I have to give up torture for now, though it is one of my favorite pastimes."

Even in his fury, the corner of Rick's mouth twitched.

I moved my gaze. "Can you watch where you're holding him?" I asked. "He's dripping all over my favorite rug." I glared at Rick. "Why is it that, since you've come into my life, bloodstains have appeared on all my favorite things?"

Rick gave me a look. "Because the best things always come covered in blood."

I was going to just let that one fly right over my head.

"What would you like me to do with him, sire?" Jeeves

asked, pointedly ignoring me.

He wouldn't when I ripped his hands off for being such a twat.

"Take him home, Sven," Rick said. He glanced at me. "I don't have minions to do the torturing. I do it all myself. Not only am I the best at inflicting pain, but it's a deterrent for those who think of crossing me. Even the most callous of my men have mercy." He gave me a pointed look. "I do not."

Again the unspoken threat had me uneasy. Did I have a 'I let a slayer fuck me senseless and we have an unnatural connection' sign plastered on my head?

"Well my work here is done," I said instead. "I'll be taking my retirement now. Do I get a gold watch and a pension?"

I'd have to find another way to get my parents in the ground; this little assignment was more than likely going to get me tasting the grave if I didn't stop. I couldn't even decide to take an extended holiday since I knew my parents would be waiting for that.

Rick glanced at me. "You're not done," he told me.

I stared at him. "I'm not done?" I repeated. "I found you a solid lead about how this faction is gaining traction, and almost died—" I paused to mentally calculate. "—three times in the process. I'm *done*."

He shook his head. "You've proved gifted, getting results not even my most trusted soldiers have been able to boast."

"It's all just dumb luck," I argued. "It's only a matter of time before one of the many, *many* attempts on my life is successful. Your health benefits suck too."

"You can handle it," he countered.

"The witch who almost killed me would beg to differ," I shot back, folding my arms.

His face changed, only slightly but it was palpable. "Witch?"

I nodded. "A nasty one too. Why didn't the idiots at Salem catch her?" I screwed up my nose. "Beetlejuice or something was her name."

Ice filled the room. "Belladonna?" he corrected in a rough voice.

I pointed at him. "Yep. That's it. What is that? The name of a cheap bottle of wine?"

He didn't find me funny. "No," he murmured eyes faraway. "The name of a witch in an ancient sect thought to be banished from this world. Locked away in the last of the wars."

I raised my brow. "There's more of her?" I asked, not relishing the thought of meeting any other witches like her.

He nodded once. "She is but the weakest of them."

"Great," I muttered. "She was powerful enough to give me a permanent dislike for the bitches with pointy hats." That didn't include Sophie, obviously. She had much better taste in headwear. But it was better for the king not to know I had a witch on my side.

Whatever side that was.

He was pensive for a long while, considering my words as I considered his. It didn't bode well that some witches banished by their own kind in alliance with vampires had broken out of their cage. Not well at all.

Rick emerged from his own head around the same time I did.

His expression stayed the same, yet his eyes traveled down my body with concern. "That's why you haven't been in contact for a week?" he deduced.

I nodded. "Required a small catnap to recharge the batteries."

His eyes searched my face. "Yet you did not engage in laevisomnus here," he said.

I shook my head. "Too much foot traffic."

His emerald eyes glistened. "May I enquire as to the location of your slumber?"

I quirked my brow. "Not on your undeath."

Another shadow of a grin. "I would offer my quarters for guaranteed safety. If you so wished."

I walked to the bar. "Safety is an illusion. And I'm guessing residing anywhere near the king the mad vampires and witches are plotting to overthrow is the furthest thing from that."

His hand gripped my wrist before I could pour my drink. "I can protect you, Isla," he promised, his voice thick.

I glanced up to him. "I don't need a male to protect me. In fact, it seems of late that I've been the protector." I gave him a pointed look to remind him of the Majestic and all the behind-the-scenes work I'd been doing. I didn't mention the behind-the-scenes work saving slayers, though this double-agent business was getting exhausting. Furthermore, I didn't even know which side I was loyal to anymore. "I'll take a pass," I said finally, ripping myself from his grasp.

"I realize this task has become somewhat of an annoyance," he began.

I raised my brow at him. "Annoyance? No, an annoyance is my hair getting stuck in my lip gloss on a windy day. This"—I waved my hand around the room—"is a fucking catastrophe. A tsunami you've brought into my life, set about destroying everything, and then trying to convince me it's just a little wave. You're delusional if you think I'm going to do any more of this shit. Delusional in the bad way, not the hot kind of crazy that makes me all tingly with the hotness of unbridled, carnal insanity. No, the kind that requires medication or euthanasia," I ranted.

His eyes, which had turned midnight right about the

'tingly' portion of my monologue, sparked with hunger and danger, and he was in my space in a split second.

I was prepared, my hand tightened around the blade inside my jacket, which I may or may not have borrowed from my 'friend' the slayer. It wasn't like he'd notice; by the looks of it, he didn't keep the best tabs on the only weapon that would keep him killing the 'creatures' he was born to exterminate.

I decided it was in much better hands with me.

"You forget yourself, Isla," he murmured, his voice even but deep and winding with meaning. "If you threaten your king, or disobey him, it doesn't matter if you've wrapped it up in your version of seduction. That act in itself will result in death." His hand went to a tendril of my hair. "The only thing you've done with your feminine wiles has me certain I'll be fucking you before I punish you," he rasped, his threat both terrifyingly morbid and erotic at the same time.

He didn't say any more, didn't move, just kept staring at me in that horribly blank yet somehow loaded stare.

I didn't want to back down. Fuck, I was a Rominskitoff; our family didn't back down. I hadn't backed down to anyone outside said family in the last four hundred and fifty-seven years.

My mind stuttered on a certain slayer who was not only still breathing, but whose lips I still tasted on my own. Whose body was still imprinted into every one of my pores.

I hoped the king didn't catch his residual scent. Then we'd stop the seduction portion of the evening and move right on to the execution. It may be frowned upon to marry and sleep with humans, but it wasn't illegal. Slayers, on the other hand? Even having a conversation with one that didn't end in you breaking their neck could be punished with imprisonment.

Sleeping with one?

Yeah, certain death.

It seemed two men—one mortal, one immortal—were producing various forms of surrender. One may be the final end of my existence, the other possibly promising the beginning. The problem was I couldn't quite distinguish one from the other.

My grip loosened on the blade, then completely released it.

His face didn't change, but he relaxed slightly and stepped back.

"Good choice, Isla," he said, betraying knowledge of my little weapon.

Damn it, I thought I'd been so stealthy.

He stepped back, buttoning the front of his jacket, eyes on me. "I've got an event at my compound in two days' time. You'll be accompanying me."

I folded my arms. We'd gone from death threats to dates in the blink of an eye. Standard practice for kings who just happened to be vampires, I presumed. "Will I now?" I challenged. "I know I'm a tempting and rather fetching choice for a date, but there's a reason that your little ball last month was the first time you'd seen me at one of those. I avoid any bureaucratic vampire gathering like I do Birkenstocks. They're not my thing, and the vampires who attend are lower than demons in my regard. I was well-behaved last time mainly because I wasn't there for long and my family had…." I tried to think of a way to euphemize the fact that they'd threatened to murder children had I not gone. "Somewhat of an incentive for me to attend," I finished. "This time, if Lucifer is feeling generous, they won't be attending and therefore I have no such incentive."

His icy gaze settled on mine. "Apart from your king's command."

I raised a brow at him. "You really need to *command*

yourself a date? You're a nice-looking monarch, I'm sure you can procure yourself a lovely vampire from a better family who is much more popular in your chosen circles. And one not likely to behead many of the guests out of boredom before the night's over," I said, only half joking. There was a reason people were uneasy to see me at such gatherings, regardless of the fact that the last incident happened well over a century ago.

He stepped forward. "You'll be coming," he declared. "I don't need to command anything when it comes to dates or the bedroom. Most women line up for the former and beg for the latter."

I gave him an even look. "I don't beg," I told him, voice hard.

That murderous coldness returned to his eyes.

"Even for your life?" he asked, the entangled promise of death if I refused left unsaid.

I tilted my chin up. "Especially for my life."

Our connection was tangible enough to be cut with a blade before a shadow of a grin crept at the corner of his lips. "Your strength has me all the more eager to break you," he murmured.

I smiled at him. "I don't break easily. Or at all."

"I don't doubt it," he returned. "My intentions are not completely noble at wanting you at this gathering."

I rose my brow once more. "No shit," I said sarcastically. "I wasn't under the impression that *any* of your intentions were noble."

He chose to ignore that, luckily for me I guessed. "I've purposefully invited most of the people I suspect to this gathering, I cannot go ahead and do any sort of investigation on them as I'll be watched the whole time. Which is why you're in my employ. Well, maybe not the whole reason," he corrected. "Even the king cannot break Theoxenia and conduct violence against those he's invited under his roof and shared blood with."

Theoxenia was the oldest and most treasured of all laws of our race. Even the most rebellious of vampires—me—obeyed it. It was ancient Greek mythology, where our race was arguably born, that hospitality be granted to guests of a blood gathering. It extended to those who accepted that hospitality and shared mortal blood with the host. Or any form of hospitality offered by the host. Should they spill Ambrogio's blood after that, they forfeited their immortality. Hence the fact that I was yet to kill anyone at a blood gathering.

Until now, it seemed.

I offered him a sly smile. "So the king wants me at his party in order to break the most ancient of all vampire laws? I'm warming up to the idea now."

He moved forward. "Not break it," he hissed. "Merely bend it. But I will break your head off your neck if you utter this to anyone." His voice smoothed over the threat.

I continued grinning. "Why of course. It's only the best secrets that offer death as the punishment for sharing them."

He stepped back, his mask firmly on. "I'll send a car for you at midnight." He gave my attire a once-over. "As enticing as the white is, I think this calls for something a little more…."

"Sinful?" I finished for him.

His eyes glittered. "Quite," he agreed before turning on his heels.

I didn't get a moment's peace. I had to go shopping.

For something that I hopefully wouldn't die in.

ELEVEN

As a vampire and couture addict, my closet was full of sinful. But I needed something that would communicate that while offering me enough movement to fight my way out of the party if need be.

Which proved a challenge at first. Why designers didn't offer dresses which lent themselves to death-match battles was beyond me.

All the best parties ended in bloodshed. Clothing should be designed for that fact.

While I walked down balmy Fifth Avenue, my perfect sinful and fighting dress swinging in the wind, my phone chimed. I'd already fielded calls from Sophie after I'd been out of the king's presence, to reassure her that he had not executed me.

Yet.

"You sure you're okay?" Sophie had asked for the

hundredth time.

"No one ever describes me as *okay*, Soph." I wandered down the street, enjoying the fact that I'd had an uneventful six hours since I left Thorne's presence. I ignored the part of me that yearned for that presence.

A big part.

"People and vampires alike describe me as beautiful, unforgettable, manic, murderous, but never merely okay."

She snorted. "Narcissism in full swing means okay," she muttered. Then there was a loaded pause. "And you killed her? The witch?"

"Yes, I did. Not a moment too soon either. Nasty piece of work that one. And apparently not the only one of her kind," I mused, remembering Rick's words.

"What?" Sophie all but hissed into the phone.

"What do you know about a witch called Belladonna?"

Static filled the line, a crackling sound making me yank the phone from my ear to make sure it didn't explode. When I was satisfied that it wouldn't, I put it back. There was still silence.

I waited.

"Are you saying that's who she was?" Sophie whispered.

I shrugged. "Apparently. And is it right that she's got some bunkmates who may be out and about?"

"Yes, Isla," Sophie said, her voice as flat as I'd ever heard it. It filled me with foreboding.

"It's not good, is it?" I guessed.

"No. Not good at all."

I rolled my eyes. "Of course. I've killed one. The rest should be a breeze."

Cue another pause. "And she didn't use magic before she died?"

I scoffed. "Of course she did. She may have been an evil, sadistic shrew but she was smart. Good thing I'm smarter. And stronger. And much, much prettier. You didn't want to see behind her mask. It was like Donald Trump without the makeup." I shuddered, reaching the foyer of my building.

Silence over the phone.

I paused. "Witchy? Have you dropped dead over there?" I asked.

"No," Sophie said, voice strange. "I'm very much alive, and glad you are too."

I laughed. "Well, in a manner of speaking."

"And you were with Thorne. For the entire week?" She changed the subject at vampire speed.

I tensed. "Yes, I was. Lying unconscious and dead, if you didn't recall," I snapped.

"But you woke up there." I heard the grin in her voice. "And to him. In his bed."

"Yes, and I got up, considered draining him and his slayer friend, thought better of it, and left."

"That's all?"

I scowled at her, wishing she could see my death glare. "That's all," I hissed.

And I may have had the most amazing sex of my afterlife in an abandoned house littered with corpses after we'd killed a witch who had almost murdered me. Then when I woke up, he had declared something dangerous like his undying love for me. I sure as shit wasn't going to tell her that. I was on my way to convincing myself it never happened. Five hundred years had me pretty good at denial for the sake of self-preservation.

Love was never undying. Especially with a mortal. It died, an ugly and bloody death.

I was the only thing that didn't.

I cannot die, which means I cannot love. Because eternity with the shadow, with the ghost of a dead love, was a forever of death.

"Riiight."

"Whatever. We need to be focusing on catching these slimeballs who turn humans and plot against our race so I can get back to my normal, peaceful life."

Sophie snorted. "You wouldn't know normal if it ripped your throat out."

"Well a decidedly abnormal vampire came up to me not one week ago and ripped my throat out. It's almost the same thing."

"And peaceful? Peace for you is when you only have one member of your family trying to kill you while you screw a demon and fight a werewolf."

"That didn't all happen at the same time," I argued for the sake of clarity. Even I had limits. "It was spread out over a week."

Sophie laughed. "Okay, so to get us back to our peaceful lives, I'll get to work on figuring out who in my community has a hand in helping vampires turn humans. I'll bet my Metallica tickets she wasn't working alone."

I perked up. "You have Metallica tickets?"

"Already have one for you. It's good incentive to survive the week."

Sophie was already doing her work, so I had to do mine.

Which meant subduing my crazy half-breed stalker once I got into my apartment and answered his seventh phone call. I'd ignored the first six.

"Isla," he practically screamed into the phone.

I screwed up my nose. "If it were possible for my eardrums to pop, I think you would have done it," I answered.

He ignored me.

"Where have you been?" he asked. "I hadn't heard from you in a week. I thought you were dead. For real." He whispered the last part as if saying it aloud would snatch my afterlife from his grasp.

"Not dead, just busy." I didn't elaborate. It wasn't that I didn't trust Scott; after all, he'd done everything he could to help Sophie and kept his mouth shut. He was like a loyal puppy, though at that point I thought kicking him might not get him off my fricking leg. It was either kill him or get used to him.

"Well I can help with whatever you need. Are we going out for humans tonight? I've already found some we could use. Plus, I've been looking into vampires who haven't been logging any kills, especially ones with previously high volumes. I'm thinking those could be the ones turning humans—"

"Jesus Christ," I hissed at Scott, reflecting on my earlier thoughts. "You don't say shit like that over the phone while you're in a building full of fucking vampires who are searching for a reason to kill you," I snapped. "Silence is golden. We'll meet after I go to this insidious gathering tomorrow night. I've got a mountain of work to do for my real job and then have to stop a vampire war. I can't babysit you too. For now, try not to do anything stupid that would get you killed—or even worse, get me involved."

I hung up on him before he painted an even bigger target on his back.

The one on mine was already getting too hard to hide.

I glanced down at my phone, grateful for the reprieve from spending six hours unmoving, staring at my computer screen.

Events of the last twenty-four hours plagued my mind. Not purely the memories of blood that that hellish witch brought to the surface, though that had me feeling a little… off.

No, it wasn't that. Or the battle. It was Thorne. Every inch of my mind seemed to be consumed with the slayer.

The human, I chanted to myself. Despite the fact that it was punishable by death to associate with slayers, it didn't follow my 'no humans' rule. There was a reason I only whored myself around the supernatural community over the past few centuries—humans died. Attachments didn't die with them, though. They stayed with me and my undying mind; hence the reason it was a little unhinged.

The thought of Thorne dying had me wanting to throw my desk out of my window. Which was precisely why he was dangerous to me and the pedestrians forty floors down.

I swirled in my chair as I snatched up my phone. "Speak," I answered.

"Isla?"

I rolled my eyes.

"Santa?" I whispered back.

There was a loaded pause. "Yes, this is Isla," Rick deduced smoothly.

"You're calling me? The king himself? Don't you have servants for that?" I asked.

Another pause. "I do. They dial for me."

I stared at the horizon. "Did you just make a joke? Oh my gosh, you did. What a wondrous day to be undead."

"Earnshaw talked," Rick clipped, obviously not liking small talk.

I relaxed in my chair. "Of course he did. He's a coward. Cowards talk. What's the goss?" I kept my voice even; this was the moment of truth to see if Sophie's spells worked. I would so kill her if they didn't and it got me dead.

"Nothing of import. Apart from how his… disciples were made," he explained, though not outright saying 'the humans he turned into vampires.' The fact that he was wary of speaking of it over the phone meant he was wary of those who could overhear him. What a world he lived in, when I was the only one he could trust.

That did not mean good things.

"You'll fill me in at this wretched ball you're throwing, I'm sure," I muttered, wincing at the prospect.

"Indeed," he agreed.

"Unless you want me to go fight bloodthirsty animals and a witch again and almost die? I can do that instead," I offered hopefully.

"No, Isla. Your job tomorrow night is to be on my arm and infiltrate the traitors."

I rolled my eyes. "James Bond made it seem so much more fun. What else has Earnshaw got that I can actually use?" I asked.

"Most of his dealings were done through an intermediary at Extermius," Rick explained.

I cocked my brow. "Interesting, but not entirely surprising. The patronage at that bar aren't lovers of the human race. I'll check it out. Tomorrow night work?"

"Isla," he warned.

I gritted my teeth. "Fine."

Rick didn't speak, but I could hear the rustling of clothes and the steady echo of footsteps on the other side of the phone.

"No, you hang up first," I cooed, my voice saccharine sweet.

"What?" His smooth voice was marred with confusion.

I spun on my chair. "Oh, were we not playing that human game to see who could sever the riveting conversation we're currently having? I thought you were struggling to hang up."

His sigh rippled through the phone. "There's one more thing. It's of little import, and actually one thing that these miscreants are doing that might benefit us."

"Whatever could that be? Killing the human responsible for those wretched *American Idol* shows? Bravo."

He ignored me, as was becoming his habit. "Apparently, they're attacking the slayer compound, in about—" He paused as if glancing down at his watch. "—twelve minutes. I would send a team out there to capture the rebels, but likely they'll be mindless soldiers who know little more than Earnshaw. I'll wait until they've exterminated those pests and then perhaps I'll send someone to pick up the leftovers," he mused.

I swallowed the ash at my throat. "Oh, don't bother yourself with that," I said, my voice easy. "I do love myself a good slayer genocide. I've got a free hour or so in my schedule, so I'll whip out and interrogate, then get rid of the leftovers," I offered.

There was a pause. "I thought you were unhappy about being involved in this any more than you had to be," he replied, voice flat but questioning nonetheless.

"Unhappy would be an understatement," I scoffed. "But I don't do things by halves, so now that I'm in, I may as well be all-in. And this might actually be fun."

"I'll assign you a team," he said after he digested my words. Something I was learning about the king was he took great care in analyzing every word of a conversation before replying. It was dangerous, especially since I had to go to extreme effort to disguise the unreasonable panic in my belly.

"Ugh. No, thanks. The stiffs will just turn my fun into something like getting my fangs ripped out," I replied. "I work better alone."

"Your confidence is admirable but your death would be… inconvenient, so I'll not permit you to go alone," he said firmly.

I clenched my fist. "I don't do well with people permitting me or forbidding me to do things, nor doubting my mad skills," I said through my fangs. "But since your concern warms the cockles of my heart, I won't go alone. Though I won't take your GI Jeeves. I've got my own team."

"You've got a *team*?" he asked, disbelief clear in his tone. "A collection of vampires who don't want you to see the grave?"

I would have smiled, if not for the bitter taste of death on my tongue. I stood quickly, shrugging on my leather jacket and darting through my office. My employees glanced up at the breeze that rustled papers on their desks, but their human eyes saw nothing. "If I didn't know you any better, Rick, I would've thought you just made something resembling a joke," I said as I bypassed the elevator to dart down the forty flights of stairs it took me to get to the parking garage. "I've got a team," I lied. Scott was one half breed who likely didn't know how to fight his way out of a ComicCon, but he was better than nothing. Actually, he was worse than nothing, considering I'd probably have to spend half my time saving him from death, but I couldn't lie to the king. I knew his practiced ears would hear it, even from my own practiced mouth. So I went for a variation of the truth.

"As you wish," he relented, surprisingly. "But if you die in this fight, I will be most displeased."

I got into my car, wasting no time in roaring through the garage. "Well I'd rather die than displease you, sire, so I'll make sure to stay on this side of the earth, at least until you're done with me," I replied sweetly.

"In that case, indefinitely," he replied, his voice ragged instead of smooth.

I narrowed my eyes at the response, but didn't have time to question it as I was met with dead air on the other side of the line.

I glanced down at my phone. "Couldn't he just say 'goodbye' once in awhile?" I asked myself as I dialed the one half-breed who would come running when I called.

I only hoped I wasn't getting him running to his death.

Or mine.

Or Thorne's.

The latter had me pressing my foot down harder on the accelerator without even considering why the thought of Thorne six feet under had my entire body shuddering.

I smelled the blood in the air before I even pulled down the dirt road to the compound I'd scouted before I'd left Thorne's. I had thought it'd be good to know the layout for a rainy day.

And it was pouring.

Thorne's house was small and isolated, wilderness on all sides save for the barn and the dirt road leading in and out of it. A few minutes away was what seemed to be a small suburban settlement in the middle of nowhere. It was nestled in the trees and off any main highways so no one could stumble upon it. At the time I'd been focusing on the burn in my throat so I couldn't do too much spying, but the little community seemed to be full of slayers.

"This is exciting." Scott's voice cut through the bitter taste that had filled the interior of the car as I skidded down the road.

For once, I was grateful for his chatter. I gave him a sideways look. "Exciting?" I repeated.

He nodded, tapping his fingers on his thigh with one hand, the other gripping the copper blade I'd given him. I'd decided against a gun which I'd had in the back, equipped with copper bullets, not putting it past him to shoot himself before we even got to the battle. If the sounds of ripping flesh and screams were anything to go by, the battle was well in play and the slayers were not doing well.

At all.

I gripped the steering wheel, calculating that I had about one minute until I reached them.

Hopefully they could hold on that long. But a minute was a long and lethal stretch of time in a battle, especially for humans.

"Yes, seeing action," Scott babbled. "And working for the king. I mean… wow. I never thought I'd be in such an important position… well, ever," he breathed.

I glanced at him again. "It's not an important position if you die while you're doing it. Do me a favor and don't do that," I requested. "Are you sure you have passable knowledge of how to use that thing?" I asked uncertainly, glancing to the blade.

Thirty seconds.

He nodded, but I didn't miss the slight twitch in his eyes.

He had no idea.

"Stick them with the pointy end," I instructed. "In the temple, preferably. The heart isn't ideal because it's not as easy to find when it's not beating, and you'll likely get your throat ripped out while you're trying to dislodge it from a very pissed-off vampire's rib cage."

He glanced down at the blade. "Temple. Got it."

Ten seconds.

"Okay, it's almost go time. You're here more as an extra body. I don't expect heroics." I could see a blur of bodies up ahead. The blood was unmistakable that time.

"And remember, don't kill the slayers. Vampires only," I told him firmly.

To his credit, he didn't even question it. Only another nod.

I slammed on my brakes before I hit a building.

"Okay, go time. Remember, your main incentive is not to die," I reminded him.

I was out of the car and snapping a rogue vampire's neck as soon as the last word left my mouth. Blood and death encircled my body as I regarded the cluster of houses, littered with bodies of humans and vampires in various states of death. I scanned the fight, listening for the thumping heartbeat that had become the soundtrack to most of my thoughts.

I was slammed back into a building before I had time to do so.

Because I'd been distracted, I had let the vampire crush my collarbone. I ignored the pain and focused on jumping up just in time to meet another onslaught.

Now that I was focused, I could see it wasn't another vampire who had broken my collarbone and pissed me off, but a red-eyed freak with snapping teeth and a disconcerting amount of strength. I didn't remember them packing the same amount of punch at the mansion.

Not having time to contemplate it, I focused on dispatching this one quickly.

The rip of flesh was satisfying. I moved to my next target just as it was bending over a woman scrambling for her knife, blood covering her face. The vampire crumpled to the side and she gazed up at me in dazed shock.

I grinned at her. "You're welcome." Then I kicked the knife into her grasp and went about saving the day.

When I had done a lazy recon of the compound, I'd

counted at least forty heartbeats in the scattered commune. Now they'd be lucky to have twenty.

I gritted my teeth when I witnessed a small familiar-looking human standing in the middle of the battle, gripping a bloodstained knife.

I took down the red-eyed freak heading to her before snatching her up and running to a building that looked like it wouldn't have as much of a chance of getting her killed.

Her eyes widened as I set her down in the middle of the room. "Isla," she breathed.

I ignored that and detached her hand from mine. "Stay here," I ordered. "And for Lilith's sake, don't die."

I left her in the house, but not before I picked up a dresser and placed it on the outside of the door.

I glanced through the battle, eyes glazing over the slayers. I noticed a familiar blond head yanking a blade out of the temple of a fallen vampire. I whistled and, surprisingly, he turned. I pulled the gun from my belt and tossed it to him.

He caught it on reflex, glancing down at it, then up to me.

"More effective than that." I nodded to the knife before throwing him an extra clip.

A low boom vibrated through my rib cage and I whirled around to see Thorne taking on two red-eyed assholes, blood streaming down his temple and more staining his gray tee. The sheer scent of it wafted through the battle, mingled with the bitter tang of death in the air, and enticed me with its sweetness. His muscles bulged as he took down the first who charged at him, then the other in a smooth and unhurried movement that contradicted the simple fact that he was human and, despite these things not being full fangers, they were still strong. Much stronger than he should have been. His movements were sure, purposeful, made without hesitation and exemplifying his experience in fighting assailants of the fanged persuasion.

After he made short work of putting a blade in each of their temples, his eyes found mine. The chaos stilled around us, like we'd slipped through a crevice in time. His gaze widened and blazed over my body, which, until then, had been in a perpetual state of chill.

I welcomed the flames and managed to claw away from the crevice that I longed to remain in. There was a battle to be fought.

My vision of Thorne was obstructed by a rather inconsiderate abomination, intent on ripping my throat out. I returned the favor before darting to Thorne.

"What are you doing here?" he growled as we both took on separate attackers.

I dispatched mine and circled behind his to snap its neck. "Isn't it obvious?" I asked after the vampire fell to the ground, leaving us facing each other. Thorne was breathing heavily, his eyes locked on mine.

I grinned at him. "I'm riding in to save the day." I gave him a wink before scanning the battle. The remaining slayers were bloodied, and their faltering heartbeats told me they wouldn't last long.

The entire area between the houses was filled with the red-eyed hybrids. From what little I'd learned about them, I knew they wouldn't be working of their own accord. Their sire had to be close by.

I glanced back to Thorne. "You do your best to make sure your friends don't become corpses decorating this place, and I'll find the vampire with the controls for all of these." I gestured to the twitching body at my feet. "And turn them off."

Thorne's hand gripped mine before I could leave him to hopefully not become a corpse.

"I'm kind of busy—"

I was cut off by the quick and brutal press of his lips against mine.

The fire that had simmered with his gaze became an inferno in the small collection of seconds that his mouth was on mine.

He released me. "Be careful," he demanded roughly.

"I'm never careful," I replied before turning to the area that was free of heartbeats and had a cold stillness that was unnatural for such a battle. The fire quickly doused in my belly when I located the source.

I ran through the door, skirting the discarded dresser that had once been barring it and coming to an abrupt stop when I saw a pale figure standing inches away from a smaller one.

Both heads darted to me. One was frantic and slightly panicked, the other cool and detached with a slim smile stretched across her face.

"So the rumors are true," she purred. "Isla Rominskitoff is batting for the other team."

I glared at her. "I have in the past, but now I like them male. You're going to have to find another rug to munch."

She quirked her brow, folding her arms casually. "Still as uncouth as always."

"Better that than dead," I snapped back. "Which is what you'll be in about two-point-five seconds."

She grinned. "Oh I wouldn't be so sure."

My eyes fastened on the child who seemed intent on dying before she reached puberty. "Run, you little idiot," I hissed.

To give her credit, she did it just in time.

The vampire in front of me pounced. I was ready for it, but we still crashed through the walls of the house, each of us landing in a crouch on the grass outside.

I straightened, circling her, as did she. "Your empty womb must have been troubling if you had to create these abominations," I said, nodding around to the red eyes that remained. "I'm sorry to say that your children are assholes."

The fist that slammed into my jaw was expected, but the pain was still not desirable. I captured her hand and snapped it so the wrist was only attached by one stubborn tendon.

I grinned at her screech of pain and wiped the blood from my mouth.

I slammed another fist into her chest, concaving her ribs so they shattered inwards.

She toppled to the ground and I stood over her. "That was so easy, it's just embarrassing," I told her, preparing to detach her shiny black head from her body.

Through the pain on her pinched face, she grinned. "Unlike you, I'm not easy."

It was then that a body barreled into my back and landed atop me on the grass. I dodged the snapping teeth, although not entirely as they tore into my neck enough to smart. I frowned at the vampire before placing my hands on either side of its head and twisting.

I tossed it aside and it was then that I realized the reason for the bitch's grin.

Every single red eye in the place had abandoned its slayer battle and was focused on me.

Great.

"Hiding behind your minions?" I asked conversationally while fighting the first wave of them. "That's just cowardly."

"That's survival," she hissed through the bodies. "These are the warriors of a new tomorrow. It will put me in the master's favor if I am the one to rid him off the Rominskitoff slut."

I gritted my teeth as I fought them off. The sounds of

gunshots had my head turned momentarily to see Thorne wading through the horde.

"Get you and your merry band of slayers out of here," I gritted. "I've got this."

He didn't glance at me. "Not a fucking chance."

I huffed and continued dispatching the wall of red eyes.

It didn't escape me that a couple of slayers, including the mousy-haired woman from the start of the battle, had joined the fray. And the kid. The twit.

Despite that, and my efforts, it seemed that things were not going to end well. I could only fight off so many, as the torn flesh that was getting ripped as quickly as it healed communicated.

I met Thorne's eyes once more. They were hard, determined. But resignation flickered in them, an acknowledgement of the inevitable fate.

Just as I was about to open my mouth and whisper a goodbye that would have sounded very similar to a declaration of an emotion I'd sworn off centuries before, every single snapping body froze. Like a robot that'd had its switches pulled, they all just stopped, standing much too straight, their previously frenzied eyes empty and unseeing.

And then they all fell to the ground in an anticlimactic synchronicity.

I blinked at the ground, then looked up to the area where I'd last heard the triumphant voice of the female vampire.

My eyes did not prepare me for what I saw.

Scott grinned at me, half his boyish face covered in blood. He had a gaping wound in his shoulder and his khakis were torn beyond repair, a blessing in my opinion. And he had a blade embedded in the temple of the vampire who had almost bested me.

Then he gave me a thumbs-up.

Silence settled heavily over the remaining survivors, which I could count as to be about three less than the number that had been there when I arrived.

The morbid atmosphere of death was stifling, but all I focused on was Scott's stupid grin and the stares of the slayers on the half breed who had saved them all.

Her death was preferable but now there was no one to interrogate, which had us back to square one. You couldn't interrogate a corpse.

"Isla!" a small voice squealed, and then something attached itself around my middle.

The scent of bubblegum radiated off the strawberry curls. I held my hands out to make sure I didn't make contact, screwing my nose up at Thorne, who was standing amidst the scattered bodies, his chest moving heavily, his body stained with blood. "Get it *off* me," I gritted out.

"I knew you'd come," she said, looking up at me through the gaps in her hair.

Thorne crossed his bloodstained arms, eyes blank, but if I weren't mistaken, there was a glint in his eye. I glared at him. "Your innocent and fragile little sibling is touching a creature of the night, a demon who drinks blood, a monster," I told him. "Shouldn't you be doing something about that?"

He cocked his brow. "I *am* doing something."

I glared down at the head of hair again. "You can release me now. I'm sure your gratitude has been communicated."

She gave me one last squeeze and then grinned up at me, not blinking at the bodies littered around her.

"You're very strange," I observed.

Cue a bigger grin. "Thanks."

"It wasn't a compliment," I muttered.

I glanced to Scott, who was watching this exchange

carefully. I didn't miss the fact that he didn't attack the remaining slayers, who were looking at us with gazes from unease to murderous. It was hanging on a precipice whether they'd attack or not, even though we'd saved their lives.

Centuries of being mortal enemies did not get cancelled out with one battle.

Though Scott wasn't as well versed on slayer law as I was, I knew that he understood this to be unusual to say the least. But he didn't blink that we were saving the slayers.

And perhaps I was insane, but I trusted him to heed my commands and keep whatever happened there on lockdown. He may have a big mouth, but secrets wouldn't slip out of it.

I was betting my afterlife on it.

Thorne stepped forward, yanking his sister into his embrace roughly, kissing her head. "You did good today, kid," he murmured. "But I want you to go with Kathy to the safe house," he instructed as he let her go.

A bloodstained woman in jeans and a tee stepped forward. She smiled warmly at the girl and then at Thorne with a definable twinkle in her eye.

I balled my fists.

I hated Kathy.

"Sure, Thorne. You've got"—she turned to me, eyes no longer bright but cold and smug. "Trash to take out."

She snatched the girl's hand.

Must not murder slayer.

Why? I had no idea.

Then my eyes fastened on steely gray ones.

Oh, that was why.

"Why are you here?" he asked, the word echoing in the open air.

I pretended not to notice the way the weary and

bloodstained slayers hung on that question. I shrugged. "I was in the neighborhood."

He narrowed his eyes, but then an unfamiliar human stepped forward, his face swelling with what I guessed was a broken cheekbone as he limped obviously. His clothes were ripped and there were various areas of torn skin where the red eyes had managed to latch on. It was impressive that he was still standing, let alone glowering at me with such a look of hatred that it must've taken physical effort to maintain.

"What does it matter why she's here?" he hissed. "She needs to die. Just like her friends, who attacked us. *Killed* Brody, Susan, Alexia."

Loss and anger were a dangerous combination.

"Friends?" I repeated softly. "Yes, the mindless vampire zombies who I just ruined my shoes killing were my friends. We just pretend to fight and murder each other, but I'll be sharing a vein with them all back at our concrete mansion where we sacrifice goats on the regular." I rolled my eyes. "How dense are you? I just risked my own afterlife to save your miserable one. 'Thanks' is the word you're looking for. I also accept Barneys vouchers." I knew he'd suffered a loss and should be handled with care, but I wasn't that vampire. I saved their lives; that was downright maternal for me. Coddling them for losing people was a surefire way to foster the softness and humanity that would ensure their extinction.

He stepped forward, gripping his knife. Scott was at my side in an instant as a couple of other men tightened their bodies, poised for attack.

Thorne snatched the man from the air before he could do anything suicidal.

"No, brother," Thorne murmured.

I gripped Scott's wrist. "Easy," I said, my voice too low for human ears.

He rolled forward on his heels. "They're thinking of attacking. After we *saved* them." His voice was cloaked in disbelief.

I gave him a sideways glance. "This isn't the movies, Scotty. We don't get thanked for our good deeds. Or medals. Or even a steak dinner. A knife in the back is the only thanks they'd give us even if we spent a hundred years doing this. We're monsters—to them, anyway." I shrugged. "They're the ones who have a snapshot of time on this earth, so complicated concepts aren't something their small brains grasp. Good versus evil is the world these people live in. It helps them forget that they're dreadfully mortal. And the evil they're so convinced is unique to the supernatural is much more rampant in their own race."

Thorne's eyes, and everyone's in the areas, were on me.

"You want to survive?" I asked the group. "I'd suggest you learn how to fight vampires when they decide to come looking for you. Seeking them out in the shadows like you've done for centuries doesn't mean a thing when something like this happens." I held out my hands. "I'm sure your heads are too far up your own asses to realize that things are happening in the supernatural world. Things that most likely mean every single one of you has a less-than-ideal chance of surviving unless you adapt. Unless you learn."

The woman I'd helped stepped forward, her face carefully blank. It wasn't warm, but it was devoid of the hatred peppered through the group. "Learn what?"

I smiled at her, showing fang. "How to fight like a vampire."

She tilted her head. "How are we meant to learn that?"

I shrugged. "Stock up on Bram Stoker, have a *Twilight* marathon. How should I know? I've done my bit for humanity." I looked to my left. "Come on, Scotty. I've got a hankering for tenderloin."

I'd been planning to leave without even glancing at Thorne, but a raspy voice stopped me.

"You can teach us."

I turned around, my eyes catching the kid, Chace, who'd managed to survive. Kudos to him.

The air turned static and deathly quiet.

"Sorry. I didn't go to college for a teaching degree. Only evil and murder." I winked at them. "But I am smart enough to know that teaching slayers how to fight vampires is beyond insane, even for me, and I make Henry VIII look well-adjusted. Plus, I know a trap when I see one, and my newest cheerleader will be as likely to learn from me as he would to stick a copper blade into my temple, or die trying if your fearless leader wasn't holding him back."

Thorne's gaze darted from the kid to me.

Chace stepped forward. "But you're not like them." He glanced to the remains of the woman Scott had killed.

I flipped my hair. "Of course I'm not. I've got much better taste in wine and shoes."

Crickets.

Tough crowd.

"You said that something's coming," he continued. "A war."

I raised my brow. "I didn't use that word, but you're not as emptyheaded as I first thought."

I didn't elaborate on his suggestion, like I knew they were expecting me to do.

"And you're fighting for humans in this war," he probed. It wasn't a question.

I folded my arms. "No. I'm fighting for *me*," I corrected. "Survival is the main goal. Saving you was an unfortunate side effect."

Lie, but at least I did it convincingly.

Unease flickered through the group as they digested my words.

"Well then, you're going to need all the bodies you can get to fight this war," the women cut in.

I nodded. "*Undead* bodies. They're less breakable than yours." I gestured to a man with an obviously broken wrist, pale and looking barely conscious. "I'm not here to make new friends. Especially not with slayers. And I'm not about to hold your hands and help you do your job. This was a one-time thing. I'd advise you start practicing a lot more, or get out of dodge. I'm not coming to the rescue next time." I gave them a pointed look. "There will be a next time."

Chace looked as if he might open his mouth to argue, but someone pushed past the kid roughly.

I folded my arms. "No Neck. I'm surprised and, if I'm honest, a little disappointed that you didn't get your femoral artery torn by one of these critters." I kicked one with my ruined pump.

His returning grimace was quite a treat when coupled with one swelling black eye and his all-around ugliness. "Fuck you. You nasty vampire cunt," he spat. "We don't need you—"

He probably would've said more but me snapping through the plaster of his bloodstained cast had him stopping.

"Sticks and stones won't break my bones," I chanted. "But you know what *will* hurt you?" I rebroke the arm that had only just began to heal.

I waited a moment to bathe in his screams.

"Insulting me. You'd do well to remember that." I eyed him. "And don't use that word to insult any woman ever again."

I stepped back, reveling in the open shock and disgust on most of the slayers' faces. That was more like it.

I glanced at Scott. "Can you do me a favor and get Mother

Teresa over there to the right people so they can identify her and hopefully make this not a wasted trip?" I asked him sweetly, nodding to the corpse of a vampire. "I'd move rather quickly, Scotty. The air is turning around here," I added, noting the way the slayers seemed very pissed off over me breaking No Neck's arm. I couldn't fathom why; surely he couldn't be that well liked.

Scott nodded once, darting to the body and hefting it over his shoulder. He paused, an uneasy look on his bloodstained face. "Are you going to be okay on your own?" he asked.

I rolled my eyes. "I think I'll remain undead without your protection," I responded dryly. "Go," I urged, then paused. "It would be best to play up the slayer fatalities to our friend. A lot."

It wouldn't do well for King Rick to know we'd left slayers alive. Saved them. And it didn't escape me that Scott was committing treason for me without blinking. After I'd been nothing but mean to him. It was touching. Not that I'd start being nice to him or anything wild.

Scott nodded once more, then was gone.

I smiled at the angry crowd. "Thanks for your patience. Now I have to talk to your leader. Try not to die in the interim."

On that note, I snatched Thorne's arm and dragged him into the house on the outer edges of the settlement. I'd gotten into the place where the American dream had vomited everywhere before Thorne wrenched his arm from mine, his eyes wild.

"I can't believe you did that," he hissed.

His fury filled the living room of the empty house.

"What, saved you and most of your friends?"

His mouth thinned. "Broke Erik's arm in front of everyone who'd just watched their friends die."

I sighed. "Vampire, remember? You keep waiting for me to turn good because my diet is slightly different than my contemporaries, you're going to get gray and old." I paused. "No, actually, wait right here for that to happen. I'd be much more able to live my death without the shadow of a slayer and the stench of his self-righteousness following me around."

He regarded me. "You're lying," he growled.

"Oh, I almost always lie. But not about this."

He stepped forward and I steeled myself from stepping back. "Everything about you is a contradiction," he murmured. "You're so coldblooded sometimes I think you could freeze a waterfall, but you make my fuckin' blood turn into Hades. You're cruel, but kindness is a side effect of that cruelty. You should be ugly to me, but fuck, are you the most beautiful creature I've ever laid eyes on. You should make me rear away in disgust, but it takes everything I have not to fuckin' tear those clothes off you and taste every inch of your damned skin." His eyes burned with desire. "You want everyone to think that you'd taste bitter, but I know for a fact it's the sweetest honey I've ever had on my tongue.

"You're some kind of twisted harmony. Everything you are, your very existence should make you gnarly and rough. Instead, you're so fuckin' smooth, so goddamn beautiful. That harmony makes me unable to kill you like I should do. Makes it impossible, in fact. That harmony brings you into my fuckin' dreams, so I can't sleep a wink without seein' your face. That harmony's gonna be fatal to me, and I can't find it in me to give a shit about that."

His lips were on mine the second he finished. His fingers tore into my hair, yanking at the roots while bruising my lips with his kiss, yanking me to him with his other hand.

I sank into it, the fire, the touch I'd been yearning for. For centuries, it seemed. Then I found sense. Reason.

I yanked myself back, darting to the middle of the room so there was a sofa between us.

"We cannot go there again," I stated.

His eyes glowed and he made to move around the sofa.

I extended my fangs, rebelling against the body that craved him. "I'm serious. I've just signed my death warrant by helping you. You try to kiss me again, I will kill you."

He stopped, never taking his eyes from me. "We can't do this now," he growled finally.

"We can't do this ever," I corrected.

He narrowed his brows. "We've got shit to talk about. You can't escape that, Isla. But for now, I've got dead to bury, injured to tend to and a council to answer to."

Despite my mood, my ears perked up. "Council? Here I was thinking that slayers were unorganized brutes with little to no organizational skills."

Thorne stayed still. "In the morning. Dawn. Your apartment."

I gave him my best glare. "I thought we'd discussed your fate should you continue the delusion that you have the right to command me," I said, my voice a whisper that rode on the promise of death.

Or at least dismemberment.

Thorne regarded me. Then he held his muscled and blood-stained arms up straight. "You want to kill me? Do it," he challenged, a glint in his eye.

I stared at him, at the cords in his neck, the rips and tears in his skin from the battle. The blood that sang to me throughout the entire exchange staining his skin. The scarred and muscled flesh of his arms willing me to do what was in my nature.

Nature was the problem. She may have designed us to be

enemies, but she'd also made that line too close to lovers. One, once crossed, you couldn't go back from.

Thorne's eyes burned into mine as he lowered his arms. "Didn't think so," he rumbled, his voice vibrating the air. "Dawn. Your apartment," he repeated. After one last gaze filled with promise and hellfire, he turned on his booted heel and walked out.

TWELVE

I WATCHED DAWN KISS THE DARK HORIZON WITH ITS presence as the cool embrace of night circled my body.

I was at my apartment. On the balcony. Waiting for him. Like an idiot.

This was after I had spent the night ensuring Scott's silence and then lying my ass off to Rick about what happened in the battle. The fact that I was still there to wait for Thorne instead of a memory to him said my lies were holding up. For now.

The party the following night might just be turned into the celebration of my final death if I wasn't careful.

I was balancing on a knife's edge. And there was only so long I could do so before I drew blood.

It would always end in blood.

Yet there I was. Waiting for dawn. Waiting for Thorne. Waiting for death.

The thrumming of a heartbeat preceded the opening and closing of my front door that I'd left unlocked. His scent filtered through the air and encircled me like a familiar lover. Not a doomed one.

There was a slight pause before the echoes of his boots mingled with the echo of his heartbeat crossed my living room and through to the balcony.

His eyes ran over me. I wasn't clad in armor. Even my designer stuff. He could cut through it all like butter. So instead I was wearing a white tee and cotton shorts. My hair was tangled in a knot atop my head, my face free of makeup.

And the heat in his gaze told me he regarded me like I should be donning wings and walking down a catwalk.

It warmed me. To the core.

Fatal.

"You're here," he observed.

I raised my brow. "It's my apartment."

He didn't reply, merely stepped onto the balcony and stayed a few feet away from me, refusing to acknowledge the dancing colors of the sunrise. Instead his eyes never strayed from my face.

We stayed like that for a long time. There was a lot to say, the sheer number of words perhaps the reason neither of us spoke.

But I don't think it was that.

Because there in the stillness of a New York dawn, cabs hurtling down the street, sirens echoing through the spaces between the buildings, his steady and roaring heartbeat, that was the most quiet, the most respite we'd had in each other's presence since we had met.

I bathed in that stillness. Let myself, even for a moment, sink into the embrace of his scent, his emotions, his presence. And gave myself a sliver of the luxury afforded to humans—simplicity.

But only a sliver.

That simple silence that was only given to those who were burdened with the inevitability of death. When you didn't have that, when eternity stretched before you, nothing was simple.

"Half of my team wants your head," he began. "The other half wants your number."

I smiled against the razors in my chest. "Give my number to the half that wants my head," I told him. "Problem solved."

He folded his arms across his chest. "This shit ain't gonna be solved by your smart mouth."

I stared at him. "At least it'll make it less dull." I clutched to my flippancy because the air around us was getting more charged, electric, like the atmosphere before a storm.

"You saved my family today," he declared. "My sister."

I resisted the urge to squirm with the statement. "How did they die?" I asked, instead of addressing the unspoken thanks. "Your parents." It was a simple piece of information that brought forth the realization that I didn't know anything about his life. Only that it would end. That should have been all I needed to know, yet I asked the question.

The taste of the air turned bitter with my words, yet his face didn't change. "Vampires. Lucille was three. They almost got her too…." His eyes went far away. "I got there in time. Or at least not too late for her. They were long gone." He sucked in a breath. "I've looked after her ever since. Training her to make sure she won't have the same fate as our family."

"She doesn't live with you?" I asked, remembering only the residual scent of bubblegum at his place.

He shook his head, running his hand over his mouth. "No, not full time. It's too dangerous for her." He gave me a pointed look. "She lives with my dad's sister. The only version of a mother she has left now."

The pain lingered in his words, an echo behind them that had yet to be dulled by the passing of the years. Anger and hate had nurtured it, kept it alive.

I nodded. "Makes sense."

He tilted his head. "What?"

"Your hatred for the entire race of vampires. They took your family from you. It's not logical, as it could have been just as likely for a homicidal maniac to kill them, or for them to be hit by a bus, which in turn wouldn't make you hate bus drivers for the rest of your life. In fact, it was most likely preferable for you, at least, that they be killed by something supernatural. Then you could attach hate and evil to a supernatural creature rather than admit evil doesn't need the supernatural to exist. It's easier to attach it to us than admit it lives within humans." I paused. "What goes bump in the night isn't what you should be fighting. Maybe it's what remains when the sun comes up." My gaze went the upcoming sunrise before flickering back to him.

His body didn't flinch with my words, yet his eyes turned liquid and his emotions became a swirl of contradictions. Anger. Hate. Lust.

He was silent for a long while. I waited.

"Why do you do it?" he asked softly. Dangerously.

"Narrow it down there, Buffy. I do a lot of different things for a lot of different reasons." I thought on it a moment. "Scratch that. I do most things for one simple reason—*because I can*."

His face stayed impassive. Unreadable. It unnerved me because he was a child, an infant human, yet he disguised his emotions better than a two-hundred-year-old immortal. In fact, everything about him rebelled against the fact that he was a human, that he wasn't as old as some of my handbags.

"Kill monsters. Survive on them," he clarified.

His line of questioning was unexpected, but I rolled with it.

I gave him a look. "Haven't you heard? I *am* a monster. It takes one to know one, and it certainly takes one to kill one. And darling, I may be encased in an attractive package that nature designed to communicate the contrary, but I am a monster. You'd do well to remember that."

My words contradicted my earlier statement, but if I reminded him of what likely had been beaten into him since he was born, maybe he would do the right thing and leave. Me? I always did the wrong thing. Like pray he didn't walk out that door.

He was across the balcony at the start of my response, perhaps even at the end of it. Then he wasn't. Then he was right up in my space, pressing me against the railing of the balcony, his fire imprinting on my cold skin, chasing away the chill that was natural to me.

His form was tight but humming with something. Something dangerous, similar to the hum I was fighting. Every inch of his body held mine in its thrall. I couldn't move even if I desired to.

"No," he rasped, gray eyes searching my face. "I used to think that. But I was wrong. I'm not ashamed to admit it." His finger was a ghost as it trailed down my cheek. "In fact, I've never been happier to have been as wrong as I was about you." He paused. "But never have things been more complicated than they are now. Beliefs that've been in place for centuries have been changed because of what you did tonight."

I laughed. "Yeah, and I just royally fucked myself over for that. Damned myself in the eyes of my race irrevocably. Not that I'm losing sleep over that. Let's just hope the oncoming war makes that little transgression slip through the cracks and keep me here for a little longer, at least."

He gripped my neck. "You're not going anywhere," he promised.

I raised my brow. "You don't have the power to make those kinds of statements," I replied, wishing I was wrong, for once. "There's a war coming. It's been brewing for centuries. Been fought in the shadows until there was no choice but to bring it to light. I don't know my fate in it, but the odds are stacked against me. There's nothing you can do to change that."

He glared at me. "There's everything *you* can do to change that," he challenged.

"No. I've solidified my fate. I'm involved to the end, most likely. I don't run and I've got a vested interest in winning this battle, if not the war." If I could find a way to expose my family and then have them executed, I considered that a victory.

"So have I," Thorne growled, eyes on me.

"No," I argued harshly. "You don't. It's past time for us to end this madness. For you to actually try to act like you hold some value over your own life." I tried to struggle from his grasp but he stopped me. I could've have broken away but I was selfish and decided to bathe in the feeling until it was nothing more than a shadow. For it would be. Soon. "There is no place for humans in this war." I eyed him. "There is no place for you, anywhere in this life. My life. My deathless life. Other than a hole in a ground and a gravestone. And I'm not having that on my shoulders."

"You're not dismissing me like that. Like I'm nothing. Like *we're* nothing."

"It's what we should be," I argued.

"Should be, maybe," he agreed. "But not what we are. Not what you are to me. And you're mine." He brushed my mouth with his thumb. "This tells me all the truth I need to know—that I'm your man." He trailed his fingers down my chin, my neck, to settle over my chest. The vibration of his heart through his hands gave me the illusion that mine was beating.

I didn't have time for illusions.

"I can't have a man," I hissed.

"You don't need a man," he agreed, his hand never leaving my chest, his eyes never leaving mine. "You're a storm, a volcano, a fucking battle. Every day with you is a fight against an unstoppable force. Beauty." He stroked a tendril of my hair. "To possess that beauty, one cannot merely be a man, because you come with a fight. A war. So you need a fucking warrior who won't fight battles for you, but who will fight the battle that *is you*. The man who will get bloody and broken and make good fuckin' friends with the reaper who knocks at the door every day he's with you. He'll do all that with a smile on his face and fire in his belly, because a true warrior craves the ultimate battle. That's what you are, Isla—the ultimate battle. *My* ultimate battle." He rested his head against mine. "And I don't surrender. To anyone. Not for you. Not even *to* you. So fight us as much as you want. You may be stronger than me, but you won't win unless you end it."

It was a challenge, an unwavering one that would have taken me a second to take up. To win. Despite whatever puzzling strength he had to keep me in place, to keep himself alive despite all odds, he was right. I was stronger.

In theory.

I wasn't strong enough to do what I should've done and snap his neck. I could no sooner do that than snap my own.

"We have to end it," I whispered against the weathering gale of his emotions. "I can't…." I searched for the word. The one I swore I'd never use.

"Love me?" he finished for me.

I blinked against the surety of his words. His willingness to utter them. "Because you do. I know it 'cause despite it all, I love you, Isla. You can't change that. You've just got to live with it, or die with it."

His words filled the dawn and swallowed the sun, or at least they seemed to.

"Where do you think this can go, Thorne?" I hissed. "What do you think we do here? I'm not going to let this love be the anchor that yanks me into the abyss and damns us all. I'm already damned, but even I have to draw the line somewhere. And I think this, whatever this is, isn't just damnation, but destruction. For both of us." I never let my gaze fall from his. "You want a life that's violent and short just because of that useless organ in your chest? You want pain and suffering to follow you as long as you clutch this romantic notion that love conquers all? Newsflash, buddy—it *will* conquer all. Everything. You, me, everyone you care about. Because it's a bitter battle against everything both of our races stand for. A vampire and a slayer isn't romantic, or soulful. It's death. Pain. Ugliness. And I'm not ready for any of those. And I'm most certainly not willing to give you the curse that my love will give."

I restrained the urge to gulp in a huge breath with the tidal wave of my words, staying still in his thrall. In his glare.

"That's why?" he said finally. "Why you resist me? Because you're focused on my mortality being a death sentence for this, for us?"

I gave his smoldering glare an even look. "Is that not enough?" I scoffed.

He surged forward. "What if that wasn't an issue?"

I glared at him. "What-ifs are for imbeciles and Republicans."

"Jesus, Isla. Answer the question," he growled.

I jutted my chin up. "I won't answer the ridiculous question because it *is* an issue. You're mortal. I'm not. The point is moot."

He let out a sigh of impatience, then cupped my face, bringing our faces together. "What if I could tell you that wasn't the case? What if mortality was a thing we weren't both plagued with?"

Something bloomed in my stomach. Something hot and uncomfortable.

Hope.

I frowned at him. "I would ask for the details," I replied.

He narrowed his brows. "I can't give you that," he clipped. "Not now. Not yet." He stroked my cheek with an unwavering gentleness. "I'm askin' you to trust me."

I steeled myself against the touch, the blossoming hope in my stomach, the way his presence burned away the rest of the world. "I don't trust anyone. You get dead by doing that," I said finally.

He clutched my chin, gentleness gone, replaced by a brutal urgency. "I'm not asking you to trust anyone," he growled. "I'm asking you to trust *me*."

The words hung in the air like an omen. Like an open door that if I stepped through, there was no going back. But perhaps I'd already stepped through that door the second I'd decided not to kill him in that alley. Maybe I was too far gone already. Walking a road that had an end. Finally.

"Okay," I whispered, the word flinging that door shut and slamming the deadbolt home. "I will. Not for good. Not even for a really long time. Or a short one," I added. "I'm not patient."

His eyes were liquid quicksilver. "I've noticed," he said dryly.

I stroked the pulsing vein at his neck idly. "But for the record, we're saying that you can't die?"

He clutched my wrist roughly, turning my palm in his hand to bring it to his mouth. "Everyone can die, Isla. Even you," he replied, voice thick. "I'm saying that it's tougher to send me to the grave than most. That I've been around for longer than you think, and that now, in the years that I've been on this earth, I've never had more to live for."

I wanted to ask a lot of questions. A lot. How long had he been on this earth? What were the semantics of his vague declaration at a hint of immortality? He breathed. His heart beat. He could be hurt almost as easily as a human, yet he healed quickly. I wanted to know precisely what he was.

But the questions died on my tongue when he took it for his own, thrusting his mouth over mine.

The urgency to cement whatever had just been declared on that balcony was beyond anything I'd ever experienced. We were a clash of wills, of nature, fighting each other for the upper hand.

I ripped off Thorne's jacket, sending it fluttering to the ground before I raked my hand down his back, the bare skin flexing and pulsing under my touch.

He growled in his throat as he detached his mouth from mine and wrenched my top off, the air kissing my exposed breasts.

The tee went flying off the balcony, hurtling down thirty stories as Thorne attached himself to my breast, his hands the back of my neck.

I ran my fingers through his inky hair as he moved down, quickly divesting me of my cotton shorts and panties so I stood naked on my balcony.

I reasoned an early riser having their morning coffee on

any number of the building surrounding mine could have seen us. I simply didn't care. My only need was to rip Thorne's shirt from his body, which was exactly what I did, exposing the wide, scarred, and muscled expanse of his chest. I longed to explore the ridges of his abs with my lips, but the second his shirt was off, Thorne yanked me to him, plastering his mouth to mine once more, lifting me.

I wrapped my legs around his waist, surrendering all control to him as he pressed my back lightly against the railing.

He used one hand to free himself from his jeans, his naked torso pressing into mine, the fire and ice of our bodies meeting in a fatal harmony.

He stayed poised at my entrance, lips hovering over mine, eyes glued on me. "Do you trust me?" he rasped, clutching me to him. I was at his mercy, hovering at the edge of the balcony with only his arms around me stopping me from falling.

I didn't hesitate. "With my death."

He attached his lips to mine and surged into me.

"We agreed on sinful, not demonic," Rick murmured in my ear as we glided through the party. "The Devil himself might rise up and decide to take you for his queen, and I'd have to fight him for that honor."

"Queen?" I repeated sarcastically. "I think a crown would slip right off my shiny head."

I swallowed my grin at the variety of undead jaws in danger of hitting the ground. The vampiric elite exceled at hiding emotions under their pale and mostly beautiful faces; my theory was because they didn't have them. But they betrayed themselves that evening, though I had to hand it to them, as the last place I expected to be was on the arm of the king at one of these things.

But there I was.

Weren't surprises great?

"Plus, the devil's already here," I added, nodding to the corner of the room. The one I needed to be focused on instead of rehashing the events of earlier that day. I was there for a purpose, namely not to get dead. Preferably to set about the demise of the woman I was looking at right then. "And it's a she. Unfortunately the she who birthed me."

I hadn't seen a lot of expressions on my mother's face. In fact, until that moment I hadn't been sure she'd been able to communicate anything but loathing and indifference.

But there we were, watching the shock ripple over her usually carefully schooled and deceptively youthful features. The way she gripped her flute of blood had me thinking she wasn't quite sure whether to be glad that the daughter she hated was on the arm of the king, or furious.

It all hung on whether she was indeed involved in the plot to murder said king, and by proxy me. Though my death would likely screw up her promises of having me raped for breeding purposes.

Rick followed my eyes. "Well even if she is doing the job of hiding her crown as the queen of Hades, there's another king downstairs who'd love to replace your mother with the newer and decidedly more interesting model," he murmured, his mouth touching my ear.

"Oh, I'd hate you to fight the Devil for little old me," I responded. "Whoever comes out on top would be severely disappointed when they realized that regardless of bloody victory, I'm not a trophy that can be snatched up as the spoils of war. I'm likely to give more a fight than the Devil himself if anyone tries to possess me. And honey, I'd win." I gave him a challenging gaze.

My words weren't exactly true. The Devil or the king of vampires may not be able to possess me, but a human slayer did. Body and soul. He'd made sure of that when he spent all day imprinting himself on me, neither us coming up for air, though one of us actually needed it to survive.

Not much talking was done, so the semantics of his own deathless life were not discussed.

And when it came time for him to leave, he'd cupped my face and those eyes radiated concern that I'd never experienced. No one worried about a vampire. Until him.

"This party, will it be dangerous?" he'd asked.

"Hopefully," I'd answered. "Otherwise, it'd be horribly dull."

His mouth thinned. "You're immortal, but not invincible. Remember that," he ordered, stroking my face. "And you're important. Remember that too. Your life is not something to be risked easily." He pressed his lips to mine fiercely. "You'll be coming to mine when you're done."

I'd blinked away the warmth of his kiss while I battled the call of his blood. "I thought we'd established that I didn't like to be ordered around."

His eyes darkened. "No. After today, we've established how much you love to be ordered around." He'd stuck around for a beat more, then left.

"Half the men in this room are considering treason to rip you out of my arms," the king continued, bringing me back to the present. His lips were at my ear to make sure no one could catch the conversation.

"The other half, I'm guessing, were already considering treason and they will most likely still rip me out of your arms, just long enough to execute me," I murmured back.

His hand tightened on mine. "Oh, even the ones with the most burning hatred in their veins for you couldn't bring themselves to end your life before ripping that dress off your body and defiling you in every way possible."

I was wearing red. Blood-red. It hugged every curve like a second skin, its straps doing well to hold my girls in despite the thin fabric. It was simple but moved with my body instead of constraining it, and the split that went up my thigh and almost to my waist made it very apparent that I wasn't wearing underwear. Only some deftly placed tape maintained my modesty. Or it would have, if I had any.

As it were, it would be perfect in a fight, my best weapon being distraction.

I sighed. "Oh, sire, Shakespeare had nothing on you. Your words are sonnets."

He chuckled, his chest vibrating as he did.

The sound bounced off the walls and cut through the fake conversation.

Even I had a moment of shock before I regained my poker face. The king did not chuckle. Or laugh. I would have bet the ability had been drained out of him at birth. The shadows of smiles I'd seen since he'd made my acquaintance were unusual enough, but at that kind of event, he was more likely to spear someone through the heart than laugh.

But the night was still young.

Mother glided over, nodding demurely at those who encountered her, looking like the cat that got the cream. Or the blood. Her daughter who had once shamed her had hooked the whale.

In her eyes, at least.

"Defcon level one," I muttered to Rick. "Brace yourself."

He stiffened until he followed my gaze, his eyes twinkling with the slightest amusement as my mother approached.

She put on an almost genuine smile, surprising me that her facial muscles still moved that way. "Isla," she said warmly, like it was normal. She reached in to give me air kisses. When she released me, she looked between me and the king before dipping her head. "Sire," she greeted.

My brothers hung back, one gripping a human with fear in her eyes and sorrow in her soul. Their eyes were masked in hatred. I returned the favor. Human property was not permitted at such gatherings unless they didn't leave through the doors they came in.

Not many vampires adhered to draining humans at these events, not this century at least. Most had become more progressive, if only for privacy about their killing habits. Not my brothers.

I swallowed my rage and once more promised myself that I'd be putting a blade through their hearts.

Not in time to save the human, though.

I'd learned to swallow whatever pain came with that thought. You couldn't save everyone.

He nodded. "Alyona," Rick greeted, his eyes on Viktor and the human roughly plastered to his side before focusing on my mother. Though his practiced tone was full of respect, I could sense the distaste that underpinned it.

My mother looked between us once more, unable to keep the calculated glee off her face. I bet she was planning the best way to weasel her way into being the queen mother and commencing world domination.

"My darling."

I glanced around, wondering who she was addressing. When it became apparent that she was talking to me, I looked back to her.

"This is the last place I expected to see you, with the king on your arm as well," my mother continued, ignoring my extended pause.

"Yes, well, it seems hell has frozen over," I replied, sipping my drink. I then tilted my head and gave her a sympathetic smile. "I'm sorry that means you won't be able to return home in the near future."

Her eye ticked slightly, but the rest of her mask stayed in place. She glanced to Rick. "My daughter, the joker. She must have you in fits of laughter, sire."

Rick's face stayed blank. "She keeps me amused," he answered dismissively. "Unfortunately, I'm not here to be amused. I'm here to host." He stepped back, nodding slightly. "If you'll excuse us, I must take Isla to amuse the rest of the guests. She is my court jester, after all."

I choked on the wine I was downing at the dry and even tone accompanying the words.

Rick ignored it, nodding to my mother in farewell before dragging me off.

I waved at her with my glass, still swallowing laughter.

Rick guided us through the crowds until we were a safe distance away.

"You have a touch with sadistic mothers," I complimented. "You have one too?"

He kept his eyes blank. "I don't have a mother. If you'll recall your history lessons, the royal Vein Line kills the queen once she's birthed an heir."

Foot in mouth once more.

"Oh yes. I did forget that frightfully brutal piece of history," I replied. "Likely did you a favor, though. If this environment is anything to go by, she would've been a snake anyway."

I probably should've told him I was sorry for his loss or treaded carefully. I didn't do careful.

Rick glanced at me. "In my years as prince, then king, not one vampire has been so callous about my mother," he observed.

I sipped my drink. "What can I say? I'm unique."

He chuckled once more.

I scanned the crowd, all of whom were staring at us while trying to pretend they weren't.

I leaned in. "As fun as this is, it's hard to spy while attached to the king," I murmured. "Perhaps you should go off and execute or at least flay some people and cause a distraction so I can go about my business."

Rick's face stayed blank. "Yes, I think you're right." He paused. "But before I do that, I'd like to show you something."

He directed us through the crowd and towards the edge of the room.

I raised my brow. "Are we going to play doctor with all of your guests within hearing distance?" I teased. "Why, you are a naughty monarch."

Rick ignored me, all but for the small upturn of his mouth.

We continued down a hallway drenched in the same trappings of aristocratic wealth, tasteless and dated tapestries alongside paintings of old, fat and boring men.

"You need a decorator from this century," I observed. "Or at least one who isn't going for Count D chic."

Rick was still silent.

It was unnerving, being in his presence and not getting even a slight gauge of his thoughts. Like he was a marble statue that walked and talked. And drank blood. And alternately threatened me with death and flirted with me.

The marble hand opened a door to a stairway that went

down.

"After you," he said, nodding.

"Age before beauty," I challenged, not liking going down to what was most likely a dungeon without possibility for escape.

Rick gave me a hard look.

I puffed out a breath. "Fine, but if you're taking me down here to kill me, I'll be annoyed. Though I will say, I'm dressed rather fetchingly for death."

I stepped my red heel onto the first stone step, then another. The slight echo of the door closing behind Rick was hopefully not the sound of my doom. We descended in silence, a slow drip of water somewhere in the bowels of the mansion the only soundtrack. The air was damp and smelled like stone and mold. And something else.

Death.

I stopped at the bottom, a long hallway yawning out in front of me, various shapes lining the walls.

Rick came to a stop beside me. "Welcome to the gallery," he said, voice flat, then put his hand on my lower back, edging me forward.

A shriveled and emaciated vampire greeted us. It could have been male or female, shoulder-length hair scraggly and clumped together. Its face was pinched and wrinkled, like a dehydrated corpse. The eyes were frighteningly alive, though, silently pleading as its fingers, which were chained above its head with copper wire, twitched.

We kept walking. The next one was much the same.

And the next.

Their clothing was the only thing that betrayed their age. It was like going through a gruesome time capsule of the trends of the twenty-first century.

I didn't say a word through the journey.

We came to a stop in front of a vampire less prune-like than the others. Her hair tumbled down her back, still shiny and healthy. The evening gown she was wearing was immaculate, if a little stained with blood.

"Hi, Selene. Nice weather we're having," I greeted her cheerfully.

Silence.

Rick brushed my side. "For those who are guilty and of no further use for informational purposes, we cut their tongues out with enchanted blades," he stated.

I nodded. "Good call. Selene never had anything worthwhile to say anyway."

Her eyes narrowed with hate.

Rick directed us to another vampire. It took effort to keep my face blank as hatred that dwarfed Selene's greeted me.

"Earnshaw. Looking well," I said.

His eyes bulged, though his body stayed statuesque.

He was covered in matted blood and some injuries were still gaping, showing they had been made by an enchanted blade.

"We've spelled him silent when we're not interrogating him."

I stilled. "You've been interrogating him?"

Rick nodded in my periphery. "He's the only true member of the rebellion we've captured alive. I'm sure there's more he's not telling us."

I swallowed, hoping that Sophie's little barriers held, or I'd be in a world of trouble.

"Did you bring me down here for better company than the guests upstairs or just a general stretching of the legs?" I asked.

Even in the dark I still caught every inch of Rick's features as he turned to face me. They were etched like the stone surrounding us, his eyes glowing green in the dim light. "I brought you down here to show you that I take betrayal very seriously. And those who betray me don't get the mercy of a quick death."

I managed to quell my panic at the weight of his words, and what was left unsaid.

"So you'll be comforted to know that those involved in this will be getting the most prudent punishment," he continued.

I hid my relief like I hid my fear as we returned to the stairs. "Yes. This has all been so very comforting," I deadpanned.

"And we're down here because this is the one place we won't be overheard." His gaze flickered to the vampires around us. "At least not by anyone who'll be seeing the light of day ever again."

I crossed my arms against the chill in the air and yet another cold premonition of death.

By the pricking of my thumb, something wicked this way comes.

"You've found out how they made them," I surmised.

Rick nodded once. "It is not an exclusively vampire process."

I did my best not to gape at that.

"Vampires who have taken human lovers and who have wanted to pass on the gift of immortality have been trying this for years, this is true," Rick continued. "But since the dawn of our race, we have had little more than a tentative peace with the other supernatural creatures. If not for a few exceptions." He gave me a pointed look. "Now it seems there is a common goal between them."

"New world order, human enslavement. I've heard the propaganda," I spat. "I'm sick of the fucking publicity script." I glared at Earnshaw, then Selene. "Rebellion is always entrenched in romance of revolution in the beginning, but reality soon moves in and fucks all romantic ideas, replacing them with blood and brutality. There's nothing romantic about a revolution, even a good one, a necessary one. Death is the one certainty. It's the sacrifice of the thing. Only in some cases is that death for a cause that's worthy of it. Most of the time, the death serves as a boneyard to build a hell on. That's what they're trying to do, create a cemetery of bones and place them as martyrs in which to create more graves."

Rick regarded me. "I don't disagree," he said finally. "Though I didn't understand you to be so… passionate towards them."

Seduction wrapped around the death in the air, which I would've been party to had Throne's touch not still been firmly around my heart.

"Call me traditional, but I do get a tad passionate about a group of people who try to kill me and my friends, plus create abominations who are a disgrace to both humans and vampires alike," I snapped. "Now tell me how're they're made so we can unmake them."

Rick glanced to Earnshaw. "They can be killed by many of the same processes used to kill a vampire. Copper has somewhat of a muted effect on them but is still fatal in the head or heart." He paused. "They can only be made by a vampire whose Vein Line has direct connection to Ambrogio. Noble blood."

Another pause, perhaps to carry the weight of the betrayal. Noble bloodlines had been those closest to the royal line for millennia.

"Makes sense," I muttered.

Rick's eyes went glacial. "It makes sense that the Vein Lines most loyal to the crown would be the ones to try to overthrow it?" His voice thickened with an ancient accent as fury got the best of him.

I nodded. "Their proximity to you at these parties is not from love, but from jealousy. Greed. The most loyal are usually the most wicked. It is not our enemies we should look to to betray us, but our friends. For we do not expect loyalty from our enemies, do we? Betrayal is only birthed from loyalty. Look at Judas. And Brutus. And Brad Pitt."

Rick's gaze was no longer tinted with anger. "You see much more than your eyes and your mouth lets on," he said finally.

I waited for him to continue.

"Once the blood of the Vein Line has been inserted into the dead human, a witch, a powerful one with ancient magic, must replicate the death spell. Not a mortal death, but the vampire death," Rick continued.

"And I'm guessing that's where Belladonna and her bunkmates come in," I surmised.

He nodded. "Yes. They're likely the only ones on the planet with magic dark enough to do such things. Which is why they were originally banished. What they practiced was brought forth from Hades himself."

Another shiver settled over me. Or inside me, the bloom of death that had lingered since killing Belladonna.

"Killing the witches is obviously going to be the top of our to-do list," I said, instead of betraying my chill.

"First we must separate the traitors," Rick said.

I glanced to the roof. "I'm thinking you have most of them up there as it is."

"I fear it to be so," Rick agreed. "Though they will regret the day they entertained the thought of crossing me. No Vein Line will be safe. I will exterminate every last one of the great families if need be," he promised.

I grinned. "Sounds fun. Let's go."

Before I could take a step, I was pressed against the rough stone, Rick's body imprinted onto every inch of me. My body responded; although I was dead, I was not in the ground.

"Centuries on this earth, surrounded by these vampires, and I have yet to meet one quite like you." His breath was ice on my face. "Strong enough to fight for herself and others, a mouth sharper than the blades which I use to behead my enemies, and strangely merciful to the race as stupid as they are mortal," he continued.

I didn't know quite what to say, so for once, I hedged my bets and stayed silent.

"You could be my queen," he invited, his voice absent of that detachedness that was ever present, even when he tried to seduce me.

The pull of his raspy voice was magnetic, bringing with it the emotions that he'd kept hidden.

I let them wash over me. Had I not been nailed down to another who clutched his hands around my nonbeating heart, they might have swayed me. Even now, I found myself tasting the promise on his lips.

"A queen." I let the word roll over my tongue. "*Your* queen. And where is this offer coming from? You don't know me."

Yes, Rick had flirted with me, but it was detached and cold and came in the same sentence as a death threat. Now I was getting the offer of a crown?

He kept his gaze on me. "I know that you are unique and strong enough to keep my interest and favor for centuries to come. That the thought of bedding you is as enticing as exterminating every traitor with my bare hands." His hand was a ghost of ice on my jaw.

I regarded his stare. "Interest, favor, sex," I mused. "And what about love? Do you not look for that in a queen?"

His body was stone. "We are immortals, Isla. We know that love is a fairytale that humans cling to in order to make it through their miserable lives. We know it does not exist."

The surety of his tone cleverly disguised the pain buried underneath it. Most likely wouldn't have recognized it, unless they'd tasted the rancid turn of a love laid dead at their feet.

Instead of addressing it, I nodded. "No, it does not. But reason does, and you seem to have that. Yet you still invite me to be your queen, even with what you *do* know of me?"

His eyes glowed. "Yes, because of what I have witnessed in you," he hissed. "You'd be the most powerful vampire on this earth. After we defeat the rebels, of course."

"Being a queen through a man is not how I'd like to gain power," I said. "In fact, power is the last thing I'd get as your queen. It would get sucked from me as I was molded to fit the crown that comes with the title. See, I like jewels and sparkly things as much as the next girl, but only if they're made for me. And that crown you're offering? That's made for someone else, someone I'd have to change into to ensure it fits on my head. And Your Highness, I don't change. Not for a man, not for a vampire, and not even for a king."

His mask returned, though he didn't take his eyes off me. "Curious. I'm interested to be the first man, vampire, and king, to change that."

He didn't say another thing, merely turned and ascended the stairs.

THIRTEEN

"Well blow me down with a fucking feather," a rough drawl boomed over the soft conversation, various heads turning in distaste.

I grinned immediately, which was good; after the evening I'd had I was in need of a grin. After the little visit downstairs and the offer of a crown amidst the rotting vampires who'd wronged the king, I was feeling a little flat. And more than a little unnerved that Earnshaw was still down there, with knowledge that could ruin me.

"Move it. Get the fuck out of my way before I use my fangs to rip that stick out of your arse," the voice continued as a large form stomped through the crowd. An auburn head turned to a woman in a purple dress who showed more cleavage than even I was comfortable displaying, which said a lot. "I might do that for you latter, lassie, but I'm sure you'd enjoy it." His thick Scottish brogue curled around the words in a rough caress that made the woman forget his uncouthness, focusing on that accent and the muscles that couldn't be contained under his gray suit.

I didn't need to see his eyes to know he gave her the signature smirk he'd perfected over the centuries to get women's panties right off.

He turned to lock his hazel gaze with mine, and his mouth parted into a full-on grin.

"Isla, as I die and don't breathe, it *is* you," he declared, clearing the last few yards in mere seconds and yanking me into his bone-crushing embrace.

I don't use that as a figure of speech either; a handful of my ribs cracked with the force of the hug. Of course he heard it but gave me one last squeeze, because he was an asshole.

"That's for leavin' me high and dry with those werewolves two centuries ago," he growled in my ear.

I laughed as he let me go, my ribs smarting as they failed to heal with the usual speed. It seemed too common of late, as if my body was punishing me for my relations with a human. "You're trying to tell me you needed little old me to save you from some overgrown dogs?" I looked him up and down. "It seems they didn't rip off any important parts. Plus, I had a party to go to at Marie Antoinette's. Good thing I went too, since it was the last one she threw."

Duncan did look good. A hundred years had passed since I'd seen the Scottish vampire, but it could've been a week. His burnt auburn locks brushed at his collar, wild and rough, framing his stubbled face and sharp masculine features. Everything about him—his stature, the muscles that I knew were more than a little impressive—screamed man. And he used that, plus his accent, to his complete advantage. The highlander had bedded more women in the centuries than he'd killed supernatural creatures, which was saying a lot since he was a hit man for hire.

He shook his head. "Still hurt me pride that a beautiful woman such as yourself couldn't wait to get away from me."

I grinned at him. "You or the snapping teeth of bloodthirsty werewolves. It was a toss-up."

He grinned back, his hands resting on my hips. "Well I'm more than glad to be in a circumstance where I'm not wielding a sword or distracted by mangy mutts so I can fully take in your magnificence," he declared, eyes roving over my body in a physical caress.

Although the look, the voice and the gentle grip of large hands on my waist might have been a winning combination for 99 percent of women on the planet, human or vampire, I just didn't feel it. I never had with Duncan, ever since we'd ran into each other while he was hunting rouge Reinvents in Eastern Europe in the 1700s, although he'd been intent on bedding me. When he couldn't, he became content with letting me help him out when I was bored and felt like killing things. Of course, he still tried relentlessly to get me in the sack, unable to believe I was immune to his charm.

"You're fuckin' glorious," he murmured, meeting my eyes. "Which begs the question, why the fuck are you here with all these arseholes?"

I gave him a look. "You wouldn't believe me if I told you. Suffice to say, it's not by choice," I said low enough so only we could hear.

Luckily the rest of the populace had decided to distance themselves from the two of us; no matter how desperate they were to find out the information between me and the king, they didn't want to rub shoulders with the likes of Duncan. Another reason why I liked him: asshole vampire repellant.

His eyes transformed from that of a teasing lothario to the ruthless killer I knew him to be.

"Who the *fuck* do I need to kill who's forcin' you to come to places like this, where your *parents*, of all vampires, attend?" he ground out, his voice as low as mine.

He knew my sordid history with Mom and Pa and was well-versed in the bloodbath that was my vampire birth.

"That would have to be me," a smooth voice cut in, and I felt Rick's presence at my back. I turned my head slightly to see him give Duncan a hard look, and the Scot's hands at my hips an even harder one.

To his credit, Duncan didn't take his hands off me. "Figures," he scoffed. "You've got good taste, Your Highness, I'll give you that. But even you and your whole fuckin' royal guard couldn't contain this one. And unfortunately, if you tried it would not end bonny for you," he said.

I raised my brow as I heard a couple of gasps from around us. That was as close to an open threat as you could get without even openly threatening the king. I knew three black-suited men had already closed in behind me as I watched two more shoulder through the crowd behind Duncan. I tensed, ready to take them down if need be. Despite whatever loyalty I felt the king had earned, Duncan had mine immediately; I would take on the king himself and his guard if it came to that.

It was only fair, as he'd done the same for me once or twice. Or three times. Granted, the monarchs had been of the human persuasion, so it wasn't exactly taxing like I feared any battle in this ballroom might be.

Rick gave a flick of his hand, which made the guards stand down and saved me from having to ruin my dress just yet.

He surprised me by grinning and yanking Duncan in for a man hug. “I don’t suspect it would, old friend,” he said while patting him on the back. I grinned as I heard Duncan’s ribs crack.

His eyes flared slightly and met mine. “Karma,” I mouthed at him.

He mouthed a filthy word in Gaelic before Rick released him.

“But considering she doesn’t seem to be having the usual reaction to all that is Duncan Campbell, I don’t think this will end bonny for you either,” he continued, mimicking Duncan’s accent perfectly.

I looked between the two of them. “You two know each other?” I asked in disbelief. The bounty hunter who once said “The only good monarch is one you can screw. The rest should be impaled,” and the king whom I guessed didn’t take kindly on such people.

Duncan showed me his fangs. “Got a contract on him once, gave it a go.” He shrugged. “Decided to have an ale with him after he put up a good fight.”

“After I beat you, you mean,” Rick corrected dryly.

“You took up a contract to kill the king of our race? And are still somehow standing here talking about it?” I clarified.

“Well, he wasn’t the king then. And to be fair, I didn’t know who he was until I was halfway through the job. Couldn’t rightly stop then, could I?”

“Jesus,” I muttered. “How you’re still here is beyond me.”

Rick gave me a half grin. “Pure pigheadedness and stubbornness, I believe, Isla. Plus, I wouldn’t put it past him to charm some witch into spelling him to make sure no assassination attempts are successful.”

His eyes only twinkled slightly as the rest of him stayed

impassive, though the warmth was the most he'd betrayed in all the time I'd known him.

I snorted. "Duncan doesn't tangle with witches. They're the only kind of females he doesn't whore around, probably because he had an unlikely incident with a curse and woman scorned," I said, grinning at Duncan before continuing. "And if such a spell existed, I'd have charmed my own witch to do so. Assassination attempts are all well and fun, but like facials, too many in too short of a time span is just downright taxing."

Duncan raised a brow as his eyes glittered with anger. "And who, my love, is stupid enough to try and kill something as lovely as you? And where do they rest their head? So I can chop it off, of course." He fingered his belt where his long, jagged-edge copper knife was strapped. He never went anywhere without it, even wore it while sleeping with women.

Not that I knew firsthand.

Obviously, I couldn't answer his question because at that point in the evening, the room blew up.

Now of course, I wasn't expecting to be thrown through the air, nor hit with a white-hot fireball, so I didn't land in a catlike crouch like a vampire would be expected to by any *Underworld* fan. No, I hit a wall painfully and tumbled down onto a glass table, shards embedding themselves into my skin and ruining my fucking dress.

The excruciating heat and burning of my skin told me that I'd been close enough to the blast to have the top layer of my skin burned off, but not close enough to be blown to pieces like some had been.

The single arm lying next to me communicated that.

Vampires may have been able to grow back limbs, but they couldn't survive being blown apart.

Which was what I told myself while I gritted my teeth

against the agonizing pain pulsing through my entire body. There's always a silver lining, even in the midst of third degree burns.

A quick glance told me my arms were the worst, almost charred to the bone. Most of my exposed skin in my dress, which was a lot, was peeled back so I looked like an extra in a B-grade horror movie.

Acrid smoke permeated the air and, based on the hacking coughs of any humans left alive, was choking anyone in the room who needed their lungs to breathe. Luckily, I needed them for swearing purposes only.

I wrested myself up to my feet, gritting my teeth at the searing pain that came with the movement. Ripping a piece of glass from my chest, I yelled, "Whoever set off that motherfucking bomb is either buying me a new dress and shoes or is going to die a *very* grisly death."

The frenzied shouts and rapid exits from the less courageous of the guests hampered the impact of my shout. Then a body came barreling into my only recently healed midsection.

I was slammed into a wall once more, but that time I didn't tumble down it.

The hand at my throat made sure of that.

Amidst the screams, the unmistakable sounds of battle communicated what this was—an ambush. Someone stupid and brazen enough to attack the king's feast, breaking the most sacred vampire law.

I struggled against the hand at my throat, every move of my limbs ripping the burns on my skin that were trying to heal back together. They would've been half healed already if it weren't for that whorish witch.

Even with my increased sight, I could barely make out my attacker through the thick smoke, apart from the fact that he was strong enough to crush my neck and I could taste his satisfaction hearing my bones crack as he did so.

Wow, the man trying his damnedest to rip my head off after trying to blow me to pieces wasn't my biggest fan. Shocker.

I gritted my teeth through the pain and kicked out with my heels, which were somehow still firmly on my feet. I had them coated with copper in case of this very situation.

I managed to spear my attacker through the chest and sink my heels through his heart.

The hand at my throat flexed and tightened to the point of worry before he released me and I managed to land on shaky feet.

I didn't have time to recover, as the sounds echoing through the smoke-filled room betrayed a battle, a lot of bad guys—or badder guys—trying their level best to kill the king.

And me, as it turned out.

"Is that all you've got, you lazy fuckers?" The twang filtered through the smoke. "Attack the king, you think you'd have bigger balls than that."

A ripping sound and accompanying screech of pain made me grin as I clutched the throat of the woman darting through the smoke with a copper blade aimed at my chest.

I held her up, noting her raven hair and emerald eyes, and the expanse of cleavage. "Now that's not very nice. For the record, this is mostly because you're trying to kill me, but at least a little bit is punishment for crimes to fashion," I said then I turned her knife around and thrust it through her exposed chest to her heart.

I threw her aside as the smoke cleared to expose Rick fighting off three different vampires at once, half of his face in the process of healing from the blast. He looked like he was handling himself okay, if the way he ripped off the first one's head like it was a mushroom had anything to do with it.

His bodyguards didn't look like they had done much protecting, their limbs scattered around his feet.

Guests caught in the crossfire littered the floor as some society ladies and gents cowered in the corners of the room, trying their best to make themselves part of the drapery.

For the number of people intent on kissing their fair king's ass, there weren't nearly as many willing to fight for him.

A knife slammed into the side of my neck as the barely healed skin exploded with pain. I whirled around, yanking the knife out to embed it into the skull of the vampire who threw it. I was satisfied with the crunch that came with the action.

I glanced to Duncan, who was suddenly beside me, face splattered with enough blood to fill a bathtub, his white fangs exposed as he grinned maniacally at me. "All right, Isla?" he asked while he choked a vampire to his chest.

I lifted my leg to impale an incoming attacker on my heel. "Oh yes, this is the way I wish all parties ended," I gritted out.

He took the head off the vamp in an easy motion, his eyes no longer on the battle but where the split of my dress had moved.

"Well me too, lassie," he breathed, his eyes hooded. "All this bloodshed is worth it for that view."

Seconds after that, he emitted a deep "whoof" as a body barreled into him, sending him flying into the same wall that I'd created a hefty dent in what could have been hours or seconds previously. Though he brought half of the marble down with him as he landed.

I grinned as he pushed himself up and went back to the vampire with a savage snarl.

"Serves you right for not being a gentleman," I muttered.

My eyes went back to the bloodbath that had improved

the party tenfold, in my opinion, and had the added benefit of dispatching any of the vampires I'd despised for centuries without having to face the Sector for inevitably doing it myself.

I searched for my family, expecting to see them fighting, of course. Just not on the right side.

My brothers and mother were nowhere to be seen, but amidst the battle I wasn't surprised to see my father discard a head like a forgotten basketball.

His glittering eyes, full of bloodlust, met mine, and he didn't hesitate to charge at me.

I braced myself for the attack, gritting my teeth at the inevitability of my death. I'd always half expected it to come at the hands of those responsible for my life and hadn't considered my chances to be high in such a battle; my father was millennia older than me, and I was still recovering from the copper at my neck and the burns on my body.

That didn't mean I wouldn't fight.

It just meant I wouldn't be surprised when I took my last glimpse of this world.

Thorne's face flickered in my mind the second before my father descended.

A ripping of flesh and bone exploded in my senses as the unmistakable sounds of death poisoned the air. It took me a millisecond to realize it wasn't my death.

I whipped around to meet those brutal eyes once more, then down at the head of the vampire who had been directly behind me, a knife in hand.

I opened my mouth and then closed it, having a moment of utter disbelief in the middle of the battle.

My father didn't wait for me to speak, nor did he seem overly concerned about my injuries. Without a word, he disappeared into the fray once more. I didn't get a chance to think because Rick was still in the midst of the furious assault, running low on bodyguards, which meant he was preoccupied with the two vampires he was wrestling, not noticing the one behind him about to land a kill shot.

I tackled the vampire around the midsection as Rick turned in what would have been just in time to see his head taken from his own neck if it weren't for me.

Me saving him was becoming a habit.

We crashed into a table, scattering the cowards who had been huddled underneath it. A rouge piece of wood speared into my calf, the vampire I'd tackled up and brandishing his deadly weapon the second I let my grip relax in pain.

I dodged the first of his swipes. Well mostly. The copper grazed a line from shoulder to shoulder, nothing more than a flesh wound.

I tried not to notice that the world seemed to be sideways as my injuries got the best of me. The previous vampires had been relatively easy to dispatch, even in my injured state, but it seemed the ones focusing on Rick were the elite squad.

And I had to be all heroic and save my king. I may have just signed my own death warrant instead.

An attacker let out a hiss as I darted forward to connect my knees with his balls. I fought dirty, I wasn't ashamed to say. Nobility in a battle got you one place—properly dead.

I clasped him to me and sank my fangs into his jugular, aiming on ripping it out, giving me a much easier job of removing his head. I managed my task at the same time as burning agony exploded in my chest. I let out a hiss of pain the same second the vampire's eyes widened in victory.

"Die, bitch," he choked through the wet sounds of his blood filling his mouth.

I winced but managed, through a sheer force of will, to

grasp the sides of his neck.

"No, thanks. I think it's your turn," I rasped, then used the last of my strength to make sure that horrible gaze was looking at the floor instead of me.

His headless body stood there for a moment. I glanced down, seeing the white hand clutched against the handle protruding from my chest cavity.

"Fuck," I murmured, yanking the hand away. As if we'd synchronized it, the headless body and I tumbled to the floor.

I lay beside the bodies and blood, staring at the ceiling. I had intended to pull the copper blade from my chest before it could puncture my heart, but my hands didn't seem to work.

Thankfully all of the pain that had plagued me this entire time seemed to wash away like the tide, leaving only blissed numbness in its place. I smiled at the tapestry hanging from the ceiling, not hearing the sounds of death or tearing of flesh. I didn't hear a thing, in fact. Strangely, I saw Jonathan, lying on the ceiling in a mirror image of my position.

He wasn't covered in blood like the last time I saw him. His eyes weren't glassy and vacant; instead, they glowed with that purity of love that had made me forget everything but the two of us.

He smiled, his tanned skin glistening against the vibrant ceiling.

I grinned back.

His hand extended upwards, like it was trying to cross the distance between us, a yawning chasm thanks to the high-ceilinged mansion. I frowned and found myself able to do the same. Where my arms were once paralyzed, they came unstuck, reaching with everything I had to grasp his hand. His hand that I knew would be warm, residual heat from the Paris summer kissing his skin.

It wouldn't be cold like the marble floor beneath me. I was certain I needed to grasp that hand and it would all be gone. The distance started to grow smaller as the cold spread through my body. I stayed on the floor yet somehow felt like I was floating.

Then the picture of him rippled as a bloodstained face yanked me away from the grip that had been mere millimeters away.

A face that was covered in blood, eyes cloaked in horror.

"Isla," he said urgently, his voice thick as it waded through the layers of ice that had encircled my body.

I frowned at him for getting in the way and attempted to struggle, but my hand fell like a weight at my side.

Rick's mouth moved as his fear-filled gaze ran over my body. His words were lost in the ice, and the last thing I saw was his wrist move to his lips before pressing it to my own.

The liquid broke through the ice like lava, uncomfortable in its heat, rivaling the blast that happened what should have been years before.

It was worse than that as it trickled down my throat, burning my insides as I lay paralyzed.

Black that I hadn't noticed dancing at the edge of my vision chose that moment to pounce, giving me reprieve from the pain.

From everything.

"Sire we must insist that we dispatch from the mansion," a grating voice pleaded. "We're already compromised. Our guards are depleted. The royal guard is en route from Geneva but they're hours away. Your men cannot protect you here for much longer."

I tasted the rage in the air and decided to keep my eyes closed to listen to this play out.

"My men couldn't even protect me on the first attack, Sven," Rick said smoothly, the ice in his voice cutting through the air. "Forgive me if I'm not relying on any of them in regards to my safety, which I'm quite capable of ensuring." There was a loaded pause as the air turned bitter and musky with the taste of rage. "In fact, relieve my current guard from their duty apart from the ones who actually managed to keep all their limbs and fight with dignity," he snapped.

"But sire—"

"Do you want to be included in that group, Sven? Because if you do, keep arguing with your king."

Please argue, Jeeves, I chanted. That would be a glorious way to start the night.

Silence and the taste of shame quickly retreated as the door shut behind me.

Drat.

"I know you're awake," a voice observed dryly, though something softer cut through the previous rage.

I opened my eyes and in one swift movement got up from the bed I'd been tucked in to stand on my bare feet. A quick glance down showed I was naked.

At least my skin was fresh and free from the burns that had previously clothed me. Though the smell of smoke and charred skin clung to my hair.

"And I'm not dead," I observed, watching Rick burst from the chair he'd been reclining in at my bedside. "Because if I was in heaven, I'd have heard you dismiss Jeeves, and the more likely residence of my afterlife would be a lot hotter and less luxurious," I continued, glancing around the opulent room. The bed I'd been in was larger than a studio apartment in Brooklyn, the rest of the space sparse but expensively decorated.

"You shouldn't be up," Rick growled, coming to stand in front of me. His gaze focused on my chest. "Not when you've taken a disturbing amount of time to heal. I fear that blade was spelled."

"I shouldn't be naked either," I shot back. I wasn't perturbed by my lack of attire, humans were caught up on it but I was pleased with what god, or depending who you talked to, the devil gave me. For fun, I gave Rick's stoic face a look. "Unless you weren't planning on having me up so soon and you were going to do naughty things with my unconscious body." I *tsked*. "My my, Your Highness. It always is the royal ones who are the most depraved."

His eyes turned glassy and glittered with rage. He clutched my shoulders with force that normally, even in my strongest state, would make me wince, but interestingly, it felt like a gentle squeeze.

I didn't have time to inspect that because Rick's face was in mine. "You were so close to dying, Isla, I could taste the fucking grave on you. You've been taunting Hades himself with your sheer proximity," he fumed. "Do you take anything seriously?" His cultured voice ran over the curse like velvet, a slight accent mingling with his words.

His fury exploded through the room, hitting the walls and washing back to coat me in its taste.

"Of course I take things seriously," I snapped. "Just not insignificant things like life and death. You start worrying about that too much and you'll find yourself in a grave quicker than you can say necrophilia."

His eyes flared and he flinched like he might actually strike me. I waited to see which way the wind would blow.

He let me go, running his hands through his hair in a decidedly human gesture of frustration.

I tilted my head at him while I took stock of my body. My naked skin was flawless and didn't betray an inch of the inferno that had embraced it… how long ago had the battle been? I extended my senses outwards and could still smell the burning of tapestries and hear the cries of injured vampires, or more likely attackers being interrogated. Rick hadn't changed out of his torn and burned clothes; the black disguised most of the blood, but there was no mistaking the smell.

It couldn't have been more than an hour, two at the very most since the explosion, and even with my abilities, I wouldn't be feeling like I'd just drained a college football team. Especially when my skin had been punctured by not one but two copper daggers, which slowed the healing process. Not to mention the second one had brushed my heart in such a way that I'd thought I'd be faced with the king of the underworld right now, not the angry and broody king of our race.

"Speaking of life and death, how am I on this side of the grave? I don't doubt my strength, but even I can't survive and heal from injuries like copper to the heart and being barbequed like a steak," I said, memories of the last moments of my consciousness flowing through me.

I momentarily stilled as that cold washed over me.

Jonathan.

I'd seen him. Almost touched him.

That meant I'd crossed the veil into the otherworld. If my skin had come into contact with his…. I shuddered as the prospect of it both excited and terrified me.

The ice of the grave had me in its clutches, but then there was heat.

My head snapped up as Rick watched me intently. He

hadn't answered me, instead observing me as I added it up.

"Your blood," I said, my voice a muted whisper.

He nodded once.

The simple nod tore through centuries of history I'd rebelled against learning in school.

Blood of a vampire couldn't heal, despite popular belief. There was a reason why we fed from humans; we needed the life force of their blood, the same force that didn't flow through ours. We were technically dead, although our bodies operated on an accelerated healing process and were able to digest food and drink. Because of that, our blood needed to be mixed with live blood in order to sustain us.

Sure, I'd known Rick's blood could hypnotize a human, but heal a vampire? That was something else entirely.

"You want to elaborate on that?" I asked finally.

He stepped forward so his body brushed my naked skin. The heat of it burned through his clothes. He'd fed recently.

"This knowledge could be the signature on your death warrant, if you utter it to anyone else," he warned.

I blinked at him. "The ink on that's been dry for centuries," I told him.

His eyes hardened. "Not here. The walls have ears," he said finally, stepping back.

"And knives," I added. "If tonight's attack was anything to go by."

He nodded. "The war has emerged from the shadows."

It was not a nice thought. "Seems to be," I agreed. "Did you get any intel?""Not from the attackers. They all burned." His voice vibrated with fury. "What I could get out of them in their death throes was little more than pleading."

I scoffed in distaste. "It's good to know the vampires fighting for the other side are complete and utter cowards."

Pleading? In the face of death. That was just embarrassing.

The king nodded. "Most behind this rebellion are. But cowardice is more dangerous than bravery in times such as these."

My tangled thoughts jumped around more than normal while digesting that information. "Duncan," I said suddenly. "Is he okay?"

On cue, the door burst open and a bloodstained Scotsman stepped through it. His suit, which had been gray earlier that night, was almost entirely a dirty brown, with the distinct metallic smell of blood. His hair was matted with soot and who knew what else, and his face had been haphazardly wiped to get the worst of his red mask off.

"Are you psychic or something?" I asked, relief palpable in my tone. I didn't have many friends, so I really didn't need the ones I did have dying on me.

He grinned. "Nope, been waitin' out there to make an entrance." He winked at me. "And securing meself a date for later this evening." His eyes went over my naked pale skin. "Unless you're offerin'?"

Rick was gone from in front of me and back in a breeze, thrusting a shirt at me with a pointed gaze at Duncan.

I shrugged into it unhurriedly.

"Well, Em, you sure know how to throw a shindig," Duncan declared, his eyes on my fingers as they fastened the white shirt that reached my midthighs.

He met Rick's steely gaze once I'd covered up all the interesting bits. "Not that I'm complaining, but I almost lost a good friend of mine tonight, which I think I would've been very fuckin' brassed off about." He gave me a soft look. "Glad you're healed and not in the ground, lassie."

"Me too," I replied cheerfully. "I plan on my death being a

little more exciting than at a stuffy monarchy party."

He turned his attention back to Rick. "Even though she's still up and about, I'm most motivated to ask who the fuck did it and who you've pissed off since we last saw each other."

Rick walked to the corner of the room and pressed a button, a bar unfolding from the wall.

Nifty.

He poured each of us glasses of whiskey. Duncan drained his before I'd even gripped the crystal properly. He darted back over to the bar to snag the bottle instead of going through the motions of pouring.

"What? I'm Scottish," he said to Rick.

Rick took a sip of his own drink. "You know who this is, Campbell."

"What? Those new world order pricks? Last I heard they were an annoying mosquito."

"Fuck, you're just as bad as Isla," Rick muttered.

"I'll take that as a compliment," Duncan said as he swigged from the crystal tumbler.

I nodded. "As you should. Not a higher one can be paid."

Rick wasn't finding us amusing. Assassination attempts had him very testy.

"As you can see, they're a little more than a mosquito now," Rick gritted out. "It's fair to say that it's not a small faction of rebellious vampires, nor is it exclusive to our race. Evidenced by the fact that both the wolves and witches experienced similar attacks tonight."

"Fuck," I muttered, thinking of Sophie, but then deciding these assholes may have been doing her a favor by dispatching the witch queen.

"My sentiments exactly," Rick muttered. "Especially with the intel you've uncovered, Isla. Using their newest abominations as weapons is going to bring about a war the likes of which will rival the Uprising."

I raised my brow. Not that I didn't think this was serious, but perhaps I hadn't been treating it like it was anything… big. History's battles like the Uprising showed magnificent and bloody battlefields that rippled through the species and filtered even to human's books.

I'd thought such rebellions were tucked in the past, the blood sunk into the soil and half-forgotten in lieu of a society that may still shed blood on a regular basis but wouldn't go to war. We considered ourselves superior to humans, who were always warring over trivial things. Yet there we were, and I hadn't even realized it to be so. I wondered idly if it had been the same for those in the war which decimated numbers on all sides before treaties were signed. Books always wrapped events up neatly, like a story that flowed with cohesion. Reality was rarely the same, splintered events clashing together with randomness until they culminated in a war. Until the bodies piled so high that all you could see was death.

"Wait a second," Duncan cut into my thoughts. "You've got *Isla* collecting intel?" His eyes flared and he glanced to me. "You said you weren't here by choice." Then his bottle smashed to the floor and he and Rick were a blur of bodies until they emerged with fresh blood coating their faces, fangs extended as they clutched each other's necks.

I sat back on the bed, crossing my legs and sipping my drink. I'd been in enough battles, plus I didn't have enough testosterone to be involved in theirs.

"What kind of shit have you got on Isla to force her to be your fuckin' little soldier? 'Cause I know she'd rather file down her own fuckin' fangs than become an employee of the monarchy," Duncan hissed, voice slightly garbled from Rick's hand at his throat.

"Her survival is her primary motivator," Rick rasped back. "Considering this faction has decided to make her one of their most wanted targets. My employ comes with my protection."

I raised a brow at that.

"Your employ didn't save me from the witch and her little monkeys who almost killed me. It was little old me who saved myself," I cut in, unable to help myself. Oh, and the slayer I slept with, but I decided to keep that little gem to myself.

Rick's eyes cut to me. "That's because the protection detail I had on you was busy chasing down the man who planted explosives in your apartment. Which they succeeded in diffusing."

I glared at the king. "You've had people following me?"

I shouldn't have been surprised, but I'd failed to think of the possibility. Ice washed over me at the thought of the king's royal guard witnessing me and Thorne in any way shape or form.

Though the fact that I was still undead meant they obviously hadn't. No matter how fond of me the king seemed, I knew he wouldn't blink at executing me. That character trait was one of the primary reasons why His Highness was growing on me.

That and he had a great ass.

Rick gave Duncan a pointed look. "Better to let me explain without trying to choke me. You can try again once you've heard the whole story."

Duncan gave him a look before he released him. "I'm only doing this because you're my mate, not that fuckin' blue blood runnin' through ye veins. You know I couldn't give a shite about that."

Rick rubbed his throat. "Precisely why you're the two

vampires I can trust at this point in time."

I laughed. "Well that's just sad. Duncan and I are the last people anyone should be trusting."

Duncan grunted in agreement.

Rick shook his head. "Honesty, which you've disguised as insolence, makes you part of a very small circle that, after tonight, has gotten smaller." His eyes went faraway before anchoring him back in the room.

He focused on me. "Yes, you were being followed. For about one day. By happy accident it was the day the bomb was planted in your apartment. Then every time they attempted to do so they'd find themselves back at my compound, unable to articulate as to why," he said, voice tight.

I restrained a smile. I was so sending Sophie a Sephora voucher.

"It seems there's much more to you than meets the eye," Rick continued. "When it became apparent that you could take care of yourself, I assigned your guards to monitor unusual activity at your apartment instead. Even then they found themselves unable to tell me about the comings and goings of your visitors."

Good thing. Or else Thorne's head would not be attached to his shoulders and I would be subject to some very uncomfortable questioning.

"So your fury is unfounded," Rick continued evenly.

I glared at him. "Not unfounded whatsoever. I take great offense at having anyone but Scott follow me. And that's because I've resigned myself to the fact that I can't kill him, so I've gotten used to him."

"Who is Scott?" Rick clipped.

I rolled my eyes. "No one you need to worry your pretty little head about. You just need to remember that if you have me followed again, you won't be just worried about this little war. You'll be worrying about the lives of the soldiers who could be protecting you instead of dying because you're a stalker who doesn't even have the guts to do the stalking himself."

I actually heard him grind his teeth. "It wasn't stalking. It was protection."

Duncan clapped him on the back. "I'd quit while you're ahead, Your Highness. Or behind. No use arguing with a regular woman under the best of circumstances, and this isn't the best of circumstances and Isla isn't a regular woman. She'll likely grind them balls to dust if you keep going much longer," he stated. "Plus, I think, if I weren't mistaken, she was the one who almost died protecting your royal ass tonight." His tone was a pleasant mixture of teasing and homicide.

Rick's eyes burned on mine.

"You're welcome," I said cheerfully. "I'm sure you'll bump up my salary for that one. Or at least my silence on the big bad king being saved by the little good Isla."

The corner of his mouth quirked, cracking the marble fury on his face. "I don't pay you anything."

I grinned. "Exactly. That's why I'm expecting a *very* generous raise."

He shook his head. "Is there ever a chance of staying on point with the two of you, even in the face of a war?"

"Fuck no" was Duncan's response as I shook my head.

Rick rubbed his neck. "Well, let's try. For our continued survival more than anything. Should that be a good motivator?"

He took our silence as affirmation.

"Right. So to fill in those who don't have the knowledge about the precarious situation we find ourselves and our race in—"

The buzzing of my phone cut the conversation short, even

on vibrate and in my purse which somebody had thoughtfully placed on the chaise across the room.

I hopped over to the sofa, holding up my finger to the very grumpy-looking king.

Side note: even with bloodstained ruins of a custom suit and covered in soot from an explosion, he was practically sinful. Who was I kidding? He looked better than he ever would.

His emerald eyes darkened in warning.

"The precariousness of our race can take a pause," I said, glancing down at Scott's name flashing on the screen and the multitude of missed calls from him.

He'd probably had some form of mental breakdown about his characters on *Star Force* or whatever it was.

"Scott, you do have the best timing," I answered, giving a wink to the stoic and pissed-off male in front of me.

My wink and easy demeanor were immediately cut off by the pained cry at the end of the phone, followed by Scott's garbled words.

"Where are you?" I hissed.

I got the location in the midst of his hysteria, then slipped on my heels, which were soot and bloodstained but still wearable.

Both Duncan and Rick had heard both sides of the conversation, so Duncan had lost his easy grin and Rick had more tension and frustration rolling off him.

"I'm sure you can fill Duncan in and make battle plans. I've got another disaster to handle," I informed them.

Rick was in my way before I tried to make it to the door. "Isla, you just survived an assassination attempt. You're not going anywhere," he growled, sounding decidedly more caveman than his usual refined monarch.

I narrowed my eyes at him. "No, *you* survived an

assassination attempt," I corrected tightly. "I was merely unlucky enough to be in the immediate vicinity. I'm sure you've got enough mute burly guards to keep you safe, so don't worry."

He narrowed his brows. "You're a prime target for these extremists, if you haven't noticed. Plus, you were responsible for a considerable dent in their numbers after this evening. We can't be sure this wasn't a retaliation."

I shook my head at Duncan when he mimed hitting Rick over the head in order to let me leave. They'd only just stopped almost killing each other.

"No, this was a planned and coordinated event," I said, impatience leaching into my tone. "No one knew I was even coming, since it's pretty well known I'm not a regular on this circuit, so it was your party, your house and you're the figurehead for the entire establishment these assholes are trying to bring down. Sure, they'd like to get their hands on me too, but I'm quite capable of protecting myself—and you, for that matter. And now I've got another damsel who needs saving, so if you'll excuse me." I gave him a dangerous look, and the air turned palpable as he debated on restraining me bodily. I could see it in his eyes. Likely he could do it, as he was stronger than me, but then Duncan would try to join in on the fun and then guards would storm the room and it'd be a big thing.

He stepped aside.

"You're getting a guard on you," he relented.

I grinned at him. "Of course. I'll feel *so* much safer." I quickly kissed Duncan on the cheek. "Great to see you, Dunc."

He squeezed my waist. "Never a dull moment, Isla," he murmured. "Sure you don't need backup?" he asked hopefully.

I shook my head. "I've got this one. You stay with our fearless leader and plan to fight a revolution. I'm sure two strapping brutes such as yourself, plus the council keeping patriarchy alive, don't need a little woman being in the way." I gave Rick a look. "Rain check on the details of my speedy recovery," I said firmly. It wasn't a question.

Rick and Duncan exchanged a glance. "I'll be in touch," he gritted out.

"Dandy," I replied.

"Try not to get killed," Duncan called to me.

"Ditto," I replied as I sped out the door.

FOURTEEN

I LOST MY TAIL WITHIN TWO MINUTES OF WEAVING through traffic heading back into the city.

Really, Rick needed new staff. I was in a cherry-red convertible, not exactly hard to miss. But I did have mad skills.

I didn't enjoy that as much as I normally would. Scott's phone call took care of that. Only when confronted with his scrambled cries about a slayer attack and his injury that wasn't healing had I realized how fond of the idiot I was.

Which had me pissed the hell off at the prospect that he might die. At the hands of slayer, no less.

"Hey, hooker," Sophie answered when I dialed her on my car Bluetooth.

"I need you to be at a warehouse near the Hudson in five minutes," I clipped, ignoring a red light and swerving past a semi that seemed intent on plowing into me. "I'm sending you the address."

"Do I need to bring weapons?" she asked, catching my tone immediately. "No, I'll take care of that. Just be there."

I hung up and spent the rest of the deceptively long trip thinking up various ways to punish the slayer who did this.

I could smell the blood before I even got out of the car.

Scott's slumped form at the corner of the empty warehouse was the source of most of it. A dead human was sprawled a few feet away from him.

"Isla," he choked out as soon as I knelt in front of him, his voice strained. "I'm sorry."

"That's the last time you apologize until we make sure you're going to live long enough to be sorry," I snapped, pushing his hand from his face that was covered in a thick blanket of blood.

As were his white tee and jeans.

And the floor surrounding him.

He winced but otherwise didn't cry out. Which was admirable considering he was missing his left eyeball, a gaping and jagged wound carved into the socket instead.

"He just came out of nowhere," he cried as I knelt in front of him, unsure of what to do. First aid wasn't exactly needed when you healed within minutes.

Pressure. That's what they do on those shows.

Four hundred years on this earth and I had no idea how to treat injuries.

I laid my hands against the bleeding wound on his face. It was rather awkward and Scott let out another pain-filled hiss. That one choked into a small sob and I gritted my teeth against it, remembering how young he was.

"How long have you been here?" I asked him, voice tight.

"Um, I'm n-not exactly s-sure," he stuttered. "It's b-been

longer than an hour, though."

"Fuck," I hissed. He'd been bleeding for an hour. And still hadn't healed.

"Am I going to die?" he asked, his rough voice little more than a whisper.

I looked into his one tear-filled eye. "Of course not," I snapped. "Don't say such stupid things. You're a half breed, so you just take longer to heal, that's all," I lied.

His eye held mine before it turned slightly glassy and started to droop.

"Don't you dare pass out," I ordered. "If you do, you'll never come out on a hunt with me again."

My threat did little, but his eyes thankfully stayed open and he stretched his bloodstained mouth into a sad grin.

"It's what I was doing," he rasped. "I found one for us." His head did a weird little jerk to the dead human. "Rapist," he coughed. "Easy to trail him here. Wanted to show you I could do it myself." He chuckled in a dry and utterly horrible sound, coated with death. "Guess I proved myself wrong."

"He's dead, isn't he? I'd say you did well," I said, my voice chock-full of fake cheerfulness. I was inwardly screaming at myself for inability to do a thing to help him.

My gaze landed on the glint of silver that hummed with its power. It was covered in blood, Scott's blood, but it was unmistakable.

"Scott," I said urgently. "The slayer who did this, did you get a look at him?"

The yawning silence between my question and his answer was full of the life draining from Scott.

"Big, like he took too many roids, you know?" he said weakly. "Bald head. A total tool."

I smiled weakly. "Erik?"

He nodded.

I gritted my teeth.

At the same moment Scott's eyes dropped closed, Sophie's scent mingled against the blood as she settled beside me.

"Shit," she hissed.

"Yeah," I agreed. I picked up the blade, embracing the pain that came with the contact. I held it up to her. "You can undo what this has done?"

She glanced at the blade as she pushed my hands away, replacing them with her own that started to glow slightly.

"I can't undo the damage, you know that," she said, her voice turning thick with magic leaching from her. "But I can save his life." She glanced at me, her eyes glowing with that same green. "You want to go make sure that no one can save the life of the one who did this?" Sophie had become rather fond of Scott too.

I grinned. "Do I fucking ever."

Content that Sophie had it covered, I bent down to Scott's head, placing my lips on it before leaving the warehouse with one destination in mind.

I clutched the blade in my hand, barely feeling the pain jarring up my arm.

I hadn't needed Scott's identification of Erik; his scent was all over the warehouse, sticking to the blade like a leech. I wasn't a werewolf so I couldn't use my nose to track the undesirable scent through the city. I could use my brain, though.

"Isla, did that explosion at the king's compound have anything to do with you?" Dante asked on the other side of the phone.

I rolled my eyes. "No, though I did happen to get my favorite dress ruined as a result," I hissed, weaving through traffic to get to the side of the city I was aiming for. There was one or two places in the human quarter where slayers were known to mingle. Humans didn't know it, but they had a small sliver of the pie that had divided New York amongst immortals when the city was first born. That's the place the slayers skulked when they weren't brave enough to head into our territory.

The only reason those establishments still stood was because most vampires had better things to do than hunt slayers on their spare time. Slayers usually came to us. Much more convenient.

I knew men like Erik wouldn't tuck themselves back in bed after mutilating innocent vampires; they were more than likely to boast about their conquests while poisoning their livers. The night was getting late, dawn only a couple of hours away, which had me thinking he wouldn't be doing any more slaying for the night.

"You were there?" Dante hissed over the background noise of the bar. "Jesus, Isla, are you okay?"

"Didn't you hear me?" I asked. "I'm not okay. My dress got ruined, I am now intimately acquainted with how uncomfortable copper to the chest is, and now I'm pissed the fuck off at a slayer who doesn't know when to cry uncle," I half yelled. "I need intel so I can make sure I let out the wrong amount of rage on the right person."

There was a split-second pause. "What do you need?"

"You still got that contact at that slayer bar in Brooklyn?"

"Fuck, Isla," the demon said by way of reply. "That's crazy, even for you."

"I didn't ask for your diagnosis of my sanity. I said goodbye to that centuries ago. I asked if you still had that contact,"

I snapped.

"Yes, I do," he answered, obviously giving up on the concerned demon routine. "What do you need from him?"

"To know if an asshole named Erik has been in the bar, and if not I need his location. I need it five minutes ago."

Dante sighed. "Got it. You not already neck deep in enough shit, you gotta add slayers to the mix?" he asked, sounding concerned.

I drummed my fingers against the steering wheel. "Oh no, this isn't trouble. This is going to be fucking brilliant."

I'm pretty sure I heard him mutter "crazy bitch" as he hung off.

Five minutes later, I had my location.

Fifteen minutes later, I kicked in the door of a dive bar in Eastern Brooklyn.

All heads turned to me, as the slayers could sense my arrival. Also, wearing a men's white dress shirt covered in blood and nothing else but ruined Jimmy Choos might have contributed to the slack-jawed reaction I got from the supposed warriors of the human race hunched over beers in a dirty bar.

"Did anyone order Girl Scout cookies?" I asked sweetly.

Before they could start getting their shit together, I wove through the tables and grabbed No Neck from his perch on the bar, slamming him against the wall.

Dante's intel held up. He was so getting a Christmas card this year.

"Hello, asshole. Didn't anyone teach you it's rude to stab other people?" I paused as he kicked his booted feet out uselessly. He reeked of alcohol. *Cheap whiskey. Figures.* I screwed up my nose. "Nope? Me neither."

I didn't waste any time pressing my borrowed blade through the same eye that he had done to Scott in a practiced sweep. The blade wasn't exactly designed for vampires to use against slayers, hence the resistance from the blade itself, but that didn't mean it didn't sink into his flesh; I just had to ignore the shooting pain in my bones. His screams worked as my lullaby. I let Erik crumple to the ground when I was satisfied with my work.

The first of his buddies to try and attack me from behind went flying into the bar, landing awkwardly and probably breaking some bones, but not enough to kill him.

I turned to the remaining patrons, who now had enough blood spilled to realize they needed to fight. They roughly circled me, each of them eying me warily. One had a gun, another a copper knife and the third a shotgun. Nothing to worry about. I didn't recognize any of them as Thorne's people, and I didn't know whether this was a bad or a good thing.

"Now, boys. I've had more than enough of battles and bloodshed tonight and I'd prefer not to kill you considering you lead such fulfilled and charitable lives." I gave the bar and their drinks a pointed look. "But if you force my hand, I will have to maim at least some of you," I continued.

Before one of them could pluck up the courage, or shake off their drunkenness, the door burst open. Without even looking, I knew who it was.

The relief from the men around me was palpable. Thorne stormed past me and the disbelieving eyes of the men, who'd presumably thought he'd enter a death match with the evil and sexy vampire immediately. Familiar faces trailed after him, eyeing me and the bloody scene with blank gazes.

Apart from Chace, of course. His young eyes popped out. Not literally, thankfully; there'd already been too much of that.

I grinned at him.

Thorne's gaze was filled with utter rage and disgust, and I

winced.

"What the fuck have you done?" he hissed, his voice at a decibel that shouldn't be heard over the screams, but the weight of accusation in it gave it an echo quality.

Each of the slayers stood in their spots, weapons drawn but not doing anything with them. Thorne was barking at someone to get a doctor while putting pressure on Erik's face. His furious gaze rarely left mine, keeping me anchored to the floor.

I flipped my hair in an effort to make it seem like that gaze didn't hurt. "An eye for an eye," I replied casually. "I know history has made the phrase metaphorical, but I take everything literally. And I take revenge very seriously. Be happy he's even breathing. Fifty percent loss of eyesight is better than one hundred percent loss of blood." I scanned the slayers who were ready to pounce. "You'd all do well to remember that, in case anyone was considering serving me a dish best served at the same temperature as my heart. I doubt *Erik* is someone you're willing to die for."

"Your men come after my *innocent* friends again, I'll burn your entire fucking compound to the ground." I gave Thorne a pointed look. "I know where you live, remember?" My gaze left his to scan the rest of those in the bar. "You slayers think you're doing humanity a favor by murdering those who qualify, but you're damning souls irreparably. You know what road's paved with good intentions, and it's not the one that saints walk on. I know how much you'd all like to believe you're doing God's work, but Lucifer makes all his worst sinners commit his wishes in the act of God."

Erik's heavy breathing and irritating cries were the only thing that followed my little speech, the cries silenced when he thankfully passed out. Or died. I was hoping for the latter, but a quick sense in his direction disappointed me with a weak heartbeat, distinguished from the rest of the men whose hearts where thrumming like sparrows.

Except Thorne's. His continued on a steady cadence, a different texture to the ones around him, so much so I could have picked him out in the middle of Times Square.

Troublesome.

As was the atmosphere of the bar. The air had an almost damp quality, like before a storm, hinting at another battle. My outfit was about as practical as the last one.

"I really need to rethink my wardrobe if things keep going like this," I muttered to myself.

Thorne's energy coursed through the bar, the attention was focused on him yet eyes on me. It wasn't lost on me that the men considered my life in his hands. What they likely didn't know was that he was moments away from condemning his men to death.

Something in Rick's blood had changed me. I could feel the texture of the air and the blood of every single human in the room in a way I hadn't before. I knew that the Hispanic one in front of me clutching a semiautomatic weapon had a metal insert in his knee which would spear through the skin if hit correctly. The lean man in front of me who looked like he should've been on Wall Street had an undiagnosed heart murmur. The man beside him hadn't slept in almost thirty hours; his organs on overdrive mingled with the adrenaline in his system would make him erratic.

How I knew these things, I had no clue. Or rather, I did and it unnerved me. But it also made my blood sing akin to the high of a draining a human who had imbibed drugs. I knew I could beat them all, and without effort. A foreign part of me introduced through this new blood urged me to do it. The vampire I had been before beckoned me with her cold arms and empty heart, tempting me with the simplicity of cruelty.

It was the thundering heart behind me that kept me rooted in place. I wouldn't make the first move.

"Stand down." His quiet command lay heavy on his shoulders and the ones of his men.

Chace lowered his immediately, looking almost relieved. The rest hesitated.

"I said stand the fuck down," he repeated on a growl.

They did, though their hatred filled the room.

"I'd love to stay and chat," I said amidst the loaded silence, "but now that we both have eyeless friends, I have other things to do, like kill the people who ruined my dress and severely pissed me off. Toodles." I finger-waved and darted through the gaps in their ranks before they could say a thing.

Thorne's throaty voice carried through the air even as I left the bar behind, walking at human speed down the street.

"Get him to a fuckin' hospital now, and figure out what the fuck is goin' on in the city tonight," he growled before his aura followed mine.

I didn't quicken my pace, though I didn't revel in having a confrontation in Brooklyn, of all places, wearing a man's shirt covered in blood after I'd gouged his friend's eye out.

Not the best situation to have the first conversation with the slayer you'd finally done the dirty with.

To be fair, his friend started the gouging.

Thorne caught up with me just as I got to my car, which thankfully wasn't up on bricks as this neighborhood would've had me believe.

He spun me around, at his hand at my neck in what would have been a whirl of motion for him. For me it happened slow enough to stop it. If I'd wanted to. But in the craziness of the past twenty-four hours, when I'd touched the grave and seen the eyes of my very dead lover, I craved the electric heat of his touch, even if it was his hand circled around my neck.

His eyes bore into mine, capturing me in their orbit and yanking me into the world of his fury and lust and concern. His emotions coated my body like a second skin.

My foreign blood both reveled and revolted with his touch, my nerve endings alight with urges to possess his mouth in a brutal kiss or snap his neck as an age-old instinct dredged up in blood urged me to do.

I stayed stock-still as his boots rested at either side of my heels, his body brushing mine as he pushed me into my car. My collarbone protested in pain as cool steel laid upon it in a dormant threat.

"Every single rule and lesson I've learned in my years fighting your kind screams at me to use this right now," he murmured, his voice a razor through my protests.

He pressed the steel in harder, the blade vibrating with his magic. It didn't break the skin, but I felt a craving for more of the pain to mingle with the pleasure of his touch, of his fury. I leaned into the blade.

His eyes flared at my small movement. "The men in there"—he nodded in the direction of the bar—"they haven't even tasted the bitter honey that is your lips, or felt the soft ridges of your peaches-and-cream skin, yet they're questioning it too.". His words should have been soft, but the underlying fury made the edges jagged and harsh. "You're making them question every single thing they've learned. They've attached to their identity. And those questions are dangerous. Fatal."

"The truth always is," I replied. "The fairy tales you've taken as gospel paint such convenient heroes and villains. I've made all that obsolete and painted people like No Neck as the villain when they're hell-bent on being the hero, willing to do whatever it takes to be one."

"You just drew blood from one of my men," he hissed. "I'm honor bound to take your life." The pressure of the knife increased further still, taunting me with its power. Then it clattered to the ground, and the hands that had encircled my neck with violence cradled it in a rough caress that rode the line between tender and brutal. A harmonious mix of the two.

His eyes were silver flames. "But all I can think about is you wearin' another man's shirt, covered in blood, and the haunted look behind your eyes that show me death has touched you tonight," he growled, pressing his forehead against mine.

I blinked at him, but for all the sarcastic remarks I could come up with in the midst of certain death, I had nothing to give him. Silence was a gift from me, and it was only his.

"What happened?" he rasped. "Who came close enough to take you from this earth when I don't have a grip on you that's tight enough for comfort? When I still can't breathe easy without tasting your scent on the air?" he growled.

"It's a long story," I breathed.

His eyes searched my face. "Yeah, and you'll tell it to me… after."

His lips descended on mine with a brutality that mirrored the violence of the night, the only difference being the tenderness that stopped the assault from becoming deadly.

Yet it still was.

Because he yanked back and, even though I knew it was for the best, that his merry team of slayers or one of Dante's friends could catch us at any moment, I wanted more. I wanted him despite what discovery meant.

I'd escaped demise countless times by fighting tooth and nail, yet I welcomed it with Thorne.

His hands at my neck once more showed me he possessed

more self-preservation.

"Keys," he ordered.

I nodded to the driver's seat.

He glanced to the interior of my car. "You left your fuckin' keys in the *ignition*?"

I found my tongue. "I had better things to worry about than finding a valet," I shot back.

His lips thinned at the reminder. "Get in the car, Isla." His voice was steel, and even though I'd most likely rip the tongue out of any other man, human or vampire, who tried to order me around, I complied.

The second my ass was in the seat, he screeched out into the night, gripping the steering wheel so hard his knuckles whitened. I could sense his blood, taste it almost. It drew me in with its allure as it had the night I'd woken up after the mansion. It wasn't thirst, as my belly was full of blood which I didn't rightly understand. It was something else. Something that didn't understand that giving into that craving was certain death.

"You want to educate me on what's happened that's torn this city apart tonight?" Thorne gritted out while he wove through traffic with ease.

I glanced at his arms, the muscles straining from the grip on the steering wheel. It was only then that I registered the scent of foreign blood atop his skin. It stained his arms and knuckles, the stark white showing grazes I'd somehow missed before.

"What happened to you?" I asked, my voice low, feeling an irrational urge to spill more blood.

"You didn't hear?"

"It's been a busy evening. I didn't have time to catch the evening news."

"There was an attack on a concert tonight in Lower Manhattan. Werewolves." He rubbed the back of his neck. "Was a fuckin' bloodbath. Got Lewis over there along with some higher-ups talkin' about an extremist shooter."

I scoffed. "Yes, that'll do wonders for the hate-filled wars your kind have already torn this world with. Blame it on the scapegoat."

His glare roasted my skin and I welcomed it. Ice had yet to recede from the edges of my psyche. It seemed it was always there, unless I was with him.

"And what's the alternative? Educate them on the fact that werewolves and vampires are warring in the streets and human causalities mean nothing to them as they stomp over them like flies?"

I glanced at my bloodstained nails. "Well that's not exactly the words I'd use," I muttered.

He slammed his fist down on the steering wheel. "Isla, this is serious!" he roared, the weight of his fury filling the car. "You almost killed one of my men tonight. Not to mention all the shit that's making the air taste bitter, like there's blood on the horizon, and you're firmly in your little world of denial, intent on making everything a joke."

I whipped my head to face him, shoving back the curtain of red that was my hair, but the curtain of rage remained. "I know!" I screamed back. "I'm well aware of how serious this is, considering I've been nearer to death these past weeks than I have this past century. I'm aware of how serious it is because I just witnessed an entire faction of vampires break the most sacred rule that governs our kind and try to blow most of the ruling families off the face of the earth. I know because they almost fucking succeeded. And because I was close enough to that blast to smell the roasting of my own flesh as it peeled off.

I know because most likely the same assholes who killed all of those humans tonight, who did that"—I glared at his bruised skin—"to you, are likely the same creatures who plunged a copper dagger into my chest so deep that I tasted the chill of the grave and saw… him," I hissed. "And because they're responsible for me almost embracing it. Instead, I've found myself in the middle of a war that may be the end of life as I know it and confronted by an attack on one of the gentlest vampires I know."

I gave him a contempt-filled look. "Oxymoron for you, I know, but that doesn't make it less true. I had to see him tasting the same death I'd chewed on tonight, merely because he wanted to help me rid the world of humans who tainted the world with their presence. He was trying to be *good,* despite what your publicity machine spits out and shoves down your throat to tell you otherwise. And he is good. The best. So on top of the stellar fucking evening I've had, I had to watch him go through that pain because your friend is infinitely more cruel than a vampire who now will be crippled for life when he's already shunned for being a half breed and a good person." I leaned forward. "I didn't hesitate in searching for my revenge, and I don't regret it, not for a second. What I don't understand is why I kept him breathing. Because of you. You robbed that from me because all I could think of was that gaze you treated me to the moment you walked through that door. I didn't want you to see me as a monster, when in reality that's all you'll ever see me as anyway."

Once I'd cut open the wound and poured my heart out, I felt tempted to suck in a ragged breath and cut through the bitter silence that followed my epic word vomit.

I wanted to look away from Thorne's penetrating gaze, to escape how the air seemed to vibrate. Heck, I considered throwing myself from the car, but he slowed down and whipped through a side street to park in an abandoned lot, still on a dark New York night.

Before I could make my escape, Thorne's hands were at my hips, yanking me across the car so I straddled him.

His shirt rode up and I ground my bare flesh against his jeans, mingling with the blood he'd spilled.

He gripped my neck. "Not once since I first saw you have I ever considered you a monster," he hissed. "A sorceress, perhaps, for the spell you've woven over me." His eyes roved over my face like he was consuming it. "If that's what it is, I hope never to get free of it."

He pulled my hair so my neck was exposed and laid his mouth on the cool skin, grazing it with his teeth. I cried out and ground against him, ripping at his jeans to get him free.

In a brutal blur of motion, we were no longer separate, his fire filling me with ecstasy. I wasn't gentle, nor did I abide by human speed as I pounded down onto him. He wasn't gentle either, gripping my neck and yanking at my hair as he met me, thrust for thrust.

No words were spoken. We were little more than animals, craving the only thing that made sense, that wasn't trying to kill us.

Each other.

Though even that might turn out to be the most fatal of them all.

I went straight for the whiskey bottle as we entered my apartment, filling my glass to the brim. Thorne didn't say a word as he disappeared down the hall. I didn't follow him, deciding to drain my drink and watch the skyline. I heard the opening and closing of my fridge and fizz of a beer bottle being opened.

He padded back into the room, taking a pull of his beer, regarding me. Electricity was whipping between us like a downed power line in the middle of the room, the fevered lovemaking on the side of the road cementing something forbidden and wrong between us, combining with all of the things that needed to be said. To be explained.

"Whose shirt?" he asked, glancing at the stained fabric in distaste.

I raised a brow. "After everything that happened tonight, that's the question you're asking?"

No verbal answer, just a stiff nod.

"Don't you think it's more important to address the fact that we're on the brink of war, your team may or may not want me dead and both of us have signed our death warrants by the mere act of being together and not killing each other?"

Thorne's eyes didn't leave mine as he crossed the room, setting his beer down on the bar before taking the empty tumbler from my hands. He did both things with gentleness and deliberate slowness, a stark contrast to him ripping the shirt's buttons off and yanking it down my arms so it tumbled to the floor.

"Nope," he clipped. "Out of all of that, my main concern is, first and foremost, you. I'll be ending those who spilled your blood, but that's for later. For now, I need to know why my woman is clothed in another man's shirt and is completely naked underneath." His calloused hands traced over my chest, the exact spot that that been opened earlier that night, then trailed between my breasts in a featherlight touch, circling my bellybutton and exploring the ridges of my hips.

I gazed at him through hooded lashes. "My dress got

ruined," I said by explanation. "And I wasn't exactly in control of the changing into the shirt."

The air flickered as my words registered. "You weren't in control?" Thorne repeated, his voice velvet.

"No. Well, of putting the shirt on, but taking off the dress, no. I was kind of… busy being unconscious."

His body stiffened. "Unconscious?" he repeated.

I smiled uneasily at his reaction. "Boy, you can taste the alpha rage in the air. Be careful, I might choke on it," I teased.

He gripped my arms tight enough to bruise if I wasn't hopped up on Rick's wacky bloody. "Isla," he warned. "You're dancin' around this shit and treating how close you were to death like it's a comedy show."

I scowled at him. "And how else am I supposed to treat it? I'm alive. Or undead. Healed and fine. Am I supposed to brood about the fact that I almost died, like you have. Focusing on *almost* is fatal, you know," I informed him. "Plus, we've got, like, a thousand other pressing matters."

He yanked me to him. "Yeah, much to my utter displeasure," he murmured. "Even if my team find a way to get right with you attacking a member of our own, the council is gonna need retribution, and Erik will be after blood."

I smiled. "Who isn't?"

He glowered at me. "How the fuck am I meant to bring the case of me and you to the council if you keep doin' shit that's gonna make them want to kill you?" he all but roared.

"They're going to have to take a number, unfortunately," I said, then stilled. "Bring the matter of me and you to the council?" I repeated.

His hands flexed at my arms. "Yeah," he answered like it was obvious.

"And why in heaven's name would you do such a thing?" I

hissed, yanking out of his arms. I needed distance for this. And booze. I swiped the bottle.

"Because," he clipped, letting me go, "my team is already guessin' that me and you enjoy more than a professional relationship, and although I trust them with my life, I'm not going to trust them with yours." His heat kissed my back, and my hair left the nape of my neck to be replaced by his mouth. "Plus, I'm not givin' you up, not for a good long while. And while you might be used to slinking in the shadows, I want to enjoy the sunshine with you."

Beautiful words. Romantic words. Pity they were a crock of shit. I whirled on him.

"You're delusional," I stated. "You think you can just tell a council that's been set in its ways for millennia that you're banging the enemy and they'll just be like, 'okay, cool'? No. That's not how this works. You're young, still bright-eyed despite all your broodiness and alpha-ness. Whatever this"—I gestured between us—"is, it's not enough to break a war that's been simmering for thousands of years gone by and most likely thousands of years to come. And however intent you are on keeping me alive, I'm going to do the same for you." My eyes burned into him. "And trust me, I'll go to great lengths to ensure that. And if you even consider telling your little council about us, you'll never see me again."

"Whatever 'this is,'" he parroted, "*is* worth starting a thousand wars for, Isla."

His body turned to marble and cracks split up the beer bottle he'd resumed drinking from during my tirade. "And I don't do well with threats," he bit out. "Especially when they involve you running."

I narrowed my eyes at him. "I don't do threats. I make promises," I replied, my voice cold. "And I don't run. Not from anything."

He stepped forward. "And you won't run from me," he declared. "From this. From us. Because if you do, I'll find you. And you won't like what happens when I do."

The threat lingered between us and I gazed into the resolve in his eyes, realizing I was fucked.

"Well, someone's been a naughty girl," a thick brogue declared.

Thorne whirled round, sending his beer shattering to the floor as he pulled his knife out, crouching in front of me in the time it took for Duncan to walk over to my bar and pour himself a drink.

He regarded Thorne and his knife casually. "A slayer, Isla? I'm impressed."

I put my hand on Thorne's shoulder, giving it a squeeze. "Down, boy. Duncan's not going to kill you," I said, though I wasn't so sure.

Duncan lifted his brow as he sipped his drink. "Aren't I?" he asked. "Well, I guess you're right. I'm at least going to wait until I get the lowdown on this particular situation and how you've managed to show yourself to a slayer and a king all in one night," he said, moving to recline on the sofa, crossing his ankles.

I tried to dart forward, but Thorne, who'd lowered his knife but hadn't sheathed it, grabbed me. "Don't sit your bloody suit all over my new sofa," I hissed.

Duncan smiled. "Don't worry, this stuff is dry. Fresh blood has yet to be spilled."

I could have detached myself easily but Thorne whipped us around, covering my naked body with his. In one movement, he'd taken off his leather jacket and covered me with it.

I glared at Thorne.

He glared back.

"Don't worry, mate, it's nothing I haven't seen before. I've seen it this very night, in fact." He winked at Thorne. "She gets around, you see."

The air around Thorne seemed to ripple. "He's the one who handled you while unconscious?" he growled, gripping his knife.

Duncan grinned. "Possessive one, isn't he?" he asked me playfully. "That means this isn't just a fuck. I forgot how utterly exciting it is with you around, Isla. You make the French Revolution seem like a night at the library." He focused on Thorne when I scowled at him. "Wasn't me who tangled with her unconscious and bloodstained body, though I would have, given the chance. Not that the king would let me. He was too busy making sure she didn't die." He gave him a hard look. "Which I think is more important considering she came pretty fuckin' close to it."

Thorne stiffened. It was at the sound of how close I was to death, I was sure, but I didn't miss the way his body visibly flinched at the mention of the king.

I guessed sleeping with one vampire was one thing when you'd dedicated your life to killing them. Sleeping with a vampire who let the king of the undead race see her naked must have been where he drew the line.

"Let's not bore him with the details, Dunc," I gritted out.

Duncan nodded. "Your wish is my command, my lady. Though I do approve of any form of rule breaking, and I'd follow you through the gates of heaven itself, I gotta ask, you sure about this?" He nodded to Thorne.

I gave Duncan a look.

He nodded. "So you know how forbidden this is?"

Another look. "Why do you think I'm doing it?"

He laughed, genuinely and long. "Let's just make sure you don't let anyone but me know about it." His grin was gone as quickly as it came. "'Cause even with the king being intent on getting into the panties that you never seem to wear, he won't hesitate to execute you once he finds out a slayer gets there first."

His words were a cool echo of my earlier thoughts. I didn't worry about Duncan blabbing; I knew enough of his secrets to have him in a dungeon for the rest of his life. Plus, I trusted him with my life. Two of the three people who had that trust were in that room.

I didn't know where Sophie was, though I hoped she was safe.

Thorne was gone from my side, his blade at Duncan's neck.

"You talk about having her executed again, it'll be the last words you utter," Thorne hissed.

Duncan raised his arm to take another sip. The movement had the blade scoring his skin. He didn't even blink.

"Happy to see you care about her enough to be suicidal," he said, his voice low but dangerous. "One thing you should learn about me is that I've known your girl here since before your grandfather fucked yer grandmammy, so you don't get to defend her honor." He grinned at me. "If she had any left, she'd be the one who did the protecting. She doesn't need an overly sensitive slayer or a disgustingly attractive vampire doing either one. But I will protect her neck. Which is why I'm here, and why you're not a pile of blood and guts on the floor. You'd do well to remember that."

The promise of death hung in the air as neither man moved. I regarded the blood under my fingernails in distaste.

Thorne leaned back, lowering the knife and stepping back. Not back to me, though; I noted the distance he kept between us with his face blank.

I straightened my shoulders, questioning why the sting of that small gesture hurt more than the flaying of my skin earlier that night.

"You're here for a reason, I presume?" I asked Duncan tightly.

He nodded. "Mainly to get away from all the bureaucratic assholes descending on the mansion." He gave me a calculated look. "The Sector was arriving just as I left."

I paced the room. "Yes, well, things are escalating. Of course the suits will get involved."

"As if they're not already involved."

I stopped and stared at Duncan. "Three hours ago, you didn't know the extent of the war. I think the word 'mosquito' was used. Now you're insinuating that the Sector is involved in overthrowing the king?"

He nodded and grinned. "I catch on quick."

I stared at him. "Not that quick."

He sighed. "Okay, so I may have visited an old bedmate of mine, and after being thoroughly satisfied, like I imagine you have been"—he winked at me and Thorne growled—"I managed to find out that the Sector has been having some regime changes implemented by our friend the king, who has them brassed off, to say the least."

I frowned. "Regime changes?" It was fair to say I didn't keep up with the rules; since I didn't follow them, what was the point? And they hadn't changed in thousands of years. Until now.

"Ones that threaten the carte blanche vampires have had over human life, or more aptly human death," Duncan explained. "They've been controversial."

"I bet they have," I muttered.

"It was the catalyst for an already unstable political climate. Some don't like the idea of blood being the only thing that gives someone authority."

I scoffed. "Can they wake up and smell the O-neg? Blood is the foundation of everything. The religious ones believe the blood that runs through Rick's veins is that of the original family, the first vampires. Of Ambrogio himself."

I didn't add that I had firsthand experience. The king's death threat echoed in my mind, but it was the threat of Thorne's fury that I'd shared a human with the king that stopped me.

"Veins can lie. And be drained."

I gave Duncan a look. "That they can."

Thorne's aura glittered around him. It didn't escape my notice that it seemed the stronger my feelings got for him the more I could see him, the twisting of his emotions becoming separate to the man himself.

I didn't need to be a witch to know that spelled danger.

"I need to be filled in on this shit, now," he growled.

Duncan drained his glass. "No, I don't think who you're fucking dictates you knowing anything," he replied, the harshness of his tone mingling with his brogue.

Thorne stepped forward at the same time as I did. I put my hand on his chest. "I know I gouged your buddy's eye out not an hour ago, but could I ask you to not try the same with Duncan?" I asked. "I've had about enough death matches in my living room."

Thorne glared at me, then Duncan. But he didn't lunge. I was calling that a win.

"You fought off an army of arseholes while seducing them at the same time, defeated death, disobeyed the king, de-eyed a slayer and then fucked one?" Duncan let out a low whistle. "I forgot just how magnificent you are, lassie. Good thing I'm stickin' around. Won't likely be bored."

"You're sticking around?" My hands were still on Thorne's chest, which had stiffened even more at Duncan's words.

Duncan nodded once. "The king himself is paying a pretty penny for my services."

I gaped at him. "You're staying because you're getting paid, not because of the war that may change the course of our race?"

He grinned, then stood. "I'm a mercenary, darlin'. War's when I make my fortune. I'd be an idiot not to capitalize on the biggest one this side of the millennia." He straightened his bloodstained suit. "Though I'll bet one lucky slayer is gettin' his share of the riches from this one. I'm gonna be going now, procure myself a permanent residence for the foreseeable future. I'll also get rid of any guards the king has seen fit to post after you lost them earlier." His face lost a bit of the teasing glint, the seriousness of his features aging his attractive face and showing the horrors of centuries that he hid remarkably well. "I'm not likely to be tellin' anyone 'bout this, you can trust that. But even someone as crazy as you wouldn't break this particular rule if she didn't think death was worth riskin'." He gave Thorne a long stare. "Mortals take such things as risking death lightly because, for them, it's a risk getting into an automobile. But listen to me now, lad. Immortals do not take on such things like feeble humans do. What she's riskin' for you is centuries lived and centuries yet to live. You best realize that."

And then he was gone.

The weight of his words joined the already heavy room.

My hand remained over Thorne's heart, the steady thump chasing away the taste of death that still lingered. After a few beats, his own scarred hand lifted up to cover mine.

"Just to be clear, I'm not plannin' on letting you get anywhere fuckin' near that grave. Ever."

I met his eyes. "Ditto."

The grave did not cater to such pious emotions as love, nor listen to promises whispered on the eve of the battle.

The grave came for everyone.

Even immortals.

Especially immortals if they happened to be star-crossed lovers.

FIFTEEN

Two Months later

I WALKED THROUGH THE DOOR AND STOPPED, TILTING MY head. "Well, that's one way to greet a visitor," I said to the men wielding knives and looking all murdery. I focused on one in particular. He wasn't holding a knife and was standing slightly removed from the mob, arms crossed over his impressive chest. He didn't much look like he'd be stepping in.

"You're not a visitor," the pimply faced one closest to me spat, shaking his knife at me. "You're a monster."

I rolled my eyes. "Kid, you gonna wave that thing around, make sure you know how to use it." I stepped forward so the tip of the steel pressed against my chest. "Oh, and that goes for the knife too," I purred.

He scuttled back so he hit his other friend's knife, yelping as it pricked his skin.

I smirked at the fiasco and my eyes met Thorne's. I swear to Chanel, his eyes glistened with amusement, though he was doing his best to hide it in front of his little class, of course. They knew I was coming to train them so their deaths weren't guaranteed in the coming battles, but they were yet to find out I was sleeping with their leader.

That might make one of their little sparrow hearts give out. No one, save Thorne and perhaps his best friend Silver, knew our alliance was something more than a weary peace treaty.

Not even the ominous council that I was yet to meet. Slayers operated in factions, each with their own leader. Thorne was in charge of the New York group and had commanded their silence over being trained by me. So far, the vampire had stayed in the bag, though I didn't know how that would last with the latest group. I had trained with everyone in his unit first. Only broke a few bones, the rest were bruises. Most of them took their injuries fairly well—apart from Erik, of course, who refused to partake.

Somehow, Thorne had managed to keep the eye incident from the council and had made it so only about a quarter of the slayers I'd trained looked at me with unbridled hatred, kind of like these. But that didn't mean all was forgiven. It most likely meant Erik was biding his time. I warned Thorne that he was likely to betray him before the month was out.

Thorne had given me an even look. "He's an asshole, but he's been with my unit for nigh on half a century."

I'd given him another look. "Vampires betray allies they've had for millennia. Time means nothing."

"We're not vampires."

I'd let him have that one but was still wary about Erik.

Thorne was part of some elite bloodline of slayers gifted with extended life spans in order to have some semblance of an even ground with vampires. Yet another thing he was loath to explain. It had been a sticking point but we didn't exactly have time to hash it out, what with all the raids on enemy camps I'd been partaking in with Sophie tagging along for fun.

It'd been quiet.

Unnervingly quiet. The kind of quiet that followed a dragon sucking in a large breath before it breathed fire all over the place.

Not good.

But that was for another time. Now I had to worry about trying to train the latest and freshest batch of slayers.

My eyes darted back to where Pizza Face was shaking and frantically dabbing at the tiny droplets of blood coming from his arm. His friend waved the knife at me. "Back, she-devil," he cried.

I gracefully dodged one of his swipes, checking my phone as I did. He did it a second time and I snatched his wrist, exerting enough pressure for him to let out a yelp similar to his friend's. When he dropped the knife, I caught it in my other hand. "I'll take this for now. We don't want you cutting yourself, do we?"

I glanced back at him. "Seriously? What is this, slayer preschool? No wonder you guys are going extinct."

He stepped forward, snatching the knife from Pizza Boy. In one lithe movement he had it against my neck. I grinned at him. "Touché."

In another, arguably lither movement, I had my own knife against his jugular. "Who do you think has a faster wrist? Fumbling human slayer barely out of diapers or kickass, beautiful and experienced vampire?"

"Experienced is a nice euphemism for old," he rasped.

I exerted just a little more pressure, enough to give him a

close shave. "You want to throw around dangerous words like that in front of the woman with a knife to your neck?" I asked, my voice sweet.

His eyes were quicksilver. "I live on the edge."

I grinned at him, lowering my knife. "Good thing I'm feeling forgiving today."

He lowered his own. "Good thing."

We shared a quick look before he turned back to the group.

"Isla is here to help us. Train you against attacks that you'll be seeing in the field. I'll be having words with anyone who tries to insult the fact that she's here." His voice was hard.

"And I'll be having more than words with that same person," I promised on a wink.

Thorne's eyes stayed blank, but the corner of his mouth twitched.

I rolled on my heels. "Okay, let's see what you've got."

"You think we've got a chance?" Chace asked, sipping his beer.

I glanced at him from my position on the sofa. "A chance at what? Winning *American Idol*?" I shook my head. "Sorry, you just can't hit those high notes."

He grinned at me before his naturally carefree face turned serious. "To make a difference in this war."

I sipped my wine, glancing to Thorne who was at the other end of the sofa, watching me, hands around his own beer. I let myself slip into a slight daydream about what those hands might do to me later.

I snapped out of it. "No, you don't have a chance at making a difference. But you've got a chance at not dying. So that's always good."

Thorne glared at me.

"What? I'm just being honest with the kid," I defended. "I've helped where I can, but even I'm not a miracle worker."

Though Thorne himself might be handy in a fight. He had the strength and speed of at least a half breed. Scott had helped out with sparring more than a couple of times, and Thorne bested him easily.

But that was Scott. It didn't count.

We'd sparred in the comfort of this abandoned warehouse-turned-practice space, but every single time it turned to sex.

Jury was out on who 'won.'

Another glance at Thorne and the way his veins pulsed in his forearms told me maybe I did.

"Isn't it hard?" Chace cut in.

I grinned at him. "That's what she said."

Thorne shook his head. "You have the maturity of a twelve-year-old," he observed.

I sipped my wine. "Thank you." I looked to Chace, who was chuckling. "Apart from the obvious, is *what* hard?"

He kept his eyes on me. "Having sex with Thorne and not… you know, biting him."

Thorne, who had at that moment been taking a sip of his beer, nearly choked on it.

His spluttering filled the air until he steadied himself. I grinned. No one could take him by surprise, not even me.

"What are you talking about?" Thorne rasped.

Chace rolled his eyes. "Come on, it's totally obvious." He waggled his eyes between the two of us like a schoolgirl.

"Is it?" I asked, slightly disappointed. "There goes my Oscar nod. And I thought I'd been doing *such* a good job."

We had. Thorne had been all business around his slayer

crew, the odd swirl in his eyes the only sign that there was something below the surface. I'd been the same. I had four hundred years of practice in my poker face. It upset me a child could see through it.

Chace grinned at me. "Well, I doubt anyone else has noticed," he relented. "Apart from Silver, obviously. But I'm observant." He gave Thorne a look. "And can keep a secret, so don't worry."

"Good," I said cheerfully. "I'd hate to snap your neck if you decided to sell this one to the tabloids."

Thorne glared at me.

I shrugged.

"I'll take it to the grave," Chace promised.

I sipped my wine. "We can only hope. And with the way this war is shaping up, that might not be too far away."

He didn't seem perturbed by his upcoming death. "So?" he probed.

"So what?"

"Is it hard not to bite him during sex? 'Cause, you know, his blood will kill you and all."

Thorne bristled and growled in his throat.

"Down, boy." I waved my hand at him. "I am somewhat aware that slayer blood is fatal, Chace," I told him dryly. "Let me ask you, considering someone's popped your cherry and had the most magical fifteen seconds of their life. Do you crave a cheeseburger when you're doing the horizontal tango?"

His face stayed blank and he shook his head slowly. Amusement rolled off him in waves. As with Thorne, though it was liberally sprinkled with fury. And lust.

I wasn't being entirely truthful. Though I snacked on the regular with psychos Scott and Lewis found, I was never sated. In fact, as of late it had been harder to even dull the burn in my throat. My body had a permanent chill to it, different than what was natural, and that only subsided when I was with Thorne. It settled in my stomach, like the pull of the grave. Troubling. The broken ribs I'd sustained after Thorne had been deliciously rough the previous night had only just healed that morning, and during training with the baby slayers they had smarted.

Not that I let that on.

Especially when Thorne's blood had an ever-increasing pull that was starting to worry me. After the rib-breaking, I had focused on the vein at his neck and had my lips fastened around it before I could blink. Luckily I could pass it off as a caress, with extreme effort. But it was concerning. Very. Especially when I had to report back to the king very soon. Whom I had been artfully dodging for the last two months.

It was great timing that he had been in Europe doing… whatever kings did. Now he was back and it was time to face the music.

"Isla." A deep voice jerked me out of my head.

Thorne was right in my face, concern rolling off him in waves.

"Are you okay?" he clipped.

The very fact that he had moved without me noting it was proof that I was not okay.

"Yes. Dandy. Just thinking of my outfit for tomorrow. Fashion is serious business."

His jaw tightened. "I'm still not happy about you going," he declared. This was far from the first time he'd made his misgivings known about me actively pursuing those involved with the rebellion. He knew little of my involvement with the king, and he knew nothing of my family's promise of my Awakening. That would not go down well.

I was learning that he was possessive to the thousandth

degree and would take it upon himself to try and do something suicidal like kill my family.

Only I could do that.

I had already had Sophie work her juju to make sure my family's spies couldn't trail me, or Thorne. It wouldn't do well at all to have them know about us.

The mere thought made me feel vaguely sick, in fact.

But all had been quiet from them too.

Another dragon that was sucking in its breath.

I focused on Thorne and the present. "Thanks for letting me know that," I replied. "It won't change a thing, but thanks just the same.

"I'm coming," he said suddenly.

I narrowed my eyes. "You are not. Unless you have a death wish I don't know about."

He held my glare. "No, but since yours is apparent, you're not going without me."

"They'll sense you within a mile," I told him triumphantly. "And most vampires won't react the way I have to you. No matter how pretty you are."

Thorne's gaze darted to Chace, who was finding the ceiling particularly fascinating at the moment.

"I can do something about that," a throaty voice declared.

Sophie's combat boots thumped against the concrete floor of the warehouse, Silver right behind her.

I narrowed my eyes at the strange pairing and then at Sophie's words once she approached us.

"There's a cloaking spell that will disguise his aura and make him little more than an average human," she continued.

A sliver of a grin edged on the corner of Thorne's face.

I glared at Sophie. "Not cool, dude. Why would you betray me in such a way?"

Her eyes were hard. “You can’t go to Mortimeus alone,” she said. “It’s too dangerous for you.”

I raised a brow. “You’re telling me it’s too dangerous going to a bar when you were the one who convinced me to crash a demon séance and I almost lost an eye?”

She didn’t smile. Or even move her lips.

Something wafted off her that I didn’t like.

“Jeez, who died? If it’s my parents I’d assume you’d be a lot happier.”

Sophie didn’t even blink. “We need to talk,” she said, her voice flat and strange.

I frowned at her. “Well… speak,” I urged.

She glanced at Chace.

“Don’t worry, I’m already going to kill him if he spills trade secrets.” I waved my hand to dismiss her concerns.

She swallowed. “How are you feeling?”

I stared at her a long moment. “Fine. I’m immortal, so no sniffles for me. Now, what’s the news?”

She stepped forward, her blank face an omen of what was to come. Even when she’d discovered her boyfriend in the 1960s was trying to kill her, she had a shadow of a grin and said he was bad in bed anyway.

“No, Isla, how are you feeling?” she repeated, giving me a look that told me she had insight into my current situation.

Thorne bristled beside me. “What is this about?” he demanded, looking from Sophie to me. “Isla?”

I glanced at him. “Why are you asking me? I’m not the one who said I had news,” I defended.

He wasn’t buying it.

“Remember Belladonna?” Sophie cut in.

A cool bitterness settled over my body. “The wine?” I asked, playing dumb.

I got two sets of narrowed eyes at that one.

"Isla," Sophie warned.

"You do a great Thorne impression," I shot at her.

She glared at me.

"Yes, I remember her. Bad magical plastic surgery job, nasty teeth, tried to kill me once or twice until I put her in the ground."

Sophie's eyes narrowed. "Well, I've been doing some digging since you told me her origins. That she was part of a coven long banished to live in captivity."

"Until someone let the dogs out," I finished for her. "Now they're playing for the wrong team."

Sophie nodded. "They were bound in that prison together, and from what I can gather from the old books, even upon their release, they stay bound. Each of the other's magic lives inside them."

A heavy silence settled over the room.

"Am I the only one not getting the punch line?" I asked after a beat.

Sophie glanced at Thorne, who was doing his best statue impression. Silver had his tattooed arms crossed, looking equally grim. Chace's face was masked in confusion.

Great, me and the meathead are in the same intelligence category.

"Since the four are bound, each spell they cast stays alive until they all perish," Sophie explained. "The witch's magic stays inside you even after her death. She practices death magic, spells that thrive from the grave, so in fact, it's even stronger with you killing her."

I threw up my hands. "Oh, I'm sorry I killed the evil witch who was doing her best to roast my blood on the inside out."

She gave me a look. "I'm not saying you made the wrong

decision in that moment, but if I'd been there like I wanted to be—"

"If you even try and weave an 'I told you so' into this conversation, I'll find myself a stake and we'll roast marshmallows off your corpse," I hissed.

Thorne raised a warning brow as Silver stepped forward slightly.

I noted the protective stance with a detached amusement, too focused on myself, but I'd circle back to it.

Sophie didn't take notice, merely grinned. "I'd like to see you try. I'd be using your rib cage as a beer cooler."

"Jesus," Thorne muttered.

Chace grinned. "You chicks are more bloodthirsty than us," he said in amazement.

I gave him a smile. "Oh it's always the most bloodthirsty between girlfriends. You're just lucky history hasn't had any wars with two girlfriends pissed at each other on either side. The world would be flattened."

I moved my attention back to Sophie, whose smile dropped off her face with alarming quickness. That did not bode well. Sophie didn't get rattled easily.

"Spill it, Sabrina," I demanded.

She gave Thorne and me a sympathetic look before speaking. "The spell will kill you." She said it quickly and simply, ripping off the proverbial Band-Aid.

Thorne's reaction was decidedly more dramatic than mine.

Mine being no reaction.

His being to fling waves of pure unadulterated fear through the air. Though he coated it in a hefty spattering of rage. "That's not fuckin' happening," he hissed, snatching me to his side as if it would stop death from being inevitable. Like taxes.

Despite that being impossible, I didn't pull out of the

embrace. Being curled against him wasn't disagreeable.

"How exactly will this spell kill me?" I asked evenly.

I didn't miss the sliver of fear twinkling in Sophie's eyes. "It's a blood spell. First it makes you relive all the blood you've ever spilled, as though it's flowing from your own body."

I shivered despite being unable to feel the crisp New York air filtering through the uninsulated warehouse. Thorne's radiating heat chased the cold away, but not in the right direction; it curled up into the deepest part of me, where even he couldn't reach.

Sophie arched her brow. "That's already begun to happen, hasn't it?"

I gave her a nod.

Who knew one jerk of my head would make Thorne's arms turn to steel and unleash rage from his pores?

He turned me in his arms so his quicksilver irises could lock onto mine. "What?"

That one word had the impact of a mallet to the head.

"What?" I parroted.

His hands and my shoulders flexed. That was going to bruise. Or it would have, had I not been vampire and all.

"Don't," he warned. "You think it might've been something to tell me that you've been experiencing half a millennium of death?"

I glowered at him. "No, I didn't. I thought it was nobody's business but mine." My words were a challenge, and likely one he would have met had Sophie not cleared her throat.

"Thorne, you couldn't have exactly done anything, anyway," she told him.

He didn't take his eyes off me. "That's not the fuckin' point."

I rolled my eyes. "But the point is to let Sophie get to hers." I turned my attention back to my friend, who I swore was grinning.

Bitch.

"Get back to the story of my demise," I instructed.

Thorne cursed under his breath and yanked my back to his front. Even in the midst of an argument, he needed contact, I was coming to understand that, and crave the same thing.

"After reliving how you took blood in the past, you'll start to get less nutrients from the blood of the present," Sophie said. "It will slowly stop sustaining you and you'll become weaker. Your injuries won't heal as quickly…." She trailed off, seeing something on my face.

Thorne couldn't see my face but he sensed it in the air.

"That's already started happening too, hasn't it?" Sophie asked quietly.

I shrugged.

"How long?" Thorne growled.

I didn't look at him. "Night at the mansion, when Earnshaw ripped my throat out.

Even Silver blanched at that news.

"That was two months ago, Isla," Thorne said slowly.

"I'm able to count the passing of days," I snapped.

"You've been letting my men train with you," he continued. "Letting them hurt you. Letting *me* hurt you."

What hurt more than anything was the emotion in Thorne's voice. The guilt.

"Please," I scoffed. "Even if I were drinking animal blood for a year, I'd still be able to beat your recruits with my eyes closed." That time I turned in his arms out of my own volition, reaching up to stroke his stubbled jaw. "Plus, you're never hurting me. And I like the pain," I murmured with a thickness to my voice. "It's not anything serious, like I've turned human. A broken bone just takes an hour instead of a minute to heal," I said cheerfully. I glanced back at Sophie. "That's as bad as it's going to get, isn't it?" I asked, already knowing the answer.

"No," she said quietly. "It's likely to get worse. It will take longer because you're stronger and more stubborn." She winked at me. "But eventually, you'll be as weak as a human. And as vulnerable as one."

Silence followed her statement, thick and heavy, and all seemingly focused on me.

I was one woman who liked attention, but not like that. Not when I was turning disturbingly into the damsel when I worked best as the villain.

"So this is a cure to vampirism?" I asked, toying with the idea of being human. Nope. Couldn't do it. Crow's feet and gray hair? No thanks.

Then something else crept into my mind. Wrinkled hands clutching the same ones that were circled around me. Growing old with Thorne instead of watching age ravage him and death take him. Despite his extended life span, he'd age eventually, I'd gleaned as much.

It was tempting.

Very.

"No," Sophie cut off my dreams. "It won't turn you human. You'll still be a vampire. Still need blood to survive. But human blood won't be what keeps you that way. You'll weaken and die."

I almost choked on the force of Thorne's grip me and the raw energy radiating off him.

I stayed calm. "Well I wish I could bring that witch back and kill her twice," I muttered. "What an inconvenience."

"Inconvenience?" Thorne repeated. "That's what we're calling your death, Isla?"

His rage had to be directed somewhere, I guessed.

I looked at him. "You don't live for five hundred years without brushing with death at least once a decade," I explained. "Me and the grim reaper are best buds. Death is a part of immortality. This is not my first rodeo." I winked at him. "There's always a way to beat the reaper."

I looked at Sophie. "Now's your cue."

She gave me a grim look. "Yeah, there is a cure to this," she said, almost reluctantly.

I gave Thorne a triumphant grin.

"Drinking the blood of a slayer," Sophie said, her words coming down like a guillotine.

Obviously, Thorne didn't take the news well. Neither did I, if I was honest, but I didn't break as many things nor use enough curse words.

After his tirade, I'd given him an expectant look. "Finished?" I didn't wait for an answer. "I'm assuming you're going to bippity-boppity-boo some other suggestions?" I asked Sophie in a carefully constructed bored tone.

She nodded. "You bet your ass I will."

"Great. Well, I've got a renewed motivation to hit some clubs tonight. Maybe I'll be able to find three dark witches there and can end them all."

I went to walk out of the warehouse, to escape the weight of stares more than anything else.

An iron grip at my wrist stopped me.

"You're not seriously fuckin' thinkin' I'll let you go now?" he all but growled at me.

I raised my brow at him. "No, I'm not seriously thinking that," I replied. "Because that would imply you have the power to 'let' me do anything. Which you do not."

His rage enveloped the room in a cloud so thick I was surprised the breathers didn't choke on it.

"You're insane," he hissed.

I tilted my head. "I'm not sure what that's got to do with it."

He stepped forward, his hot breath on my face. "You heard Sophie. Every fuckin' day you're getting weaker. You want to go into the vampire den like that?"

I rolled my eyes. "I grew up in the vampire den. I'll survive."

His hand bit into my wrist. "It's dangerous."

"What isn't? The most dangerous thing you could do would be to put me in a padded room, despite what psychiatrists recommend." I looked to Sophie, who was uncomfortably watching the exchange like a spectator would a car crash.

"I'm not likely to drop dead, properly at least, in the next twenty-four hours, am I?" I asked her sharply.

"Not of unnatural causes," she replied.

I held up my hands to Thorne. "See, as safe as houses. Now, I'm going. And I'll tell you now, you won't like what happens if you try to stop me."

The hurricane in his eyes regarded what was likely the typhoon in mine. "Out," he growled, not taking his eyes off me but making it apparent that he was speaking to everyone else.

The echo of feet on concrete told me his command was being obeyed. The retreating heartbeats would have also, but Thorne's was a roar in my ears.

"If this is you going all caveman on me, I'd advise against it. The Neanderthals didn't fare well in history. I'd have to call some historians to let them know one survived extinction, and they'll likely put you in a museum quicker than you can say 'misogynistic,'" I snapped.

He snatched my face in his hands. "You didn't tell me. Any

of it."

I widened my eyes at him. "And?" I prompted, failing to see why it outraged him.

"*And*, Isla, I should have fuckin' known," he roared.

"Why? Unless you're also ruler of the universe in your spare time, you couldn't have done anything."

He narrowed his eyes. "That's not the point. You're *mine*. And you've been slipping through my fingers, all the shit you've been doing, the danger you've been putting yourself in." He shuddered. Actually shuddered. Thorne, who was scared of nothing, chilled at the prospect of me in danger.

"Well I didn't know the extent of it," I protested.

"Would that have changed anything?"

I pouted. "Likely not."

He ground his teeth together. "Fuck, Isla. Have you got any self-preservation?"

I jutted my chin out. "I have a lot. I quite like being undead, and I intend to stay that way. It's not like I asked to be blackmailed by the king into being his 007 in order to get my parents killed and then got myself in a war where witches cursed me, is it?" I snapped.

"Exactly why you shouldn't go," he snapped back.

"And what should I do instead? Sit patiently and knit while the menfolk take up their swords to be the heroes?" I glared at him. "Clue in. It's been my sword that's saved you more than the other way around, and it's going to be me who saves myself too. Genius though she is, I'm going to have to disagree with Bonnie Tyler here. I don't need a hero. And I sure as shit am not holding out for one."

Thorne gritted his teeth so hard I worried they might shatter. He stayed silent.

"I'm going," I declared.

We glared at each other, each bathing in the other's fury. Thorne sighed and yanked my body so it was flush to his, resting his forehead against mine.

"I don't like this," he murmured. "You're so strong. A fuckin' warrior, at that. You don't know it, and you'll never admit it, but you're a rose. Beautiful and precious. See, it's your job to be the warrior you're born to be, but it's mine to protect that rose. That's why I'm not planning on leaving your side until we can get this curse lifted. Likely not after that, either."

His soft yet hard voice, plus the words, should've sent warmth shooting up my spine. Instead it brought forth the chill already lingering.

His rose.

I yanked myself from his touch with a ferocity that surprised even me. "No, it's not your job to protect a *vampire*, Thorne. Your job is to kill them, remember? A witch has already done half the job for you," I hissed. "Instead of promising vengeance on her, why don't you thank her?"

And I left.

Or more precisely, I ran. Me. Ran. I never ran from a fight. Never.

Ghosts, on the other hand, I ran from. Especially when they brought forth the reminder of who the truly delicate one in this arrangement was.

He found me not two hours later. Just as the sun was setting, its farewell peeking through the glistening skyscrapers. I leaned against the balcony, sipping my fourth whiskey and reveling in the slight buzz that came with it. There might have been a lot of downsides to this little curse, but at least I could get drunk easier.

Silver linings, people.

So maybe the slight inebriation was what had me spilling the bloodbath that was my history and my birth into immortality.

"My earliest memory is of screaming," I whispered. "Of a woman's scream. It wasn't exactly loud, or at least not how I remember. It was something worse than that. Raw and so full of desperation, like her very soul was clawing out her throat, searching for escape from her body." I glanced out at the horizon. "I'm curious, so I went looking. I knew it was a bad sound but I wasn't old enough to understand everything about it. When I saw her, I discovered how much blood the human body had. What the body could survive." I paused. "What doesn't kill you doesn't make you stronger. The human who coined that ridiculous phrase obviously hadn't met a member of the Rominskitoff family. What doesn't kill you damages your soul beyond repair, so to this day I question whether there was anything left inside that woman to die when her heart stopped beating. She'd died—her truest soul, at least. It'd been ripped, torn, cut, brutalized and murdered long before her lungs took her last breath."

I traced Thorne's still jaw with my eyes. "I was four," I told him. "And despite what you might think, I wasn't born with the ability to stomach that kind of cruelty. Just like any other creature in the universe, I was born with a purity of ignorance, naivety. Nature versus nurture is a true concept. We may have been designed with the ability to be the cruelest of them all, but I think that one doesn't need fangs or immortality for that. No, cruelty is learned, nurtured. And I witnessed the evil that had blossomed in my brothers. That my family would try to water with screams like that one. Something pivotal in me rebelled, revolted against it. In my naïve and pure mind, I urged those empty eyes to give me whatever soul was left, for me to take care of." I met his eyes. "That's what kept me from truly becoming… whatever I was destined to become. I won't say I didn't become 'evil' because I don't think anyone in the world is pure enough to say that, least of all me. But I didn't cause such irreparable damage to any living creature… until…."

Thorne stepped forward as if he sensed the way the words lodged in my throat, that they were scraping at my insides. I held my hand up to stop him. He did so, folding his arms so the muscles in his forearms flexed, his face hard.

"I was a rebellious child, but not in the contemporary understanding of the word. I'm under the impression 'rebellious children' cause mischief and general misdeeds. I revolted against that. I made friends with the humans in the village I grew up in. It was hard, considering their parents' fear of my family." I took a sip. "They knew what we were, you see. In the old days, when everything was simpler and there were no power switches or ages of reason to chase away the monsters, people accepted it. Feared us, surely. The village had a taste to it, that fear. No plants would grow, though the unyielding Russian landscapes could explain that, I think it was the toxic emotion."

He stepped closer to me yet seemed to sense that distance was pivotal.

"Children don't accommodate fear like adults do," I continued. "They feel it, sure, but it doesn't take root the same. It can be chased away until age makes it an immovable force. So I made friends. I grew up with cruelty and yet I kept it at bay by nurturing that little piece of that nameless woman's soul. I let hatred for them, my wretched family, fester until I was in my early twenties. Most likely years away from my change, which meant my parents assumed humanity was temporary. I didn't know whether they expected me to run, or if they even cared, but I did. I didn't go as far as I'd planned. Everything was new to me, you see? I was sequestered in that castle for years, too vulnerable in my human state to be around my family's enemies, of which we had many. Well, apart from Mortimeus, but I didn't think that really counted. I was the freak there too, though my classmates were never bold enough to openly comment on that. Not when I was of the ancient Vein Lines." I met Thorne's eyes. "I planned to lose myself in the throngs of humans who were so very foreign to me. It was like an alien planet, but I liked it. Loved it."

"He was the first one I'd recognized a soul in." I laughed coldly. "Or I thought perhaps he recognized one in me."

The memories that came with speaking of such times were replaced by fresher ones, though unlike their dated counterparts, they were murky, frayed around the edges. In my experience, time didn't dim memories; no, it made them starker. I could describe the last rose on the bodice of my dress, and the curl to Jonathan's mustache, along with the canapés served at the party where we met.

"He called me a rose," I choked out. "His white rose. "What he didn't see was that I couldn't be something so pure. Or maybe I could. If only so you could see the blood that much better when it spilled. And it spilled all over that stark and simple life I'd created in a dream of stupidity and fantasy. Under the haze of that deadly mix of chemicals you humans call love. It's ironic, really, that that's what you all live for, strive for. When, more often than not, that's what you die for." I paused. "Well, it's what I died for, at least. One week into a marriage that had me convinced the first twenty years of my life were merely a dream. Can you imagine the stupidity of youth? The horrors tattooed on my soul were easily forgotten under the blindness of love. Or what I thought was love," I corrected. "I forgot that vampires existed, or that I was one of them. Hang around monsters for long enough, you can convince yourself you are one. Hang around humans, you forget that monsters exist, which is dangerous in itself because they never stopped existing, just stared back at you in the mirror, hiding in plain sight."

I laughed again. "I remembered, though. When my pretty dress and my pretty life were stained with the blood of almost everyone I'd ever met. The floor was scattered with them. A child I'd played with at a party. His baby brother whose cheek I'd pinched with an empty womb and a fool's hope." I flinched. "And him. Jonathan. My husband." I glanced up at Thorne. "You can die of a broken heart, you know. Because when a vampire grows into itself, the human part of us, it has to die. It's nature. Our genetic makeup. I died that day. Of a broken heart. And unlike all other wounds, even immortality couldn't fix that."

We were silent for a long time after that. To be fair, I'd hit him with an emotional freight train.

I was captured by his gaze

He slowly unfolded his arms. "You didn't tell me."

Not a question. Just a statement.

I searched those eyes, feeling an overwhelming urge to escape the conversation, to escape my own head. Problem was, I could run from real-life demons, but I couldn't outrun the ones residing in my soul, hiding in the shadows.

His eyes offered a promise that I wouldn't face them alone. And for once, I didn't want to.

"I didn't tell you because, if you haven't noticed, this—us—hasn't really accommodated time for us to talk about things other than otherworldly wars and the general bad idea of us being together. I bet you don't even know what star sign I am."

He quirked his brow.

"Scorpio, by the way," I muttered.

He didn't say anything, just waited. Funny, I was the one with eternity but he had more patience than me, acting as if every second wasn't sand in the hourglass of his death.

Or mine, as the case may be.

Then he surged forward, every inch of his body swallowing mine.

"I couldn't do it," I whispered. "See you taken away from me as a result of what I am. I can't have you fighting my battles, Thorne, because if you fail it's because of me. I'm at peace with the fact that I may die myself, I can live with my every increasingly mortality. But I can't live with that. I won't survive that."

He cupped my face. "I already go to battle for you," he growled. "Every day is a battle against these vampires who want your head, the rest of the supernatural community who are either scorned lovers or murderous rebels, my own kind who'll kill you the second they learn about us." He yanked me to him, squeezing my ass and sending ripples of pleasure up my spine. "And you," he murmured. "You're the greatest battle of all, and I'm counting myself as the luckiest son of a bitch on the planet to be able to fight for you. Which I will. Every day. Always. And I'll be right by your side when we wipe your family off the face of this earth. I'll fuckin' bathe in their blood for what they did to you," he seethed.

I searched his face and smiled at his ferocity. "We're *so* meant to be together," I said.

His eyes silenced my smile. "Yes, baby, we are. And I'm

gonna make sure we stay that way. Forever."

He meant it. That promise.

The problem was—to humans, at least—forever was drenched in ambiguity.

Forever was sixty years, maybe six hundred. Or maybe six hours.

SIXTEEN

Spending yet another evening at the king's compound, which had been newly fireproofed, was not how I wanted to round off this day. I'd been at the office doing my day job since six and had been up all night with Thorne. After laying my bloody history down at my feet, I had two options to stave off the grave: battle or sex. It wasn't a choice when I was around Thorne, though it did tire my ever-weakening body.

Not that I was complaining.

And not that I'd told him. He even toyed with the idea of following me to work, as if I'd accidently slit my wrists on a paper cutter or something.

Luckily he had other things to do, since we were hitting Extermius later to follow a lead Dante had given us.

But Rick had called to say he was back from Europe and

I'd been summoned.

I didn't know why. Two months had passed with zilch. No new info and no leads, much to my chagrin. And I doubted he wanted to see me to give me a snow globe he'd picked up in Prague.

Nor hear about how two months with Thorne had attached him to every part of my being.

Whatever.

Thorne would not have been happy about me doing anything remotely dangerous in my newly fragile condition. Which was precisely why I didn't tell him. That and I hadn't heard from him all day.

I was fine. A death spell making me as weak as a mortal was not going to stop me from living my life.

And hopefully not my death.

Sophie was scouring through every text she could on those witch bitches to find a loophole that didn't include me drinking the blood of a slayer. Not a cure when the blood of a slayer was fatal.

Rock, hard place.

After going through the new and slightly invasive security procedures I would've enjoyed had it been my slayer boyfriend doing it and not an angular-faced mute vampire, I waltzed through the hallways.

Ice prickled up my skin at the pure stillness of it all. The silence. I couldn't shake the feeling that I needed to turn on my red-soled heel and run.

But I didn't run.

So I continued, ignoring the ice until something replaced it. Something that made dread a knife in my heart.

I knew what was behind the ornate doors a human servant opened before my hand had grasped the knob.

The roar permeated my ears and his presence whipped through me like liquid electricity.

Seeing him trussed up in front of a room full of vampires, one eye swollen shut and what I immediately deduced was a fatal wound in his torso, cut me open. Drawn and quartered with that single image, without a blade, without blood, the pain rivaled anything a weapon could cause. Every single fiber of my being screamed with agony as the vision of him tore through me. As his pain-filled eyes flared at the sight of me.

At what was in them.

Love was what brought the pain.

Fear was what almost brought me to my knees. Because even from that single glance, I knew. That fear wasn't for his death, coming quick and fast like a thunderstorm in a Texan summer.

No, it was for me.

And that utter selfless devotion for the creature he loved, the creature that brought about his destruction, made every measured step I made towards the king standing in front of my slayer the most pain I'd ever experienced in half a millennium.

One look was more excruciating than four hundred years of pain. It even swallowed that afternoon in Paris when I was young and naïve.

Because I wasn't young or naïve anymore. And I was deeper than I had been then, despite my intentions to act shallow. He'd filled me up, every crevice, to the brim. And now there he was, full of holes draining the only thing in my deathless existence that mattered to me.

His life.

"Rick, I like what you've done with the place," I remarked casually, glancing around. "Is it new carpet?" I clicked my fingers as if in realization. "No, the trussed-up slayer. Adds to the ambience of the room. Bravo to your new decorator."

It took every ounce of my self-control to keep my tone light and sarcastic, eyes glued to the king's and not rip his throat out.

I walked slowly through the room, scanning the people there for the face of my betrayer.

My mother's satisfied glint met mine. I grinned at her through the knives in my belly. I would not give her the gift of seeing my heartbreak.

I straightened my shoulders and met Rick's eyes before zeroing in on a small rosebud of blood on his stark white cuff.

Try as I might, I couldn't tear myself away from the small stain. Thorne's blood.

The icy monarch who I'd grown deceptively fond of was now above dear old Ma on my kill list.

It had been seconds, too long to be staring at a cuff, but not long enough to pull myself together. I did, though. And somehow didn't look in the direction of the vibrating pound. I met emerald eyes that glittered with their sheer coldness. Lack of emotion. Of any form of humanity.

"Not that I don't love a good slayer execution, but don't we have bigger fish to fry?" I glanced to the small crowd. "And I'm sure these fine families have much better things to do than this."

He stayed silent as he measured my words. I knew at that moment that he knew.

That our presence was not a happy accident.

It was a sentence. For both of us.

I had nothing to lose.

Without hesitation, I darted past the king, one destination in mind.

Two guards slowed me down but I snapped their necks, my eyes on Thorne's.

His steely gaze no doubt only followed a blur, but there was no mistaking his roar when my right femur snapped, bringing me painfully to my knees where a burning copper blade rested against my neck.

I struggled, which only sent steaming blood trickling down my chest.

Thorne's roar intensified as his struggles mirrored my own, even without his injuries healing like mine. Though my own process was slow. Maybe nonexistent. I couldn't feel the pain amidst the agony of knowing Thorne was right there, dying, and I could do nothing.

"Not in my years as king have I been as surprised and disappointed as I am now," Rick purred in my ear, his voice liquid death.

The knife pressed deeper into my neck, sinking through my flesh like butter. I failed to grant him the satisfaction of the scream I yearned to release.

"You would do well not to struggle unless you want your slayer to watch me slice off your head." He glanced up at the man whose shouts turned into unintelligible grunts as his exertion drained the life from him.

"My plans for tonight did not include killing, Isla," Rick continued, addressing Thorne. "If you stop that incessant struggling, maybe we'll keep to those plans."

Thorne stopped immediately.

The silence and the depth of that simple gesture temporarily sucked the air out of the cavernous room.

Then Rick yanked me up. I let out a hiss through my teeth as the bone rebroke that was in the process of healing. Cool blood mingled with white-hot pain when the bone tore through the skin of my leg. It radiated continually with every step.

We were on a makeshift stage, Thorne trussed up on a T-shaped structure, his arms chained on either side of him at shoulder height. I wondered how long Rick had been torturing him, drawing his blood in front of the bloodthirsty crowd.

Thorne's fury choked me. His fear filtered through my veins like acid, his love shredding my insides.

Rick paid no notice, keeping the blade to my throat as he yanked me towards a set of restraints similar to Thorne's. Though these were copper and significantly more reinforced.

I continued my struggle the moment realization hit. Letting myself be put in those meant my death. And, more importantly, Thorne's.

No way was I giving up that easily.

I wasn't a quitter.

Gritting my teeth against the pain in my leg, I whipped my head back, cracking it on Rick's, which made him relax his grasp enough for me to dart away. I came close enough to Thorne to smell the bitterness of his death combined with the sweetness of his blood. Small cuts peppered his muscled body, the veins flexing with the exertion from fighting.

I met his eyes for one second, slipping down that crevice in time we'd made for ourselves.

In that vortex, I was propelled back into memories as my mind struggled to save me from plunging into insanity at seeing Thorne journeying to the grave. Whatever he had that was more than human, whatever had saved him countless times, was failing him now.

Because of me.

"Demon. Thirty years ago," Thorne rumbled as I traced a crescent scar on his left pec. Little of his torso was untouched from the memories of his life.

I glanced up, jostling only slightly so I stayed in his arms but could meet his gaze. "Thirty," I repeated.

He nodded once.

I explored his face. Weathered for sure. Tan that was permanent now, in the midst of New York winter. Up closer, I could see the small white line at the top of his lip. Another scar. His eyes betrayed age much older than the thirty or so that the very faint lines at the edges of them suggested. How I hadn't seen it before I didn't know. Maybe it was because every meeting until that point had been under life-or-death circumstances; I'd barely had time to keep my head on my shoulders, definitely not puzzle over the depths in his eyes that didn't match up with the years on his masculine and attractive face.

"How old are you?" I asked him.

His eyes twinkled slightly as he traced circles on my naked back. "Thirty-five."

I grinned. "And how long have you been thirty-five?"

The corner of his mouth twitched. "A while," he responded.

In that moment, the pure obscurity of all of this, coupled with the reference to a movie that I had been sure he hadn't seen, became too much for me. I laughed. Full-on laughed. Genuinely, not sardonically or sarcastically. An actual laugh.

When I was done, there was no residual humor in Thorne's eyes, but something else. Something intense, though that seemed to be his default around me. Usually it was tinted with a heavy dose of fury.

Not then, though.

"I've never seen you do that," he said, his voice thick.

I frowned. "What? Make a sarcastic movie reference? I'm sure that's not true. I'm half movie quotes, half sarcasm and the rest nonsense."

He pushed the auburn hair from my face. "No, laugh," he rasped, watching my face. "You make a lot of jokes, Isla, but it's just occurred to me that that's the first time you've truly laughed. It's rather beautiful. You're rather beautiful."

The compliment, so simple, so genuine, took me off guard. "I guess there's a lot to joke about but not much to laugh about lately," I told him honestly.

"We're going to have to change that."

I gave him a look. "Yes, there's heaps of time for laughs in the midst of a supernatural war that I'm somehow in the middle of whilst I'm in love with a slayer who is something other than human and has refused to tell me quite what. Oh, and this current relationship could get me killed if anyone in my race, most of whom are just looking for a reason to get me executed, finds out. We'll pencil in the hilarity between battles," I deadpanned.

His emotions turned the moment I spoke, swirling with sweetness and bitterness that was better than the best blood in the world.

"You love me," he rasped.

I raised my brow. "That's *what you got from that?"*

He moved so I was pinned to the bed, his muscled form pressing into me, his heart vibrating against my chest.

His mouth covered mine and he thrust into me. "I love you too," he grunted. "That other shit? It's nothing to that," he promised.

The heat from the memory was chased away as a cool hand clutched my neck and yanked me back from where I'd reached for Thorne.

Rick plunged his knife directly into my heart. At least that's what I thought. Though it only brushed the organ that was pulsating with pain when the blade broke my skin, hurtling through my chest cavity.

I did let out a scream that time.

Thorne's pain filled the room and wrapped me in enough strength to silence myself.

His fury meant exerting energy that he sorely needed to stay alive.

I didn't look at the steely gray eyes I knew were burning into me. Instead, I met the emerald ones.

"You go nice into those cuffs and maybe he'll live." Rick nodded to Thorne while removing the knife. "You don't, you fight." He moved his eyes to two burly vampires. "To the death with my two best. You win, you go free, your treasonous transgressions forgotten."

A murmured whisper rode over the small crowd at his words, the outrage palpable. I could most likely win against two of even the king's best. My fighting skills were not exactly a secret—I'd advertised them in that very room not two months before when I'd been saving the king's life—so him offering such a thing was tantamount to a pardon.

Vampires didn't get pardons. They got put in Rick's gallery, as I'd learned. Or publicly executed.

The king was feeling merciful. Or at least sentimental.

The wave of protest came and went as quickly as it took for emerald eyes to silence them with a glare.

Even their outrage of such an offer to a vampire such as me wasn't enough to make them do something as suicidal as speak against the most ruthless king we'd ever had.

They expected me to take the fight, of course.

And most who knew me at least a little, like my mother and father who were sitting mere feet from me, knew that I'd win.

Without hesitation, I stood and moved to the copper restraints.

Whereas the king's offer was met with a roar, my gesture

was met with an even thicker silence than Thorne's. I nearly choked on it.

"Don't you fuckin' dare," a rough voice ordered.

Even half dead, restrained in a room full of vampires literally out for his blood, he managed to give weight to such a command. "You *fight*," he growled.

The weight of the silence had nothing on the weight of those words, the stare that kissed the side of my cheek.

I addressed neither and ignored him. Me thrusting my hand up to be cuffed was enough of a response.

I couldn't look at Thorne. Not yet. It would kill me to see the grave in his eyes. To know I put it there. I would only welcome death if it came with the reward of his life.

Instead I looked to the face of my captor

"Don't do this," I pleaded, my voice rough.

His body jolted, only slightly, while his face stayed impassive.

He turned to the room. "Out, all of you," he barked.

Their disappointment was palpable. They had been there to see something that many, including my family, had been waiting for for centuries.

My death.

In the blink of a human eye, the spectators were gone. The room felt fuller without their presence, even though the cavernous space was only occupied by the three of us.

Rick turned back to me, his eyes twinkling with something that hadn't been there before. Something I couldn't name. "You beg now? For this human? This slayer? You didn't beg for your own life that night in your apartment, yet you're willing to do so for his."

"I don't beg."

"Even for your life?"

"Especially for my life."

I didn't lower my gaze. "I don't beg for my life. My soul? That's a different story."

Thorne's energy sizzled as my words entered the air. "You want to kill someone, asshole?" he growled. "Kill me. You're fuckin' amping to do so. Do it now. Isla has no part in this."

"Shut up, Thorne," I hissed, my eyes moving.

"Never," he rasped, his voice filled with death. "Not gonna watch you give yourself up without a fight. You want a fight, Emrick? Fight me," he invited, rattling his binds. "Don't you fuckin' dare taint this world any more by removing her from it. Not even the grave will save you if you do. I'll chase you to the fuckin' afterlife. Fight me. Let her go."

Rick glanced between us, laughing coldly in a bitter sound that poisoned the air. "Fight you? Now?" He gave Thorne's midsection a pointed look. "Rather unnecessary."

He stepped back to me, clutching my neck in the grip that was akin to two semis pressing on either side of my jugular. In other words, not pleasant.

The chill of his breath kissed my eyelids as he leaned forward. "What is it about them?" he hissed. "The humans? What is it that makes you not want to kill them?" His glance wavered down to the floor. To the ever-increasing pool of blood. I could smell it. It was a pulse, a life force, vibrating through the room, reaching my pointed heel. That pulse was receding, weakening. "To save them?" he continued, eyes back to me.

I didn't waver from his eyes. I couldn't look down at the blood. The body so full of strength and life and me, containing what was left of my soul. It was withering and dying and I couldn't watch that. I was already feeling that death clutch me in its icy grip. It was much tighter than the king's grip, no matter how strong he was.

"They're weak," I whispered. Choked, really. "They die. They get sick. Age."

His brows furrowed. "Yes. Which is why they're nothing."

I shook my head. "It's why they're *everything*." I blinked. "They change. They are a never-finished project. Their very nature accommodates death, but it also accommodates life. Love.

"Us? We're done, right? The finished, more improved version of God's first time around. We don't die. We don't age. We aren't plagued with the soul that becomes man's demise. We get to walk this earth without the shadow of death kissing our shoulders, which means we don't need to change. As a species, we're bloodthirsty, emotionless, cruel, and that's all we're going to be. No more change." I swallowed, the air scraping my lungs like a thousand razor blades. I cast my glance past the ever-increasing pool of blood to the man it was coming from. The lightly tanned skin was turning gray, lifeless. The magnetic eyes were glued to me, intent, flaming with so much emotion. Physically seeing that life in his eyes at the midst of death, it hurt. More than anything.

But I carried on.

"They change," I croaked. "Through the centuries, we've seen them turn from savage illiterates to creatures who produced *A Tale of Two Cities*, *Romeo and Juliet*, who introduced compassion into an ever-cruel world. They encompass all of our soulless depravity, that's true, but they also possess something our superior species cannot. The other side of the coin. The binary opposition." I met the silver eyes that were draining of the fight that surrounded his soul. "Love that means so much more than whatever we can have. Because we're safe with our immortal love. Because forever means forever, though it rarely lasts. Forever, in reality, is a long time. For love to wither, die, become boring." I nodded to Thorne. "But for them, forever is sixty years, sixty days, sixty seconds. It's not fixed. They love even though they know the life they've attached that emotion to is so very fragile, temporal. That life that has the power to destroy them will, inevitably, when it ends. But they keep doing it, despite everything. And that's why we'll never win. Because we don't know death, we don't know *life*. It means nothing to us. And that's our curse." I wrenched my eyes away from his. "And that's why I save them. Because it's our curse, not theirs. And every innocent life that's ended because someone was hungry, bored or turned on is never just singular. It's multiple little deaths for those connected to that life."

My eyes no longer saw the dungeon. I was in Paris, my gaze flickering over the littered bodies of those I had come to love.

To Jonathan, who I had come to breathe for, to exist for.

And I died a thousand little deaths then.

But I survived. And endured.

But this time I wouldn't. There would be no pieces to pick up if I had to taste Thorne's death. Live in a silence that didn't have his steady heartbeat filling me.

I jutted my chin up. "So you can sit on your fucking solid gold throne with your arrogance and superiority and immortality and pretend to lord over the human race. But in reality, you are never going to be better than them, because you won't ever change. You won't ever die, but you won't ever *live*. And that is the only glory I'll get from my death. Not much, not nearly enough, but it'll do."

I met his eyes through all of the pain and death and utter destruction that was coursing through my veins. "But if you kill me, you best make sure that I'm dead. Otherwise, I swear to Ambrogio, I will come after you with a ferocity that even you, oh fearless leader, couldn't dream of in your wildest nightmares," I promised.

Rick's eyes inspected me. "That's the idea," he muttered, and then there was a resounding crack followed by a thundering yell so full of pain and suffering that it sent agony unlike I'd ever experienced through every part of me.

Then there was nothing.

"I will kill you," a rough voice promised.

"Wait until we've made it out of this alive first," a calmer voice responded, its elegance scraped by an undertone of something.

Uneasiness. Concern, perhaps.

It was hard to inspect through the fog I was fighting. It was like nothing was corporal, real. My last memories were of death, yet I was reasonably sure that this wasn't heaven. Or hell.

The raspy voice coupled with the resounding heartbeat told me it wasn't hell.

He wouldn't be in hell.

And the arms cradling me to the chest that was the source of that beat wasn't hell either. Though I reasoned heaven wouldn't be so full of murder threats.

"If Isla doesn't make it through this…." The arms around me flexed as pain peppered through the emotions that were more tangible, anchoring me to the earth.

Though the earth was jerking with bumps and we seemed to be hurtling at an uncommon speed. In a car, I reasoned. And I was horizontal, half splayed in Thorne's arms. His heat burned the air but didn't break through the ice I was trapped in.

I was yet to find purchase on my body or my eyelids, which

seemed determined to stay firmly shut.

"She's a vampire. She'll make it through," the cold voice snapped. "You're here and you're *human*."

"Not quite, Emrick. And maybe before you pulled this fuckin' stunt you might have tried to think of anyone but yourself," Thorne roared, every inch of his tone filled with utter devastation and rage. There was a lot of that.

Confusion flickered around my floating mind. Thorne seemed to be alive—cue glorious rain dance at that. But he also seemed to be pissed. Another glorious rain dance. Alive enough to be pissed was fine with me.

But he was conversing with Rick in a way that was decidedly familiar.

Too familiar for a slayer of noble blood and the king of all vampires.

Granted, I was a vampire of noble blood in love with the slayer, but we were an exception to the rule.

Or so I thought.

"Thinking of myself? I risked everything on this, on the two of you tonight," Rick hissed, igniting a cool inferno of anger. "I was provided with concrete proof of Isla's betrayal in front of the Sector and had no fucking choice but to do what I did. By not only letting the two of you survive but escape, I've thrown this world, my world, my fucking *life* into turmoil."

"Heaven forbid Emrick's carefully structured life gets shaken up," Thorne yelled back. "If you haven't noticed, we're at war. Your crown was bound to topple off at some point. Be grateful your head didn't come with it. It still might if you've killed the woman I love."

"The vampire you love."

Another squeeze. My limbs were tingling with feeling. Soon I might be able to move them, though I was gaining a disturbing amount of information playing the coma victim.

"The *woman* I love," Thorne repeated.

A heavy silence settled.

"Despite being that, she is still a vampire. She'll heal." His voice was softer. Or as soft as a polished stone could be.

"Maybe you'd have learned how wrong you are if you'd bothered to speak to her instead of using her as a weapon in your war and a tool in your monarchy," Thorne hissed. "But she won't. Not after she's been cursed by a witch, who she was fighting for you."

Another heavy silence.

"What?"

"I don't have time to explain." Smells and sounds exploded as we burst from a car into a familiar woodsy-smelling area. "I've got to try and save the *woman* I love."

Then various heartbeats entered the fray.

"Holy fuck, Thorne. You're covered in blood," a masculine voice seethed.

"Is Isla…?" Sophie's voice was small.

I managed to find purchase on my vocal cords. "Surprise, bitches. I bet you'd thought you'd seen the last of me," I croaked, my voice foreign.

In the time it took for me to open my eyes following my excellently timed *American Horror Story* reference, no one spoke. No one even breathed.

Steely gray eyes were the first thing I saw. They swirled like a storm, then closed for one beat as if the strength to hold them open had failed him. His arms flexed, bringing me up so his lips pressed to my forehead.

"You're not allowed to pull that shit again, Isla," he growled, voice thick.

"What, dying? Only if you promise the same," I replied, my

voice losing its earlier bravado. I moved my arm that seemed to be made of solid steel to stroke the skin of his face, then narrowed my eyes downwards to where the gaping wound should've been. "I'm sure I haven't been out long enough for you to recover from having your insides on your outsides," I said, suspicious.

That's when Rick stepped forward. On pure instinct, I wrenched my body from Thorne's arms—only possible because he wasn't expecting it—and lunged at Rick, my fingers around his neck in an instant.

"And the last time I saw you, I made a promise," I rasped. "Seems you didn't manage to make good on yours, which was killing me and the man I love, so I get to make good on mine." I smiled through the gray creeping into my vision and the way my limbs were turning to lead.

It was through sheer force of will that I was standing, and the power of the memory of tasting Thorne's death that I kept my grip on Rick.

Thorne's heat was at my back. "Isla," he warned. "You're gonna have to hold that thought," he instructed softly.

My knees shook.

I ignored it and kept my gaze locked on Rick. "I don't do well with delayed gratification, Thorne. And if you don't recall, this vampire almost killed us both. We'll get back to the details of your speedy recovery *after* I've finished off the king."

Thorne's hands settled on my hips. "You'll need him for an explanation, considering he's the reason we're both standing here." He may have been talking me down from murder, but there was no disguising the homicide in his tone. The barely concealed fury that whipped around him like a cape.

I wanted to disagree, but I wasn't standing any longer. The ground surged up to meet me in a swift movement and would have embraced me had Thorne's arms not caught me.

Rick had moved to do the same but Thorne beat him, despite his vampiric speed.

I was gathered in his arms, tasting his concern and fear as he strode to the sofa, resting me on it. He pushed the hair from my face gently, his features marble. His thumb brushed over my lips. "Isla," he rasped.

I'd been ignoring it, but the utter devastation in his voice brought it up so I couldn't ignore it any longer.

"I'm dying," I surmised.

He flinched. "No. You won't dare leave me," he growled.

I smiled weakly at him. "Not a choice, I'm afraid." I'd known for a while, since well before Sophie's little announcement. One wasn't ignorant to their own demise, when death was no longer outside and foreign but inside and familiar. I'd figured that any fight I'd gotten into might be my last, but I hadn't planned on anyone getting the best of me.

But I hadn't planned on falling in love with a slayer, or being willing to die for him either.

Yet I wouldn't change a thing. Thorne was right in front of me, breathing, heart beating. Existing. That was worth dying for.

His eyes stayed on mine before he ripped them from me. "Emrick," he barked.

I didn't expect the king to come running at his command, but he was beside him in an instant, cold eyes betraying something.

"Your blood. Now," Thorne growled.

I frowned at him. "How do you know about that?" I snapped.

"It won't work," Sophie said softly, stepping forward and looking anywhere but me.

I got it. I'd brought death into the room; no one wanted eye contact with that.

"She's had it once before, correct?" she addressed Rick.

If he was surprised by her knowledge of that, he didn't show it, merely nodded once.

Thorne, on the other hand, was fuming. "She has?" he gritted.

"*She* is right here, and not dead yet," I cut in, trying to push up from the sofa.

A firm hand at my chest stopped me, not that he needed to; my arms didn't seem to want to obey.

It worried me, the quickening of my demise. Though I guessed demise did come quick. It rarely offered a chance to find a way to beat it. That wasn't how death worked. I should know—I'd dealt it for long enough.

Thorne glared at me. "You didn't tell me," he accused.

I rolled my eyes. "Well telling you about all of the times I almost died would give no time for sex. And I rather like sex."

Sophie was the only one who grinned.

Deathbed humor was not a big seller. Note to self.

"She's had it once. It saved her, and is likely the reason why the spell has taken this long to take hold," Sophie continued, grin gone. "It won't help now. Nothing will. Except your blood." She gazed at Thorne.

Everyone in the room knew about that little gem, apart from Rick.

"But that will kill her," he observed. His voice somehow had the power of a roar, yet he didn't raise it higher than his normal tone. It held notes of helplessness and anger while maintaining his cool and impersonal tenor.

"We're aware," Thorne gritted out.

"Witch-22," I offered. "Nasty creatures." I glanced at

Sophie. “Present company excluded, of course. Though I don’t exclude your bedroom activities. They’re nasty. Even Christian Grey would blush.”

“Isla,” Thorne snapped. He gave me a reproachful glare which I didn’t reciprocate only because it was masking raw fear and my upcoming demise. His hand was clutched tightly to my neck as he turned to address Sophie. Though his eyes didn’t stray from mine, like he was afraid that if he broke the contact I might just drift away.

To be fair, I was fairly certain of that too.

“Track the witches,” he commanded her. “We’ll kill them all. That kills the spell.”

Sophie shook her head. “I’ve tried that, but they’re cloaked. And even if I could, their deaths likely wouldn’t reverse the spell. Not when it’s this far gone.”

“So in other words, I’m fucked,” I deduced.

Three glares.

“You can’t glare at the dying girl. It’s just mean,” I snapped.

Thorne’s volcano of fury was about to pop but Sophie beat him to it.

“Stop,” she yelled, her voice raw. “You just stop joking and acting normal. Like you aren’t being the biggest bitch of them all by leaving me alone on this godforsaken planet. You can’t joke about it, Isla,” she hissed.

Tears rolled down her face, mascara coming with it. Such a display confronted me with what the grayness at the sides of my vision told me was inescapable.

“I’m sorry I’m dying,” I whispered with a slight grin.

She blinked through the tears, her eyes meeting mine for a split second before she wrenched them away. Then she surged forward, her hands glowing as raw power echoed through the room. Thorne was thrust aside as she laid those glowing hands on my chest.

The effect was similar to what I thought a human might feel when those pad things tried to shock their heart back into rhythm. Uncomfortable, to say the least, but the sheer volume of power radiating from Sophie was more than that. It made me think of the sun and its unending energy.

She had been holding back.

Then it was gone and she stumbled slightly before Silver rushed to catch her. She sagged in his arms, wiping the blood from her nose distractedly as she came back beside me, placing her hands on my chest.

I didn't need to see the gray pallor to her face to know it hadn't worked. The pull of the grave had only paused with her touch. It was back now.

I smiled weakly at her. "You're just going to have to use that power for something that would make me proud. A good tribute to me would be blowing up a Croc factory or beheading the witch council," I requested.

Her eyes glistened. "This is too cruel. You only just found it," she choked out. I didn't need to look to Thorne to know he was my it.

In fact, I couldn't look at him; tasting his sorrow was pain enough.

I gave her hand a gentle squeeze, jerking with the residual power of her magic. "It's a cruel world, and we all just die in it, Hermione," I said softly. "Do me a favor and cause a lot of trouble before you do."

She nodded once and then wrenched her hand from my grip so she could dart out of the room.

I didn't blame her. I was uncomfortable with all of this too, would escape it if I could. Though if you inspected it, death was an escape. Just not the one I wanted.

Silver came to kiss my head firmly before chasing after Sophie.

I was left with the two men in the room who formed somewhat of a fatal harmony.

Fire and ice.

I blinked up as Thorne strode to kneel beside me once more. "If I had more time, I would really like to know how you two know each other," I told him. "And also watch you wrestle naked."

Rick's mouth turned up slightly.

Thorne stayed stoic. "You need to leave," he gritted.

Rick's body turned to stone. "I won't—"

"Leave," Thorne repeated, that one word shaking with the fury it encompassed. And the pain.

Rick's eyes turned liquid as I glimpsed the humanity in them. "I regret this, Isla. More than you know."

Then he was gone.

Just the two of us remained.

Silence reigned.

Thorne's eyes never left mine as he traced my face with his finger. "This can't be real," he whispered. I hid my flinch at the way all of his strength was just… gone. He sagged with the weight of everything on his shoulders. "You can't be leaving. Not when I've gone through hell to find you."

I smiled weakly. "Well you can go through hell to find me again, if you ever meet the same fate." I tasted bile at the thought. "Which you won't. But if you're ever on holiday in hell, I'll be there. Catching a tan."

He cupped my face. "You're not leavin' me," he choked out. "Not for another world."

His sorrow cut into every part of me. "I don't want to," I whispered. "But death isn't something we escape. In order to be immortal, one must live with death, become its comrade, its lover, its sibling and its enemy." I sucked in every detail of his face, his scent, as if I could take it with me. "Immortality only works if you don't form attachments. That's not a life. It's not. It's a death. I've been dead for four hundred years already, Thorne. I'll not regret a moment of life I've had with you."

His hands gripped my neck as if he could hold onto my life force. "We haven't had enough time," he rasped, pleading.

"I doubt a thousand years would have been enough," I told him. I stroked his neck and the pull of his blood sang to me. "I don't want this coldness inside me to be what takes me," I whispered. Even as I spoke, it spread like a cancer. "I want it to be tasting you, so I can leave with you inside me." I paused. "That sounds grosser than I meant," I added with a weak grin.

Thorne didn't smile because he knew what I meant. "No," he growled. "I'll not be the one to kill you."

"You're not going to do that. Didn't you hear? I was dead when you met me. You *resurrected* me. There was only so long the grave would wait." I met his eyes.

His own quicksilver irises gazed back, bursting with pain so raw it chased at the poison magic in my veins for what would finally kill me.

He moved his mouth so it plastered against mine in a kiss so furious it imprinted part of his soul onto my lips. I would have lived forever like that if I could.

I found myself cursing all the wasted moments I'd spent with him, not doing this, not treating every second of his presence like the heaven it was.

And it was hell.

Thorne lifted his lips from mine as if he could sense the cold creeping up my throat.

"I love you, Isla," he rasped, eyes wet. "I'll find you," he promised. "Wherever you are."

I blinked away the redness in my vision. "I love you," I whispered back. Then I leaned forward as he exposed his neck to me.

I sank my fangs into his skin and welcomed the grave.

The End

DEATH IS NEVER FATAL WHEN YOU'RE IMMORTAL...

ACKNOWLEDGEMENTS

Writing is a solitary job but there is no way that I could do any of this alone. I'm so lucky to have so many special people in my life that put up with my crazy and talk me down when I've had one too many coffees. Or wines.

Mum. You've always been my biggest cheerleader, my best friend and my sometimes therapist. You're the person responsible for all of this. You shared your love of books with me and that's where this all started. I'd never be who I am today if it wasn't for you.

My **Dad.** You're not here with us but you're the reason why I can shoot a gun, ride a motorbike, shop like a champ, and believe in myself. I miss you every day.

Amo Jones. What can I say about you? I can safely say I'd not have whatever is left of my sanity without you. I'm so very glad I met you. You're stuck with me now.

Andrea and **Caro**. You two ladies are so very special and your generosity and support is amazing. You're stuck with me too.

This book wouldn't be what it is without my wonderful team of betas. These special ladies helped to make this book what it is. **Ginny, Amy, Sarah**, and **Judy**… you are wonderful.

Polly and **Emma.** My best girls. I love you. I don't what's tighter, our jeans or our friendship.

And to **you, the reader**. Thank you. Thank you for reading my books. Thanks for every e-mail, comment, and review you give me. I treasure each and every one.

ABOUT THE AUTHOR

ANNE MALCOM has been an avid reader since before she can remember, her mother responsible for her love of reading. It started with magical journeys into the world of Hogwarts and Middle Earth, then as she grew up her reading tastes grew with her. Her love of reading doesn't discriminate, she reads across many genres, although classics like Little Women and Gone with the Wind will hold special places in her heart. She also can't get enough romance, especially when some possessive alpha males throw their weight around.

One day, in a reading slump, Cade and Gwen's story came to her and started taking up space in her head until she put their story into words. Now that she has started, it doesn't look like she's going to stop anytime soon, with many more characters demanding their story be told as well.

Raised in small town New Zealand, Anne had a truly special childhood, growing up in one of the most beautiful countries in the world. She has backpacked across Europe, ridden camels in the Sahara and eaten her way through Italy, loving every moment. For now, she's back at home in New Zealand and quite happy. But who knows when the travel bug will bite her again.

OTHER BOOKS

The Sons of Templar

Making the Cut

Firestorm

Outside the Lines

Out of the Ashes

Beyond the Horizon

Dauntless

Unquiet Mind

Echoes of Silence

Skeletons of Us